W9-CAS-958

FROM THE INTRODUCTION

"The French, in painting as well as in literature and in life, seem to have been endowed with a keen sense for the concrete . . . they admit what their eyes report to them, and they have the courage of their perceptions. The fundamental virtues of the writers here represented, most of all Balzac, Merimée, de Maupassant and Camus, are the forcefulness of sensations intensely felt and the vividness of the images . . . French authors also appear to have cherished, more than most others, a passion for an almost ascetic economy."

HENRI PEYRE

The short novel with its demands of directness and economy has been, for the French, the most important form for conveying the unique genius of their literature.

SEVEN FRENCH SHORT NOVEL MASTERPIECES

with an Introduction by
HENRI PEYRE

POPULAR LIBRARY • NEW YORK

POPULAR LIBRARY EDITION

ACKNOWLEDGMENTS

The Pastoral Symphony by André Gide. Copyright 1931 by Alfred A. Knopf, Inc.; renewed 1959. Reprinted from TWO SYMPHONIES, by André Gide, translated by Dorothy Bussy, by permission of Alfred A. Knopf, Inc.

The Growing Stone by Albert Camus. Copyright © 1958 by Alfred A. Knopf, Inc. Reprinted from EXILE AND THE KINGDOM, by Albert Camus, translated by Justin O'Brien, by permission of Alfred A. Knopf, Inc.

CONTENTS

INTRODUCTION

The short novel, or long short story, or "récit," as it is often called so as to distinguish it from the novel proper and from the regular short story and from the even briefer "conte," has long been an original feature of the literatures of France and of Germany. As novels, in the twentieth century, seem to have grown longer and longer and are being likened to sprawling sagas, to meandering rivers and to metaphysical epics claiming to call the world and man's existence into question, many a reader has relished the less ambitious and more poetical and suggestive "courts romans." The plot, in those manageable briefer novels, counts for less than in the intricate big pieces of fictional machinery which often grind four or five parallel stories into a nondescript and indigestible paste. The elaborate portrayal of a vast society, the rise and fall of bourgeois or aristocratic dynasties, the philosophical digressions or historical dissertations indulged by Balzac, Tolstoi, Dostoevsky, Proust can hardly be squeezed into the economical compass of a short novel. Nor can the author patiently attempt to convey the slow erosion worked by time and the tragic ageing of characters gradually vanquished by the wear and tear of life. The most successful authors of short novels have always known how and when to relinquish to the novelists, or to the longer novels which they themselves wrote at other moments, the laborious analysis of character and the intricacies of plots which would not fit into their more artistic and more limited mold.

On the other hand, the short novel or récit does not suffer from some of the limitations which have detracted from the value of the short story in the eyes of many twentieth century readers. Too many short stories are dashed off by novelists as a side activity or consist of superfluous episodes discarded from a novel in progress. Others appear to be tailor cut for magazines with limited space and for readers who expect the conventional effects of abrupt beginning, short and snappy paragraphs, brutal incidents, and contrived surprise in the

7

conclusion. The technique of the short story has been codified
into rules which are taught to apprentices in college courses.
The affectation of objectivity and the working up of a hurried
tension have been turned into artificial devices. The concentration on sharp outlines and on exterior attitudes, at the
expense of any insight into the inner torments of the characters, can become mere trickery. Too sure a mastery over technique, in the short story, on the stage, on the screen, may
entail the stifling of the author's personality. One of the best
critics of the short story, Sean O'Faolain, was fond of re-
calling the one essential question which another Irishman, the
poet A.E., used to ask of any author: "Out of how deep a life
does he speak?"

The French, in painting as well as in literature and in life,
seem to have been endowed with a keen sense for the concrete, an avoidance of ethereal and Pre-raphaelite figures, a
refusal to close their eyes to the facts that lovers have lips,
that the noblest souls have to be incarnated in fallible corpo-
real envelopes. They admit what their eyes report to them
and, as Henry James put it, they have the courage of their
perceptions, just as the English have the courage of their
opinions. The fundamental virtues of the writers here represented, most of all of Balzac, Mérimée, Maupassant and Camus, are the forcefulness of sensations intensely felt and the
vividness of the images into which those sensations are often
transfigured.

French authors also appear to have cherished, more than
most others, a passion for an almost ascetic economy. Stendhal, Mérimée, Flaubert, Gide all professed a preference for
sparse sentences, conciseness of style, concrete words closely
adhering to their vision of objects and a clear, disillusioned
way of looking at things, at others, and at themselves. Willa
Cather and Ernest Hemingway appreciated those qualities in
Stendhal and Mérimée, as John Galsworthy and Joseph Con-
rad did in Maupassant. Joyce and Kafka admired Flaubert for
his faultless control of his material and the elaborate yet
unobtrusive symbolic structure which gave unity and rigor to
his stories. Imagination and reverie are certainly not banished
from Balzac's *Girl with the Golden Eyes* and from *A Simple
Heart*; passion stirs and burns within the hearts of the Princess of Clèves and of the Pastor in Gide's story. But sentiment, flights of imagination and ideological digressions are
kept severely under control. That same expert on the short
story, Sean O'Faolain, paid tribute to the best French practi-
tioners of the genre in these terms: "France clearly is, as she

has always been, the breeding ground of the personal and original way of looking at things, expounded with intelligence and defended with disruptive passion, a virtue as fruitful in art as it is fatal in politics."

The earliest short novels in France were some of the medieval *fabliaux* in which the men and women of the centuries of chivalry, of courtly love and of ardent Catholic faith found an outlet for their sense of comedy and sought a revenge against the idealization of the Church and of women. Monks and the same frail sex to whom singers of old and respectful knights paid their tributes, since it had been that of the Madonna, were the butt of their boisterous but wholesome sarcasm. The several books which make up the Rabelaisian romance are in truth short novels, loosely linked. Other Renaissance writers, who had not yet discovered the possibilities open to the novel, then in its infancy, attempted to broaden the tale, inherited from Boccaccio and Chaucer, into a more spacious genre and to shun the conventional descriptions and the brutal adventures which mar, for us, the novelettes of Antoine de la Salle, Brantôme and Bonaventure des Périers. But even when the classical age of French literature, by the middle of the seventeenth century, had introduced a taste for restraint and conciseness in expression and for the study of the inner man behind the social and exterior individual, the contemporaries of Corneille, Molière and Racine proved slow in assigning limits to the sprawling novels of impossible adventures which were then in vogue. The Spaniards had anticipated them with the picturesque and entertaining *Exemplary Novels* of Cervantes, which are in fact long short stories, as the contradictory but inevitable phrase goes. The first truly modern and searchingly psychological short novel in France is *The Princess of Clèves*; its heroine is a woman and its author is, to this day, the sole truly preeminent writer of fiction in the French language who is a woman. Only in our own age have gifted women novelists such as Marguerite Duras, Nathalie Sarraute, Françoise Mallet-Joris and Françoise Sagan rediscovered the striking affinities which women-writers seem to have for the *récit*.

Mme de La Fayette had a castle in Auvergne where her husband, whom she apparently esteemed more than she loved him, preferred to live; she was most often at the Court and in the salons of her friends, the haughty moralist Duke of La Rochefoucauld and the queen of all letter-writers, Mme de Sévigné. She had already written two long short stories when she published anonymously, in 1678, just as the French classical tragedy was giving signs of exhaustion, her tragic analysis of three characters torn between their chaotic passion and their loyalty to themselves. The scene is laid in the previous century, at the court of Henri II of France, who reigned between 1547 and 1559. It is thus picturesquely colored with the gay and reckless spirit of the Renaissance. Parties, balls, tournaments and love intrigues are the chief concern of that licentious Court. That evocation of a magnificent past serves as a foil to the lucid self-control and to the moral rectitude of the heroine.

She is married to a man older than she is, somewhat severe and paternal to her, as Mr. Karenin is to Anna in Tolstoi's novel. He continues to love her with devotion and passion after marriage. She strains every nerve to return his love. She is courted by the most admired bachelor at the Court, the Duke of Nemours: she fears that she may not long be able to resist his advances. Her mother, who had brought her up in the distrust of the amorous affairs which other women indulged, dies, and leaves her daughter unprotected. She has no children and apparently little piety. Her sole resort is in her Cartesian lucidity and in her self-respect which prompts her to behave like one of Corneille's heroines. But she finds herself in a Racinian situation, aware of her inner chaos and suspecting that the sacrifices she is consenting to her virtue are made perhaps but to an imaginary and over-refined sense of duty. She fails to reach any peace of mind.

In the central scene of the "récit," she confesses to her husband the feeling which is growing in her for M. de Nemours; she seeks comfort and protection in him. He is too much of a man of honor to play the role of the outraged husband: pathetically, he forces himself to act nobly but he soon dies, heart-stricken. It is to the credit of Mme de La Fayette that she has created the first moving and deeply attractive character of a husband in modern fiction. The Princess, after much inner turmoil, decides to reject the offer of marriage of the Duke of Nemours. She yields to no social prejudice, to no exaggerated fidelity to the memory of a husband who died, after all, on her account; but she dreads the fickleness of men, the disappointments which fulfilled love brings in its train, and she strangely fears love itself, a fear of spiritual turmoil which will be depicted more than once in later French fiction. As in Racine's tragedies, as in Sartre's *No Exit* and many a modern play, the three characters, all intent on probing unflinchingly their desires and their emotional urges, are locked together in a narrow prison (here the microcosm of the Court) where the attractions of the senses are inextricably bound up with distrust and hatred.

The psychological fiction initiated by that epoch-making story was cultivated in the eighteenth century by the abbé Prévost in *Manon Lescaut*, by Laclos in *Les Liaisons dangereuses* and, with more philosophical and ironical implications and less attention to character study, in Voltaire's brief novels. The nineteenth century was in France as in Britain and Russia, the supreme age of fiction. Stendhal and Zola wrote few short novels, partly because the social criticism and the analysis of motives which they judged to be fundamental to their fiction and their demonstration of psychological and physiological laws demanded the vast scope of a full-fledged novel. But Balzac, universal in his mastery of all fictional media, wrote the most superb short stories in the French language and some of the most original short novels: *Colonel Chabert, La Recherche de l'Absolu, La Vieille Fille* and *La Fille aux yeux d'or*.

The latter has puzzled many readers to this day. It has several elements of a cloak and dagger story, with the mysterious Spanish girl, Paquita (in truth, she was supposed to have been born in the West Indies from an unknown father, and a mother from Georgia near the Black Sea), the labyrinthine recesses of the house where she is sequestered, the lover brought blindfolded in a carriage, the eunuch, the unexplained murder at the end. Balzac, before Edgar Allen Poe and Dostoevski, took pleasure in incorporating the thrills of mystery stories into his fiction; he alternated them with long moralistic developments on vice, corruption and the unscrupulous greed of ambitious seducers. The hero, Marsay, is one of those handsome, irresistible Balzacian young men out to conquer Paris, and women. The passionate Paquita with her flaming golden eyes adores him at once, leads him to her mysterious bedroom and insists on dressing him up as a woman before their first love night. Balzac keeps the secret half-hidden from his readers: but, for modern readers who are familiar with Proust's *Captive* and other sequestered characters, it is clear that the novelist was depicting a strange case of Lesbian love. The woman who held Dolores a captive and murders her at the end in her jealousy happens to be no other than Marsay's own half sister, the marquise de San Real. The most striking originality of the short novel lies in the evocation of Paris which opens it, one of the most vividly artistic ever done in words by any writer of a country where the myth of Paris has been constantly celebrated in literature.

Prosper Mérimée, born in 1803, was only four years younger than Balzac; but he stands in sharp contrast to him. He was a deliberate unromantic in the romantic age, spurning flights of imagination, the expression of sensibility, pathos, bombast and all excess in style. Walter Pater, in one of his *Miscellaneous Studies*, praised him for his directness of vision and for never "using two words where one would do better, . . . an art of which there are few examples in English." Ernest Hemingway mastered that art triumphantly in our age.

He travelled in Spain in the eighteen thirties, where he met the mother of the future Empress Eugénie and her young daughter, visited archeological sites and observed gypsies. In 1845, he published *Carmen*. The tone of the short novel, which begins and ends in a sedulously nonchalant manner, is objective and detached. The character of Don José, the prey to fatality and the victim of the "femme fatale," is a trifle conventional. But the Spanish gypsy, with her large eyes, her intoxicating bunch of flowers, and the feline suppleness of her every move, is a diabolically entrancing character. Strangely enough, when Bizet's opera, with a libretto faithfully based on Mérimée's story, was first performed in Paris, in 1875, it was very coolly received by the audiences. Only in 1883 did it score a genuine success. Mérimée's story is now safely ranked among the classics of fiction.

Flaubert's *Un Coeur Simple* is its closest rival in popularity with both grownups and pupils over the world. It appeared in *Trois Contes*, in 1877, three years before the author's death. It too is a masterpiece of selectivity and of objectivity. The melancholy story of a life devoid of adventures, altogether consecrated to charity and to devotion to an ungrateful family, then to a ludicrous but touching piety, is related impassively. Flaubert always held that he painted as he saw, "in the sincerity of his heart," but his affection for the humble servant ironically called Félicité, for his native Normandy whose setting he conjured up here for the last time, pierces through the deliberately cool and brief paragraphs of the story. The fastidious artistry of the realistic tale enhances its deep humanity.

Even more than his master and model Flaubert, Maupassant is often considered as a brutal and incisive portrayer of the drab and of the sordid and as an inveterate pessimist. His short life was a melancholy one; he brooded over the bitter ironies of many a lowly existence, watched his brother become insane and died at forty-three after two years of madness. His philosophy was nihilistic, but he never forsook the faith in art, which Flaubert had instilled into him as a substitute for religion. John Galsworthy, in a volume of essays entitled *Castles in Spain* (1927), declared him to be "in the essentials of style, the prince of teachers. The vigor of his vision and his thought, the economy and clarity of the expression in which he clothed them, have not yet been surpassed."

The parsimony of language, the dexterous contriving of surprise, the delicate building up of tension make *Yvette* one of his gentlest and warmest works, far less brutal than most of his realistic short stories of peasants, lower middle class clerks, and whores. Yvette, the daughter of a high class courtesan, courted in her turn by one of her mother's male friends who hoped to become her first lover, is one of the very few "jeunes filles" delineated in French fiction with tact, charm and truthfulness. She plays with fire, little realizing the perils she is running. When she understands what the rakish gentleman in search of amorous excitement wants from her and what her mother's life has been, she elaborately prepares to commit suicide. Her attempt fails and the novel, a rare occurrence in Maupassant, ends happily with her rescue from the brink of death.

Gide's *La Symphonie pastorale,* in contrast to the striving toward an accurate and objective painting of real life which was the concern of Mérimée, Flaubert and Maupassant, is permeated by Symbolist influences and poses religious and ethical problems. The title ambiguously recalls Beethoven's Symphony which the pastor has taken the blind girl to hear; it also suggests the poetical and almost musical drama which wrecks the pastor's faith. The pastor becomes spiritually blind as the blind girl recovers her eyesight. In the process of saving the forlorn child and of molding her mind, he insidiously enjoys pinning all the affections of her heart on him. He also feels his devotion to her turn into love and he convinces himself that he needs her love in order to continue loving and serving Christ. He argues inwardly against the heritage to Christianity which came from St. Paul and theology and for a more instinctive and radiant worship, in his eyes truer to the teaching of Christ and of St. Francis.

Gide, who was always at his very best in shorter novels or "récits," has written in *The Pastoral Symphony* the most expertly condensed and the most pathetic of his narrative works. The restraint and the speed with which the tale is told afford us only glimpses of the pastor's wife, Amelia, of their son Jacques, who clashed with his father, even of the blind girl's swift growth into a lucid person who prefers suicide to working havoc unwillingly in the family which welcomed her.

Gide's own inner anguish and his desperate search for sincerity to oneself are mirrored in that small masterpiece which he wrote in the middle of his life, in 1919-1920.

The collection of six stories from which *The Growing Stone* (*La Pierre qui pousse*) is drawn is the last one published in the lifetime of Albert Camus, in 1957. He was killed in an automobile accident two years later. The exiles are the Frenchmen who, like him, lived in Africa, loved the land and yet felt like exiles among the Arabs, "wretched lords of a strange kingdom." Those same Frenchmen felt like alienated men in a France with which they were hardly familiar. Camus himself went to France for the first time at the age of twenty-three. The kingdom would be that in which Europeans and Africans, a French engineer like M. D'Arrast in *The Growing Stone* and the Brazilian negro who insists, out of superstition, upon carrying a stone too heavy for him, employers and workmen, rich and poor might be reconciled and live harmoniously.

The meaning of the story is not clearly brought out by the author. The French engineer relieves the native who collapsed under the burden of the stone, in a land where a miraculous statue of Christ, when broken into bits, was supposed to grow again into one piece. But he carries the stone, not to the shrine of the Virgin, but to the poor negro's cabin. One is reminded of the myth of Sisyphus, dear to Camus. The gesture symbolizes the solidarity of the European with more primitive human beings and the conviction expressed already by Camus in *The Plague*, that it is best to be "a saint without God" and to help men live and save themselves, outside any organized religion. The evocation of the Brazilian scenery is achieved in a terse, glowing prose. A deep, instinctive sense of human brotherhood illuminates that enigmatic short novel. No obtrusive moral is pointed out by the author, but it is implied in the story. A few months after Camus had published that volume of long stories, on December 10, 1957, as he received the Nobel prize in Stockholm, he declared, in words which nobly define the function of literature and to the seven writers here represented, all devotees of a truth which is also beauty and solidarity: "I cannot live as a person without my art. And yet I have never set that art above everything else. . . . It is a means of stirring the greatest number of men by providing them with a privileged image of our common joys and woes."

HENRI PEYRE
Yale University

THE PRINCESS OF CLÈVES
by Madame de Lafayette

After 25 years in the country, Madame Marie-Madelaine, Comtesse de Lafayette, settled in Paris in 1659, and was quickly befriended by some of the most glittering personages of French literature, among them Mme. de Sévigné and the Duc de la Rochefoucauld. These illustrious writers helped provide consolation for an unhappy marriage, and perhaps influenced her work. An early novel, Zaïde, published under the pseudonym Segrais, is in the précieux tradition, affected, over-refined and full of exaggeration. Her subsequent work, however, establishes her as a novelist of psychological insight in a style devoid of affectation and sentimentality. Her masterpiece, The Princess of Clèves, written in 1678, may justly be described as the first novel of character. In this work, the actions develop from the feelings and motivations of the characters, rather than from the caprice or whim of the novelist. Like most of her later work, it is a study of married life, a field which had previously not been tilled. Mme. de Lafayette drew on her own experiences to tell of the unhappy marriage of Mlle. de Chârtres, and her frustrated love for the gallant Duc de Nemours. The working out of this tragic affair represents, as in Corneille's tragedies, the conflict between duty and private passions. It was Mme. de Lafayette's own assessment that doing one's duty does not necessarily guarantee happiness.

PART I.

There never was in France so brilliant a display of magnificence and gallantry as during the last years of the reign of Henri II. This monarch was gallant, handsome, and susceptible; although his love for Diane de Poitiers, Duchess of Valentinois, had lasted twenty years, its ardor had not diminished, as his conduct testified.

He was remarkably skilful in physical exercises, and devoted much attention to them; every day was filled with hunting and tennis, dancing, running at the ring, and sports of that kind. The favorite colors and the initials of Madame de Valentinois were to be seen everywhere, and she herself used to appear dressed as richly as Mademoiselle de la Marck, her granddaughter, who was then about to be married.

The fact that the queen was there, accounted for her presence. This princess, although she had passed her first youth, was still beautiful; she was fond of splendor, magnificence, and pleasure. The king had married her while still Duke of Orléans, in the lifetime of his elder brother, the dauphin, who afterward died at Tournon, mourned as a worthy heir to the position of Francis I., his father.

The queen's ambition made her like to reign. She seemed indifferent to the king's attachment to the Duchess of Valentinois, and never betrayed any jealousy; but she was so skilled a dissembler that it was hard to discover her real feelings, and she was compelled by policy to keep the duchess near her if she wanted to see anything of the king. As for him, he liked the society of women, even of those with whom he was not at all in love. He was with the queen every day at her audience, when all the most attractive lords and ladies were sure to appear.

At no court had there ever been gathered together so many lovely women and brave men. It seemed as if Nature had made an effort to show her highest beauty in the greatest lords and ladies. Madame Elisabeth of France, afterwards queen of Spain, began to show her wonderful intelligence and that unrivalled beauty which was so fatal to her. Mary Stuart, the queen of Scotland, who had just married the dauphin and was called the crown princess, or dauphiness, was faultless in mind and body. She had been brought up at the French court and had acquired all its polish; she was endowed by Nature with so strong a love for the softer graces that in spite of her youth she admired and understood them perfectly. Her mother-in-law, the queen, and Madame, the king's sister, were also fond of poetry, of comedy, and of music. The interest which King Francis I. had felt in poetry and letters still prevailed in France, and since the king, his son, was devoted to physical exercise, pleasures of all sorts were to be found at the court. But what rendered the court especially fine and majestic was the great number of princes and lords of exceptional merit;

those I am about to name were, in their different ways, the ornament and the admiration of their age.

The King of Navarre inspired universal respect by his exalted rank and his royal bearing. He excelled in the art of war; but the Duke of Guise had shown himself so strong a rival that he had often laid aside his command to enter the duke's service as a private soldier in the most dangerous battles. This duke had manifested such admirable bravery with such remarkable success that he was an object of envy to every great commander. He had many conspicuous qualities besides his personal courage,—he possessed a vast and profound intelligence, a noble, lofty mind, and equal capacity for war and affairs. His brother, the Cardinal of Lorraine, was born with an unbridled ambition, and had acquired vast learning; this he turned to his profit by using it in defence of Catholicism, which had begun to be attacked. The Chevalier de Guise, afterwards known as the Grand Prior, was loved by all; he was handsome, witty, clever, and his courage was renowned throughout Europe. The short, ill-favored body of the Prince of Condé held a great and haughty soul, and an intelligence that endeared him to even the most beautiful women. The Duke of Nevers, famous for his military prowess and his important services to the state, though somewhat advanced in years was adored by all the court. He had three handsome sons,—the second, known as the Prince of Clèves, was worthy to bear that proud title; he was brave and grand, and was withal endowed with a prudence rare in the young. The Vidame of Chartres, a scion of the old house of Vendôme, a name not despised by princes of the blood, had won equal triumphs in war and gallantry; he was handsome, attractive, brave, hardy, generous; all his good qualities were distinct and striking,—in short, he was the only man fit to be compared, if such comparison be possible, with the Duke of Nemours. This nobleman was a masterpiece of Nature; the least of his fascinations was his extreme beauty; he was the handsomest man in the world. What made him superior to every one else was his unrivalled courage and a charm manifested in his mind, his expression, and his actions, such as no other showed. He possessed a certain playfulness that was equally attractive to men and women; he was unusually skilful in physical exercises; and he dressed in a way that every one tried in vain to imitate; moreover his bearing was such that all eyes followed him wherever he appeared. There was no lady in the court who would not have been flattered by his attentions; few of those to whom he had devoted himself could boast of having resisted him; and even many in whom he had shown no interest made very clear their affection for him. He was so gentle and courteous that he could not refuse some attentions to those who tried to please him,—hence he had many mistresses; but it was hard to say whom he really loved. He was often to be seen with the dauphiness; her beauty, her gentleness, her desire to please every one, and the special regard she showed for this prince, made some imagine that he dared to raise his eyes to her. The Guises, whose niece she was, had acquired influence and position by her marriage; they aspired to an equality with the princes of the blood and to a share of the power exercised by the Constable of Montmorency. It was to the constable that the king confided the greater part of the cares of state, while he treated the Duke of Guise and the Marshal of Saint-André as his favorites. But those attached to his person by favor or position could only keep their place by submitting to the Duchess of Valentinois, who, although no longer young or beautiful, ruled him so despotically that she may be said to have been the mistress of his person and of the state.

The king had always loved the constable, and at the beginning of his reign had summoned him from the exile into which he had been sent by Francis I. The court was divided between the Guises and the constable, who was the favorite of the princes of the blood. Both parties had always struggled for the favor of the Duchess of Valentinois. The Duke of Aumale, brother of the Duke of Guise, had married one of her daughters. The constable aspired to the same alliance, not satisfied with having married his eldest son to Madame Diane, a daughter of the king by a lady of Piedmont who entered a convent after the birth of her child. The promises which Monsieur de Montmorency had made to Mademoiselle de Piennes, one of the queen's maids-of-honor, had proved a serious obstacle to this match; and although the king had removed it with extreme patience and kindness, the constable still felt insecure until he had won over the Duchess of Valentinois and had separated her from the Guises, whose greatness had begun to alarm her. She had delayed in every way in her power the marriage between the dauphin and the Queen of Scotland; this young queen's beauty and intelligence, and the position given to the Guises by this marriage, were very odious to her. She especially detested the Cardinal of Lorraine, who had addressed her in bitter, even contemptuous terms.

She saw that he was intriguing with the queen; hence the constable found her ready to join forces with him by bringing about the marriage of Mademoiselle de la Marck, her granddaughter, to Monsieur d'Anville, his second son, who succeeded to his post in the reign of Charles IX. The constable did not expect that Monsieur d'Anville would have any objections to this marriage, as had been the case with Monsieur de Montmorency; but though the reasons were more hidden, the difficulties were no less obstinate. Monsieur d'Anville was desperately in love with the crown princess; and although his passion was hopeless, he could not persuade himself to contract other ties. The Marshal of Saint-André was almost the only courtier who had taken sides with neither faction; he was one of the favorites, but this position he held simply by his own merits. Ever since he had been the dauphin, the king had been attached to this nobleman, and later had made him marshal of France, at an age when men are satisfied with lesser honors. His advance gave him a distinction which he maintained by his personal worth and charm, by a costly table and rich surroundings, and by more splendor than any private individual had yet displayed. The king's generosity warranted this sumptuousness. There was no limit to this monarch's generosity to those he loved. He did not possess every great quality, but he had many, and among them the love of war and a good knowledge of it. This accounted for his many successes; and if we except the battle of St. Quentin, his reign was an unbroken series of victories. He had won the battle of Renty in person, Piedmont had been conquered, the English had been driven from France, and the Emperor Charles V. had seen his good fortune desert him before the city of Metz, which he had besieged in vain with all the forces of the Empire and of Spain. Nevertheless, since the defeat of St. Quentin had diminished our hope of conquest, and fortune seemed to favor one king as much as the other, they were gradually led to favor peace.

The Dowager Duchess of Lorraine had begun to lead the way to a cessation of hostilities at the time of the dauphin's marriage, and ever since then there had been secret negotiations. At last Cercamp, in the Province of Artois, was chosen as the place of meeting. The Cardinal of Lorraine, the constable, and the Marshal of Saint-André appeared in behalf of the King of France; the Duke of Alva and the Prince of Orange in behalf of Philip II. The Duke and Duchess of Lorraine were the mediators. The leading articles were the marriage of Madame Elisabeth of France to Don Carlos, Infanta of Spain, and that of Madame, the king's sister, with Monsieur de Savoie.

Meanwhile the king remained on the frontier, and there heard of the death of Mary, queen of England. He sent the Count of Randan to Elizabeth to congratulate her on ascending the throne. She was very glad to receive him, because her rights were so insecure that it was of great service to her to have them acknowledged by the king. The count found her well informed about the interests of France and the capabilities of those who composed the court, but especially familiar with the reputation of the Duke of Nemours. She spoke of this nobleman so often and with such warmth that when Monsieur de Randan returned and recounted his journey to the king, he told him that there was nothing to which Monsieur de Nemours could not aspire, and that she would be capable of marrying him. That very evening the king spoke to this nobleman, and made Monsieur de Randan repeat to him his conversation with Elizabeth, urging him to essay this great fortune. At first Monsieur de Nemours thought that the king was jesting; but when he saw his mistake he said,—

"At any rate, sire, if I undertake a fantastic enterprise under the advice and in behalf of your Majesty, I beg of you to keep it secret until success shall justify me before the public, and to guard me from appearing vain enough to suppose that a queen who has never seen me should wish to marry me from love."

The king promised to speak of the plan to no one but the constable, and agreed that secrecy was essential for its success. Monsieur de Randan advised Monsieur de Nemours to visit England as a simple traveller; but the latter could not make up his mind to do this. He sent Lignerolles, an intelligent young man, one of his favorites, to ascertain the queen's feeling and to try to open the matter. Meanwhile he went to see the Duke of Savoy, who was then at Brussels with the King of Spain. The death of Mary of England raised great obstacles to any treaty of peace; the commission broke up at the end of November, and the king returned to Paris.

At that moment there appeared at court a young lady to whom all eyes were turned, and we may well believe that she was possessed of faultless beauty, since she aroused admiration where all were well accustomed to the sight of handsome women. Of the same family as the Vidame of Chartres, she was one of the greatest heiresses in France. Her father had died young, leaving her under the charge of his wife, Madame de Chartres, whose kindness, virtue, and worth were beyond praise. After her husband's death she had withdrawn from court for many years; during this period she had devoted herself to the education of her daughter, not merely cultivating her mind and her beauty, but also seeking to inspire her with the love of virtue and to make her attractive. Most mothers imagine that it is enough never to speak of gallantry to their daughters to guard them from it forever. Madame de Chartres was of a very different opinion; she often drew pictures of love to her daughter, showing her its fascinations, in order to give her a better understanding of its perils. She told her how insincere men are, how false and deceitful; she described the domestic miseries which illicit love-affairs entail, and, on the other hand, pictured to her the peaceful happiness of a virtuous woman's life, as well as the distinction and elevation which virtue gives to a woman of rank and beauty. She taught her, too, how hard it was to preserve this virtue without extreme care, and without that one sure means of securing a wife's happiness, which is to love her husband and to be loved by him.

This heiress was, then, one of the greatest matches in France, and although she was very young, many propositions of marriage had been made to her. Madame de Chartres, who was extremely proud, found almost nothing worthy of her daughter, and the girl being in her sixteenth year, she was anxious to take her to court. The Vidame went to welcome here on her arrival, and was much struck by the marvellous beauty of Mademoiselle de Chartres,—and with good reason: her delicate complexion and her blond hair gave her a unique brilliancy; her features were regular, and her face and person were full of grace and charm.

The day after her arrival she went to match some precious stones at the house of an Italian who dealt in them. He had come from Florence with the queen, and had grown so rich by his business that his house seemed that of some great nobleman rather than of a merchant. The Prince of Clèves happened to come in while she was there; he was so struck by her beauty that he could not conceal his surprise, and Mademoiselle de Chartres could not keep from blushing when she saw his astonishment: she succeeded, however, in regaining her composure without paying any further attention to the prince than civility required for a man of his evident importance. Monsieur de Clèves gazed at her admiringly, wondering who this beauty was whom he did not know. He perceived from her bearing and her suite that she must be a lady of high rank. She was so young that he thought she must be unmarried; but since she had not her mother with her, and the Italian, who did not know her, addressed her as "madame," he was in great doubt, and stared at her with continual surprise. He saw that his glances embarrassed her, unlike most young women, who always take pleasure in seeing the effect of their beauty; it even seemed to him that his presence made her anxious to go away, and in fact she left very soon. Monsieur de Clèves consoled himself for her departure with the hope of finding out who she was, and was much disappointed to learn that no one knew. He was so struck by her beauty and evident modesty that from that moment he conceived for her the greatest love and esteem. That evening he called on Madame, the king's sister.

This princess was held in high esteem on account of her influence with the king, her brother; and this influence was so great that when the king made peace he consented to restore Piedmont to enable her to marry Monsieur de Savoie. Although she had always meant to marry, she had determined to give her hand to none but a sovereign, and had for that reason refused the King of Navarre when he was Duke of Vendôme, and had always felt an interest in Monsieur de Savoie after seeing him at Nice on the occasion of the interview between Francis I. and Pope Paul III. Since she possessed great intelligence and a fine taste, she drew pleasant persons about her, and at certain hours the whole court used to visit her.

Thither Monsieur de Clèves went, as was his habit. He was so full of the wit and beauty of Mademoiselle de Chartres that he could speak of nothing else; he talked freely of his adventure, and set no limit to his praise of the young woman he had seen but did not know. Madame said to him that there was no such person as he described, and that if there were, every one would have known about her. Madame de Dampierre, her lady-in-waiting and a friend of Madame de Chartres, when she heard the conversation moved near the princess and said to her in a low voice that doubtless it was Mademoiselle de Chartres whom Monsieur de Clèves had seen. Madame turned towards him and said that if he would return the next day, she would show him this beauty who had so impressed him. Mademoiselle de Chartres made her appearance the next day. The queen received her with every imaginable attention, and she was greeted with such admiration by every one that she heard around her nothing but praise. This she received with such noble modesty that she seemed not to hear it, or at least not to be affected by it. Then she visited the apartments of Madame, the king's sister. The princess, after praising her beauty, told her the surprise she had given to Monsieur de Clèves. A moment after, that person appeared.

"Come," she said to him, "see if I have not kept my word, and if, when I point out Mademoiselle de Chartres to you, I do not show you the beauty you sought; at any rate, thank me for telling her how much you already admire her."

Monsieur de Clèves was filled with joy to find that this young woman whom he had found so attractive was of a rank proportionate to her beauty. He went up to her and asked her to remember that he had been the first to admire her, and that without knowing her he had felt all the respect and esteem that were her due.

The Chevalier de Guise, his friend, and he left the house together. At first they praised Mademoiselle de Chartres without stint; then they found that they were praising her too much, and both stopped saying what they thought of her: but they were compelled to talk about her on the following days whenever they met. This new beauty was for a long time the general subject of conversation. The queen praised her warmly and showed an extraordinary regard for her; the dauphiness made her one of her favorites, and begged Madame de Chartres to bring her to see her very often; the daughters of the king invited her to all their entertainments,—in short, she was loved and admired by the whole court, except by Madame de Valentinois. It was not that this new beauty gave her any uneasiness,—her long experience had made her sure of the king,—but she so hated the Vidame of Chartres, whom she had desired to ally with herself by the marriage of one of her daughters, while he had joined the queen's party, that she could not look with favor on any one who bore his name and seemed to enjoy his friendship.

The Prince of Clèves fell passionately in love with Mademoiselle de Chartres, and was eager to marry her; but he feared lest the pride of Madame de Chartres should prevent her from giving her daughter to a man who was not the eldest of his family. Yet this family was so distinguished, and the Count of Eu, who was the head of the house, had just married a woman so near to royalty, that it was timidity rather than any true reason that inspired the fear of Monsieur de Clèves. He had many rivals; the Chevalier de Guise seemed to him the most formidable, on account of his birth, his ability, and the brilliant position of his family. This prince had fallen in love with Mademoiselle de Chartres the first day he saw her; he had noticed the passion of Monsieur de Clèves just as the latter had noticed his. Though the two men were friends, the separation which resulted from this rivalry gave them no chance to explain themselves, and their friendship cooled without their having courage to come to an understanding. The good fortune of Monsieur de Clèves in being the first to see Mademoiselle de Chartres seemed to him a happy omen, and to promise him some advantage over his rivals; but he foresaw serious obstacles on the part of the Duke of Nevers, his father. This duke was bound to the Duchess of Valentinois by many ties; she was an enemy of the Vidame, and this was reason enough to prevent the Duke of Nevers from consenting that his son should think of that nobleman's niece.

Madame de Chartres, who had already taken such pains to fill her daughter with a love of virtue, did not remit them in this place where they were still so necessary, and bad examples were so frequent. Ambition and gallantry were the sole occupation of the court, busying men and women alike. There were so many interests and so many different intrigues in which women took part that love was always mingled with politics, and politics with love. No one was calm or indifferent; every one sought to rise, to please, to serve, or to injure; no one was weary or idle, every one was taken up with pleasure or intrigue. The ladies had their special interest in the queen, in the crown princess, in the Queen of Navarre, in Madame the king's sister, or in the Duchess of Valentinois, according to their inclinations, their sense of right, or their humor. Those who had passed their first youth and assumed an austere virtue, were devoted to the queen; those who were younger and sought pleasure and gallantry, paid their court to the crown princess. The Queen of Navarre had her favorites; she was young, and had much influence over her husband the king, who was allied with the constable, and hence highly esteemed. Madame the king's sister still preserved some of her beauty, and gathered several ladies about herself. The Duchess of Valentinois was sought by all those whom she deigned to regard; but the women she liked were few, and with the exception of those who enjoyed her intimacy and confidence, and whose disposition bore some likeness to her

own, she received only on the days when she assumed to hold
a court like the queen.

All these different cliques were separated by rivalry and
envy. Then, too, the women who belonged to each one of
them were also jealous of one another, either about their
chances of advancement, or about their lovers; often their
interests were complicated by other pettier, but no less important questions. Hence there was in this court a sort of well-
ordered agitation, which rendered it very charming, but also
very dangerous, for a young woman. Madame de Chartres
saw this peril, and thought only of protecting her daughter
from it. She besought her, not as a mother, but as a friend, to
confide to her all the sweet speeches that might be made to
her, and promised her aid in all those matters which so often
embarrass the young.

The Chevalier de Guise made his feelings for Mademoiselle
de Chartres and his intentions so manifest that every one
could see them; yet he well knew the very grave difficulties
that stood in his way. He was aware that he was not a desira-
ble match, because his fortune was too small for his rank. He
knew, too, that his brothers would disapprove of his
marrying, through fear of the loss of position which sometimes befalls great families through the marriage of younger
sons. The Cardinal of Lorraine soon proved to him that his
fears were well grounded, for he denounced the chevalier's
love for Mademoiselle de Chartres very warmly, though he
concealed his true reasons. The cardinal nourished a hatred
for the Vidame, which was hidden at the time, and only broke
out later. He would have preferred to see his brother ally
himself with any other family than that of the Vidame, and
gave such public expression to his dislike that Madame de
Chartres was plainly offended. She took great pains to show
that the Cardinal of Lorraine had no cause for fear, and that
she herself never contemplated the match. The Vidame
adopted the same course, and with a better understanding of
the cardinal's objection, because he knew the underlying reason.

The Prince of Clèves had concealed his passion quite as
little as had the Chevalier de Guise. The Duke of Nevers was
sorry to hear of this attachment, but thought that his son
would forget it at a word from him; great was his surprise
when he found him determined to marry Mademoiselle de
Chartres. He opposed this determination with a warmth so ill

concealed that the whole court soon had wind of it, and it came to the knowledge of her mother. She had never doubted that Monsieur de Nevers would regard this match as an advantageous one for his son, and was much surprised that both the house of Clèves and that of Guise dreaded the alliance instead of desiring it. She was so chagrined that she sought to marry her daughter to some one who could raise her above those who fancied themselves superior to her; and after carefully going over the ground, pitched on the prince dauphin, the son of the Duke of Montpensier. He was of the right age to marry, and held the highest position at court. Since Madame de Chartres was a very clever woman, and was aided by the Vidame, who at that time had great influence, while her daughter was in every way a good match, she played her cards so cleverly and successfully that Monsieur de Montpensier appeared to desire the marriage, and it seemed as if nothing could stand in its way.

The Vidame, though aware of Monsieur d'Anville's devotion to the crown princess, still thought that he might make use of the influence which she had over him to induce him to speak well of Mademoiselle de Chartres to the king and to the Prince of Montpensier, whose intimate friend he was. He mentioned this to the princess, who took up the matter eagerly, since it promised advancement to a young woman of whom she had become very fond. This she told the Vidame, assuring him that though she knew she should offend her uncle, the Cardinal of Lorraine, this would be no objection, because she had good grounds for disliking him, since he every day furthered the queen's interests in opposition to her own.

Persons in love are always glad of any excuse for talking about the object of their affection. As soon as the Vidame had gone, the crown princess ordered Châtelart, the favorite of Monsieur d'Anville and the confidant of his love for her, to tell him to be at the queen's reception that evening. Châtelart received this command with great delight. He belonged to a good family of Dauphiné, but his merit and intelligence had raised him to a higher place than his birth warranted. He was received and treated with kindness by all the great lords at the court, and the favor of the family of Montmorency had attached him especially to Monsieur d'Anville. He was handsome and skilled in all physical exercises; he sang agreeably, wrote verses, and had a gallant, ardent nature, which so attracted Monsieur d'Anville that he made him a confidant of his love for the crown princess. The confidence brought him into the society of that lady, and thus began that unhappy passion, which robbed him of his reason and finally cost him his life.

Monsieur d'Anville did not fail to make his appearance that evening in the queen's drawing-room; he was pleased that the dauphiness had chosen him to aid her, and he promised faithfully to obey her commands. But Madame de Valentinois had heard of the contemplated marriage and had laid her plans to thwart it; she had been so successful in arousing the king's opposition that when Monsieur d'Anville spoke of it, he showed his disapproval, and commanded him to apprise the Prince of Montpensier of it. It is easy to imagine the feelings of Madame de Chartres at the failure of a plan she had so much desired, especially when her ill-success gave so great an advantage to her enemies and did so much harm to her daughter.

The crown princess kindly expressed to Mademoiselle de Chartres her regrets at not being able to further her interests. "You see," she said, "I have but very little power; I am so detested by the queen and the Duchess of Valentinois that they or their attendants always oppose everything I desire. Still," she added, "I have always tried to please them, and they hate me only on account of my mother, who used to fill them with uneasiness and jealousy. The king had been in love with her before he loved Madame de Valentinois, and in his early married life, before he had any children, though he loved this duchess, he seemed bent on dissolving that marriage to marry the queen my mother. Madame de Valentinois dreaded the woman he had loved so well, lest her wit and beauty should diminish her own power, and entered into an alliance with the constable, who was also opposed to the king's marrying a sister of the Guises. They won over the late king; and though he hated the Duchess of Valentinois as much as he loved the queen, he joined with them in preventing the king from dissolving his marriage. In order to make this impossible, they arranged my mother's marriage with the King of Scotland, whose first wife had been Madame Magdeleine, the king's sister,—this they did because it was the first thing that offered; though they broke the promises that had been made to the King of England, who was deeply in love with her. In fact, this matter nearly caused a falling out between the two kings. Henry VIII. could not be consoled for not marrying my mother; and whenever any other French princess was proposed to him, he used to say that she would never take the place of the one they had taken from him. It is true that my mother was a perfect beauty, and it is remarkable that when she was the widow of a duke of Longueville, three kings should have wanted to marry her. It was her misfortune to be married to the least important of them all, and to be sent to a kingdom where she has found nothing but unhappiness. I am told that I am like her; I dread the same sad fate, and whatever happiness seems to be awaiting me, I doubt if I ever enjoy it."

Mademoiselle de Chartres assured the crown princess that these gloomy presentiments were so fantastic that they could not long disturb her, and that she ought not to doubt that her good fortune would give the lie to her fears.

Henceforth no one dared to think of Mademoiselle de Chartres, through fear of displeasing the king or of not succeeding in winning a young woman who had aspired to a prince of the blood. None of these considerations moved Monsieur de Clèves. The death of his father, the Duke of Nevers, which happened at that time, left him free to follow his own inclinations, and as soon as the period of mourning had passed, he thought of nothing but marrying Mademoiselle de Chartres. He was glad to make his proposal at a time when circumstances had driven away all rivals and when he felt almost sure that she would not refuse him. What dimmed his joy was the fear of not being agreeable to her; and he would have preferred the happiness of pleasing her to the certainty of marrying her when she did not love him.

The Chevalier de Guise had somewhat aroused his jealousy; but since this was inspired more by his rival's merits than by the conduct of Mademoiselle de Chartres, he thought of nothing but ascertaining whether by good fortune she would approve of his designs. He met her only at the queen's rooms or in company, yet he managed to speak to her of his intentions and hopes in the most respectful way; he begged her to let him know how she felt towards him, and told her that his feelings for her were such that he should be forever unhappy if she obeyed her mother only from a sense of duty.

Mademoiselle de Chartres, having a very noble heart, was really grateful to the Prince of Clèves for what he did. This gratitude lent to her answer a certain gentleness, which was quite sufficient to feed the hope of a man as much in love as he was, and he counted on attaining at least a part of what he desired.

Mademoiselle repeated this conversation to her mother, who said that Monsieur de Clèves was of such high birth, possessed so many fine qualities, and seemed so discreet for a man of his age, that if she inclined to marry him she would herself gladly give her consent. Mademoiselle de Chartres replied that she had noticed the same fine qualities, and that she would rather marry him than any one else, but that she had no special love for him.

The next day the prince had his offer formally made to Madame de Chartres; she accepted it, being willing to give her daughter a husband she did not love. The marriage settlement was drawn up, the king was told of it, and the marriage became known to every one.

Monsieur de Clèves was very happy, although not perfectly satisfied; it gave him much pain to see that what Mademoiselle de Chartres felt for him was only esteem and gratitude, and he could not flatter himself that she nourished any warmer feeling; for had she done so, she would have readily shown it in their closer intimacy. Within a few days he complained to her of this.

"Is it possible," he said, "that I may not be happy in my marriage? Yet assuredly I am not happy. You have a sort of kindly feeling for me which cannot satisfy me; you are not impatient, uneasy, or grieved; you are as indifferent to my love as if this were given to your purse, and not to your charms."

"You do wrong to complain," she replied. "I do not know what more you can ask; it seems to me that you have no right to demand anything more."

"It is true," he said, "that you have a certain air with which I should be satisfied if there were anything behind it; but instead of your being restrained by a sense of propriety, it is a sense of propriety which inspires your actions. I do not touch your feelings or your heart; my presence causes you neither pleasure nor pain."

"You cannot doubt," she made answer, "that I am glad to see you, and I blush so often when I do see you that you may be sure that the sight of you affects me."

"I am not deceived by your blushes," he urged; "they come from modesty, and not from any thrill of your heart, and I do not exaggerate their importance."

Mademoiselle de Chartres did not know what to answer; these distinctions were outside of her experience. Monsieur de Clèves saw only too well how far removed she was from feeling for him as he should have liked, when he saw that she had no idea of what that feeling was.

The Chevalier de Guise returned from a journey a few days before the wedding. He had seen so many insurmountable obstacles in the way of his marrying Mademoiselle de Chartres that he knew he had no chance of success; yet he was evidently distressed at seeing her become the wife of another. This grief did not extinguish his passion, and he remained quite as much in love as before. Mademoiselle de Chartres had not been ignorant of his devotion. On his return he let her know that she was the cause of the deep gloom that marked his face; and he had so much merit and charm that it was almost impossible to make him unhappy without regretting it. Hence she was depressed; but this pity went no further, and she told her mother how much pain this prince's love caused her.

Madame de Chartres admired her daughter's frankness, and with good reason, for it could not be fuller or simpler; she regretted, however, that her heart was not touched, especially when she saw that the prince had not affected it any more than the others. Hence she took great pains to attach her to her future husband, and to impress upon her what she owed him for the interest he had taken in her before he knew who she was, and for the proof he had given of his love in choosing her at a time when no one else ventured to think of her.

The marriage ceremony took place at the Louvre, and in the evening the king and queen, with all the court, supped at the house of Madame de Chartres, who received them with great splendor. The Chevalier de Guise did not venture to make himself conspicuous by staying away, but his dejection was evident.

Monsieur de Clèves did not find that Mademoiselle de Chartres had altered her feelings when she changed her name. His position as her husband gave him greater privileges, but no different place in her heart. Though he had married her, he did not cease to be her lover, because there was always left something for him to desire; and though she lived on the best of terms with him, he was not yet perfectly happy. He preserved for her a violent and restless passion, which marred his joy. Jealousy had no part in it, for never had a husband been further from feeling it, or a wife from inspiring it. Yet she was exposed to all the temptations of the court, visiting the queen and the king's sister every day. All the young and fashionable men met her at her own house and at that of her brother-in-law, the Duke of Nevers, whose doors were always open; but she always had an air that inspired respect, and seemed so remote from gallantry that the Marshal of Saint-André, though bold and protected by the king's favor, was touched by her beauty without venturing to show it except by delicate attentions. There were many others who felt as did the marshal; and Madame de Chartres added to her daughter's natural modesty such a keen sense of propriety that she made her seem like a woman to be sighed for in vain.

The Duchess of Lorraine, while trying to bring about peace, had also tried to arrange the marriage of her son, the Duke of Lorraine, and had succeeded; he was to marry Madame Claude of France, the king's second daughter. The wedding had been settled for the month of February.

Meanwhile the Duke of Nemours had remained at Brussels, completely taken up with his plans for England. He was always sending and receiving messengers. His hopes grew from day to day, and at last Lignerolles told him that it was time for him to appear and finish in person what had been so well begun. He received this news with all the satisfaction that an ambitious man can feel at seeing himself raised to a throne simply through his reputation. He had gradually grown so accustomed to the contemplation of this great piece of good fortune that whereas at first he had regarded it as an impossibility, all difficulties had vanished, and he foresaw no obstacles.

He at once despatched to Paris orders for a magnificent outfit, that he might make his appearance in England with a splendor proportionate to his designs, and also hastened to court to be present at the wedding of the Duke of Lorraine. He arrived the day before the formal betrothal, and that same evening went to report to the king the condition of affairs and to receive his advice and commands about his future conduct. Thence he went to pay his respects to the queens. Madame de Clèves was not there, so that she did not see him, and was not even aware of his arrival. She had heard every one speak of this prince as the handsomest and most agreeable man at court, and Madame the Dauphiness had spoken of him so often and in such terms that she felt some curiosity to see him.

Madame de Clèves spent the day of the betrothal at home dressing herself for the ball in the evening at the Louvre. When she made her appearance, her beauty and the splendor of her dress aroused general admiration. The ball opened, and while she was dancing with Monsieur de Guise, there was a certain commotion at the door of the ball-room, as if some one were entering for whom way was being made. Madame de Clèves finished her dance, and while she was looking about for another partner, the king called out to her to take the gentleman who had just arrived. She turned, and saw a man, who she thought must be Monsieur de Nemours, stepping over some seats to reach the place where the dancing was going on. No one ever saw this prince for the first time without amazement; and this evening he was more striking than ever in the rich attire which set off his natural beauty to such great advantage; and it was also hard to see Madame de Clèves for the first time without astonishment.

Monsieur de Nemours was so amazed by her beauty that when he drew near her and bowed to her he could not conceal his wonder and delight. When they began their dance, a murmur of admiration ran through the ball-room. The king and the queens remembered that the pair had never met, and saw how strange it was that they should be dancing together without being acquainted. They summoned them when they had finished the set, and without giving them a chance to speak to any one, asked if each would not like to know who the other was, and whether either had any idea.

"As for me, Madame," said Monsieur de Nemours, "I have no doubts; but since Madame de Clèves has not the same reasons for guessing who I am that I have for recognizing her, I must beg your Majesty to be good enough to tell her my name."

"I fancy," said the dauphiness, "that she knows it as well as you know hers."

"I assure you, Madame," said Madame de Clèves, who seemed a little embarrassed, "that I cannot guess so well as you think."

"You can guess very well," replied the dauphiness, "and you are very kind to Monsieur de Nemours in your unwillingness to acknowledge that you recognize him without ever having seen him before."

The queen interrupted the conversation, that the ball might go on, and Monsieur de Nemours danced with the dauphiness. This lady was a perfect beauty, and had always appeared to be one in the eyes of Monsieur de Nemours before he went to Flanders; but all that evening he admired no one but Madame de Clèves.

The Chevalier de Guise, who never ceased worshipping her, was standing near, and this incident caused him evident pain. He regarded it as a sure sign that fate meant that Monsieur de Nemours should fall in love with Madame de Clèves; and whether it was that he saw something in her face, or that jealousy sharpened his fears, he believed that she had been moved by the sight of this prince, and he could not keep from telling her that Monsieur de Nemours was very fortunate in making her acquaintance in such a gallant and unusual way.

Madame de Clèves went home so full of what had happened at the ball that though it was very late, she went to her mother's room to tell her about it; and she praised Monsieur de Nemours with a certain air that made Madame de Chartres entertain the same suspicion as the Chevalier de Guise.

The next day the wedding took place; Madame de Clèves there saw the Duke of Nemours, and was even more struck by his admirable grace and dignity than before.

On succeeding days she met him at the drawing-room of the dauphiness, saw him playing tennis with the king and riding at the ring, and heard him talk; and she always found him so superior to every one else, and so much outshining all in conversation wherever he might be, by the grace of his person and the charm of his wit, that he soon made a deep impression on her heart.

Then, too, the desire to please made the Duke of Nemours, who was already deeply interested, more charming than ever; and since they met often, and found each other more attractive than any one else at court, they naturally experienced great delight in being together.

The Duchess of Valentinois took part in all the merry-making, and the king showed her all the interest and attention that he had done when first in love with her. Madame de Clèves, who was then of an age at which it is usual to believe that no woman can ever be loved after she is twenty-five years old, regarded with great amazement the king's attachment to this duchess, who was a grandmother and had just married her granddaughter. She often spoke of it to Madame de Chartres. "Is it possible," she asked, "that the king has been in love so long? How could he get interested in a woman much older than himself, and who had been his father's mistress, as well as that of a great many other men, as I have heard?"

"It is true," was the answer, "that neither merit nor fidelity inspired the king's passion, or has kept it alive. And this is something which is scarcely to be excused; for had this

woman had youth and beauty as well as rank, had she loved
no one else, had she loved the king with untiring constancy,
for himself alone, and not solely for his wealth and position,
and had she used her power for worthy objects such as the
king desired, it would have been easy to admire his great
devotion to her. If," Madame de Chartres went on, "I were
not afraid that you would say of me what is always said of
women of my age, that we like to talk about old times, I would
tell you the beginning of the king's love for this duchess; and
many things that happened at the court of the late king bear
much resemblance to what is now going on."

"So far from accusing you of repeating old stories," said
Madame de Clèves, "I regret that you have told me so little
about the present, and that you have not taught me the
different interests and intrigues of the court. I am so ignorant
of them that a few days ago I thought the constable was on
the best of terms with the queen."

"You were very far from the truth," replied Madame de
Chartres. "The queen hates the constable, and if she ever gets
any power he will learn it very quickly. She knows that he has
often told the king that of all his children it is only his bastards
who look like him."

"I should never have imagined this hatred," interrupted
Madame de Clèves, "after seeing the zeal with which the
queen wrote to the constable when he was in prison, the joy
she manifested at his return, and the familiarity of her address
as regards him."

"If you judge from appearances here," replied Madame de
Chartres, "you will be often mistaken; what appears is seldom
the truth.

"But to return to Madame de Valentinois: you know her
name is Diane de Poitiers. She is of illustrious family, being
descended from the old dukes of Aquitaine; her grandmother
was a natural daughter of Louis XI.,—in short, there is no
common blood in her veins. Saint-Vallier, her father, was
implicated in the affair of the Constable of Bourbon, of which
you have heard, was condemned to be beheaded, and was led
to the scaffold. His daughter, who was remarkably beautiful,
and had already pleased the late king, managed, I don't know
how, to save her father's life. His pardon was granted him
when he was expecting the mortal stroke; but fear had so
possessed him that he did not recover consciousness, but died
a few days later. His daughter made her appearance at court
as the king's mistress. His journey to Italy and his imprison-

ment interrupted this passion. When he returned from Spain and Madame Régente went to meet him at Bayonne, she had with her all her young women, among whom was Mademoiselle de Pisseleu, afterwards Duchess of Estampes. The king fell in love with her, though she was inferior in birth, beauty, and intelligence to Madame de Valentinois: the only advantage she had was that she was younger. I have often heard her say that she was born on the day that Diane de Poitiers was married; but that remark was more malicious than truthful, for I am much mistaken if the Duchess of Valentinois did not marry Monsieur de Brézé, grand seneschal of Normandy, at the same time that the king fell in love with Madame d'Estampes. Never was there fiercer hatred than existed between those two women. The Duchess of Valentinois could not forgive Madame d'Estampes for depriving her of the title of the king's mistress. Madame d'Estampes was madly jealous of Madame de Valentinois because the king maintained his relations with her. This king was never rigorously faithful to his mistresses; there was always one who had the title and the honors, but the ladies of what was called the little band shared his attentions. The death of his oldest son, it was supposed by poison, at Tournon, was a great blow to him. He had much less love for his second son, the present king, who was in every way far less to his taste, and whom he even regarded as lacking courage and spirit. He was lamenting this one day to Madame de Valentinois, whereupon she said she would like to make him fall in love with her, that he might become livelier and more agreeable. She succeeded, as you know. This love has lasted more than twenty years, without being dimmed by time or circumstances.

"At first the late king objected to it,—whether because he was still enough in love with Madame de Valentinois to feel jealous, or because he was influenced by Madame d'Estampes, who was in despair when the dauphin became attached to her enemy, is uncertain; however that may be, he viewed this passion with an anger and a disapproval that were apparent every day. His son feared neither his wrath nor his hate; and since nothing could induce him to abate or to conceal his attachment, the king was forced to endure it as best he could. His son's opposition to his wishes estranged him still more, and attached him more closely to the Duke of Orléans, his third son. This prince was handsome, energetic, ambitious, of a somewhat tempestuous nature, which needed to be controlled, but who in time would become a really fine man.

"The elder son's rank as dauphin and the father's preference for the Duke of Orléans inspired a rivalry between them which amounted to hatred. This rivalry had begun in their childhood, and lasted until the death of the latter. When the emperor entered French territory he gave his whole preference to the Duke of Orléans. This so pained the dauphin that when the emperor was at Chantilly he tried to compel the constable to arrest him, without waiting for the king's orders; but the constable refused. Afterward the king blamed him for not following his son's advice; and this had a good deal to do with his leaving the court.

"The division between the two brothers induced the Duchess of Estampes to rely on the Duke of Orléans for protection against the influence which Madame de Valentinois had over the king. In this she succeeded; the duke, without falling in love with her, was as warm in defence of her interests as was the dauphin in defence of those of Madame de Valentinois. Hence there were two cabals in the court such as you can imagine; but the intrigues were not limited to two women's quarrels.

"The emperor, who had maintained his friendship for the Duke of Orléans, had frequently offered him the duchy of Milan. In the subsequent negotiations about peace, he raised hopes in the breast of the duke that he would give him the seventeen provinces and his daughter's hand. The dauphin, however, desired neither peace nor this marriage. He made use of the constable, whom he has always loved, to convince the king how important it was not to give to his successor a brother so powerful as would be the Duke of Orléans in alliance with the emperor and governing the seventeen provinces. The constable agreed the more heartily with the dauphin's views because he also opposed those of Madame d'Estampes, who was his avowed enemy, and ardently desired that the power of the Duke of Orléans should be increased.

"At that time the dauphin was in command of the king's army in Champagne, and had reduced that of the emperor to such extremities that it would have utterly perished had not the Duchess of Estampes, fearing that too great success would prevent our granting peace and consenting to the marriage, secretly sent word to the enemy to surprise Epernay and Château-Thierry, which were full of supplies. This they did, and thereby saved their whole army.

"This duchess did not long profit by her treason. Soon afterward the Duke of Orléans died at Farmoutier of some contagious disease. He loved one of the most beautiful women of the court, and was beloved by her. I shall not tell you who it was, because her life since that time has been most decorous; and she has tried so hard to have her affection for the prince forgotten that she deserves to have her reputation left untarnished. It so happened that she heard of her husband's death on the same day that she heard of that of Monsieur d'-Orléans; consequently she was able to conceal her real grief without an effort.

"The king did not long survive his son's decease,—he died two years later. He urged the dauphin to make use of the services of the Cardinal of Tournon and of the Amiral d'An-nebauld, without saying a word about the constable, who at that time was banished to Chantilly. Nevertheless, the first thing the present king did after his father's death was to call the constable back and intrust him with the management of affairs.

"Madame d'Estampes was sent away, and became the victim of all the ill-treatment she might have expected from an all-powerful enemy. The Duchess of Valentinois took full vengeance on this duchess and on all who had displeased her. Her power over the king seemed the greater because it had not appeared while he was dauphin. During the twelve years of his reign she has been in everything absolute mistress. She disposes of places and controls affairs of every sort; she secured the dismissal of the Cardinal of Tournon, of the Chancelier Olivier, and of Villeroy. Those who have endeavored to open the king's eyes to her conduct have been ruined for their pains. The Count of Taix, commander-in-chief of the artillery, who did not like her, could not keep from talking about her love affairs, and especially about one with the Count of Brissac, of whom the king was already very jealous. Yet she managed so well that the Count of Taix was disgraced and deprived of his position; and impossible as it may sound, he was succeeded by the Count of Brissac, whom she afterward made a marshal of France. Still, the king's jealousy became so violent that he could not endure having this marshal remain at court; but though usually jealousy is a hot and violent passion, it is modified and tempered in him by his extreme respect for his mistress, so that the only means he ventured to use to rid himself of his rival was by intrusting to him the government of Piedmont. There he has spent several years; last winter, however, he returned, under the pretext of asking for men and supplies for the army under his command. Possibly the

desire of seeing Madame de Valentinois and dread of being
forgotten had something to do with this journey. The king
received him very coldly. The Guises, who do not like him
did not dare betray their feelings, on account of Madame de
Valentinois, so they made use of the Vidame, his open enemy,
to prevent his getting any of the things he wanted. It was not
hard to injure him. The king hated him, and was made uneasy
by his presence; consequently he was obliged to go back without getting any advantage from his journey,—unless, possibly,
he had rekindled in the heart of Madame de Valentinois
feelings which absence had nearly extinguished. The king has
had many other grounds for jealousy, but either he has not
known them, or he has not dared to complain.

"I am not sure, my dear," added Madame de Chartres,
"that you may not think I have told you more than you cared
to hear."

"Not at all," answered Madame de Clèves; "and if I were
not afraid of tiring you, I should ask you many more questions."

Monsieur de Nemours' love for Madame de Clèves was at
first so violent that he lost all interest in those he had formerly
loved, and with whom he had kept up relations during his
absence. He not merely did not seek any excuses for deserting
them, he would not even listen to their complaints or reply to
their reproaches. The dauphiness, for whom he had nourished
very warm feelings, was soon forgotten by the side of Madame de Clèves. His impatience for his journey to England
began to abate, and he ceased to hasten his preparations for
departure. He often visited the crown princess, because Madame de Clèves was frequently in her apartments, and he was
not unwilling to give some justification to the widespread suspicions about his feelings for the dauphiness. Madame de
Clèves seemed to him so rare a prize that he decided to conceal all signs of his love rather than let it be generally known.
He never spoke of it even to his intimate friend the Vidame de
Chartres, to whom he usually confided everything. He was so
cautious and discreet that no one suspected his love for Madame de Clèves except the Chevalier de Guise; and the lady
herself would scarcely have perceived it had not her own
interest in him made her watch him very closely, so that she
became sure of it.

Madame de Clèves did not find herself so disposed to tell
her mother what she thought of this prince's feelings as had
been the case with her other lovers; and without definitely

deciding on reserve, she yet never spoke of the subject. But Madame de Chartres soon perceived this, as well as her daughter's interest in him. This knowledge gave her distinct pain, for she well understood how dangerous it was for Madame de Clèves to be loved by a man like Monsieur de Nemours, especially when she was already disposed to admire him. An incident that happened a few days later confirmed her suspicions of this liking.

The Marshal of Saint-André, who was always on the lookout for opportunities to display his magnificence, made a pretext of desiring to show his house, which had just been finished, and invited the king to do him the honor of supping there with the queens. The marshal was also glad to be able to show to Madame de Clèves his lavish splendor.

A few days before the one of the supper, the dauphin, whose health was delicate, had been ailing and had seen no one. His wife, the crown princess, had spent the whole day with him, and toward evening, as he felt better, he received all the persons of quality who were in his ante-chamber. The crown princess went to her own apartment, where she found Madame de Clèves and a few other ladies with whom she was most intimate.

Since it was already late, and the crown princess was not dressed, she did not go to the queen, but sent word she could not come; she then had her jewels brought, to decide what she should wear at the Marshal of Saint-André's ball, and to give some, according to a promise she had made, to Madame de Clèves. While they were thus occupied, the Prince of Condé, whose rank gave him free admission everywhere, entered. The crown princess said to him that he doubtless came from her husband, and asked what was going on in his apartments.

"They are having a discussion, Madame, with Monsieur de Nemours," he answered. "He defends the side he has taken so eagerly that he must have a personal interest in it. I fancy he has a mistress who makes him uneasy when she goes to a ball, for he maintains that it makes a lover unhappy to see the woman he loves at such a place."

"What!" said the dauphiness, "Monsieur de Nemours does not want his mistress to go to a ball? I thought husbands might object, but I never supposed that lovers could have such a feeling."

"Monsieur de Nemours," replied the Prince of Condé, "declares that a ball is most distressing to lovers, whether they are loved or not. He says if their love is returned, they have the pain of being loved less for several days; that there is not a woman in the world who is not prevented from thinking of her lover by the demands of her toilet, which entirely engrosses her attention; that women dress for every one as well as for those they love; that when they are at the ball they are anxious to please all who look at them; that when they are proud of their beauty, they feel a pleasure in which the lover plays but a small part. He says, too, that one who sighs in vain suffers even more when he sees his mistress at an entertainment; that the more she is admired by the public, the more one suffers at not being loved, through fear lest her beauty should kindle some love happier than his own; finally, that there is no pain so keen as seeing one's mistress at a ball, except knowing that she is there while absent one's self."

Madame de Clèves, though pretending not to hear what the Prince of Condé was saying, listened attentively. She readily understood her share in the opinion expressed by Monsieur de Nemours, especially when he spoke of his grief at not being at the ball with his mistress, because he was not to be at that given by the Marshal of Saint-André, being ordered by the king to go to meet the Duke of Ferrara.

The crown princess laughed with the Prince of Condé, and expressed her disapproval of the views of Monsieur de Nemours. "There is only one condition, Madame," said the prince, "on which Monsieur de Nemours is willing that his mistress should go to a ball, and that is that he himself should give her permission. He said that last year when he gave a ball to your Majesty, he thought that his mistress did him a great favor in coming to it, though she seemed to be there only as one of your suite; that it is always a kindness to a lover to take part in any entertainment that he gives; and that it is also agreeable to a lover to have his mistress see him the host of the whole court and doing the honors fittingly."

"Monsieur de Nemours did well," said the dauphiness, with a smile, "to let his mistress go to that ball; for so many women claimed that position that if they had not come, there would have been scarcely any one there."

As soon as the Prince of Condé had begun to speak of what Monsieur de Nemours thought of the ball, Madame de Clèves was very anxious not to go to that of the Marshal of Saint-André. She readily agreed that it was not fitting for a woman to go to the house of a man who was in love with her, and she was glad to have so good a reason for doing a kindness to Monsieur de Nemours. Nevertheless, she took away the jewels which the crown princess had given her; that evening, however, when she showed them to her mother, she told her that she did not mean to wear them, that the Marshal of Saint-André had made his love for her so manifest that she felt sure he meant to have it thought that she was to have some part in the entertainment he was to give to the king, and that under the pretext of doing honor to the king he would pay her attentions which might perhaps prove embarrassing.

Madame de Chartres argued for some time against her daughter's decision, which she thought singular, but at last yielded, and told her she must pretend to be ill, in order to have a good excuse for not going, because her real reasons would not be approved and should not be suspected. Madame de Clèves gladly consented to stay at home for a few days, in order not to meet Monsieur de Nemours, who left without having the pleasure of knowing that she was not going to the ball.

The duke returned the day after the ball, and heard that she had not been there; but inasmuch as he did not know that his talk with the dauphin had been repeated to her, he was far from thinking that he was fortunate enough to be the cause of her absence.

The next day, when Monsieur de Nemours was calling on the queen and talking with the dauphiness, Madame de Chartres and Madame de Clèves happened to come in and approached this princess. Madame de Clèves was not in full dress, as if she were not very well, though her countenance belied her attire.

"You look so well," said the crown princess, "that I can scarcely believe that you have been ill. I fancy that the Prince of Condé, when he told you what Monsieur de Nemours thought about the ball, convinced you that you would do a kindness to the Marshal of Saint-André by going to his ball, and that that was the reason you stayed away."

Madame de Clèves blushed at the dauphiness's accurate guess which she thus expressed before Monsieur de Nemours.

Madame de Chartres saw at once why her daughter did not go to the ball, and in order to throw Monsieur de Nemours off the track, she at once addressed the dauphiness with an air of sincerity. "I assure you, Madame," she said, "that your Majesty pays an honor to my daughter which she does not deserve. She was really ill; but I am sure that if I had not forbidden it, she would have accompanied you, unfit as she was, to have the pleasure of seeing the wonderful entertainment last evening."

The dauphiness believed what Madame de Chartres said,

and Monsieur de Nemours was vexed to see how probable her story was; nevertheless the confusion of Madame de Clèves made him suspect that the dauphiness's conjecture was not without some foundation in fact. At first Madame de Clèves had been annoyed because Monsieur de Nemours had reason to suppose that it was he who had kept her from going to the ball, and then she felt regret that her mother had entirely removed the grounds for this supposition.

Although the attempt to make peace at Cercamp had failed, negotiations still continued, and matters had assumed such a shape that toward the end of February a meeting was held at Câteau-Cambresis. The same commissioners had assembled there, and the departure of the Marshal of Saint-André freed Monsieur de Nemours from a rival who was more to be dreaded on account of his close observation of all those who approached Madame de Clèves than from any real success of his own.

Madame de Chartres did not wish to let her daughter see that she knew her feeling for this prince, lest she should make her suspicious of the advice she wanted to give her. One day she began to talk about him. She spoke of him in warm terms, but craftily praised his discretion in being unable to fall really in love and in seeking only pleasure, not a serious attachment, in his relations with women. "To be sure," she went on, "he has been suspected of a great passion for the dauphiness; I notice that he visits her very often, and I advise you to avoid talking with him as much as possible, especially in private, because you are on such terms with the crown princess that people would say that you were their confidant, and you know how disagreeable that would be. I think that if the report continues, you would do well to see less of the crown princess, that you may not be connected with love-affairs of that sort."

Madame de Clèves had never heard Monsieur de Nemours and the dauphiness talked about, and was much surprised by what her mother said. She was so sure that she had misunderstood the prince's feelings for her that she changed color. Madame de Chartres noticed this, but company coming in at that moment, Madame de Clèves went home and locked herself up in her room.

It is impossible to express her grief when her mother's words opened her eyes to the interest she took in Monsieur de Nemours; she had never dared to acknowledge it to herself. Then she saw that her feelings for him were what Monsieur de Clèves had so often supplicated, and she felt the mortification of having them for another than a husband who so well deserved them. She felt hurt and embarrassed, fearing that Monsieur de Nemours might have used her as a pretext for seeing the dauphiness; and this thought decided her to tell Madame de Chartres what she had hitherto kept secret.

The next morning she went to her mother to carry out this decision; but Madame de Chartres was a little feverish, and did not care to talk with her. The illness seemed so slight, however, that Madame de Clèves called on the dauphiness after dinner, and found her in her room with two or three ladies with whom she was on intimate terms.

"We were talking about Monsieur de Nemours," said the queen when she saw her, "and were surprised to see how much he is changed since his return from Brussels; before he went, he had an infinite number of mistresses, and it was a positive disadvantage to him, because he used to be kind both to those who were worthy and to those who were not. Since his return, however, he will have nothing to do with any of them. There has never been such a change. His spirits, moreover, seem to be affected, as he is much less cheerful than usual."

Madame de Clèves made no answer; she thought with a sense of shame that she would have taken all that they said about the change in him for a proof of his passion if she had not been undeceived. She was somewhat vexed with the dauphiness for trying to explain and for expressing surprise at something of which she must know the real reason better than any one else. She could not keep from showing her annoyance, and when the other ladies withdrew, she went up to the crown princess and said in a low voice,—

"Is it for my benefit that you have just spoken, and do you want to hide from me that you are the cause of the altered conduct of Monsieur de Nemours?"

"You are unjust," said the crown princess; "you know that I never keep anything from you. It is true that before he went to Brussels, Monsieur de Nemours meant to have me understand that he did not hate me; but since his return he seems to have forgotten all about it, and I confess that I am a little curious about the reason of this change. I shall probably find it out," she went on, "as the Vidame de Chartres, his intimate friend, is in love with a young woman over whom I have some power, and I shall know from her what has made this change."

The dauphiness spoke with an air that carried conviction to

Madame de Clèves, who found herself calmer and happier than she had been before. When she went back to her mother, she found her much worse than when she had left her. She was more feverish, and for some days it seemed as if she were going to be really ill. Madame de Clèves was in great distress, and did not leave her mother's room. Monsieur de Clèves spent nearly all his time there too, both to comfort his wife and to have the pleasure of seeing her: his love had not lessened.

Monsieur de Nemours, who had always been one of his friends, had not neglected him since his return from Brussels. During the illness of Madame de Chartres he found it possible to see Madame de Clèves very often, under pretence of calling on her husband or of stopping to take him to walk. He even sought him at hours when he knew he was not in; then he would say that he would wait for him, and used to stay in the ante-chamber of Madame de Chartres, where were assembled many persons of quality. Madame de Clèves would often look in, and although she was in great anxiety, she seemed no less beautiful to Monsieur de Nemours. He showed her how much he sympathized with her distress, and soon convinced her that it was not with the dauphiness that he was in love.

She could not keep from being embarrassed, and yet delighted to see him; but when he was out of her sight and she remembered that this pleasure was the beginning of an unhappy passion, she felt she almost hated him, so much did the idea of guilty love pain her.

Madame de Chartres rapidly grew worse, and soon her life was despaired of; she heard the doctors' opinion of her danger with a courage proportionate to her virtue and piety. After they had left her, she dismissed all who were present, and sent for Madame de Clèves.

"We have to part, my daughter," she said, holding out her hand; "and the peril in which you are and the need you have of me, double my pain in leaving you. You have an affection for Monsieur de Nemours; I do not ask you to confess it, as I am no longer able to make use of your sincerity in order to guide you. It is long since I perceived this affection, but I have been averse to speaking to you about it, lest you should become aware of it yourself. Now you know it only too well. You are on the edge of a precipice: a great effort, a violent struggle, alone can save you. Think of what you owe your husband, think of what you owe yourself, and remember that you are in danger of losing that reputation which you have acquired and which I have so ardently desired for you. Take strength and courage, my daughter: withdraw from the court; compel your husband to take you away. Do not be afraid of making a difficult decision. Terrible as it may appear at first, it will in the end be pleasanter than the consequences of a love-affair. If any other reasons than virtue and duty can persuade you to what I wish, let me say that if anything is capable of destroying the happiness I hope for in another world, it would be seeing you fall like so many women; but if this misfortune must come to you, I welcome death that I may not see it."

Madame de Clèves's tears fell on her mother's hand, which she held clasped in her own, and Madame de Chartres saw that she was moved. "Good-by, my daughter," she said; "let us put an end to a conversation which moves us both too deeply, and remember, if you can, all I have just said to you."

With these words she turned away and bade her daughter call her women, without hearing or saying more. Madame de Clèves left her mother's room in a state that may be imagined, and Madame de Chartres thought of nothing but preparing herself for death. She lingered two days more, but refused again to see her daughter,—the only person she loved.

Madame de Clèves was in sore distress; her husband never left her side, and as soon as Madame de Chartres had died, he took her into the country, to get her away from a place which continually renewed her grief, which was intense. Although her love and gratitude to her mother counted for a great deal, the need she felt of her support against Monsieur de Nemours made the blow even more painful. She lamented being left to herself when she had her emotions so little under control, and when she so needed some one to pity her and give her strength. Her husband's kindness made her wish more than ever to be always true to him. She showed him more affection and kindliness than she had ever done before, and she wanted him always by her side; for it seemed to her that her attachment to him would prove a defence against Monsieur de Nemours.

This prince went to visit Monsieur de Clèves in the country, and did his best to see Madame de Clèves; but she declined to receive him, knowing that she could not fail to find him charming. Moreover, she resolutely determined to avoid every occasion of meeting him, so far as she was able.

Monsieur de Clèves repaired to Paris to pay his respects at court, promising his wife to return the next day; but he did not return till the day after.

"I expected you all day yesterday," Madame de Clèves said

to him when he arrived, "and I ought to find fault with you for not returning when you promised. You know that if I could feel a new sorrow in the state I am in, it would be at the death of Madame de Tournon, of which I heard this morning. I should have been distressed by it even if I had not known her. It is always painful when a young and beautiful woman like her dies after an illness of only two days, and much more so when it is one of the persons I liked best in the world, and who seemed as modest as she was worthy."

"I was sorry not to return yesterday," answered Monsieur de Clèves; "but it was so imperatively necessary that I should console an unhappy man that I could not possibly leave him. As for Madame de Tournon, I advise you not to be too profoundly distressed, if you mourn her as an upright woman who deserved your esteem."

"You surprise me," said Madame de Clèves, "as I have often heard you say that there was no woman at court whom you esteemed more highly."

"That is true," he answered; "but women are incomprehensible, and the more I see of them, the happier I feel that I have married you, and I cannot be sufficiently grateful for my good fortune."

"You think better of me than I deserve," exclaimed Madame de Clèves, with a sigh, "and it is much too soon to think me worthy of you. But tell me, please, what has undeceived you about Madame de Tournon."

"I have long been undeceived in regard to her," he replied, "and have long known that she loved the Count of Sancerre, to whom she held out hopes that she would marry him."

"I can scarcely believe," interrupted Madame de Clèves, "that Madame de Tournon, after the extraordinary reluctance to matrimony which she showed after she became a widow, and after her public assertions that she would never marry again, should have given Sancerre any hopes."

"If she had given them only to him," replied Monsieur de Clèves, "there would be little occasion for surprise; but what is astounding is that she also gave them to Estouteville at the same time, and I will tell you the whole story."

PART II.

"You know," Monsieur de Clèves continued, "what good friends Sancerre and I are; yet when, about two years ago, he fell in love with Madame de Tournon, he took great pains to conceal it from me, as well as from every one else, and I was far from suspecting it. Madame de Tournon appeared still inconsolable for her husband's death, and was still living in the most absolute retirement. Sancerre's sister was almost the only person she saw, and it was at her house that the count fell in love with her.

"One evening when there was to be a play at the Louvre, and while they were waiting for the king and Madame de Valentinois in order to begin, word was brought that she was ill and that the king would not come. Every one guessed that the duchess's illness was some quarrel with the king. We knew how jealous he had been of the Marshal of Brissac during his stay at court; but the marshal had gone back to Piedmont a few days before, and we could not imagine the cause of this falling-out.

"While I was talking about it with Sancerre, Monsieur d'-Anville came into the hall and whispered to me that the king was in a state of distress and anger most piteous to see; that when he and Madame de Valentinois were reconciled a few days before, after their quarrels about the Marshal of Brissac, the king had given her a ring and asked her to wear it. While she was dressing for the play, he had noticed its absence, and had asked her the reason. She seemed surprised to miss it, and asked her women for it; but they, unfortunately, perhaps because they had not been put on their guard, said that it was some four or five days since they had seen it.

" 'That exactly corresponded with the date of the Marshal of Brissac's departure,' Monsieur d'Anville went on; 'and the king is convinced that she gave him the ring when she bade him good-by. This thought has so aroused all his jealousy, which was by no means wholly extinguished, that, contrary to his usual custom, he flew into a rage and reproached her bitterly. He has gone back to his room in great distress, whether because he thinks that Madame de Valentinois has given away his ring, or because he fears that he has displeased her by his wrath, I do not know.'

"As soon as Monsieur d'Anville had finished, I went up to Sancerre to tell him the news, assuring him that it was a secret that had just been told me, and was to go no farther.

"The next morning I called rather early on my sister-in-law, and found Madame de Tournon there. She did not like Madame de Valentinois, and knew very well that my sister-in-law also had no reason for being fond of her. Sancerre had seen her when he left the play, and had told her about the king's quarrel with the duchess; this she had come to repeat to my sister-in-law, either not knowing or not remembering that it was I who had told her lover.

"When I came in, my sister-in-law said to Madame de Tournon that I could be trusted with what she had just told her, and without waiting for permission she repeated to me word for word everything I had told Sancerre the previous evening. You will understand my surprise. I looked at Madame de Tournon, who seemed embarrassed, and her embarrassment aroused my suspicions. I had mentioned the matter to no one but Sancerre, who had left me after the play, without saying where he was going; but I remembered hearing him praise Madame de Tournon very warmly. All these things opened my eyes, and I soon decided that there was a love-affair between them, and that he had seen her after he left me.

"I was so annoyed to find that he kept the matter secret from me that I said a good many things that made it clear to Madame de Tournon that she had been imprudent; as I handed her to her carriage, I assured her that I envied the happiness of the person who had informed her of the falling out of the king and Madame de Valentinois.

"At once I went to see Sancerre; I reproached him, and said that I knew of his passion for Madame de Tournon, but I did not say how I had found it out. He felt obliged to make a complete confession. I then told him how it was I had discovered his secret, and he told me all about the affair; he said that inasmuch as he was a younger son, and far from having any claims to such an honor, she was yet determined to marry him. No one could be more surprised than I was. I urged Sancerre to hasten his marriage, and told him that he would be justified in fearing anything from a woman who was so full of craft that she could play so false a part before the public. He said in reply that her grief had been sincere, but that it had yielded before her affection for him, and that she could not suddenly make this great change manifest. He brought up many other things in her defence, which showed me clearly how much in love he was; he assured me that he would persuade her to let me know all about the passion he had for her, since it was she who had let out the secret,—and in fact he compelled her to consent, though with much difficulty, and I was from that time fully admitted to their confidence.

"I have never seen a woman so honorable and agreeable toward her lover; yet I was always pained by her affectation of grief. Sancerre was so much in love, and so well satisfied with the way she treated him, that he was almost afraid to urge their marriage, lest she should think that he was moved thereto by interest rather than passion. Still, he often talked to her about it, and she seemed to have decided to marry him; she even began to leave her retirement and to reappear in the world,—she used to come to my sister-in-law's at the time when part of the court used to be there. Sancerre came very seldom; but those who were there every evening and met her often, found her very charming.

"Shortly after she began to come out again into society, Sancerre imagined that he detected some coolness in her love for him. He spoke to me about it several times without rousing any anxiety in me by his complaints; but when at length he told me that instead of hastening, she seemed to be postponing their marriage, I began to think that he had good grounds for uneasiness. I said that even if Madame de Tournon's passion should lessen after lasting for two years, he ought not to be surprised; that even if it did not lessen, and though it should not be strong enough to persuade her to marry him, he ought not to complain; since their marriage would injure her much in the eyes of the public, not only because he was not a very good match for her, but because it would affect her reputation: hence that all he could reasonably desire was that she should not deceive him and feed him with false hopes. I also said that if she had not the courage to marry him, or if she should confess that she loved some one else, he ought not to be angry or complain, but preserve his esteem and gratitude for her.

"'I give you the advice,' I said to him, 'which I should take myself; for I am so touched by sincerity that I believe that if my mistress, or my wife, were to confess that any one pleased her, I should be distressed without being angered, and should lay aside the character of lover or husband to advise and sympathize with her.'"

At these words Madame de Clèves blushed, finding a certain likeness to her own condition which surprised her and distressed her for some time.

"Sancerre spoke to Madame de Tournon," Monsieur de Clèves went on, "telling her everything I had advised; but she reassured him with such tact and seemed so pained by his suspicions that she entirely dispelled them. Nevertheless she postponed their marriage until after a long journey which he was about to make; but her conduct was so discreet up to the time of his departure, and she seemed so grieved at parting with him, that I, as well as he, believed that she truly loved

him. He went away about three months ago. During his absence I saw Madame de Tournon very seldom; you have
taken up all my time, and I only knew that Sancerre was to
return soon.

"The day before yesterday, on my arrival in Paris, I heard
that she was dead. I at once sent to his house to find out if
they had heard from him, and was told that he had arrived
the day before,—the very day of Madame de Tournon's
death. I went at once to see him, knowing very well in what a
state I should find him; but his agony far exceeded what I had
imagined. Never have I seen such deep and tender grief. As
soon as he saw me, he embraced me, bursting into tears. 'I
shall never see her again,' he said, 'I shall never see her again;
she is dead! I was not worthy of her; but I shall soon follow
her.'

"After that he was silent; then from time to time he repeated: 'She is dead, and I shall never see her again!' Thereupon he would again burst into tears, and seemed out of his
head. He told me he had received but few letters from her
while away, but that this did not surprise him, because he well
knew her aversion to running any risk in writing letters. He
had no doubt that she would have married him on his return;
and he looked upon her as the most amiable and faithful
woman who had ever lived; he believed that she loved him
tenderly, and that he had lost her at the moment when he
made sure of winning her forever. These thoughts plunged
him into the deepest distress, by which he was wholly overcome, and I confess that I was deeply moved.

"Nevertheless, I was obliged to leave him to go to the king,
but I promised to return soon. This I did; but imagine my
surprise when I found that he was in an entirely different
mood. He was pacing up and down his room with a wild face,
and he stopped as if he were beside himself and said: 'Come;
come! see the most desperate man in the world; I am ten
thousand times unhappier than I was before, and what I have
just heard of Madame de Tournon is worse than her death.'

"I thought that his grief had crazed him, for I could imagine nothing more terrible than the death of a loved mistress
who returns one's love. I told him that so long as his grief had
been within bounds I had understood and sympathized with
it; but that I should cease to pity him if he gave way to
despair and lost his mind. 'I wish I could lose it, and my life
too,' he exclaimed. 'Madame de Tournon was unfaithful to
me; and I ascertained her infidelity and treachery the day

after I heard of her death, at a time when my soul was filled with the deepest grief and the tenderest love that were ever felt,—at a time when my heart was filled with the thought of her as the most perfect creature that had ever lived, and the most generous to me. I find that I was mistaken in her, and that she does not deserve my tears; nevertheless, I have the same grief from her death as if she had been faithful to me, and I suffer from her infidelity as if she were not dead. Had I known of her changed feeling before she died, I should have been wild with wrath and jealousy, and should have been in some way hardened against the blow of her death; but now I can get no consolation from it or hate her.'

"You may judge of my surprise at what Sancerre told me; I asked him how he found this out. He told me that the moment I had left his room, Estouteville, an intimate friend of his, though he knew nothing of his love for Madame de Tournon, had come to see him; that as soon as he had sat down, he burst into tears and said he begged his pardon for not having told him before what he was about to say; that he begged him to take pity on him; that he had come to open his heart to him; and that he saw before him a man utterly crushed by the death of Madame de Tournon.

" 'That name,' said Sancerre, 'surprised me so that my first impulse was to tell him that I was much more distressed than he; but I was unable to speak a word. He went on and told me that he had been in love with her for six months; that he had always meant to tell me, but she had forbidden it so firmly that he had not dared to disobey her; that almost ever since he fell in love with her she had taken a tender interest in him; that he only visited her secretly; that he had had the pleasure of consoling her for the loss of her husband; and, finally, that he was on the point of marrying her at the time of her death, but that this marriage, which would have been one of love, would have appeared to be one of duty and obedience, because she had won over her father to command this marriage, in order that there should not be any great change in her conduct, which had indicated an unwillingness to contract a second marriage.

" 'While Estouteville was speaking,' Sancerre went on, 'I fully believed him, because what he said seemed likely, and the time he had mentioned as that when he fell in love with Madame de Tournon coincided with that of her altered treatment of me. But a moment after, I thought him a liar, or at least out of his senses, and I was ready to tell him so. I thought, however, I would first make sure; hence I began to question him and to show that I had my doubts. At last I was so persistent in the search of my unhappiness that he asked if I knew Madame de Tournon's handwriting, and placed on my bed four of her letters and her portrait. My brother happened to come in at that moment. Estouteville's face was so stained with tears that he had to go away in order not to be seen in that state; he told me that he would come back that evening to get the things he left. I sent my brother away, pretending that I was not feeling well, being impatient to read the letters, and still hoping to find something which would convince me that Estouteville was mistaken. But, alas, what did I not find! What tenderness, what protestations, what promises to marry him, what letters! She had never written me any like them. So,' he went on, 'I suffer at the same time grief for her death and for her faithlessness,—two misfortunes which have often been compared, but have never been felt at the same time by one person. I confess, to my shame, that I feel much more keenly her death than her change; I cannot find her guilty enough to deserve to die. If she were still alive, I should have the pleasure of reproaching her, of avenging myself by showing her how great was her injustice. But I shall never see her again,' He repeated, 'I shall never see her again,—that is the bitterest blow of all; I would gladly give up my life for hers. What a wish! If she were to return, she would live for Estouteville. How happy I was yesterday!' he exclaimed, 'how happy I was then! I was the most sorely distressed man in the world; but my distress was in the order of nature, and I drew some comfort from the thought that I could never be consoled. To-day all my feelings are false ones; I pay to the pretended love she felt for me the same tribute that I thought due to a real affection. I can neither hate nor love her memory; I am incapable of consolation or of grief. At least,' he said, turning suddenly toward me, 'let me, I beg of you, never see Estouteville again; his very name fills me with horror. I know very well that I have no reason to blame him; it is my own fault for concealing from him my love for Madame de Tournon: if he had known of it, he would perhaps have never cared for her, and she would not have been unfaithful to me. He came to see me to confide his grief; I really pity him. Yes, and with good reason,' he exclaimed; 'he loved Madame de Tournon and was loved by her. He will never see her again; yet I feel that I cannot keep from hating him. Once more, I beg of you never to let me see him again.'

"Thereupon Sancerre burst again into tears, mourning Madame de Tournon, saying to her the tenderest things imaginable; thence he changed to hatred, complaints, reproaches, and denunciations of her conduct. When I saw him in this desperate state I knew that I should need some aid in calming him, so I sent for his brother, whom I had just left with the king. I went out to speak to him in the hall before he came in, and I told him what a state Sancerre was in. We gave orders that he was not to see Estouteville, and spent a good part of the night trying to persuade him to listen to reason. This morning I found him in still deeper distress; his brother is staying with him, and I have returned to you."

"No one could be more surprised than I am," said Madame de Clèves, "for I thought Madame de Tournon incapable of both love and deception."

"Address and dissimulation," answered Monsieur de Clèves, "could not go further. Notice that when Sancerre thought she had changed toward him, she really had, and had begun to love Estouteville. She told her new lover that he consoled her for her husband's death, and that it was he who was the cause of her returning to society; while it seemed to Sancerre that it was because we had decided that she should no longer appear to be in such deep affliction. She was able to persuade Estouteville to conceal their relations, and to seem obliged to marry him by her father's orders, as if it were the result of her care for her reputation,—and this in order to abandon Sancerre without leaving him ground for complaint. I must go back," continued Monsieur de Clèves, "to see this unhappy man, and I think you had better return to Paris. It is time for you to see company and to begin to receive the number of visits that await you."

Madame de Clèves gave her consent, and they returned the next day. She found herself more tranquil about Monsieur de Nemours than she had been; Madame de Chartres' dying words and her deep grief had for a time dulled her feelings, and she thought they had entirely changed.

The evening of Madame de Clèves's arrival the dauphiness came to see her, and after expressing her sympathy with her affliction, said that in order to drive away her sad thoughts she would tell her everything that had taken place at court during her absence, and narrated many incidents. "But what I most want to tell you," she added, "is that it is certain that Monsieur de Nemours is passionately in love, and that his most intimate friends are not only not in his confidence, but they can't even guess whom it is whom he loves. Yet this love is strong enough to make him neglect, or rather give up, the hope of a crown."

The dauphiness then told Madame de Clèves the whole plan about England. "I heard what I have just told you," she went on, "from Monsieur d'Anville; and he said to me this morning that the king sent last evening for Monsieur de Nemours, after reading some letters from Lignerolles, who is anxious to return, and had written to the king that he was unable to explain to the Queen of England Monsieur de Nemours' delay; that she is beginning to be offended; and that although she has given no positive answer, she had said enough to warrant him in starting. The king read this letter to Monsieur de Nemours, who instead of talking seriously, as he had done in the beginning, only laughed and joked about Lignerolles' hopes. He said that the whole of Europe would blame his imprudence if he were to presume to go to England as a claimant for the queen's hand without being assured of success. 'It seems to me too,' he went on, 'that I should not choose the present time for my journey, when the King of Spain is doing his best to marry her. In a love-affair he would not be a very formidable rival; but I think that in a question of marrying, your Majesty would not advise me to try my chances against him.' 'I do advise you so in the present circumstances,' answered the king. 'But you have no occasion to fear him. I know that he has other thoughts, and even if he had not, Queen Mary was too unhappy under the Spanish yoke for one to believe that her sister wishes to assume it, or would let herself be dazzled by the splendor of so many united crowns.' 'If she does not let herself be dazzled by them,' went on Monsieur de Nemours, 'probably she will wish to marry for love; she has loved Lord Courtenay for several years. Queen Mary also loved him, and she would have married him, with the consent of the whole of England, had she not known that the youth and beauty of her sister Elizabeth attracted him more than the desire of reigning. Your Majesty knows that her violent jealousy caused her to throw them both into prison, then to exile Lord Courtenay, and finally decided her to marry the King of Spain. I believe that Elizabeth, now that she is on the throne, will soon recall this lord and thus choose a man she has loved, who is very attractive, and who has suffered so much for her, rather than another whom she has never seen.' 'I should agree with you,' replied the king, 'if Courtenay were still living; but some days ago I heard that he had died at Padua, where he was living in banishment. I see very well,' he added, as he left Monsieur de Nemours, 'that it will be necessary to celebrate your marriage as we should celebrate the dauphin's, by sending ambassadors to marry the Queen of England by procuration.'

"Monsieur d'Anville and the Vidame, who were present while the king was talking with Monsieur de Nemours, are convinced that it is this great passion which has dissuaded him from this plan. The Vidame, who is more intimate than any one with him, said to Madame de Martigues that the prince is changed beyond recognition; and what amazes him still more is that he never finds him engaged or absent, so that he supposes he never meets the woman he loves; and what is so surprising, is to see Monsieur de Nemours in love with a woman who does not return his passion."

All this story that the dauphiness told her was as poison to Madame de Clèves. It was impossible for her not to feel sure that she was the woman whose name was unknown; and she was overwhelmed with gratitude and tenderness when she learned from one who had the best means of knowing that this prince, who had already aroused her interest, hid his passion from every one, and for love of her gave up his chances of a crown. It is impossible to describe her agitation. If the dauphiness had observed her with any care, she would at once have seen that the story she had just repeated was by no means without interest to her; but having no suspicion of the truth, she went on without noticing her. "Monsieur d'Anville," she added, "who, as I said, told me all this, thinks that I know more about it than he does, and he has so high an opinion of my charms that he is convinced that I am the only person who can make such a great change in Monsieur de Nemours."

Madame de Clèves was agitated by this last remark of the crown princess, though not in the same way as a few moments before. "I should readily agree with Monsieur d'Anville," she replied, "and it is certainly probable, Madame, that no one but a princess like you could make him indifferent to the Queen of England."

"I should at once acknowledge it," said the dauphiness, "if I knew that was the case, and I should know if it were true. Love-affairs of that sort do not escape the notice of those who inspire them; they are the first to perceive them. Monsieur de Nemours has never paid me any but the most insignificant attentions; but there is nevertheless so great a difference between his way with me and his present conduct that I can assure you I am not the cause of the indifference he shows for the crown of England.

"I forget everything while I am with you," she went on, "and it had slipped my mind that I must go to see Madame Elisabeth. You know that peace is nearly concluded; but what you don't know is that the King of Spain would not agree to a single article except on the condition that he, instead of the prince Don Carlos, his son, should marry this princess. The king had great difficulty in agreeing to this; at last he yielded, and has gone to tell Madame. I fancy she will be inconsolable; it certainly cannot be pleasant to marry a man of the age and temper of the King of Spain, especially for her, who, in all the pride of youth and beauty, expected to marry a young prince for whom she has a fancy, though she has never seen him. I don't know whether the king will find her as docile as he wishes, and he has asked me to go to see her; for he knows that she is fond of me, and imagines that I have some influence over her. I shall then make a very different visit, for I must go to congratulate Madame, the king's sister. Everything is arranged for her marriage with Monsieur de Savoie, and he will be here shortly. Never was a person of the age of that princess so glad to marry. The court will be finer and larger than it has ever been, and in spite of your afflictions you must come and help us show the foreigners that we have some famous beauties here."

Then the dauphiness left Madame de Clèves, and the next day Madame Elisabeth's marriage was known to every one. A few days later the king and the queens called on Madame de Clèves. Monsieur de Nemours, who had awaited her return with extreme impatience, and was very desirous of speaking to her alone, put off his call until every one should have left and it was unlikely that others would come in. His plan was successful, and he arrived just as the latest visitors were taking their departure.

The princess was still lying down; it was warm, and the sight of Monsieur de Nemours gave her face an additional color, which did not lessen her beauty. He sat down opposite her with the timidity and shyness that real passion gives. It was some time before he spoke; Madame de Clèves was equally confused, so that they kept a long silence. At last Monsieur de Nemours took courage, and expressed his sympathy with her grief. Madame de Clèves, who was glad to keep the conversation on this safe topic, spoke for some time about the loss she had experienced; and finally she said that when time should have dimmed the intensity of her grief, it would still leave a deep and lasting impression, and that her whole nature had been changed by it.

"Great afflictions and violent passions," replied Monsieur de Nemours, "do greatly alter people; as for me, I am entirely changed since I returned from Flanders. Many persons have noticed this alteration, and even the dauphiness spoke of it last evening."

"It is true," said Madame de Clèves, "that she has noticed it, and I think I have heard her say something about it."

"I am not sorry, Madame," Monsieur de Nemours continued, "that she perceived it, but I should prefer that she should not be the only one to notice it. There are persons to whom one does not dare to give any other marks of the love one feels for them than those which do not affect them in any but an indirect way; and since one does not dare to show one's love, one would at least desire that they should see that one wishes not to be loved by any one else. One would like to have them know that there is no beauty, of whatever rank, whom one would not regard with indifference, and that there is no crown which one would wish to buy at the price of never seeing them. Women generally judge the love one has for them," he went on, "by the pains one takes to please them and to pursue them; but that is an easy matter, provided they are charming. What is difficult is not to yield to the pleasure of pursuing them,—it is to avoid them, from fear of showing to the public or to them one's feelings; and the most distinctive mark of a true attachment is to become entirely different from what one was, to be indifferent to ambition or pleasure after having devoted one's whole life to one or the other."

Madame de Clèves readily understood the reference to her in these words. It seemed to her that she ought to answer them and express her disapproval; it also seemed to her that she ought not to listen to them or show that she took his remarks to herself: she believed that she ought to speak, and also that she ought to say nothing. The remarks of Monsieur de Nemours pleased and offended her equally; she saw in them a confirmation of what the crown princess had made her think,—she found them full of gallantry and respect, but also bold and only too clear. Her interest in the prince caused an agitation which she could not control. The vaguest words of a man one likes produce more emotion than the open declarations of a man one does not like. Hence she sat without saying a word, and Monsieur de Nemours noticed her silence, which would have seemed to him a happy omen, if the arrival of Monsieur de Clèves had not put an end to the talk and to his visit.

The Prince de Clèves had come to tell his wife the latest news about Sancerre; but she had no great curiosity about the rest of that affair. She was so interested in what had just happened that she would hardly hide her inattention. When she was able to think it all over, she perceived that she had been mistaken when she fancied that she had become indifferent to Monsieur de Nemours. His words had made all the impression he could desire, and had thoroughly convinced her of his passion. His actions harmonized too well with his words for her to have any further doubts on the subject. She did not any longer indulge in the hope of not loving him; she merely determined to give him no further sign of it. This was a difficult undertaking,—how difficult she knew already. She was aware that her only chance of success lay in avoiding the prince, and her mourning enabled her to live in retirement; she made it a pretext for not going to places where she might meet him. She was in great dejection; her mother's death appeared to be the cause, and she sought no other.

Monsieur de Nemours was in despair at not seeing her oftener; and knowing that he should not meet her at any assembly or entertainment at which the whole court was present, he could not make up his mind to go to them; he pretended a great interest in hunting, and made up hunting-parties on the days of the queens' assemblies. For a long time a slight indisposition served as a pretext for staying at home, and thus escaping going to places where he knew that Madame de Clèves would not be.

Monsieur de Clèves was ailing at nearly the same time, and Madame de Clèves never left his room during his illness; but when he was better and began to see company, and among others Monsieur de Nemours, who, under the pretext of being still weak, used to spend a good part of every day with him, she determined not to stay there. Nevertheless, she could not make up her mind to leave during his first visits; it was so long since she had seen him that she was anxious to meet him again. He too managed to make her listen to him, by what seemed like general talk; though she understood, from its reference to what he had said in his previous visit to her, that he went hunting to get an opportunity for meditation, and that he stayed away from the assemblies because she was not there.

At last Madame de Clèves put into execution her decision to leave her husband's room when the duke should be there, though she found it a difficult task. Monsieur de Nemours observed that she avoided him, and was much pained.

Monsieur de Clèves did not at first notice his wife's conduct; but at last he saw that she was unwilling to stay in his room when company was present. He spoke to her about it, and she replied that she did not think it quite proper that she should meet every evening all the young men of the court. She begged him to let her lead a more retired life than she had done before, because the presence of her mother, who was renowned for her virtue, had authorized many things impossible for a woman of her age.

Monsieur de Clèves, who was generally kind and pleasant to his wife, was not so on this occasion; he told her he was averse to any change in her conduct. She was tempted to tell him that there was a report that Monsieur de Nemours was in love with her; but she did not feel able to mention his name. She was also ashamed to assign a false reason, and to hide the truth from a man who had so good an opinion of her.

A few days later, the king happened to be with the queen when she was receiving, and the company was talking about horoscopes and predictions. Opinions were divided about the credence that ought to be given to them. The queen was inclined to believe in them; she maintained that after so many predictions had come true, it was impossible to doubt the exactness of this science. Others again held that the small number of lucky hits out of the numerous predictions that were made, proved that they were merely the result of chance.

"In former times," said the king, "I was very curious about the future; but I was told so much that was false or improbable that I became convinced that we can know nothing certain. A few years ago a famous astrologer came here. Every one went to see him, I as well as the rest, but without saying who I was; and I carried with me Monsieur de Guise and D'-Escars, sending them into the room in front of me. Nevertheless the astrologer addressed me first, as if he thought I was their master; perhaps he knew me, although he said something to me which seemed to show that he did not know who I was. He prophesied that I should be killed in a duel; then he told Monsieur de Guise that he would be killed from behind, and

D'Escars that he would have his skull broken by a kick from a horse. Monsieur de Guise was almost angry at hearing this, —as if he were accused of running away; D'Escars was no more pleased at learning that he was going to perish by such an unfortunate accident,—so that we all left the astrologer in extreme discontent. I have no idea what will happen to Monsieur de Guise or to D'Escars, but it is very unlikely that I shall be killed in a duel. The King of Spain and I have just made peace; and even if we had not, I doubt if we should resort to a personal combat, and it seems unlikely that I should challenge him, as my father challenged Charles V."

After the king had mentioned the unhappy end which had been foretold him, those who had supported astrology gave up and agreed that it was unworthy of belief. "For my part," said Monsieur de Nemours, "I am the last man in the world to place any confidence in it;" and turning to Madame de Clèves, near whom he was, he said in a low voice: "I was told that I should be made happy by the kindness of the woman for whom I should have the most violent and the most respectful passion. You may judge, Madame, whether I ought to believe in predictions."

The dauphiness, who fancied, from what Monsieur de Nemours had said aloud, that he was mentioning some absurd prophecy that had been made about him, asked him what he was saying to Madame de Clèves. He would have been embarrassed by this question if he had had less presence of mind; but he answered without hesitation: "I was saying, Madame, that it had been predicted about me that I should rise to a lofty position to which I should not even dare to aspire."

"If that is the only prediction that has been made about you," replied the dauphiness, smiling, and thinking of the English scheme, "I do not advise you to denounce astrology; you might find good reasons for supporting it."

Madame de Clèves understood what the crown princess referred to; but she also understood that the happiness of which Monsieur de Nemours spoke, was not that of being king of England.

As it was some time since her mother's death, Madame de Clèves had to appear again in society and to resume her visits at court. She met Monsieur de Nemours at the dauphiness's and at her own house, whither he often came with young nobles of his own age, in order not to be talked about; but she never saw him without an agitation which he readily perceived.

In spite of the care she took to escape his glances and to talk less with him than with others, certain things inadvertently escaped her which convinced this prince that she was not indifferent to him. A less observant man than he would not, perhaps, have noticed them; but so many women had been in love with him that it was hard for him not to know when he was loved. He perceived that the Chevalier de Guise was his rival, and that prince knew that Monsieur de Nemours was his. He was the only man at court who would have discovered this truth; his interest had rendered him more clear-sighted than the others. The knowledge they had of each other's feelings so embittered their relations that although there was no open breach, they were opposed in everything. In running at the ring and in all the amusements in which the king took part they were always on different sides, and their rivalry was too intense to be hidden.

The English scheme often recurred to Madame de Clèves, and she felt that Monsieur de Nemours would not be able to withstand the king's advice and Lignerolles' urging. She noticed with pain that this last had not yet returned, and she awaited him with impatience. If she had followed his movements, she would have learned the condition of that matter; but the same feeling that inspired her curiosity compelled her to conceal it, and she contented herself with making inquiries about the beauty, intelligence, and character of Queen Elizabeth. A portrait of her was carried to the palace, and she found Elizabeth more beautiful than was pleasant to her, and she could not refrain from saying that it must flatter her.

"I don't think so," replied the dauphiness, who was present. "Elizabeth has a great reputation as a beauty and as the possessor of a mind far above the common, and I know that all my life she has been held up to me as an example. She ought to be attractive if she is like Anne Boleyn, her mother. Never was there a more amiable woman or one more charming both in appearance and disposition. I have been told that her face was exceptionally vivacious, and that she in no way resembled most English beauties."

"It seems to me," said Madame de Clèves, "that I have heard that she was born in France."

"Those who think so," replied the crown princess, "are in error, and I will tell you her history in a few words. She was born of a good English family. Henry VIII. had been in love with her sister and her mother, and it had even been suspected that she was his daughter. She came here with the sister of

Henry VII., who married Louis XII. This young and gallant princess found it very hard to leave the court of France after her husband's death; but Anne Boleyn, who shared her mistress's feelings, decided to stay. The late king was in love with her, and she remained as maid of honor to Queen Claude. This queen died, and Madame Marguerite, the king's sister, the Duchess of Alençon, since then Queen of Navarre, whose stories you have seen, added Anne to her suite; it was from her that this queen received her inclination toward the new religion. Then Anne returned to England, where she delighted every one. She had French manners, which please all nations; she sang well, and danced charmingly. She was made a lady in waiting to Queen Catherine of Aragon, and King Henry VIII. fell desperately in love with her.

"Cardinal Wolsey, his favorite and prime minister, desired to be made pope; and being dissatisfied with the emperor for not supporting his claims, he resolved to avenge himself by allying the king his master with France. He suggested to Henry VIII. that his marriage with the emperor's aunt was null and void, and proposed to him to marry the Duchess of Alençon, whose husband had just died. Anne Boleyn, being an ambitious woman, looked on this divorce as a possible step to the throne. She began to instil into the King of England the principles of Lutheranism, and persuaded the late king to urge at Rome Henry's divorce, in the hope of his marriage with Madame d'Alençon. Cardinal Wolsey contrived to be sent to France on other pretexts to arrange this affair; but his master would not consent to have the proposition made, and sent orders to Calais that this marriage was not to be mentioned.

"On his return from France, Cardinal Wolsey was received with honors equal to those paid to the king himself; never did a favorite display such haughtiness and vanity. He arranged an interview between the two kings, which took place at Boulogne. Francis I. offered his hand to Henry VIII., who was unwilling to take it; they treated each other with great splendor, each giving the other clothes like those he himself wore. I remember having heard that those the late king sent to the King of England were of crimson satin trimmed with pearls and diamonds arranged in triangles, the cloak of white velvet embroidered with gold. After spending a few days at Boulogne, they went to Calais. Anne Boleyn was quartered in the house with Henry VIII. in the queen's suite, and Francis I. made her the same presents and paid her the same honors as if she had been a queen herself. At last, after being in love with her for nine years, Henry married her, without waiting for the annulment of his first marriage, which he had long been asking of Rome. The pope at once excommunicated him; this so enraged Henry that he declared himself the head of the Church, and carried all England into the unhappy change of religion in which you now see it.

"Anne Boleyn did not long enjoy her grandeur, for one day, when she thought her position assured by the death of Catherine of Aragon, she happened to be present with all the court when the Viscount Rochford, her brother, was running at the ring. The king was suddenly overwhelmed by such an access of jealousy that he instantly left the spot, hastened to London, and gave orders for the arrest of the queen, the Viscount Rochford, and many others whom he believed to be the queen's lovers or confidants. Although this jealousy seemed the work of a moment it had for some time been instigated by the Viscountess Rochford, who could not endure her husband's intimacy with the queen, and represented it to the king as criminal intimacy; consequently he, being already in love with Jane Seymour, thought only of getting rid of Anne Boleyn. In less than three weeks he succeeded in having the queen and her brother brought to trial and beheaded, and he married Jane Seymour. He had afterward several wives, whom he either divorced or put to death, among others Catherine Howard, who had been the confidant of the Viscountess of Rochford, and was beheaded with her. Hence she was punished for the crimes with which she had blackened Anne Boleyn, and Henry VIII., having reached a monstrous size, died."

All the ladies present thanked the dauphiness for teaching them so much about the English court, and among others Madame de Clèves, who could not refrain from asking more questions about Queen Elizabeth.

The dauphiness had miniatures painted of all the beauties of the court to send to the queen her mother. The day when that of Madame de Clèves was receiving the last touches the crown princess came to spend the afternoon with her. Monsieur de Nemours was also there, for he neglected no opportunity of seeing Madame de Clèves, although he never seemed to court her society. She was so beautiful that day that he would surely have fallen in love with her then if he had not done so already; but he did not dare to sit with his eyes fixed on her, while she feared lest he should show too plainly the pleasure he found in looking at her.

The crown princess asked Monsieur de Clèves for a minia-ture he had of his wife, to compare it with the one that was painting. All who were there expressed their opinion of both, and Madame de Clèves asked the painter to make a little correction in the hair of the old one. The artist took the miniature out of its case, and after working on it, set it down on the table.

For a long time Monsieur de Nemours had been desiring to have a portrait of Madame de Clèves. When he saw this one, though it belonged to her husband, whom he tenderly loved, he could not resist the temptation to steal it; he thought that among the many persons present he should not be suspected.

The dauphiness was seated on the bed, speaking low to Madame de Clèves, who was standing in front of her. One of the curtains was only partly closed, and Madame de Clèves was able to see Monsieur de Nemours, whose back was against the table at the foot of the bed, without turning his head pick up something from this table. She at once guessed that it was her portrait, and she was so embarrassed that the crown princess noticed she was not listening to her, and asked her what she was looking at. At these words Monsieur de Nemours turned round and met Madame de Clèves' eyes fas-tened on him; he felt sure that she must have seen what he had just done.

Madame de Clèves was greatly embarrassed. Her reason bade her ask for her portrait; but if she asked for it openly, she would announce to every one the prince's feelings for her, and by asking for it privately, she would give him an opportu-nity to speak to her of his love, so that at last she judged it better to let him keep it,—and she was very glad to be able to grant him a favor without his knowing that she did it of her own choice. Monsieur de Nemours, who observed her embar-rassment and guessed its cause, came up to her and said in a low voice: "If you saw what I ventured to do, be good enough, Madame, to let me suppose that you know nothing about it; I do not dare to ask anything more." Then he went away, without waiting for an answer.

The dauphiness, accompanied by all her ladies, went out for a walk. Monsieur de Nemours locked himself up in his own room, being unable to contain his joy at having in his possession a portrait of Madame de Clèves. He felt all the happiness that love can give. He loved the most charming woman of the court, and felt that in spite of herself she loved him; he saw in everything she did the agitation and embarrassment which love evokes in the innocence of early youth.

That evening every one looked carefully for the portrait; when they found the case, no one supposed that it had been stolen, but that it had been dropped somewhere. Monsieur de Clèves was distressed at its loss, and after hunting for it in vain, told his wife, but evidently in jest, that she doubtless had some mysterious lover to whom she had given the portrait, or who had stolen it, for no one but a lover would care for the portrait without the case.

Although these words were not said seriously, they made a deep impression on the mind of Madame de Clèves and filled her with remorse. She thought of the violence of her love for Monsieur de Nemours, and perceived that she could not control either her words or her face. She reflected that Lignerolles had returned, and that the English scheme had no terrors for her; that she had no longer grounds for suspecting the dauphiness; and finally, that, as she was without further defence, her only safety was in flight. Since, however, she knew she could not go away, she saw that she was in a most perilous condition, and ready to fall into what she judged to be the greatest possible misfortune,—namely, betraying to Monsieur de Nemours the interest she felt in him. She recalled everything her mother had said to her on her death-bed, and her advice to try everything rather than enter upon a love-affair. She remembered what her husband had said about her sincerity when he was speaking about Madame de Tournon, and it seemed to her that it was her duty to confess her passion for Monsieur de Nemours. She pondered over this for a long time; then she was astonished that the thought occurred to her: she deemed it madness, and fell back into the agony of indecision.

PART III.

When peace was signed, Madame Elisabeth, though with great repugnance, determined to obey her father the king. The Duke of Alva had been deputed to marry her in the name of the Catholic king, and he was expected to arrive shortly. The Duke of Savoy was also expected; he was to marry Madame the king's sister, and the two weddings were to take place at the same time. The king thought of nothing but making these events illustrious by entertainments at which he could display all the brilliancy and splendor of his court. It was suggested that plays and ballets should be sumptuously set upon the stage; but the king thought that too meagre a form of entertainment, and desired something more magnificent. He determined to have a tournament at which the foreigners might enter, and to admit the populace as spectators. All the princes and young noblemen gladly furthered the king's plan, and especially the Duke of Ferrara, Monsieur de Guise, and Monsieur de Nemours, who surpassed all others in exercises of this sort. The king chose them to be, with himself, the four champions of the tournament.

It was announced throughout the whole kingdom that a tournament would be opened in the city of Paris on the fifteenth day of June by His Very Christian Majesty and by the Prince Alphonso of Este Duke of Ferrara, Francis of Lorraine Duke of Guise, and James of Savoy Duke of Nemours, who were ready to meet all comers. The first combat was to be on horseback, with four antagonists, with four assaults with the lance, and one for the ladies; the second combat with swords, either singly or in couples, as should be determined; the third combat on foot, three assaults with the pike, and six with the sword. The champions were to supply the lances, swords, and pikes, from which the assailants might choose their weapons. Any one striking a horse in the attack was to be put out of the ranks. There would be four masters of the camp who should have command, and those of the assailants who should be most successful would receive a prize, of a value to be determined by the judges. All the assailants, French or foreign, were to be obliged to come and touch one or more of the shields hanging by the steps at the end of the lists; there they would find an officer to receive and enroll them according to their rank and the shields they had touched. The assailants were to have a gentleman bring their shields, with their arms, to be hung by the steps three days before the beginning of the tournament, otherwise they would not be received without the permission of the champions.

A great field was made ready near the Bastile, extending from the castle of Tournelles, across the Rue St. Antoine, to the royal mews. On each side scaffolding was raised, with rows of seats and covered boxes and galleries, fine to look upon, and capable of holding a vast number of spectators. All the princes and lords were thinking of nothing but their preparations to make a magnificent appearance, and were busily occupied in working some device into their initials or mottoes that should flatter the woman they loved.

A few days before the Duke of Alva's arrival the king went to play tennis with Monsieur de Nemours, the Chevalier de Guise, and the Vidame of Chartres. The queens went with their suites, and Madame de Clèves among the others, to watch the game. After it was over, and they were leaving the court, Châtelart went up to the dauphiness and told her that he had just found a loveletter that had fallen from Monsieur de Nemours' pocket. The crown princess, who was always curious about everything that concerned that prince, told Châtelart to give it to her; she took it, and followed the queen her mother-in-law, who was going with the king to see the preparations for the tournament. After they had been there some time the king sent for some horses which he had recently bought. Though they had not been broken, he wanted to mount them, and he also had them saddled for the gentlemen with him. The king and Monsieur de Nemours got on the most fiery ones, and they tried to spring at one another. Monsieur de Nemours, fearful of injuring the king, backed his horse suddenly against a post with such violence that he was dismounted. The attendants ran up to him and thought he was seriously injured; Madame de Clèves thought him more hurt than did the others. Her interest in him inspired an agitation which she did not think of concealing; she went up to him with the queens, and her color was so changed that a man less interested than the Chevalier de Guise would have noticed it. He remarked it at once, and gave much more attention to the condition of Madame de Clèves than to that of Monsieur de Nemours. This prince was so stunned by the fall that his head had to be supported by those about him. When he came to himself, the first person he saw was Madame de Clèves; he read on her face all the pity she felt, and his expression showed that he was grateful. He then thanked the queens for their kindness, and apologized for appearing before them in such a state. The king ordered him to go home and lie down.

After Madame de Clèves had recovered from her fright she began to recall the way she had betrayed it. The Chevalier de Guise did not leave her long to enjoy the hope that no one had observed it. As he gave her his hand to lead her from the field, he said: "I am more to be pitied, Madame, than Monsieur de Nemours. Pardon me if I abandon the profound reserve which I have always shown in regard to you, and if I betray the keen grief I feel at what I have just seen; it is the first time that I have been bold enough to speak to you, and it will be the last. Death, or at any rate an eternal separation, will remove me from a place where I cannot live, now that I have lost the sad consolation of believing that all those who dare to look upon you are as unhappy as I."

Madame de Clèves answered with a few disjointed words, as if she did not understand what the Chevalier de Guise meant. At any other time she would have been offended at his speaking of his feelings for her; but at that moment she thought only of her pain at perceiving that he had detected her own for Monsieur de Nemours. The Chevalier de Guise was so overwhelmed and pained by this discovery that he at once resolved never to think of winning Madame de Clèves' love; but the abandonment of a design which had seemed so difficult and glorious required one of equal moment to take its place, hence he thought of going to take Rhodes,—a plan he had already meditated. When he died, in the flower of his youth, just when he had acquired a reputation as one of the greatest princes of his century, his only regret was that he had not been able to carry out that noble project, which seemed on the point of accomplishment.

Madame de Clèves at once went to the queen, with her mind intent on what had just happened. Monsieur de Nemours came there soon afterward, in magnificent attire, as if he had forgotten what had just happened. He appeared even gayer than usual, and his delight at what he thought he had seen added to his content. Every one was surprised to see him, and asked him how he felt, except Madame de Clèves, who remained by the fire-place, as if she did not see him. The king came out of his room, and observing him there, called him to ask about his mishap. As Monsieur de Nemours passed by Madame de Clèves, he said in a low voice: "I have received to-day, Madame, tokens of your pity, but not those I most deserve." Madame de Clèves had suspected that the prince had noticed her emotion at his accident, and his words showed her that she was not mistaken. She was deeply pained to see that she could not control her emotions, and had even made them manifest to the Chevalier de Guise. It distressed her, too, to perceive that Monsieur de Nemours had read them; but this distress was tempered by a certain pleasure.

The dauphiness, who was impatient to know what was in the letter that Châtelart had given her, went up to Madame de Clèves. "Read this letter," she said; "it is addressed to Monsieur de Nemours, and apparently is from that mistress for whom he has left all the others. If you cannot read it now, keep it; come to me this evening and give it back to me, and

tell me whether you know the handwriting." With these words
the crown princess turned away from Madame de Clèves,
leaving her so astonished and agitated that she could scarcely
move. Her emotion and impatience were so great that she
could not stay longer with the queen, and she went home,
though it was much earlier than her usual hour of leaving.
Her hands, in which she held the letter, trembled; her
thoughts were all confused, and she felt an unendurable pain
such as she had never known. As soon as she was safe in her
room she opened the letter, and read as follows:—

"I love you too much to let you think that the change you
see in me is the result of my fickleness; I want you to know
that the real cause is your infidelity. You are surprised that I
say your 'infidelity;' you have concealed it so craftily, and I
have taken such pains to hide from you my knowledge of it,
that you are naturally astonished that I should have detected
it. I am myself surprised that I have been able to keep it from
you. Never was there any grief like mine; I imagined that you
felt for me a violent passion. I did not conceal what I felt for
you, and at the time when I let you see it, I learned that you
were deceiving me, that you loved another, and, according to
all appearances, were sacrificing me to a new mistress. I knew
it the day of the running at the ring, and that is why I was not
there. I pretended to be ill, in order to conceal my emotion;
but I really became so, for my body could not stand the
intense agitation. When I began to get better, I pretended to
be still suffering, in order to have an excuse for not seeing or
writing to you; I wanted time to decide how I should act
toward you. Twenty times at least I formed and changed my
decision; but at last I judged you unworthy to see my grief,
and I determined to hide it from you. I wished to wound your
pride by letting you see my love for you fade away. I thought
thus to diminish the price of the sacrifice you made of it; I did
not wish you to have the pleasure of showing how much I
loved you in order to appear more amiable. I resolved to write
to you indifferent, dull letters, to suggest to the woman to
whom you gave them that you were loved less. I did not wish
her to have the pleasure of learning that I knew of her
triumph over me, or to add to her triumph by my despair and
reproaches. I thought I could not punish you sufficiently by
breaking with you, and that I should inflict but a slight pain if
I ceased to love you when you had ceased to love me. I
thought you must love me, if you were to know the pang of

not being loved, which tormented me so sorely. I thought that if anything could rekindle the feelings you had had for me, it was by showing that my own were changed, but to show this by pretending to hide it from you, as if I had not strength to tell you. I decided on this; but how hard it was to do so, and when I saw you, how almost impossible to carry it out! Hundreds of times I was ready to spoil all with my reproaches and tears. The state of my health helped me to conceal my emotion and distress. Afterward I was borne up by the pleasure of dissimulating to you as you dissimulated to me; nevertheless I did myself such violence to tell you and to write to you that I loved you, that you saw sooner than I had intended that I had not meant to let you see that my feelings were altered. You were wounded, and complained to me. I tried to reassure you, but in such an artificial way that you were more convinced than ever that I did not love you. At last I succeeded in what I had meant to do. The capriciousness of your heart made you turn again toward me when you saw me leaving you. I have tasted all the joy of vengeance; it has seemed to me that you loved me better than ever, and I have shown you that I did not love you. I have had reason to believe that you had entirely abandoned her for whom you had left me. I have also had grounds for supposing that you never spoke to her of me. But your return and your desertion have not been able to make good your fickleness; your heart has been divided between me and another; you have deceived me: that is enough to deprive me of the pleasure of being loved by you as I thought I deserved, and to fix me in the resolution that I had formed never to see you again, which so surprises you."

Madame de Clèves read and re-read this letter several times without understanding it; all that she made out was that Monsieur de Nemours did not love her as she had thought, and that he loved other women, whom he deceived as he did her. This was a grievous blow to a woman of her character, who was deeply in love, and had just shown this to a man whom she deemed unworthy, in sight of another whom she maltreated for love of his rival. Never was sorrow more bitter! It seemed to her that what had happened that day gave it a special sting, and that if Monsieur de Nemours had not had reason to suppose that she loved him, she would not care whether he had loved another woman. But she deceived herself; the pang she found so unendurable was that of jealousy, with all its hideous accompaniments. This letter showed her that Monsieur de Nemours had had a love-affair for some time. She thought that it attested the writer's cleverness and worth, and she seemed a woman who deserved to be loved. She appeared to have more courage than herself, and she envied her the strength of character she showed in concealing her feelings from Monsieur de Nemours. The end of the letter showed that the woman thought herself still loved; she imagined that his constant discretion, which had so touched her, was perhaps only the effect of his love for the other, whom he feared to offend. In a word, all her thoughts only fed her grief and despair. How often she thought of herself; how often of her mother's counsels! How bitterly she regretted that she had not withdrawn from the world, in spite of Monsieur de Clèves, or that she had not followed her plan of confessing to him her feeling for Monsieur de Nemours! She judged that she would have done better to tell everything to a husband whose generosity she knew, and who would be interested in keeping her secret, than to betray it to a man unworthy of it, who was moved to love of her by no other feeling than pride or vanity. In a word, she deemed every evil that could befall her, every misery to which she might be reduced, insignificant by the side of letting Monsieur de Nemours see that she loved him, and knowing that he loved another woman. Her only consolation was that henceforth she need have no fear of herself, and that she was entirely cured of her love for him.

She gave no thought to the dauphiness's command to come to her that evening; she went to bed and pretended to be indisposed, so that when Monsieur de Clèves came back from seeing the king, he was told that she was asleep. But she was far from enjoying the calmness that induces sleep. She spent the night in self-reproach and in reading over the letter.

Madame de Clèves was not the only person whose rest was disturbed by this letter. The Vidame of Chartres, who had lost it, not Monsieur de Nemours, was very uneasy about it. He had spent the evening with Monsieur de Guise, who had given a grand supper to his brother-in-law, the Duke of Ferrara, and all the young men of the court. It so happened that during the supper the conversation turned to bright letters, and the Vidame said he had in his pocket the brightest letter that ever was written. He was asked to show it to them, but he refused. Monsieur de Nemours thereupon declared that he had never had it, and was only boasting. The Vidame replied that he tempted him to commit an indiscretion, but he would not show the letter, though he would read a few passages that would prove that few men ever received one like it. At the same time he felt for the letter, but could not find it; he sought everywhere in vain. They laughed at his discomfiture, but he seemed so uneasy that they soon stopped talking about it. He left before the others, hastening home to see if he had left the missing letter there. While he was still hunting for it, a first *valet de chambre* of the queen came to tell him that the Vicomtesse d'Uzès thought it well to let him know that they were talking at the queen's apartment about a love-letter he had dropped from his pocket while he was playing tennis; that they had repeated a good deal that was in the letter; that the queen had expressed a strong desire to see it; that she had asked one of her gentlemen-in-waiting for it; but he had answered that he had given it to Châtelart.

The *valet de chambre* said many other things to the Vidame which only added to his distress. He went out at once to see a gentleman who was a great friend of Châtelart; he made him get out of bed, although it was very late, to go and ask for the letter, without telling him who wanted it or who had written it. Châtelart, who was confident that it had been written to Monsieur de Nemours, and that he was in love with the dauphiness, felt sure that he knew who had asked for it. He replied, with malicious joy, that he had handed the letter to the dauphiness. The gentleman brought this answer back to the Vidame of Chartres; it gave him only fresh uneasiness. After long hesitation about what he should do, he decided that Monsieur de Nemours was the only man who could aid him.

The Vidame thereupon went to the house of the duke, and entered his bedroom at about daybreak. This prince was sleeping calmly; what he had seen that day of Madame de Clèves gave him only agreeable thoughts. He was much surprised when he was awakened by the Vidame, and he asked him whether this had been done out of revenge for what he had said at the supper. The Vidame's countenance showed that he had come on some serious matter. "I have come," he said, "to confide to you the most important event of my life. I know very well that you have no cause to be grateful, because I do this at a moment when I need your aid; but I know that I should have sunk in your esteem if without being compelled by necessity I had told you what I am about to say. Some time yesterday I dropped the letter of which I was speaking

last evening; it is of extreme importance that no one should
know that it was written to me. It has been seen by a number
of persons who were at the tennis-court when I dropped it.
Now, you were there too, and I beg of you to say that it was
you who lost it."

"You must suppose that I am not in love with any woman,"
answered Monsieur de Nemours, smiling, "to make such a
proposition to me, and to imagine that there is no one with
whom I might fall out if I let it be thought that I receive
letters of that sort."

"I beg you," said the Vidame, "to listen to me seriously. If
you have a mistress, as I do not doubt, though I have no idea
who she is, it will be easy for you to explain yourself, and I
will tell you how to do it. Even if you do not have an explanation with her, your falling-out will last but a few moments;
whereas I by this mischance bring dishonor to a woman who
has loved me passionately, and is one of the most estimable
women in the world; and moreover, from another quarter I
bring upon myself an implacable hatred, which will certainly
cost me my fortune, and may cost me something more."

"I do not understand what you tell me," replied Monsieur
de Nemours; "but you imply that the current rumors about
the interest a great princess takes in you are not entirely
without foundation."

"They are not," exclaimed the Vidame; "but would to God
they were! In that case I should not be in my present trouble.
But I must tell you what has happened, to give you an idea of
what I have to fear.

"Ever since I have been at court, the queen has always
treated me with much distinction and amiability, and I have
reason to believe that she has had a kindly feeling for me; yet
there was nothing marked about it, and I had never dreamed
of other feelings toward me than those of respect. I was even
much in love with Madame de Themines; the sight of her is
enough to prove that a man can have a great deal of love for
her when she loves him,—and she loved me. Nearly two years
ago, when the court was at Fontainebleau, I happened to talk
with the queen two or three times when very few people were
there. It seemed to me that I pleased her, and that she was
interested in all that I said. One day especially we were
talking about confidence. I said I did not confide wholly in
any one; that one always repented absolute unreserve sooner
or later; and that I knew a number of things of which I had
never spoken to any one. The queen said that she thought

better of me for that; that she had not found any one in France who had any reserve; and that this had troubled her greatly, because it had prevented her confiding in any one; that one must have somebody to talk to, especially persons of her rank. The following days she several times resumed the same conversation, and told me many tolerably secret things that were happening. At last it seemed to me that she wanted to test my reserve, and that she wished to intrust me with some of her own secrets. This thought attached me to her; I was flattered by the distinction, and I paid her my court with more assiduity than usual. One evening, when the king and all the ladies had gone out to ride in the forest, she remained at home, because she did not feel well, and I stayed with her. She went down to the edge of the pond and let go of the equerry's hand, to walk more freely. After she had made a few turns, she came near me and bade me follow her. 'I want to speak to you,' she said, 'and you will see from what I wish to say that I am a friend of yours.' Then she stopped and gazed at me intently. 'You are in love,' she went on, 'and because you do not confide in any one, you think that your love is not known; but it is known even to the persons interested. You are watched; it is known where you see your mistress: a plan has been made to surprise you. I do not know who she is, I do not ask you; I only wish to save you from the misfortunes into which you may fall.' Observe, please, the snare the queen set for me, and how difficult it was to escape it. She wanted to find out whether I was in love; and by not asking with whom, and by showing that her sole intention was to aid me, she prevented my thinking that she was speaking to me from curiosity or with premeditation.

"Nevertheless, in the face of all appearances I made out the truth. I was in love with Madame de Themines; but though she loved me, I was not fortunate enough to meet her in any private place where we could be surprised, hence I saw that it was not she whom the queen meant. I knew too that I had a love-affair with a woman less beautiful and less severe than Madame de Themines, and it was not impossible that the place where I used to meet her had been discovered; but since I took but little interest in her, it was easy for me to escape from perils of that sort by ceasing to see her. Hence I decided to confess nothing to the queen, but to assure her that I had long since given up the desire to win the love of such women as might smile on me, because I deemed them unworthy of an honorable man's devotion, and it would take women far above them to fascinate me. 'You are not frank,' replied the queen; 'I know the opposite of what you say. The way in which I speak to you binds you to conceal nothing from me. I want you to be one of my friends,' she went on; 'but when I give you that place, I must know all your ties. Consider whether you care to purchase it at the price of informing me; I give you two days to think it over. But be careful what you say to me at the expiration of that time, and remember that if I find out afterward that you have deceived me, I shall never pardon you so long a I live.' Thereupon the queen left me, without awaiting my reply.

"You may well imagine that I was much impressed by what she had just said. The two days she had given me for consideration did not seem to me too long. I perceived that she wished to know whether I was in love, and hoped that I was not. I saw the importance of the decision I was about to make. My vanity was not a little flattered by a love-affair with a queen, and a queen who was still so charming. To be sure, I love Madame de Themines, and although I was unfaithful to her in a way with that other woman I mentioned, I could not make up my mind to break with her. I also saw the danger to which I exposed myself in deceiving the queen, and how hard it would be to deceive her; yet I could not decide to refuse what fortune offered me, and I determined to risk the consequences of my evil conduct. I broke with that woman with whom my relations might be discovered, and I hoped to conceal those I had with Madame de Themines.

"At the expiration of the two days that the queen had granted me, as I was entering a room where all her ladies were assembled, she said to me aloud, with a seriousness that surprised me,—

" 'Have you thought over that matter of which I spoke to you, and do you know the truth about it?'

" 'Yes, Madame,' I replied, 'and it is as I told your Majesty.'

" 'Come this evening at the hour that I shall write to you, and I will give you the rest of my orders.'

"I made a deep bow, without answering, and did not fail to appear at the hour set. I found her in the gallery with her secretary and some of her ladies. As soon as she saw me, she came up to me and led me to the other end of the gallery.

" 'Well!' she said, 'is it after due reflection that you have nothing to say to me, and does not my treatment of you deserve that you should speak to me frankly?'

" 'It is because I am frank with you, Madame,' I replied,

'that I have nothing to tell you; and I swear to your Majesty, with all the respect I owe you, that I am not in love with any lady of the court.'

" 'I am willing to believe it,' resumed the queen, 'because I wish to; and I wish it because I desire that you should be unreservedly attached to me; and I could not possibly be satisfied with your friendship if you were in love. One may trust those who are, but it is impossible to have confidence in their secrecy. They are too inattentive and have too many distractions; their mistress is their main interest,—and that would not suit the way in which I want you to be attached to me. Remember, it is on account of your oath that you are free that I choose you for the recipient of my confidence. Remember that I wish yours without reserve, that I want you to have no friend, man or woman, except such as shall be agreeable to me, and that you will give up every aim except pleasing me. I shall not let harm come to your fortune,—I shall look after that more zealously than you do; and whatever I do for you, I shall consider myself more than paid if I find that you are to me what I hope. I choose you in order to confide in you all my anxieties, and to help me endure them. You will see that they are not light. To all appearance I suffer no pain from the king's attachment to Madame de Valentinois; but I can scarcely bear it. She controls the king; she is false to him; she despises me; all my people are devoted to her. My daughter-in-law, the crown princess, is vain of her beauty and of her uncle's power, and pays no respect to me. The Constable of Montmorency is master of the king and of the kingdom; he hates me, and has given me tokens of his hatred which I can never forget. The Marshal of Saint-André is an audacious young favorite, who treats me no better than do the others. The full list of my sufferings would arouse your compassion. Hitherto I have not dared to trust any one; I do put confidence in you: act in such a way that I shall not repent of it, and be my sole consolation.'

"The queen's eyes filled with tears as she said these last words, and I was on the point of throwing myself at her feet, so deeply was I moved by the kindness she showed me. Since that day she has had perfect confidence in me; she never takes a step without talking it over with me, and my alliance with her still lasts.

PART IV.

"Still, though much taken up by my new intimacy with the queen, I was bound to Madame de Themines by a feeling which I could not overcome. It seemed to me that her love for me was waning; and although if I had been wise I should have taken advantage of this change I saw in her to try to forget her, as it was, my love for her redoubled, and I managed so ill that the queen in time learned something about this attachment. Persons of her nation are always inclined to jealousy, and possibly her feelings toward me were warmer than she herself supposed. But at last the report that I was in love gave her such distress and grief that I very often felt sure that I had wholly lost her favor. I reassured her by my attentions, submissiveness, and by many false oaths; but I could not have long deceived her if Madame de Themines' altered demeanor had not at last set me free in spite of myself. She made me see that she loved me no longer, and I was so sure of this that I felt compelled to cease persecuting her with my attentions. Some time after, she wrote me the letter that I have lost. That told me that she knew about my relations with the other woman I mentioned, and that this was the reason of the change. Since, then, there was no one to divide my attentions, the queen was tolerably satisfied with me; but inasmuch as my feeling for her was not of a sort to render me incapable of another attachment, and it is impossible for a man to control his heart by force of will, I fell in love with Madame de Martigues, in whom I had been much interested before, when she was a Villemontais and maid-of-honor to the dauphiness. I had reason for believing that she did not hate me, and that she was pleased with my discreet conduct, although she did not understand all its reasons. The queen has no suspicions about this affair, but there is another which torments her a great deal. Since Madame de Martigues is always with the crown princess, I go there oftener than usual. The queen has taken it into her head that it is with this princess that I am in love. The dauphiness's rank, which is equal to her own, and her advantages of youth and beauty, inspire a jealousy which amounts to madness, and she cannot conceal her hatred of her daughter-in-law. The Cardinal of Lorraine, who seems to me to have been for a long time an aspirant for the queen's good graces, and who sees me occupying a place that he would like to fill, under the pretence of bringing about a reconciliation between her and the crown princess is looking into the causes of their dissension. I do not doubt that he has found out the real cause of the queen's bitterness, and I fancy that he has done me many an evil turn, though without showing his hand. That is the state of affairs now. Judge then what will be the effect of the letter I lost when I was unfortunate enough to put it into my pocket to return it to Madame de Themines. If the queen sees this letter, she will know that I have deceived her, and that at almost the same time when I was false to her on account of Madame de Themines, I was false to Madame de Themines on account of another woman. Judge then what sort of an opinion she will have of me, and whether she will ever believe me again. If she does not see this letter, what shall I say to her? She knows that it has been in the dauphiness's hands; she will think that Châtelart recognized that princess's handwriting, and that the letter is from her; she will imagine that she is perhaps the woman whose jealousy is mentioned,—in a word, there is nothing which she may not think, and there is nothing I may not fear from her thoughts. Add to this that I am sincerely interested in Madame de Martigues, that the crown princess will certainly show her this letter, and that she will believe it was written very recently. So I shall be embroiled both with the women I love best in the world and with the woman from whom I have most to fear. Consider now whether I am not justified in begging you to say that the letter is yours and in asking you as a favor to try to get it from the dauphiness."

"It is very plain," said Monsieur de Nemours, "that one could hardly be in more serious perplexity than you are; and you must confess that you got into it by your own fault. I have been accused of being a faithless lover and of carrying on several love-affairs at the same time; but I am nothing by the side of you, for I should never have dreamed of doing what you have done. Could you suppose it possible to keep on good terms with Madame de Themines when you formed your alliance with the queen; and did you hope to become intimate with the queen and yet succeed deceiving her? She is an Italian and a queen, and hence suspicious, jealous, and haughty. When your good luck rather than your good conduct got you out of one entanglement, you got into a new one, and imagined that here, amid the whole court, you could love Madame de Martigues without the queen's knowing anything about it. You could not have been too careful to rid her of the mortification of having taken the first steps. She has a violent passion for you. You are too discreet to say so, and I am too discreet to ask any questions; but she loves you, she distrusts you, and the facts justify her."

"Is it for you to overwhelm me with reproaches?" interrupted the Vidame. "Ought not your experience to make you indulgent to my faults? Still, I am willing to confess that I did wrong; but consider, I beg of you, how to get me out of my present complications. It seems to me that you must see the crown princess as soon as she is up, and ask her for the letter as if it were yours."

"I have already told you," replied Monsieur de Nemours, "that this is a somewhat extraordinary request, and one that, the circumstances being what they are, I do not find very easy to grant. Then, too, if the letter was seen to fall from your pocket, how can I convince them that it fell from mine?"

"I thought I had said that they told the dauphiness that it was from yours that it fell."

"What!" said Monsieur de Nemours with some asperity, for he saw at once that this mistake might complicate matters with Madame de Clèves. "So the dauphiness has been told that I dropped this letter?"

"Yes," answered the Vidame; "that is what they told her,— and the mistake arose in this way: there were several of the queen's gentlemen in one of the rooms by the tennis-court where our clothes were hanging, and when we sent for them the letter dropped; these gentlemen took it up and read it aloud. Some thought it was written to you; others, that it was written to me. Châtelart, who took it, and from whom I have just tried to get it, said he had given it to the crown princess as a letter of yours; those who mentioned it to the queen unfortunately said it was mine,—so you can easily do what I wish, and get me out of this terrible complication."

Monsieur de Nemours had always been very fond of the Vidame of Chartres, and his relationship to Madame de Clèves rendered him still dearer. Nevertheless, he could not make up his mind to run the risk of her hearing of this letter as something in which he was concerned. He began to meditate profoundly, and the Vidame, guessing the nature of his thoughts, said: "I really believe you are afraid of falling out with your mistress; and I should be inclined to think that it is about the dauphiness that you are anxious, were it not that your freedom from any jealousy of Monsieur d'Anville forbids the thought. But however that may be, you must not sacrifice your peace of mind to mine, and I will make it possible for you to prove to the woman you love that this letter was written to me, and not to you. Here is a note from Madame d'Amboise; she is a friend of Madame de Themines, and to her she has confided all her feelings about me. In this note she asks me for her friend's letter,—the one I lost. My name is on the note, and its contents prove beyond the possibility of doubt that the letter she asks for is the one that has been picked up. I intrust this note to you, and I am willing that you should show it to your mistress in order to clear yourself. I beg of you not to lose a moment, but to go to the dauphiness this morning."

Monsieur de Nemours gave his promise to the Vidame of Chartres and took Madame d'Amboise's note. But his intention was not to see the crown princess; he thought he had something more urgent to do. He felt sure that she had already spoken about this letter to Madame de Clèves, and he could not endure that a woman he loved so much should have any reason for thinking that he was attached to any other.

He went to her house as soon as he thought she might be awake, and sent up word that he would not ask to have the honor at such an extraordinary hour if it were not on very important business. Madame de Clèves was not yet up; she was much embittered and agitated by the gloomy thoughts that had tormented her all night. She was extremely surprised when she heard that Monsieur de Nemours wanted to see her. Grieved as she was, she did not hesitate to send him word that she was ill, and unable to see him.

He was not pained by this refusal; an act of coolness at a time when she might be jealous was no unfavorable omen. He went to Monsieur de Clèves' apartments and told him that he had just called on his wife; that he was very sorry he could not see her, because he wished to speak to her of a matter of importance in which the Vidame of Chartres was interested. In a few words he told Monsieur de Clèves how serious the matter was, and Monsieur de Clèves took him at once to his wife's room. Nothing but the darkness enabled her to hide her agitation and surprise at seeing Monsieur de Nemours brought into her room by her husband. Monsieur de Clèves said that there was some question about a letter, and the Vidame's interests required her aid; he added that Monsieur de Nemours would tell her what was to be done, and that he should go to the king, who had just sent for him.

Monsieur de Nemours was left alone with Madame de

Clèves,—which was exactly what he wanted. "I have come, Madame," he began, "to ask you if the dauphiness has not spoken to you about a letter which Châtelart gave her."

"She said something about it to me," answered Madame de Clèves; "but I don't understand how this letter concerns my uncle, and I am able to assure you that his name is not mentioned in it."

"True, Madame," Monsieur de Nemours went on, "his name is not mentioned; nevertheless, it was written to him, and it is of the utmost importance to him that you should get it out of her hands."

"I fail to understand," said Madame de Clèves, "how it concerns him that this letter should not be seen, and why it should be asked for in his name."

"If you will kindly listen to me," said Monsieur de Nemours, "I will speedily explain the matter to you, and you will soon see that the Vidame is so implicated that I should not have said anything about it even to the Prince of Clèves if I had not needed his assistance in order to have the honor of seeing you."

"I think that all that you might take the trouble to say to me would be useless," replied Madame de Clèves, somewhat tartly; "and it is much better that you should go to the crown princess and tell her frankly your interest in this letter, since it has been said that it belongs to you."

The vexation that Monsieur de Nemours saw in Madame de Clèves gave him the keenest pleasure he had yet known, and fully consoled him for his impatience to explain himself. "I do not know, Madame," he began, "what may have been said to the dauphiness; but this letter does not concern me personally, and it was written to the Vidame."

"That I believe," replied Madame de Clèves; "but the dauphiness has been told the contrary, and it will not seem to her likely that the Vidame's letters should fall out of your pockets. That is why, unless you have some good reason for concealing the truth from her, I advise you to confess it to her."

"I have nothing to confess to her," he went on; "the letter is none of mine, and if there is any one I wish to convince of this, it is not the crown princess. But, Madame, since the Vidame's fate is at stake, permit me to tell you some things which you will find quite worth listening to."

The silence of Madame de Clèves showed that she was willing to listen, and Monsieur de Nemours repeated in as few words as possible what the Vidame had told him. Although

this might well have surprised, or at least interested, her,
Madame de Clèves listened with such marked indifference that
she seemed to doubt it or to find it unworthy of her attention.
She maintained this indifference until Monsieur de Nemours
mentioned Madame d'Amboise's note to the Vidame of
Chartres, which was the proof of all he had just been saying.
Since Madame de Clèves knew that she was a friend of
Madame de Themines, it seemed to her possible that Monsieur de Nemours had been speaking the truth, and she began
to think that possibly the letter in question had not been
written to him. This thought suddenly dispelled her indifference. The prince read her the note, which exonerated
him completely, and then handed it to her for examination,
telling her that perhaps she knew the handwriting; she was
compelled to take it and to read the address, and indeed every
word, in order to make sure that the letter asked for was the
one in her possession. Monsieur de Nemours said everything
he could think of to convince her; and since a pleasant truth
is readily believed, he succeeded in proving to Madame de
Clèves that he had no part whatsoever in the letter.

Then she began to reflect on the Vidame's troubles and
danger, to blame his evil conduct, and to desire means to aid
him. She was surprised at the queen's behavior; she confessed
to Monsieur de Nemours that the letter was in her possession,
—in a word, so soon as she thought him innocent, she interested herself at once with the utmost cordiality in the very
things that at first left her perfectly indifferent. They agreed
that it was not necessary to return the letter to the crown
princess, lest she should show it to Madame de Martigues,
who knew Madame de Themines' handwriting, and would at
once have guessed, from her interest in the Vidame, that the
letter had been written to him. They also thought that it was
better not to confide to the dauphiness the part concerning her
mother-in-law, the queen. Madame de Clèves, under the pretext of her concern for her uncle's affairs, gladly promised to
keep every secret that Monsieur de Nemours might intrust to
her.

This prince would have talked with her about other things
than the Vidame's affairs, and would have taken advantage of
this opportunity to speak to her with greater freedom than he
had ever done, were it not that word was brought to Madame
de Clèves that the dauphiness had sent for her; Monsieur de
Nemours consequently was obliged to withdraw. He went to

see the Vidame, to tell him that after leaving him he had thought it better to see his niece, Madame de Clèves, than to go straight to the dauphiness. He brought forward many good arguments in support of what he had done and to make success seem probable.

Meanwhile Madame de Clèves dressed in all haste to go to the crown princess. She had scarcely entered the room when the dauphiness called her to her, and said in a low voice,—

"I have been waiting two hours for you, and never had more difficulty in concealing the truth than I have had this morning. The queen has heard about the letter I gave you yesterday, and thinks it was the Vidame of Chartres who dropped it; you know she takes a good deal of interest in him. She wanted to see the letter, and sent to ask Châtelart for it; he told her he had given it to me, and then they came to ask me for it, under the pretext that it was a very bright letter, which the queen was anxious to see. I did not dare say that you had it; I feared she would think that it had been placed in your hands because the Vidame is your uncle, and that there was some understanding between you and me. It has already occurred to me that she did not like his seeing me often; so I said the letter was in the pocket of the clothes I wore yesterday, and that those who had the key of the room in which they were locked had gone out. So give me the letter at once, that I may send it to her; and let me look at it before I send it, to see if I know the handwriting."

Madame de Clèves was even more embarrassed than she had expected. "I don't know, Madame," she answered, "what you will do; for Monsieur de Clèves, to whom I had given it, gave it back to Monsieur de Nemours, who came this morning to get him to ask you to return it to him. Monsieur de Clèves was imprudent enough to say that it was in his possession, and weak enough to yield to Monsieur de Nemours' entreaties and to give it to him."

"You have put me in the greatest possible embarrassment," said the dauphiness, "and you did very wrong to return the letter to Monsieur de Nemours; since I gave it you, you ought not to have returned it without my permission. What can I say to the queen, and what will she think? She will believe, and on good grounds, that this letter concerns me, and that there is something between the Vidame and me. She will never believe that the letter belongs to Monsieur de Nemours."

"I am extremely sorry," answered Madame de Clèves, "for the trouble I have caused,—I see just how great it is; but it is Monsieur de Clèves' fault, not mine."

"It is yours," retorted the dauphiness, "because you gave him the letter. There is not another woman in the world who would confide to her husband everything she knows."

"I acknowledge that I was wrong, Madame," said Madame de Clèves; "but think rather of repairing than of discussing my fault."

"Don't you remember pretty well what was in the letter?" asked the crown princess.

"Yes, Madame," was the reply; "I remember it, for I read it over more than once."

"In that case, you must go at once and write it in a disguised hand. This copy I will send to the queen. She will not show it to any one who has seen the original; and even if she should, I shall always maintain that it was the one that Châtelart gave me, and he will not dare to deny it."

Madame de Clèves agreed to this plan, and all the more readily because she thought she would send for Monsieur de Nemours to let her have the letter again, in order to copy it word for word, and so far as possible imitate the handwriting; in this way she thought the queen could not fail to be deceived. As soon as she got home she told her husband about the dauphiness's embarrassment, and begged him to send for Monsieur de Nemours; this was done, and he came at once. Madame de Clèves repeated to him what she had just told her husband, and asked him for the letter. Monsieur de Nemours replied that he had already given it back to the Vidame de Chartres, who was so glad to see it again and to be out of danger that he had at once sent it to Madame de Themines. Madame de Clèves was in new trouble; but at last, after discussing the matter together, they determined to write the letter from memory. They locked themselves up to work, left word at the door that no one was to be let in, and sent off Monsieur de Nemours' servants. This appearance of mystery and of confidence was far from unpleasant to this prince, and even to Madame de Clèves. The presence of her husband and the thought that she was furthering the Vidame's interests almost calmed her scruples. She felt only the pleasure of seeing Monsieur de Nemours; it was a fuller and purer joy than any she had ever felt, and it inspired her with a liveliness and ease that Monsieur de Nemours had never seen in her, and his love for her was only deepened. Since he had never before had such

pleasant moments, his own spirits rose, and when Madame de
Clèves wanted to recall the letter and to write, he, instead of
aiding her seriously, did nothing but interrupt her with idle
jests. Madame de Clèves was quite as merry; so that they had
been long shut up together, and twice word had come from
the dauphiness urging Madame de Clèves to make haste, before half the letter was written.

Monsieur de Nemours was only too happy to prolong so
pleasant a visit, and forgot his friend's interests. Madame de
Clèves was amusing herself, and forgot those of her uncle. At
last, at four o'clock, the letter was hardly finished, and the
handwriting was so unlike that of the original that it was
impossible that the queen should not at once detect the truth;
and she was not deceived by it. Although they did their best
to convince her that the letter was written to Monsieur de
Nemours, she remained convinced, not only that it was addressed to the Vidame de Chartres, but that the dauphiness
had something to do with it, and that there was some understanding between him and her. This thought so intensified her
hatred of this princess that she never forgave her, and perse-
cuted her till she drove her from France.

As for the Vidame of Chartres, he was ruined so far as she
was concerned; and whether it was that the Cardinal of Lorraine had already acquired an ascendency over her, or that
the affair of this letter, in which she saw that she had been
deceived, opened her eyes to the other deceptions of which
the Vidame had been guilty, it is certain that he could never
bring about a satisfactory reconciliation. Their intimacy was
at an end, and she accomplished his ruin afterward at the time
of the conspiracy of Amboise, in which he was implicated.

After the letter had been sent to the crown princess, Monsieur de Clèves and Monsieur de Nemours went away. Madame de Clèves was left alone; and as soon as she was deprived
of the presence of the man she loved, she seemed to awaken
from a dream. She thought with surprise of the difference
between her state of mind the previous evening and that she
then felt; she pictured the coldness and harshness she had
shown to Monsieur de Nemours so long as she had supposed
that Madame de Themines' letter had been written to him,
and the tranquillity and happiness that had succeeded them
when he had proved to her that this letter in no way concerned him. When she recalled that the day before she had
reproached herself, as if it were a crime, for having shown an
interest that mere compassion had called forth, and that by

her harshness she had betrayed a feeling of jealousy,—a certain proof of affection,—she scarcely recognized herself. When she thought further that Monsieur de Nemours saw that she was aware of his love; when he saw that, in spite of this, she treated him with perfect cordiality in her husband's presence,—indeed that she had treated him with more kindness than ever before, that she was the cause of her husband's sending for him, and that they had just passed an afternoon together privately,—she saw that there was an understanding between herself and Monsieur de Nemours; that she was deceiving a husband who deserved to be deceived less than any husband in the world; and she was ashamed to appear so unworthy of esteem even before the eyes of her lover. But what pained her more than all the rest was the memory of the state in which she had passed the night, and the acute grief she had suffered from the thought that Monsieur de Nemours loved another and that she had been deceived.

Up to that time she had not known the stings of mistrust and jealousy; her only thought had been to keep from loving Monsieur de Nemours, and she had not yet begun to fear that he loved another. Although the suspicions that this letter had aroused were wholly removed, they opened her eyes to the danger of being deceived, and gave her impressions of mistrust and jealousy such as she had never felt before. She was astounded that she had never yet thought how improbable it was that a man like Monsieur de Nemours, who had always treated women with such fickleness, should be capable of a sincere and lasting attachment. She thought it almost impossible that she could ever be satisfied with his love. "But if I could be," she asked herself, "what could I do with it? Do I wish it? Could I return it? Do I wish to begin a love-affair? Do I wish to fail in my duty to Monsieur de Clèves? Do I wish to expose myself to the cruel repentance and mortal anguish that are inseparable from love? I am overwhelmed by an affection which carries me away in spite of myself; all my resolutions are vain; I thought yesterday what I think to-day, and I act to-day in direct contradiction to my resolutions of yesterday. I must tear myself away from the society of Monsieur de Nemours; I must go to the country, strange as the trip may seem; and if Monsieur de Clèves persists in opposing it, or in demanding my reasons, perhaps I shall do him and myself the wrong of telling them to him." She held firm to this resolution, and spent the evening at home, instead of going to find out from the dauphiness what had become of the Vidame's pretended letter.

When Monsieur de Clèves came home she told him she wanted to go into the country; that she was not feeling well, and needed a change of air. Monsieur de Clèves, who felt sure from her appearance that there was nothing serious ailed her, at first laughed at the proposed trip, and told her that she forgot the approaching marriages of the princesses and the tournament, and that she would not have time enough to make her preparations for appearing in due splendor along-side the other ladies. Her husband's arguments did not move her; she begged him, when he went to Compiègne with the king, to let her go to Coulommiers,—a country-house they were building at a day's journey from Paris. Monsieur de Clèves gave his consent; so she went off with the intention of not returning at once, and the king left for a short stay at Compiègne.

Monsieur de Nemours felt very bad at not seeing Madame de Clèves again after the pleasant afternoon he had spent with her, which had so fired his hopes. His impatience to meet her once more left him no peace; so that when the king returned to Paris he determined to make a visit to his sister, the Duchess of Mercœur, who lived in the country not far from Coulommiers. He proposed to the Vidame to go with him; the latter gladly consented, to the delight of Monsieur de Nemours, who hoped to make sure of seeing Madame de Clèves by calling in company with the Vidame.

Madame de Mercœur was delighted to see them, and at once began to devise plans for their amusement. While they were deer-hunting, Monsieur de Nemours lost his way in the forest; and when he asked what road he should take, he was told that he was near Coulommiers. When he heard this word, "Coulommiers," he at once, without thinking, without forming any plan, dashed off in that direction. He got once more into the forest, and followed such paths as seemed to him to lead to the castle. These paths led to a summer-house, which consisted of a large room with two closets, one opening on a flower-garden separated from the forest by a fence, and the other opening on one of the walks of the park. He entered the summer-house, and was about to stop and admire it, when he saw Monsieur and Madame de Clèves coming along the path, followed by a number of servants. Surprised at seeing Monsieur de Clèves, whom he had left with the king, his first impulse was to hide. He entered the closet near the flower-garden, with the intention of escaping by a door opening into the forest; but when he saw Madame de Clèves and her husband sitting in the summer-house, while their servants stayed in the park, whence they could not reach him without coming by Monsieur and Madame de Clèves, he could not resist the temptation to watch her, or overcome his curiosity to listen to her conversation with her husband, of whom he was more jealous than of any of his rivals.

He heard Monsieur de Clèves say to his wife: "But why don't you wish to return to Paris? What can keep you in the country? For some time you have had a taste for solitude which surprises me and pains me, because it keeps us apart. I find you in even lower spirits than usual, and I am afraid something distresses you."

"I have nothing on my mind," she answered, with some embarrassment; "but the bustle of a court is so great, and our house is always so thronged, that it is impossible for mind and body not to be tired and to need rest."

"Rest," he answered, "is not needed by persons of your age. Neither at home nor at court do you get tired, and I should be rather inclined to fear that you are glad to get away from me."

"If you thought that, you would do me great injustice," she replied, with ever-growing embarrassment; "but I beg of you to leave me here. If you could stay too I should be very glad, provided you would stay alone, and did not care for the throng of people who almost never leave you."

"Ah, Madame," exclaimed Monsieur de Clèves, "your air and your words show me that you have reasons for wishing to be alone which I don't know, and which I beg of you to tell me."

For a long time the prince besought her to tell him the reason, but in vain; and after she had refused in a way that only redoubled his curiosity, she stood for a time silent, with eyes cast down; then, raising her eyes to his, she said suddenly,—

"Don't compel me to confess something which I have often meant to tell you, but had not the strength. Only remember that prudence does not require that a woman of my age, who is mistress of her actions, should remain exposed to the temptations of the court."

"What is it you suggest, Madame?" exclaimed Monsieur de Clèves. "I should not dare to say, for fear of offending you."

Madame de Clèves did not answer, and her silence confirming her husband's suspicions, he went on,—

"You are silent, and your silence tells me I am not mistaken."

"Well, sir," she answered, falling on her knees, "I am going to make you a confession such as no woman has ever made to her husband; the innocence of my actions and of my intentions gives me strength to do so. It is true that I have reasons for keeping aloof from the court, and I wish to avoid the perils that sometimes beset women of my age. I have never given the slightest sign of weakness, and I should never fear displaying any, if you would leave me free to withdraw from court, or if Madame de Chartres still lived to guide my actions. Whatever the dangers of the course I take, I pursue it with pleasure, in order to keep myself worthy of you. I beg your pardon a thousand times if my feelings offend you; at any rate I shall never offend you by my actions. Remember that to do what I am now doing requires more friendship and esteem for a husband than any one has ever had. Guide me, take pity on me, love me, if you can."

All the time she was speaking, Monsieur de Clèves sat with his head in his hands; he was really beside himself, and did not once think of lifting his wife up. But when she had finished, and he looked down and saw her, her face wet with tears, and yet so beautiful, he thought he should die of grief. He kissed her, and helped her to her feet.

"Do you, Madame, take pity on me," he said, "for I deserve it; and excuse me if in the first moments of a grief so poignant as mine I do not respond as I should to your appeal. You seem to me worthier of esteem and admiration than any woman that ever lived; but I also regard myself as the unhappiest of men. The first moment that I saw you, I was filled with love of you; neither your indifference to me nor the fact that you are my wife has cooled it: it still lives. I have never been able to make you love me, and I see that you fear you love another. And who, Madame, is the happy man that inspires this fear? Since when has he charmed you? What has he done to please you? What was the road he took to your heart? I found some consolation for not having touched it in the thought that it was beyond any one's reach; but another has succeeded where I have failed. I have all the jealousy of a husband and of a lover; but it is impossible to suffer as a husband after what you have told me. Your noble conduct makes me feel perfectly secure, and even consoles me as a lover. Your confidence and your sincerity are infinitely dear to me; you think well enough of me not to suppose that I shall take any unfair advantage of this confession. You are right, Madame,—I shall not; and I shall not love you less. You make me happy by the greatest proof of fidelity that a woman ever gave her husband; but, Madame, go on and tell me who it is you are trying to avoid."

"I entreat you, do not ask me," she replied; "I have determined not to tell you, and I think that the more prudent course."

"Have no fear, Madame," said Monsieur de Clèves; "I know the world too well to suppose that respect for a husband ever prevents men falling in love with his wife. He ought to hate those who do so, but without complaining; so once more, Madame, I beg of you to tell me what I want to know."

"You would urge me in vain," she answered; "I have strength enough to keep back what I think I ought not to say. My avowal is not the result of weakness, and it requires more courage to confess this truth than to undertake to hide it."

Monsieur de Nemours lost not a single word of this conversation, and Madame de Clèves' last remark made him quite as jealous as it made her husband. He was himself so desperately in love with her that he supposed every one else was just as much so. It was true in fact that he had many rivals, but he imagined even more than there were; and he began to wonder whom Madame de Clèves could mean. He had often believed that she did not dislike him, and he had formed this opinion from things which now seemed so slight that he could not imagine he had kindled a love so intense that it called for this desperate remedy. He was almost beside himself with excitement, and could not forgive Monsieur de Clèves for not insisting on knowing the name his wife was hiding.

Monsieur de Clèves, however, was doing his best to find it out, and after he had entreated her in vain, she said: "It seems to me that you ought to be satisfied with my sincerity; do not ask me anything more, and do not give me reason to repent what I have just done. Content yourself with the assurance I give you that no one of my actions has betrayed my feelings, and that not a word has ever been said to me at which I could take offence."

"Ah, Madame," Monsieur de Clèves suddenly exclaimed, "I cannot believe you! I remember your embarrassment the day your portrait was lost. You gave it away, Madame,—you gave away that portrait which was so dear to me, and belonged to me so legitimately. You could not hide your feelings; it is known that you are in love: your virtue has so far preserved you from the rest."

"Is it possible," the princess burst forth, "that you could suspect any misrepresentation in a confession like mine, which there was no ground for my making? Believe what I say: I purchase at a high price the confidence that I ask of you. I beg of you, believe that I did not give away the portrait; it is true that I saw it taken, but I did not wish to show that I saw it, lest I should be exposed to hearing things which no one had yet dared to say."

"How then did you see his love?" asked Monsieur de Clèves. "What marks of love were given to you?"

"Spare me the mortification," was her answer, "of repeating all the details which I am ashamed to have noticed, and have only convinced me of my weakness."

"You are right, Madame," he said, "I am unjust. Deny me when I shall ask such things, but do not be angry if I ask them."

At this moment some of the servants who were without, came to tell Monsieur de Clèves that a gentleman had come with a command from the king that he should be in Paris that evening. Monsieur de Clèves was obliged to leave at once, and he could say to his wife nothing except that he begged her to return the next day, and besought her to believe that though he was sorely distressed, he felt for her an affection and esteem which ought to satisfy her.

When he had gone, and Madame de Clèves was alone and began to think of what she had done, she was so amazed that she could scarcely believe it true. She thought that she had wholly alienated her husband's love and esteem, and had thrown herself into an abyss from which escape was impossible. She asked herself why she had done this perilous thing, and saw that she had stumbled into it without intention. The strangeness of such a confession, for which she knew no precedent, showed her all her danger.

But when she began to think that this remedy, violent as it was, was the only one that could protect her against Monsieur de Nemours, she felt that she could not regret it, and that she had not gone too far. She spent the whole night in uncertainty, anxiety, and fear; but at last she grew calm. She felt a vague satisfaction in having given this proof of fidelity to a husband who so well deserved it, who had such affection and esteem for her, and who had just shown these by the way in which he had received her avowal.

Meanwhile Monsieur de Nemours had left the place where he had overheard a conversation which touched him keenly, and had hastened into the forest. What Madame de Clèves had said about the portrait gave him new life, by showing him that it was he whom she did not hate. He first gave himself up to this joy; but it was not of long duration, for he reflected that the same thing which showed him that he had touched the heart of Madame de Clèves, ought to convince him that he would never receive any token of it, and that it was impossible to gain any influence over a woman who resorted to so strange a remedy. He felt, nevertheless, great pleasure in having brought her to this extremity. He felt a certain pride in making himself loved by a woman so different from all others of her sex,—in a word, he felt a hundred times happier and unhappier. Night came upon him in the forest, and he had great difficulty in finding the way back to Madame de Mercœur's. He reached there at daybreak. He found it very hard to explain what had delayed him, but he made the best excuses he could, and returned to Paris that same day with the Vidame.

Monsieur de Nemours was so full of his passion and so surprised by what he had heard that he committed a very common imprudence,—that of speaking in general terms of his own feelings and of describing his own adventures under borrowed names. On his way back he turned the conversation to love: he spoke of the pleasure of being in love with a worthy woman; he mentioned the singular effects of this passion; and, finally, not being able to keep to himself his astonishment at what Madame de Clèves had done, he told the whole story to the Vidame, without naming her and without saying that he had any part in it. But he manifested such warmth and admiration that the Vidame at once suspected that the story concerned the prince himself. He urged him strongly to acknowledge this; he said that he had long known that he nourished a violent passion, and that it was wrong not to trust in a man who had confided to him the secret of his life. Monsieur de Nemours was too much in love to acknowledge his love; he had always hidden it from the Vidame, though he loved him better than any man at court. He answered that one of his friends had told him this adventure, and had made him promise not to speak of it, and he besought him to keep his secret. The Vidame promised not to speak of it; nevertheless, Monsieur de Nemours repented having told him.

Meanwhile, Monsieur de Clèves had gone to the king, his heart sick with a mortal wound. Never had a husband felt warmer love or higher respect for his wife. What he had heard had not lessened his respect, but this had assumed a new form. His most earnest desire was to know who had succeeded in pleasing her. Monsieur de Nemours was the first to occur to him, as the most fascinating man at court, and the Chevalier de Guise and the Marshal of Saint-André as two men who had tried to please her and had paid her much attention; so that he decided it must be one of these three. He reached the Louvre, and the king took him into his study to tell him that he had chosen him to carry Madame to Spain; that he had thought that the prince would discharge this duty better than any one; and that no one would do so much credit to France as Madame de Clèves. Monsieur de Clèves accepted this appointment with due respect, and even looked upon it as something that would remove his wife from court without attracting any attention; but the date of their departure was still too remote to relieve his present embarrassment. He wrote at once to Madame de Clèves to tell her what the king had said, and added that he was very anxious that she should come to Paris. She returned in obedience to his request, and when they met, each found the other in the deepest gloom.

Monsieur de Clèves addressed her in the most honorable terms, and seemed well worthy of the confidence she had placed in him.

"I have no uneasiness about your conduct," he said; "you have more strength and virtue than you think. It is not dread of the future that distresses me; I am only distressed at seeing that you have for another feelings that I have not been able to inspire in you."

"I do not know how to answer you," she said; "I am ready to die with shame when I speak to you. Spare me, I beg of you, these painful conversations. Regulate my conduct; let me see no one,—that is all I ask; but permit me never to speak of a thing which makes me seem so little worthy of you, and which I regard as so unworthy of me."

"You are right, Madame," he answered; "I abuse your gentleness and your confidence. But do you too take some pity on the state into which you have cast me, and remember that whatever you have told me, you conceal from me a name which excites an unendurable curiosity. Still, I do not ask you to gratify it; but I must say that I believe the man I must envy to be the Marshal of Saint-André, the Duke of Nemours, or the Chevalier de Guise."

"I shall not answer," she said, blushing, "and I shall give you no occasion for lessening or strengthening your suspicions; but if you try to find out by watching me, you will surely make me so embarrassed that every one will notice it. In Heaven's name," she went on, "invent some illness, that I may see no one!"

"No, Madame," he replied, "it would soon be found that it was not real; and moreover I want to place my confidence in you alone,—that is the course my heart recommends, and my reason too. In your present mood, by leaving you free, I protect you by a closer guard than I could persuade myself to set about you."

Monsieur de Clèves was right; the confidence he showed in his wife proved a stronger protection against Monsieur de Nemours and inspired her to make austerer resolutions than any form of constraint could have done. She went to the Louvre and visited the dauphiness as usual; but she avoided Monsieur de Nemours with so much care that she took away nearly all his happiness at thinking that she loved him. He saw nothing in her actions which did not prove the contrary. He was almost ready to believe that what he had heard was a dream, so unlikely did it appear. The only thing that assured him that he was not mistaken was the extreme sadness of Madame de Clèves, in spite of all her efforts to conceal it. Possibly kind words and glances would not have so fanned Monsieur de Nemours' love as did this austere conduct.

One evening, when Monsieur and Madame de Clèves were with the queen, some one said that it was reported that the king was going to name another nobleman of the court to accompany Madame to Spain. Monsieur de Clèves fixed his eyes on his wife when the speaker added that it would be either the Chevalier de Guise or the Marshal of Saint-André. He noticed that she showed no agitation at either of these names, or at the mention of their joining the party. This led him to think that it was neither of these that she dreaded to see; and wishing to determine the matter, he went to the room where the king was. After a short absence he returned to his wife and whispered to her that he had just learned that it would be Monsieur de Nemours who would go with them to Spain.

The name of Monsieur de Nemours and the thought of

seeing him every day during a long journey, in her husband's presence, so agitated Madame de Clèves that she could not conceal it, and wishing to assign other reasons, she answered,—

"The choice of that gentleman will be very disagreeable for you; he will divide all the honors, and I think you ought to try to have some one else appointed."

"It is not love of glory, Madame," said Monsieur de Clèves, "that makes you dread that Monsieur de Nemours should come with me. Your regret springs from another cause. This regret tells me what another woman would have told by her delight. But do not be alarmed; what I have just told you is not true: I made it up to make sure of a thing which I had only too long inclined to believe." With these words he went away, not wishing by his presence to add to his wife's evident embarrassment.

At that moment Monsieur de Nemours entered, and at once noticed Madame de Clèves' condition. He went up to her, and said in a low voice that he respected her too much to ask what made her so thoughtful. His voice aroused her from her revery; and looking at him, without hearing what he said, full of her own thoughts and fearful that her husband would see him by her side, she said: "In Heaven's name, leave me alone!"

"Alas! Madame," he replied, "I leave you only too much alone. Of what can you complain? I do not dare to speak to you, or even to look at you; I never come near you without trembling. How have I brought such a remark on myself, and why do you make me seem to have something to do with the depression in which I find you?"

Madame de Clèves deeply regretted that she had given Monsieur de Nemours an opportunity to speak to her more frankly than he had ever done. She left him without giving him any answer, and went home in a state of agitation such as she had never known. Her husband soon noticed this; he perceived that she was afraid lest he should speak to her about what had just happened. He followed her into her room and said to her,—

"Do not try to avoid me, Madame; I shall say nothing that could displease you. I beg your pardon for surprising you as I did; I am sufficiently punished by what I learned. Monsieur de Nemours was the man whom I most feared. I see your danger: control yourself for your own sake, and, if possible, for mine. I do not ask this as your husband, but as a man, all of whose happiness you make, and who feels for you a tenderer and stronger love than he whom your heart prefers." Monsieur de Clèves nearly broke down at these last words, which he could hardly utter. His wife was much moved, and bursting into tears, she embraced him with a gentleness and a sorrow that almost brought him to the same condition. They remained for some time perfectly silent, and separated without having strength to utter a word.

The preparations for Madame Elisabeth's marriage were completed, and the Duke of Alva arrived for the ceremony. He was received with all the pomp and formality that the occasion required. The king sent the Prince of Condé, the Cardinals of Lorraine and Guise, the Dukes of Lorraine, Ferrara, Aumale, Bouillon, Guise, and Nemours to meet him. They were accompanied by many gentlemen and a great number of pages wearing their liveries. The king himself received the Duke of Alva at the first door of the Louvre with two hundred gentlemen in waiting, with the constable at their head. As the duke drew near the king, he wished to embrace his knees; but the king prevented him, and made him walk by his side to call on the queen and on Madame Elisabeth, to whom the Duke of Alva brought a magnificent present from his master. He then called on Madame Marguerite, the king's sister, to convey to her the compliments of Monsieur de Savoie, and to assure her that he would arrive in a few days. There were large receptions at the Louvre, to show the Duke of Alva and the Prince of Orange, who accompanied him, the beauties of the court.

Madame de Clèves did not dare to stay away, much as she desired it, through fear of displeasing her husband, who gave her special orders to go. What made him even more determined was the absence of Monsieur de Nemours. He had gone to meet Monsieur de Savoie, and after that prince's arrival he was obliged to be with him almost all the time, to help him in his preparations for the wedding ceremonies; hence Madame de Clèves did not meet him so often as usual, and she was able to enjoy a little peace.

The Vidame of Chartres had not forgotten the talk he had had with Monsieur de Nemours. He had made up his mind that the adventure this prince had told him was his own, and he watched him so closely that perhaps he would have made out the truth, had not the arrival of the Duke of Alva and of Monsieur de Savoie so changed and busied the court that he had no further opportunity. His desire for more information, or, rather, the natural tendency to tell all one knows to the woman one loves, made him mention to Madame de Martigues the extraordinary conduct of the woman who had confessed to her husband the love she felt for another man. He assured her that it was Monsieur de Nemours who had inspired this violent passion, and he besought her to aid him in observing this prince. Madame de Martigues was greatly interested in what the Vidame had told her, and her curiosity about the dauphiness's relations with Monsieur de Nemours made her more anxious than ever to get to the bottom of the affair.

A few days before the one set for the wedding the crown princess gave a supper to her father-in-law the king and the Duchess of Valentinois. Madame de Clèves, who was delayed in dressing, started for the Louvre a little later than usual, and on her way met a gentleman coming from the dauphiness to fetch her. When she entered the room the crown princess called out to her from the bed on which she was lying that she had been waiting for her with the utmost impatience.

"I fancy, Madame," she replied, "that I have no cause to be grateful to you for this impatience; it is doubtless for some other reason that you were eager to see me."

"You are right," said the dauphiness; "but, nevertheless, you ought to be obliged to me, for I am going to tell you something that I am sure you will be very glad to hear."

Madame de Clèves knelt down by the side of the bed in such a way that, fortunately for her, her face was in the dark. "You know," said the crown princess, "how anxious we have been to find out the cause of the change in the Duke of Nemours; I think I have found out, and it is something that will surprise you. He is desperately in love with one of the most beautiful women of the court, and the lady returns his love."

These words, which Madame de Clèves could not take to herself, because she thought that no one knew of her love for this prince, gave her a pang that may be easily imagined.

"I see nothing in that," she replied, "which is surprising for a man of his age and appearance."

"But that," resumed the dauphiness, "is not the surprising part; what is amazing is the fact that this woman who loves Monsieur de Nemours has never given him any token of it, and that her fear that she may not always be able to control her passion has caused her to confess it to her husband to persuade him to take her away from court. And it is Mon-

sieur de Nemours himself who is the authority for what I
say."

If Madame de Clèves had been grieved at first by thinking
that the affair is no way concerned her, these last words of the
dauphiness filled her with despair, since they made it sure that
it did concern her only too deeply. She could make no reply,
but remained with her head resting on the bed while the
dauphiness went on talking, too much taken up with what she
was saying to notice her embarrassment. When Madame de
Clèves had recovered some of her self-control, she answered,—

"This does not sound like a very probable story, and I
wonder who told it to you."

"It was Madame de Martigues, who heard it from the Vidame. You know he is her lover; he told it to her as a secret,
and he heard it from the Duke of Nemours. It is true that the
Duke of Nemours did not mention the lady's name and did
not even acknowledge that it was he who was loved; but the
Vidame de Chartres has no doubt about that."

As the dauphiness pronounced these last words, some one
drew near the bed. Madame de Clèves was turned away so
that she could not see who it was; but she knew when the
dauphiness exlaimed, with an air of surprise and amusement,
"There he is himself, and I am going to ask how much truth
there is in it."

Madame de Clèves knew that it must be the Duke of Nemours, and so it was. Without turning toward him, she leaned
over to the crown princess and whispered to her to be careful
not to say a word about this adventure, that he had told it to
the Vidame in confidence, and that this would very possibly
set them by the ears. The dauphiness answered laughingly that
she was absurdly prudent, and turned toward Monsieur de
Nemours. He was arrayed for the evening entertainment, and
addressed her with all his usual grace.

"I believe, Madame," he began, "that I can think, without
impertinence, that you were talking about me when I came in,
that you wanted to ask me something, and that Madame de
Clèves objected."

"You are right," replied the dauphiness; "but I shall not be
as obliging to her as I usually am. I want to know whether a
story I have heard is true, and whether you are the man who
is in love with and is loved by a lady of the court who
carefully conceals her passion from you and has confessed it
to her husband."

Madame de Clèves' agitation and embarrassment cannot be conceived, and she would have welcomed death as an escape from her sufferings; but Monsieur de Nemours was even more embarrassed, if that is possible. This statement from the lips of the dauphiness, who, he had reason to believe, did not hate him, in the presence of Madame de Clèves, whom he loved better than any woman at court, and who also loved him, so overwhelmed him that he could not control his face. The embarrassment into which his blunder had plunged Madame de Clèves, and the thought of the good reason he gave her to hate him, made it impossible for him to answer. The dauphiness, noticing his intense confusion, said to Madame de Clèves: "Look at him, look at him, and see whether this is not his own story!"

Meanwhile Monsieur de Nemours, recovering from his first agitation, and recognizing the importance of escaping from this dangerous complication, suddenly recovered his presence of mind and regained his composure.

"I must acknowledge, Madame," he said, "that no one could be more surprised and distressed than I am by the Vidame de Chartres' treachery in repeating the adventure of one of my friends which I told to him in confidence. I might easily revenge myself," he went on, smiling in a way that almost dispelled the dauphiness's suspicions; "since he has confided to me matters of considerable importance. But I fail to understand why you do me the honor of implicating me in this affair. The Vidame cannot say that it concerns me, because I told him the very opposite. It may do very well to represent me as a man in love; but it will hardly do to represent me as a man who is loved,—which, Madame, is what you do."

Monsieur de Nemours was very glad to say something to the dauphiness which had some connection with his appearance in former times, in order to divert her thoughts. She caught his meaning; but without referring to these last words of his, she continued to harp on his evident confusion.

"I was embarrassed, Madame," he replied, "out of zeal for my friend and from fear of the reproaches he would be justified in making to me for repeating a thing dearer to him than life. Nevertheless, he only told me half, and did not mention the name of the woman he loves. I simply know that he is more in love and more to be pitied than any man in the world."

"Do you find him so worthy of pity," asked the crown princess, "because he is loved?"

"Are you sure that he is?" he answered; "and do you think that a woman who felt a real love would confide it to her husband? This woman, I am sure, knows nothing about love, and has mistaken for it a faint feeling of gratitude for his devotion to her. My friend cannot nourish any hope; but, wretched as he is, he has at least the consolation of having made her fearful of loving him, and he would not change his fate for that of any man in the world."

"Your friend's love is easily satisfied," said the crown princess, "and I begin to think that you can't be talking about yourself; I am inclned to agree with Madame de Clèves, who maintains that there can be no truth in the whole story."

"I don't think there can be," said Madame de Clèves, who had not yet said a word; "and if it were true, how could it become known? It is extremely unlikely that a woman capable of such an extraordinary thing would have the weakness to tell of it. Evidently a husband would not think of doing such a thing, unless he were a husband very unworthy of the confidence that was placed in him."

Monsieur de Nemours, who saw that Madame de Clèves' suspicions had fallen on her husband, was very glad to strengthen them; he knew that he was his strongest rival.

"Jealousy," he replied, "and the desire to find out more than he had been told, may induce a husband to commit a great many indiscretions."

Madame de Clèves was at the end of her strength; and being unable to carry on the conversation further, she was about to say that she did not feel well, when, fortunately for her, the Duchess of Valentinois came in to tell the dauphiness that the king would arrive very soon. The crown princess accordingly went into her room to dress; whereupon Monsieur de Nemours came up to Madame de Clèves as she was about to follow her, and said,—

"Madame, I would give my life to speak to you a moment; but of all the important things I should have to say to you, nothing seems to me more important than to beg you to believe that if I have said anything which might seem to refer to the dauphiness, I have done so for reasons which do not concern her."

Madame de Clèves pretended not to hear him, but moved away without looking at him and joined the suite of the king, who had just come in. There being a great crowd present, her foot caught in her dress, and she made a misstep; she took advantage of this excuse to leave a place where she had no strength to stay longer, and went away pretending that she could not stand.

Monsieur de Clèves went to the Louvre, and being surprised not to see his wife, he was told of the accident that had just happened to her. He left at once, to find out how she was; he found her in bed, and she told him that she was but slightly hurt. When he had been with her for some time he saw that she was exceedingly sad; this surprised him, and he asked her, "What is the matter? You seem to suffer in some other way than that you have told me."

"I could not be in greater distress than I am," she answered. "What use did you make of the extraordinary, I might say foolish, confidence I had in you? Was I not worthy of secrecy on your part? And even if I was unworthy of it, did not your own interest urge it? Was it necessary that your curiosity to know a name which I ought not to tell you, could force you to confide in any one else in order to discover it? Nothing but curiosity could have led you to commit such an imprudence. The consequences have been most disastrous; the story is known, and has just been told to me, without any notion that I was the person most concerned."

"What do you say, Madame?" he replied. "You accuse me of having repeated what passed between us, and you tell me the story is known! I shall not defend myself from the charge of repeating it; you can't believe it, and you must have taken to yourself something said about some other woman."

"Oh, sir," she said, "in the whole world there is not another case like mine; there is not another woman capable of doing what I have done! Chance could not make any one invent it; no one has ever imagined it,—the very thought never entered any one's mind but mine. The dauphiness has just told me the whole story; she heard it from the Vidame of Chartres, and he had it from Monsieur de Nemours."

"Monsieur de Nemours!" exclaimed Monsieur de Clèves, with a gesture expressive of the wildest despair. "What, Monsieur de Nemours knows that you love him and that I know it!"

"You always want to fix on Monsieur de Nemours rather than any one else," she replied; "I told you that I should never say anything about your suspicions. I cannot say whether Monsieur de Nemours knows my share in this affair, or the part you assign to him; but he told it to the Vidame de

Chartres, saying that he had it from one of his friends, who did not give the name of the woman. This friend of Monsieur de Nemours must be one of your friends, and you must have told the story to him in an effort to get some information."

"Is there a friend in the world," he exclaimed, "to whom any one would make a confidence of that sort? And would any one try to confirm his suspicions by telling another what one would wish to hide from one's self? Consider rather to whom you have spoken. It is more likely that the secret got out from you than from me. You could not endure your misery alone, and you sought solace in making a confidant of some friend who has played you false."

"Do not torment me further," she burst forth, "and do not be so cruel as to charge me with a fault which you have committed. Could you suspect me of that? And because I was capable of speaking to you, am I capable of speaking of it to any one else?"

His wife's confession had so convinced Monsieur de Clèves of her frankness, and she so warmly denied having mentioned the incident to any one, that Monsieur de Clèves did not know what to think. For his own part, he was sure that he had repeated nothing; it was something nobody could have guessed: it was known, and it must have become known through one of them. But what caused the liveliest grief was the knowledge that this secret was in somebody's hands, and apparently would be soon divulged.

Madame de Clèves' thoughts were nearly the same; she held it equally impossible that her husband should have spoken and should not have spoken. What Monsieur de Nemours had said, that curiosity might make a husband indiscreet, seemed to apply so well to just the state of mind in which Monsieur de Clèves was, that she could not think it was a mere strange coincidence; and this probability compelled her to believe that Monsieur de Clèves had abused her confidence in him. They were both so busy with their thoughts that they for a long time did not speak, and when they broke the silence, it was but to repeat what they had already said very often, and they felt farther apart than they had ever been.

It is easy to picture the way they passed the night. Monsieur de Clèves' constancy had been nearly worn out by his effort to endure the unhappiness of seeing his wife, whom he adored, touched with love for another man. His courage was wellnigh exhausted; he even doubted whether this was an op-

portunity to make use of it, in a matter in which his pride and
honor were so sorely wounded. He no longer knew what to
think of his wife; he could not decide what course of action
he should urge her to take, or how he should himself act; on
all sides he saw nothing but precipices and steep abysses. At
last, after long distress and uncertainty, reflecting that he
should soon have to go to Spain, he made up his mind to do
nothing that should confirm any one's suspicions or knowledge of his unhappy condition. He went to Madame de Clèves
and told her that it was not worth while to discuss which of
them had betrayed their secret, but that it was very important
to prove that the story that had been told was a mere inven-
tion in no way referring to her; that it depended on her to
convince Monsieur de Nemours and the rest of this; that she
had only to treat him with the severity and coldness which she
ought to have for a man who made love to her, and that in
this way she would soon dispel the notion that she had any
interest in him. Hence, he argued, there was no need of her
distressing herself about what he might have thought, because
if henceforth she should betray no weakness, his opinion
would necessarily change; and above all, he urged upon her
the necessity of going to the palace and into the world as
much as usual.

When he had finished, Monsieur de Clèves left his wife
without awaiting her answer. She thought what he had said very
reasonable, and her indignation against Monsieur de Nemours
made her think it would be very easy to carry it out; but she
found it very hard to appear at all the wedding festivities with
a calm face and an easy mind. Nevertheless, since she had
been selected to carry the train of the dauphiness's dress,—a
special honor to her alone of all the princesses,—she could
not decline it without exciting much attention and wonder.
Hence she resolved to make a great effort to control herself;
but the rest of the day she devoted to preparations and to
indulging the feelings that harassed her. She shut herself up
alone in her room. What most distressed her was to have
grounds for complaint against Monsieur de Nemours, with no
chance of excusing him. She felt sure that he had told the
story to the Vidame,—this he had acknowledged; and she felt
sure too, from the way in whch he spoke of it, that he knew
that she was implicated. What excuse could be found for so
great a piece of imprudence, and what had become of the
prince's discretion, that had once so touched her? "He was
discreet," she said to herself, "so long as he thought himself

unhappy; but the mere thought of happiness, vague as it was, put an end to his discretion. He could not imagine that he was loved without wishing it to be known. He had said everything he could say. I have not confessed that it was he whom I loved; he suspected it, and showed his suspicions. If he had been sure of it, he would have done the same thing. I did wrong to think that there ever was a man capable of concealing what flattered his vanity. Yet it is for this man, whom I thought so different from other men, that I find myself in the same plight as other women whom I so little resemble. I have lost the love and esteem of a husband who ought to make me happy; soon every one will look upon me as a woman possessed by a mad and violent passion. The man for whom I feel it is no longer ignorant of it, and it is to escape just these evils that I have imperilled all my peace of mind, and even my life." These sad reflections were followed by a torrent of tears; but whatever the grief by which she felt herself overwhelmed, she knew that she could have endured it if she had been satisfied with Monsieur de Nemours.

This prince's state of mind was no more tranquil. His imprudence in unbosoming himself to the Vidame of Chartres, and the cruel results of this imprudence, caused him great pain. He could not without intense mortification recall Madame de Clèves' agitation and embarrassment. He could not forgive himself for having spoken about that affair in terms which, though courteous in themselves, must have seemed coarse and impolite, since they had implied to Madame de Clèves that he knew that she was the woman who was deeply in love, and with him. All that he could wish was a conversation with her; but he thought this more to be dreaded than desired. "What should I have to say to her?" he exclaimed. "Should I once more undertake to tell her what I have already made too clear to her? Shall I let her see that I know she loves me,—I, who have never dared to tell her that I love her? Shall I begin by speaking to her openly of my passion, in order to appear like a man emboldened by hope? Can I think merely of going near her, and should I dare to embarrass her by my presence? How could I justify myself? I have no excuse, I am unworthy to appear before Madame de Clèves, and I do not venture to hope that she will ever look at me again. By my own fault, I have given her a better protection against me than any she sought, and sought perhaps in vain. By my imprudence I have lost the happiness and pride of being loved by the most charming and estimable woman in the world. If I had

lost this happiness without her suffering, without having inflicted on her a bitter blow, that would be some consolation;
and at this moment I feel more keenly the harm I have done
her than I did when I was in her presence."

Monsieur de Nemours long tortured himself with these
thoughts. The desire to see Madame de Clèves perpetually
haunted him, and he began to look about for means of com-
municating with her. He thought of writing to her; but he
considered, after his blunder, and in view of her character,
that the best thing he could do would be to show his profound
respect, and by silence and evident distress to make it clear
that he did not dare to meet her, and to wait until time,
chance, or her own interest in him should work in his favor.
He resolved also to forbear from reproaching the Vidame of
Chartres for his treachery, lest he should confirm his suspicions.

The betrothal of Madame Elisabeth, which was to take
place on the morrow, and the wedding, which was to be
celebrated on the following day, so occupied the court that
Madame de Clèves and Monsieur de Nemours had no
difficulty in concealing their grief and annoyance from the
public. The dauphiness referred only lightly to their talk with
Monsieur de Nemours, and Monsieur de Clèves took pains not
to say anything more to his wife about what had happened, so
that soon she found herself more at ease than she had supposed possible.

The betrothal was celebrated at the Louvre; and after the
banquet and the ball, the whole royal household went to the
bishop's palace to pass the night, as was the custom. The next
morning the Duke of Alva, who always dressed very simply,
put on a coat of cloth of gold, mingled with red, yellow, and
black, and all covered with precious stones; on his head he
wore a crown. The Prince of Orange, arrayed in equal splendor, came with his servants, and all the Spaniards with theirs,
to fetch the Duke of Alva from the Villeroy mansion, where
he was staying; and they started, walking four abreast, for the
bishop's palace. As soon as they arrived, they went in due
order to the church. The king conducted Madame Elisabeth,
who also wore a crown; her dress was held by Mesdemoiselles
de Montpensier and De Longueville; then came the queen, but
not wearing a crown; after her came the dauphiness, the
king's sister, Madame de Lorraine, and the Queen of Navarre,
with princesses holding their trains. The queens and princesses
had all their maids-of-honor magnificently dressed in the same

colors that they themselves wore, so that the maids-of-honor could be at once distinguished by the colors of their dresses. They ascended the platform set up in the church, and the wedding ceremony took place. Then they returned to dinner at the bishop's palace, and at about five left for the palace, to be present at the banquet to which the parliament, the sovereign courts, and the city officials had been invited. The king, the queens, the princes, and princesses ate at the marble table in the great hall of the palace, the Duke of Alva being seated near the new Queen of Spain. Below the steps of the marble table, on the king's right hand, was a table for the ambassadors, the archbishops, and the knights of the order, and on the other side a table for the members of parliament.

The Duke of Guise, dressed in a robe of cloth of gold, was the king's major-domo, the Prince of Condé his head butler, the Duke of Nemours his cupbearer. After the tables were removed, the ball began; it was interrupted by the ballets and by extraordinary shows; then it was renewed, until, after midnight, the king and all the court returned to the Louvre. Though Madame de Clèves was very much depressed, she yet appeared in the eyes of every one, and especially in those of Monsieur de Nemours, incomparably beautiful. He did not dare to speak to her, although the confusion of the ceremony gave him many opportunities; but his demeanor was so dejected, and he showed such fear of approaching her, that she began to deem him less blameworthy, though he had not said a word in excuse of his conduct. His behavior was the same on the succeeding days, and continued to produce the same impression on Madame de Clèves.

At last the day of the tournament came. The queens betook themselves to the galleries and the raised seats set apart for them. The four champions appeared at the end of the lists, with a number of horses and servants, who formed the most magnificent spectacle ever seen in France.

The king's colors were plain black and white, which he always wore for the sake of Madame de Valentinois, who was a widow. The Duke of Ferrara and all his suite wore yellow and red. Monsieur de Guise appeared in pink and white: no one knew why he wore these colors; but it was remembered that they were those of a beautiful woman whom he had loved before she was married, and still loved, though he did not dare to show it. Monsieur de Nemours wore yellow and black,—why, no one knew. Madame de Clèves, however, had no difficulty in guessing: she remembered telling him one day that she liked yellow, and was sorry she was a blonde, because she could never wear that color. He believed that he could appear in it without indiscretion, because since Madame de Clèves never wore it, no one could suspect that it was hers.

Never was there seen greater skill than the four champions displayed. Although the king was the best horseman in the kingdom, it was hard to know to whom to give the palm. Monsieur de Nemours showed a grace in all he did that inclined in his favor women less interested than Madame de Clèves. As soon as she saw him at the end of the lists she felt an unusual emotion, and every time he ran she could scarcely conceal her joy when he escaped without harm.

Toward evening, when all was nearly over, and the company on the point of withdrawing, the evil fate of the country made the king wish to break another lance. He ordered the Count of Montgomery, who was very skilful, to enter the lists. The count begged the king to excuse him, and made every apology he could think of; but the king, with some annoyance, sent him word that he insisted upon it. The queen sent a message to the king beseeching him not to run again, saying that he had done so well he ought to be satisfied, and that she entreated him to come to her. He answered that it was for love of her that he was going to run again, and entered the field. She sent Monsieur de Savoie to beg him again to come; but all was in vain. He started, the lances broke, and a splinter from that of the Count of Montgomery struck him in the eye and remained in it. He fell at once to the ground. His equerries and Monsieur de Montgomery, one of the marshals of the field, ran up to him, and were alarmed to see him so severely wounded. The king was not alarmed; he said it was a slight matter, and that he forgave the count. It is easy to conceive the excitement and distress caused by this unhappy accident after a day devoted to merry-making. As soon as the king had been carried to his bed the surgeons examined his wound, which they found very serious. The constable at that moment recalled the prediction made to the king that he should be slain in single combat, and he had no doubt that the prophecy would come true.

As soon as the King of Spain, who was then in Brussels, heard of this accident, he sent his physician, a man of vast experience; but he thought the king's state desperate.

The court, thus distracted and torn by conflicting interests, was much excited on the eve of this great event; but all dissensions were quieted, and there seemed to be no other cause of anxiety than the king's health. The queens, the princes, and the princesses scarcely left his ante-chamber.

Madame de Clèves, knowing that she was compelled to be there and to meet Monsieur de Nemours, and that she could not hide from her husband the embarrassment that the sight of him would produce; knowing too that the mere presence of this prince would excuse him and overthrow all her plans,— decided to feign illness. The court was too busy to notice her conduct or to make out how much was true and how much feigned in her illness. Her husband alone could know the truth; but she was not sorry to have him know it, so she remained at home, thinking little of the great change that was impending, and perfectly free to indulge in her own reflections. Every one was with the king, Monsieur de Clèves came at certain hours to tell her the news. He treated her as he had always done, except that when they were alone his manner was a little colder and stiffer. He never spoke to her again about what had happened, and she lacked the strength and deemed it unwise to reopen the subject.

Monsieur de Nemours, who had expected to find a few moments to speak to Madame de Clèves, was much surprised and pained not to have even the pleasure of seeing her. The king grew so much worse that on the seventh day his physicians gave him up. He received the news of his approaching death with wonderful firmness, all the more admirable because he died by such an unfortunate accident, in the prime of life, full of happiness, adored by his subjects, and loved by a mistress whom he madly worshipped. The evening before his death he had Madame his sister married with Monsieur de Savoie, very quietly.

It is easy to conceive in what state was Madame de Valentinois. The queen did not permit her to see the king, and sent to her to ask for the king's seals and for the crown jewels, which were in her keeping. The duchess asked if the king was dead; and when they told her no, she said: "Then I have no master, and no one can compel me to return what he intrusted to my hands."

As soon as he had died, at the castle of Tournelles, the Duke of Ferrara, the Duke of Guise, and the Duke of Nemours conducted to the Louvre the queen-dowager, the king, and his wife the queen. Monsieur de Nemours escorted the queen-dowager. Just as they were starting, she drew back a little and told her daughter-in-law she was to go first; but it was easy to see that there was more vexation than politeness in this compliment.

PART V.

The Cardinal of Lorraine had acquired complete ascendency over the mind of the queen-dowager; the Vidame de Chartres had completely fallen from her good graces, but his love for Madame de Martigues and his enjoyment of his freedom had prevented him from suffering from this change as much as he might have done. During the ten days of the king's illness and cardinal had had abundant leisure to form his plans and to persuade the queen to take measures in conformity with his projects; hence as soon as the king was dead, the queen ordered the constable to remain at the castle of Tournelles to keep watch by the body of the late king and to take charge of the customary ceremonies. This order kept him aloof from everything and prevented all action on his part. He sent a messenger to the King of Navarre to summon him in all diligence, in order that they might combine to oppose the promotion that evidently awaited the Guises. The command of the army was given to the Duke of Guise; that of the treasury to the Cardinal of Lorraine; the Duchess of Valentinois was driven from the court; the Cardinal of Tournon, the avowed enemy of the constable, was recalled, as well as the Chancelier Olivier, the open enemy of the Duchess of Valentinois, so that the aspect of the court was completely changed. The Duke of Guise was made equal to the princes of the blood, and allowed to carry the king's mantle at the funeral; he and his brothers were placed high in authority, not merely through the cardinal's influence over the queen, but also because she believed that she could overthrow them if they should offend her, while she would not be able to overthrow the constable, who was supported by the princess of the blood.

After the funeral the constable went to the Louvre, but met with a cold reception from the king. He desired to speak with the king in private; but the king called the Guises and told him in their presence that he advised him to seek retirement, that the treasury and the command of the army were already disposed of, and that whenever he might need his counsels he should summon him. The queen-dowager received him even more coldly than the king; she went so far as to remind him of his insulting remrk to the late king about his children not looking like him. The King of Navarre arrived, and was received no better. The Prince of Condé, who was less patient than his brother, complained bitterly, but all in vain; he was exiled from court under the pretext of sending him to Flanders to sign the ratification of the treaty of peace. The King of Navarre was shown a forged letter of the King of Spain which accused him of making attempts on his territory, and he was made to fear for his own possessions, and induced to return to his kingdom. The queen made this easy for him by assigning to him the duty of escorting Madame Elisabeth; she even obliged him to start before her, so that there was no one left at court to oppose the power of the household of Guise.

Although it was most unfortunate for Monsieur de Clèves that he could not escort Madame Elisabeth, he still could not complain, in view of the lofty rank of the man who was preferred; but the deprivation of the dignity was not what pained him, but rather that his wife lost an opportunity of absenting herself from court without exciting comment.

A few days after the king's death it was decided that the court should go to Rheims for the coronation. Madame de Clèves, who had hitherto stayed at home under pretence of illness, begged her husband to excuse her from accompanying the court, and to let her go to Coulommiers to get strength from the change of air. He replied that he would not ask her whether it was care for her health that compelled her to give up the journey, but that he was willing she should not take it. He readily consented to a plan he had already decided on. High as was his opinion of his wife's virtue, he saw very clearly that it was not well for her to be exposed longer to meeting a man she loved.

Monsieur de Nemours soon learned that Madame de Clèves was not to accompany the court. He could not bear to think of leaving without seeing her; and the day before he was to start he called on her as late as he could, in order to find her alone. Fortune favored him, and as he entered the courtyard he met Madame de Nevers and Madame de Martigues coming out. They told him they had left her alone. He went upstairs in a state of agitation that can only be compared with that of Madame de Clèves when his name was announced. Her fear that he would mention his love; her apprehension lest she should give him a favorable answer; the anxiety that this visit would give her husband; the difficulty of repeating or concealing everything that happened,—all crowded on her mind at once, and so embarrassed her that she determined to avoid the thing she desired most in the world. She sent one of her maids to Monsieur de Nemours, who was in the hall, to tell him that she was not feeling well, and much regretted that she could not have the honor of receiving him. It was a grievous blow to him that he could not see Madame de Clèves because she was unwilling to receive him. He was to leave the next day, and there was no chance of his meeting her. He had not spoken to her since their conversation at the crown princess's, and he had reason to believe that his mistake in speaking to the Vidame had shattered all his hopes; consequently, he went away in deep dejection.

As soon as Madame de Clèves had somewhat recovered from the agitation of the prince's threatened visit, all the arguments that had made her decline it vanished from her mind; she even thought she had made a mistake, and if she had dared, and there had still been time, she would have called him back.

Madame de Nevers and Madame de Martigues, after leaving her, went to the crown princess's and found Monsieur de Clèves there. The princess asked them where they had been. They said they had just come from Madame de Clèves', where they had spent the afternoon with a number of persons, and that they had left no one there except Monsieur de Nemours. These words, which they thought thoroughly insignificant, were quite the opposite for Monsieur de Clèves, although it must have been evident to him that Monsieur de Nemours could easily find opportunities to speak to his wife. Nevertheless, the thought that he was with her alone, and able to speak to her of his love, seemed to him at that moment such a new and unendurable thing that his jealousy flamed out with greater fury than ever. He was not able to stay longer with the dauphiness, but left, not knowing why he did so, or whether he meant to interrupt Monsieur de Nemours. As soon as he got home he looked to see if that gentleman was still there; and when he had the consolation of finding him gone, he rejoiced to think that he could not have stayed long. He fancied that perhaps it was not Monsieur de Nemours of whom he ought to be jealous; and although he did not really doubt it, he tried his best to do so: but so many things pointed in that direction that he could not long enjoy the happiness of uncertainty. He went straight to his wife's room, and after a little talk on indifferent matters, he could not refrain from asking her what she had done and whom she had

seen. Observing that she did not mention Monsieur de Nemours, he asked her, trembling with excitement, if those were
all she had seen, in order to give her an opportunity to mention
him, and thus save him from the pain of thinking she was
capable of deception. Since she had not seen him, she said
nothing about him; whereupon Monsieur de Clèves, in a tone
that betrayed his distress, asked:

"And Monsieur de Nemours, didn't you see him, or have
you forgotten him?"

"I did not see him, in point of fact; I was not feeling well,
and I sent my regrets by one of my maids."

"Then you were ill for him alone," he went on, "since you
received everybody else? Why this difference for him? Why is
he not the same to you as all the rest? Why should you dread
meeting him? Why do you show him that you make use of the
power his passion gives you over him? Would you dare to
refuse to see him if you did not know that he is able to
distinguish your severity from incivility? Why should you be
severe to him? From a person in your position, Madame,
everything is a favor except indifference."

"I never thought," answered Madame de Clèves, "that however suspicious you might be of Monsieur de Nemours, you
would reproach me for not seeing him."

"I do, however," he went on, "and with good cause. Why
do you decline to see him, if he has not said anything to you?
But, Madame, he has spoken to you; had his silence been the
only sign of his passion, it would have made no such deep
impression. You have not been able to tell me the whole
truth; you have even repented telling me the little you did,
and you have not the strength to go on. I am more unhappy
than I supposed,—I am the unhappiest of men. You are my
wife, I love you devotedly, and I see you love another man!
He is the most fascinating man at court, he sees you every
day, he knows that you love him. And I," he exclaimed,—"I
could bring myself to believe that you would overcome your
passion for him! I must have lost my reason when I imagined
such a thing possible."

"I don't know," replied Madame de Clèves, sadly, "whether
you were wrong in judging such extraordinary conduct as
mine so favorably; I don't feel sure that I was right in
thinking that you would do me justice."

"Do not doubt it, Madame," said Monsieur de Clèves. "You
were mistaken; you expected of me things quite as impossible
as what I expected of you. How could you expect me to retain

my self-control? Have you forgotten that I loved you madly and that I was your husband? Either case is enough to drive a man wild: what must it be when the two combine? And see what they do! I am torn by wild and uncertain feelings that I cannot control; I find myself no longer worthy of you,—you seem no more worthy of me. I adore you, and I hate you; I offend you, and I beg your pardon; I admire you, and I am ashamed of my admiration,—in a word, I have lost all my calmness, all my reason. I do not know how I have been able to live since you spoke with me at Coulommiers, and since the day when you learned from the dauphiness that your adventure was known. I cannot conjecture how it came out, or what passed between Monsieur de Nemours and you on this subject. You will never tell me, and I don't ask you to tell me; I beg of you only to remember that you have made me the unhappiest man in the world."

With those words Monsieur de Clèves left his wife's room, and went away the next morning without seeing her, although he wrote her a letter full of grief, consideration, and gentleness. She wrote him a touching answer, containing such assurances about her past and future conduct that, since they sprang from the truth and were her real feelings, the letter carried great weight with Monsieur de Clèves and calmed him somewhat. Moreover, since Monsieur de Nemours was also on his way to join the king, her husband had the consolation of knowing that he was separated from Madame de Clèves. Whenever she spoke with her husband, the love he showed her, the uprightness of his treatment of her, her own affection for him, and her sense of duty, made an impression on her heart which effaced all thought of Monsieur de Nemours. But this was only for a time; the remembrance of him soon returned with greater force than ever.

The first days after that prince had left, she scarcely noticed his absence; then it began to appear painful,—for since she began to love him, hardly a day had passed in which she had not either feared or hoped to see him; and it was to her a melancholy thought that chance could no longer make her meet him.

She went to Coulommiers, taking with her copies she had had made of the large pictures with which Madame de Valentinois had adorned her fine house at Anet. All the memorable events of the king's reign were represented in these pictures. Among others was one of the Siege of Metz, with excellent likenesses of the principal officers, among whom was Monsieur de Nemours; and that was perhaps why Madame de Clèves cared for the pictures.

Madame de Martigues, having been unable to accompany the court, promised to spend a few days with her at Coulommiers. The queen's favor, which they both enjoyed, did not make them jealous or hostile; they were good friends, although they did not confide to each other everything. Madame de Clèves new that Madame de Martigues loved the Vidame, but Madame de Martigues did not know that Madame de Clèves loved Monsieur de Nemours and was loved by him. The fact that she was a niece of the Vidame endeared her to Madame de Martigues; and Madame de Clèves was drawn toward her as a woman who, like herself, was in love, and with her lover's most intimate friend.

Madame de Martigues kept her promise, and went to Coulommiers. She found Madame de Clèves leading a most retired life,—indeed, she had sought absolute solitude, spending her evenings in the gardens, unaccompanied by her servants. She used to go into the summer-house where Monsieur de Nemours had overheard her talking with her husband, and enter the closet which opened on the garden. Her women and the servants would stay in the summer-house or in the other closet, coming to her only when they were called. Madame de Martigues had never seen Coulommiers; she was delighted with all the loveliness she found there, and especially with the comfort of this summer-house, in which she and Madame de Clèves spent every evening. Their solitude after dark, in the most beautiful place in the world, made easy prolonged talks between these two young women, who were both in love; and although they did not confide in each other, they delighted in talking together. Madame de Martigues would have been very sorry to leave Coulommiers if she had not been going to meet the Vidame; she went to Chambort, where was the whole court.

The new king was crowned at Rheims by the Cardinal of Lorraine, and the rest of the summer was to be spent at the castle of Chambort, then newly built. The queen manifested great pleasure at seeing Madame de Martigues again; and after giving expression to her joy, she asked after Madame de Clèves and what she was doing in the country. Monsieur de Nemours and Monsieur de Clèves were then with the queen. Madame de Martigues, who had been delighted with Coulommiers, described its beauty, and spoke at great length of the summer-house in the wood and of the pleasant evenings she had passed there with Madame de Clèves. Monsieur de Nemours, who was sufficiently familiar with the place to know what Madame de Martigues was talking about, thought that it might be possible to see Madame de Clèves there without being seen by her. He questioned Madame de Martigues, in order to get further information; and Monsieur de Clèves, who had kept his eyes on him while Madame de Martigues was talking, fancied that he detected his design. The questions that Monsieur de Nemours asked only strengthened his suspicions, so that he felt sure the duke intended to go to see his wife. He was right; this plan so attracted Monsieur de Nemours that after spending the night in devising plans to carry it into execution, the next morning he asked leave of the king to go to Paris on some pretext he had invented.

Monsieur de Clèves had no doubt about his reasons for going away, but he determined to seek information on his wife's conduct, and no longer to remain in cruel uncertainty. He desired to leave at the same time with Monsieur de Nemours, and from some place of concealment to discover what success he might have; but he feared lest their simultaneous absence might attract attention, or that Monsieur de Nemours might get wind of it and adopt other measures; so he determined to rely on one of the gentlemen in his suite, in whose fidelity and intelligence he felt confidence. He told him in what trouble he was, and what Madame de Clèves' virtue had been hitherto, and ordered him to follow in Monsieur de Nemours' footsteps, to watch him closely, and to see if he did not go to Coulommiers and enter the garden by night.

This gentleman, who was well suited for the duty, discharged it with the utmost exactness. He followed Monsieur de Nemours to a village half a league from Coulommiers, where the prince stopped, and the gentleman easily guessed that this was to await the approach of night. He did not think it well to wait there too, but passed through the village and made his way into the forest, to a spot which he thought Monsieur de Nemours would have to pass. He was not mistaken; as soon as night had fallen, he heard footsteps, and though it was dark, he easily recognized Monsieur de Nemours. He saw him walk about the garden as if to find out if he could hear some one, and to choose the most convenient spot for entering it. The palings were very high, and there were some beyond to bar the way, so that it was not easy to get in; nevertheless, Monsieur de Nemours succeeded. As soon as he had made his way into the garden, he had no difficulty in

making out where Madame de Clèves was, as he saw many
lights in the closet. All the windows were open; and creeping
along the palings, he approached it with an emotion that can
easily be imagined. He hid behind one of the long windows by
which one entered the closet, to see what Madame de Clèves
was doing. He saw that she was alone; she was so beautiful
that he could scarcely control his rapture at the spectacle. It
was warm, and her head and shoulders had no other covering
than her loosely fastened hair. She was on a couch behind a
table, on which were many baskets of ribbons; she was
picking some out, and Monsieur de Nemours observed that
they were of the same colors that he had worn in the tournament. He saw that she was fastening bows on a very peculiar
stick that he had carried for some time and had given to his
sister, from whom Madame de Clèves had taken it, without
seeming to recognize it as belonging to Monsieur de Nemours.
When she had finished her work with a grace and gentleness
that reflected on her face the feelings that filled her heart, she
took a light and drew near to a large table opposite the picture of the Siege of Metz, in which was the portrait of Monsieur de Nemours; then she sat down and gazed at this portrait with a rapt attention such as love alone could give.

It would be impossible to describe everything that Monsieur de Nemours felt at this moment. To see, in the deep
night, in the most beautiful spot in the world, the woman he
adored; to see her without her seeing him, busied with things
that bore reference to him and to the hidden love she felt for
him,—all that is something no other lover ever enjoyed or
imagined.

Monsieur de Nemours was so entranced that he stood motionless, contemplating Madame de Clèves, without remembering that every moment was precious. When he had come to
his senses again, he thought he ought to wait till she came into
the garden before speaking to her; this he reflected would be
safer, because then she would be farther from her maids.
When, however, he saw that she remained in the closet, he
decided to go in there. When he tried to do it, he was overwhelmed with agitation and with the fear of displeasing her.
He could not bear the thought of seeing the face, just before
so gentle, suddenly darken with anger and surprise.

He thought it madness, not his undertaking to see Madame
de Clèves without being seen, but to think of showing himself;
he saw everything that he had not before thought of. It seemed
to him foolhardy to surprise at midnight a woman to whom

he had never spoken of his love. He thought he had no right to assume that she would consent to listen to him, and he knew she would have good grounds for indignation at the danger to which he exposed her from possible consequences of his acts. All his courage abandoned him, and more than once he was on the point of deciding that he would go back without seeing her. But he was so anxious to speak to her, and so encouraged by what he had seen, that he pushed on a few steps, though in such agitation that his scarf caught on the window and made a noise. Madame de Clèves turned her head; and whether it was that her mind was full of this prince, or that his face was actually in the light, she thought that she recognized him; and without hesitation or turning toward him, she rejoined her maids. She was so agitated that she had to trump up an excuse of not feeling well; and she said it also to attract their attention and thus give Monsieur de Nemours time to beat a retreat. After a little reflection she decided that she had been mistaken, and that the vision of Monsieur de Nemours was a mere illusion. She knew that he had been at Chambort, and she judged it extremely unlikely that he could have undertaken so perilous an enterprise; several times she was on the point of going back into the closet to see if there was any one in the garden. Perhaps she hoped as much as she feared to find Monsieur de Nemours there; but at last reason and prudence prevailed over every other feeling, and she decided that she should do better to stay where she was than to seek any further information. She was long in making up her mind to leave a place near which he might be, and it was almost morning when she returned to the castle.

Monsieur de Nemours stayed in the garden as long as he saw a light. He had not given up all hope of seeing Madame de Clèves again, although he was sure that she had recognized him and had only left in order to avoid him; but when he saw the servants locking the doors, he knew that he had no further chance. He retraced his steps, passing by the place where the friend of Monsieur de Clèves was in waiting. This gentleman followed him to the village, whence he had started in the evening. Monsieur de Nemours determined to spend the whole day there, in order to return to Coulommiers that night, to see if Madame de Clèves would be cruel enough to flee from him, or not to let him look at her. Although he was highly delighted to find that her mind was occupied with him, he was deeply pained to see her so instinctively taking flight.

Never was there a tenderer or intenser love than that which animated this prince. He strolled beneath the willows beside a little brook which ran behind the house in which he was concealed. He kept himself out of sight as much as possible, that no one might know of his presence. He gave himself up to the transports of love, and his heart was so full that he could not keep from shedding a few tears; but these were not of grief, they were tempered with all the sweetness that only love can give.

He recalled all Madame de Clèves actions since he had fallen in love with her,—the honorable and modest severity with which she had treated him, although she loved him. "For she does indeed love me," he exclaimed; "she loves me,—I cannot doubt it. The most fervent protestations, the greatest favors, are no surer tokens, than those I have received; and yet she treats me with the same austerity as if she hated me. I thought time would bring a change, but I can expect nothing more from it; I see her always on her guard against me and against herself. If she did not love me, I should try to please her; but I do please her, she loves me, and hides her love. What then am I to hope,—what change in my fate can I expect. What! the most charming woman in the world loves me, and I cannot enjoy the supreme happiness that comes from the first certainty of being loved, except in the agony of being ill treated! Show, fair princess," he called aloud, "that you love me; show me what you really feel! If you will only once let me hear from you what your feelings are, I am willing that you should resume for ever the severity with which you overwhelm me. At least look at me with those eyes that I saw gazing at my portrait. Could you look at it with such gentleness, and then flee from me so cruelly? What do you fear? Why do you so dread my love? You love me, and you hide your love to no purpose; you have yourself given me tokens of it unawares. I know my good fortune: let me enjoy it, and cease making me unhappy. Is it possible that Madame de Clèves loves me, and I am still unhappy? How beautiful she was last night! How could I resist my longing to fling myself at her feet? Had I done so, I might have prevented her flight; my respectful bearing would have reassured her. But perhaps she did not recognize me,—I distress myself more than I should; and the sight of a man at such an extraordinary hour frightened her."

These thoughts haunted Monsieur de Nemours all day. He awaited the night with impatience, and when it had come he took once more the road to Coulommiers. The friend of Monsieur de Clèves, having assumed a disguise to avoid being recognized, followed him as he had done the previous evening, and saw him enter the same garden. Then Monsieur de Nemours preceived that Madame de Clèves was unwilling to run the risk of his trying to see her; every entrance was closed. He wandered in every direction to find some light, but his search was vain.

Madame de Clèves, suspecting that Monsieur de Nemours might come back, stayed in her own room; she feared lest strength to flee should be denied her, and she did not wish to risk the possibility of speaking to him in a manner that might contradict her previous conduct. Although Monsieur de Nemours had no hope of seeing her, he could not make up his mind to leave at once a place where she had been so often. He spent the whole night in the garden, finding some slight consolation in at least gazing on the same objects which she saw every day. The sun had risen before he thought of leaving; but at last the fear of being observed compelled him to go.

It was impossible for him to return without seeing Madame de Clèves; hence he went to see Madame de Mercœur, who was then living in her house not far from Coulommiers. She was extremely surprised at her brother's arrival. He invented some specious excuse for his journey, which completely deceived her, and at last managed so cleverly that she herself proposed their calling on Madame de Clèves. This plan they carried out that very day, and Monsieur de Nemours told his sister that he would leave her at Coulommiers to return with all speed to the king. He devised this plan of parting from her at Coulommiers in the hope that she would be the first to leave; in this way he imagined he could not fail to have an opportunity of speaking to Madame de Clèves.

When they reached Coulommiers, they found Madame de Clèves walking in a broad path along the edge of the flower-garden. The sight of Monsieur de Nemours embarrassed her not a little, and made her sure that it was he whom she had seen the previous night. This conviction filled her with anger that he should have been so bold and imprudent. He noticed with pain her evident coldness. The talk ran on insignificant subjects, and yet he succeeded in displaying so much wit and amiability, and so much admiration for Madame de Clèves, that he finally dispelled some of her coolness, in spite of her determination not to be appeased.

When he had got over his first timidity, he expressed great

curiosity to see the summer-house in the wood; he described it
as the most delightful spot in the world, and with so many
details that Madame de Mercœur said he must have often seen
it, to be so familiar with all its beauty.

"Still, I do not believe," answered Madame de Clèves, "that
Monsieur de Nemours has ever been in it; it has been finished
only a very short time."

"It is not long, either, since I was there," he retorted,
looking at her; "and I do not know whether I ought not to be
very glad that you have forgotten having seen me there."

Madame de Mercœur, who was busy looking at the garden,
paid no attention to what her brother was saying. Madame de
Clèves, blushing, and casting down her eyes so as not to see
Monsieur de Nemours, said:

"I do not remember ever having seen you there, and if you
ever have been there, it was without my knowledge."

"It is true, Madame," he said, "that I have been there
without your permission, and I have spent there the most
blissful and the most wretched moments of my life."

Madame de Clèves knew only too well what he meant; but
she made no answer. She was thinking how she should keep
Madame de Mercœur from going into the closet which contained the portrait of Monsieur de Nemours: this she did not
want her to see. She succeeded so well that the time passed
imperceptibly, and Madame de Mercœur spoke of leaving; but
when Madame de Clèves noticed that Madame de Mercœur
and her brother were not going away together, she saw the
impending danger, and was as much embarrassed as she had
been in Paris, and she decided on the same course. Her fear
lest this visit should only confirm her husband's suspicions
helped her to form this decision, and in order to prevent
Monsieur de Nemours from being alone with her, she told
Madame de Mercœur that she would accompany her to the
edge of the forest, and ordered her carriage to follow her.
This prince's grief at finding Madame de Clèves as austere as
ever was so keen that he turned pale. Madame de Mercœur
asked him if he was ill; but he looked at Madame de Clèves
without being seen by any one, and let her see that he was
suffering from nothing but despair. Nevertheless, he was compelled to let them go without daring to follow them; and after
what he had said, he could not go back with his sister. He
returned to Paris, and left it the next day.

Monsieur de Clèves' friend had watched him all the while.
He also returned to Paris; and when he saw that Monsieur de

Nemours had left for Chambort, he took the post in order to get there before him, and to make his report about his expedition. His master was awaiting his return to determine his life's unhappiness.

As soon as Monsieur de Clèves saw him, he read in his expression and his silence that he had brought only bad news. He remained for some time overwhelmed with grief, his head bowed, unable to speak; then he motioned to him to withdraw. "Go," he said; "I see what you have to tell me, but I am not strong enough to hear it."

"I have nothing to report," answered the gentleman, "from which it is possible to form an accurate judgment. It is true that Monsieur de Nemours entered the garden in the woods two nights running, and called at Coulommiers the next day with Madame de Mercœur."

"That is enough," replied Monsieur de Clèves, "that is enough;" and then, again motioning to him to leave, he added, "I have no need of further information."

The gentleman was forced to leave his master plunged in despair. Never, perhaps, has there been more poignant grief, and few men who possessed so much spirit and so affectionate a heart as Monsieur de Clèves have suffered the agony of discovering at the same time a wife's infidelity and the mortification of being deceived by a woman.

Monsieur de Clèves was overwhelmed by this grievous blow. That same night he was seized with a fever of such severity that at once his life was in peril. Word was sent to Madame de Clèves, and she went to him with all speed. He was worse when she reached him, and she noticed something cold and icy in his manner toward her that greatly surprised and pained her. He even seemed to be annoyed at the attention she paid him; but at last she thought this was perhaps a result of his illness.

As soon as Madame de Clèves had arrived at Blois, where the court was at that time, Monsieur de Nemours was filled with joy at knowing that she was in the same place as himself. He tried to see her, and called at the house every day, under pretext of inquiring after Monsieur de Clèves; but it was all in vain. She never left her husband's room, and was very anxious about him. Monsieur de Nemours regretted that she suffered so much; he readily saw how this grief would be likely to rekindle her love for Monsieur de Clèves, and how this affection would prove a dangerous foe to the love she bore in her heart. This feeling depressed him for some time; but the extreme seriousness of Monsieur de Clèves' illness soon gave him new hopes. He saw that Madame de Clèves would soon be free to follow her own wishes, and that in the future he might find lasting happiness. This thought filled him with almost painful rapture, and he banished it from his mind, lest he should be too miserable if his hopes were disappointed.

Meanwhile Monsieur de Clèves was almost given up. One of the last days of his illness, after he had passed a very bad night, he said, toward morning, that he would like to rest. Madame de Clèves alone stayed in his room. It seemed to her that instead of resting, he was very uneasy; she went up to him and knelt down by his bed, with her face covered with tears. Monsieur de Clèves had made up his mind to say nothing about his grievance against her; but her attentions and her sorrow, which seemed genuine, and which he sometimes regarded as tokens of deceit and treachery, produced such conflicting and painful feelings that he could not repress them.

"You, Madame," he said, "are shedding a great many tears for a death of which you are the cause, and which cannot give you the sorrow which you display. I am no longer able to reproach you," he went on, in a voice weakened by illness and grief, "but I am dying of the cruel suffering you have inflicted on me. Was it necessary that so extraordinary an action as that of speaking to me as you did at Coulommiers should have so little result? Why confide to me your love for Monsieur de Nemours, if your virtue was not strong enough to resist it? I loved you so that I was glad to be deceived,—I confess it to my shame; I have since longed for the false tranquillity of which you robbed me. Why did you not leave me in the calm blindness in which so many husbands are happy? I should perhaps have never known that you loved Monsieur de Nemours. I am dying," he went on; "but bear it in mind that you make me welcome death, and that since you have robbed me of the love and esteem I felt for you, I dread living. What would life be to me, if I had to spend it with a woman I have loved so much and who has so cruelly deceived me, or if I had to live apart from her, after a scene of violence utterly repugnant to my disposition and to the love I bear you? My love for you, Madame, has been far deeper than you know; I have concealed the greater part of it, from fear of tormenting you or of lessening your esteem by a manner unbecoming to a husband; I really deserved your affection. I say it once more: I die without regret, since I could not win this, and now can no longer wish for it. Farewell,

Madame. Some day you will mourn a man who had for you a
true and lawful love. You will know the misery that overtakes
women who fall into these entanglements, and you will learn
the difference between being loved as I loved you, and being
loved by men who, while protesting their love, seek only the
honor of misleading you. But my death will leave you free,
and you will be able to make Monsieur de Nemours happy
without doing anything criminal. What do I care what may
happen when I shall be no more? Must I be weak enough to
look upon it?"

Madame de Clèves was so far from imagining that her
husband could suspect her that she listened to him without
understanding what he was saying, and supposing that he was
blaming her interest in Monsieur de Nemours. At last, suddenly grasping his meaning, she exclaimed,—

"I a criminal! The very thought of it never entered my
head. The severest virtue could command no different course
of conduct than mine, and I have not done one thing of which
I should not be glad to have you an eye-witness."

"Should you have been glad," asked Monsieur de Clèves,
looking at her somewhat disdainfully, "to have had me for an
eye-witness of the nights you spent with Monsieur de Nemours? Ah! Madame, am I speaking of you when I speak of a
woman who has spent nights with a man?"

"No," she answered, "no; it is not of me that you are
speaking,—I have never passed nights or moments with Monsieur de Nemours; he has never seen me in private; I have
never had anything to do with him or listened to him, and I
will swear—"

"Say no more," interrupted Monsieur de Clèves; "false
oaths or a confession would give me equal pain."

Madame de Clèves could not answer; her tears and her
grief choked her. At last, making a great effort, she said:
"Look at me, at least; listen to me. If it concerned me alone, I
should endure these reproaches; but it is your life that is at
stake. Listen to me for your own sake; it is impossible that,
with all the truth on my side, I should not convince you of
my innocence."

"Would to God that you could convince me!" he exclaimed.
"But what can you say to me? Was not Monsieur de Nemours
at Coulommiers with his sister, and had he not passed the two
previous nights with you in the garden in the forest?"

"If that is my crime," she replied, "I can clear myself
easily. I don't ask you to believe me, but believe your serv-

ants: ask them if I was in the garden the evening Monsieur de Nemours came to Coulommiers, and if I didn't leave it the evening before, two hours earlier than usual."

She then told him how she had imagined she saw some one in the garden, and confessed that she had thought it was Monsieur de Nemours. She spoke with such earnestness, and the truth, even when improbable, carries such weight, that Monsieur de Clèves was almost convinced of her innocence.

"I do not know," he said, "whether I dare believe you; I am so near death that I do not want to see anything that might make me long to live. Your explanation comes too late; but it will always be a consolation to think that you are worthy of the esteem I have had for you. I beg of you to let me have the additional consolation of knowing that my memory will be dear to you, and that if it had depended on you, you would have had for me the feeling you have had for another."

He wanted to go on; but a sudden faintness made it impossible, and Madame de Clèves summoned the physicians. They found him almost lifeless. Nevertheless, he lingered a few days longer, and at last died, having displayed admirable firmness.

Madame de Clèves was almost crazed by the intensity of her grief. The queen at once came to see her, and carried her to a convent, without her knowing whither she was going. Her sisters-in-law brought her to Paris before she was yet able to realize her afflictions. When she began to be strong enough to think about it, and saw what a husband she had lost, and reflected that she was the cause of his death by means of her love for another man, the horror she felt at herself and at Monsieur de Nemours cannot be described.

At first this prince did not venture to pay her any other attentions than such as etiquette required. He knew Madame de Clèves well enough to be sure that anything more marked would displease her; but what he learned later assured him that he would have to maintain this reserve for a long time. One of his equerries told him that Monsieur de Clèves' gentleman, a friend of his, had told him, in his deep regret for the loss of his master, that Monsieur de Nemours' trip to Coulommiers was the cause of his death. Monsieur de Nemours was extremely surprised to hear this; but on thinking it over, he made out a part of the truth, and conjectured what would be the feelings of Madame de Clèves, and how she would detest him if she thought her husband's illness had been

due to jealousy. He thought that the best thing would be not
to have his name brought to her notice, and he regulated his
conduct accordingly, painful as he found it.

The prince went to Paris, and could not refrain from
calling on Madame de Clèves to ask how she was. He was
informed that she saw no one, and had even given orders that
she was not to be told who had inquired after her. Possibly
these rigid orders were given solely on account of the prince,
and to avoid hearing his name mentioned. But Monsieur de
Nemours was too desperately in love to be able to live with
absolutely no chance of seeing Madame de Clèves. He resolved to try every means, no matter how difficult, to escape
from such an unendurable condition of affairs.

The princess's grief passed all bounds of reason. Her dying
husband,—dying for her sake, and filled with such tender love
for her,—was never absent from her mind; she continually
recalled everything she owed him, and blamed herself for not
having loved him,—as if that were a thing that depended on
her will. Her sole consolation was the thought that she
mourned him as he deserved, and that for the rest of her life
she would only do what he would have approved if he had
lived.

She had often wondered how he knew that Monsieur de
Nemours had come to Coulommiers; she did not suspect that
the prince had spoken of it, and it even seemed to her that it
was immaterial whether he had said anything about it, so
thoroughly rid of her passion did she feel. Nevertheless, she
was deeply distressed to think that he was the cause of her
husband's death, and she remembered with sorrow the fear
that had tormented Monsieur de Clèves on his deathbed lest
she should marry him; but all these various sources of grief
were lost in that over her husband's death, and the others
sank into insignificance.

After many months had passed, she recovered from her
violent grief, becoming sad and languid. Madame de Martigues made a visit to Paris, and saw her repeatedly during her
stay there. She talked with her about the court and of all that
had happened; and although Madame de Clèves seemed to
take no interest, Madame de Martigues went on talking in
order to divert her. She told her all about the Vidame, Monsieur de Guise, and all the other men of note.

"As for Monsieur de Nemours," she said, "I do not know
whether his occupations have taken the place of gallantry, but

he is less cheerful than he used to be; he shuns the society of women; he continually runs up to Paris, and I believe is here now."

Monsieur de Nemours' name surprised Madame de Clèves and made her blush; she changed the subject, and Madame de Martigues did not notice her confusion.

The next day, the princess being anxious to find some occupation suitable for her condition, went to see a man living close by who worked in silk in a peculiar way, with the intention of undertaking something of the sort herself. After looking at what he had to show, her eyes fell on the door of a room in which she thought there were some more, and asked to have it opened. The man replied that he did not have the key, and that it was occupied by a man who came there sometimes to draw the fine houses and gardens to be seen from the windows. "He is the handsomest man in the world," he went on, "and does not seem obliged to support himself by his work. Whenever he comes here, I see him always looking at the houses and gardens, but I have never seen him at work."

Madame de Clèves listened with great attention; what Madame de Martigues had said about Monsieur de Nemours coming sometimes to Paris, as well as her vision of this handsome man who had taken quarters near her house, made her think of that prince, and suggested that he was trying to see her. This thought produced in her an agitation which she could not understand. She went to the windows to see on what they looked, and saw that it was on her garden and her own apartment; and when she was in her room she saw the same window to which she had been told that the stranger used to come. The conjecture that it was Monsieur de Nemours entirely altered the current of her thoughts; she no longer felt the sad tranquillity which she had begun to enjoy, —she was uneasy and agitated. At last, unable to endure her loneliness, she went out to take the air in a garden in the faubourgs, where she expected to find solitude. At first she supposed no one was there; the place seemed deserted, and she strolled about for some little time.

After passing through a little thicket, she saw at the end of the path, in the most retired part of the garden, a sort of summer-house open on all sides, and she turned in that direction. When she had got near it, she saw a man lying on the benches who seemed sunk in deep thought, and she recognized Monsieur de Nemours. At the sight of him she stopped short; but her servants, who were following her, made some noise that aroused him. Without looking at them, he arose, to avoid their company, and turned into another path, bowing deeply, so that he was unable to see whom he was saluting.

Had Monsieur de Nemours known from whom he was running away, he would have eagerly retraced his steps; but as it was, he followed the path and went out by a side-gate, at which his carriage was waiting. This incident made a deep impression on Madame de Clèves' heart; all her love was suddenly rekindled with its former fervor. She went on and sat down in the place which Monsieur de Nemours had just left, and there she remained, completely overwhelmed. Her mind was full of this prince, more fascinating than any man in the world; loving her long with respect and constancy; giving up everything for her; respecting even her grief; trying to see her, without himself being seen; abandoning the court, where he was a favorite, to look upon the walls behind which she was immured, to come and muse in places where he could not hope to meet her,—in short, a man worthy to be loved for his love alone, and for whom she felt a passion so violent that she would have loved him even if he had not loved her, and one moreover of a lofty nature perfectly in harmony with her own. Duty and virtue could not restrain her emotions; every obstacle vanished; and of all her past she remembered nothing but her love for Monsieur de Nemours and his for her.

All these thoughts were new to the princess; she had been so lost in grief for her husband's death that she had given them no attention. With the sight of Monsieur de Nemours they all recurred to her. But when they came fastest, and she remembered that this same man whom now she thought of as able to marry her was the one she had loved during her husband's lifetime and was the cause of his death; that on his deathbed he had manifested his fear lest she should marry him,—her rigid virtue was so pained by the thought that it seemed to her quite as grievous a crime to marry Monsieur de Nemours as it had been to love him while her husband was living. She gave herself up to these reflections, which were so hostile to her happiness, and confirmed them by many arguments concerning her peace of mind and the evils she foresaw in case she married him. At last, after spending two hours there, she returned home, convinced that she ought to avoid the sight of him as a real obstacle to her duty.

But this conviction, the product of reason and virtue, did not control her heart, which remained attached to Monsieur

de Nemours with a violence that reduced her to a most restless and pitiable state. That night was one of the unhappiest
she had ever known. In the morning her first thought was to
go to see if there was anyone at the window which commanded
her house; she looked out and saw Monsieur de Nemours.
This surprised her, and she drew back so quickly that he felt
sure she must have recognized him. This he had long wished
might happen, since he had devised this method of seeing her;
and when it seemed hopeless, he used to go and meditate in
the garden where she had seen him.

Worn out at last by grief and uncertainty, the duke made
up his mind to find some way to determining his fate. "Why
should I wait?" he asked. "I have long known she loved me;
she is free, and duty no longer stands in her way. Why should
she force me to see her without being seen by her and with no
chance to speak to her? Can love have so absolutely destroyed
my reason and my boldness that I am not what I was when in
love before? I was bound to respect Madame de Clèves' grief;
but I have respected it too long, and I am giving her time to
forget the affection she feels for me."

Thereupon he began to devise some way of seeing her. He
fancied that there was no good reason for concealing his love
from the Vidame of Chartres, and he resolved to speak to him
and to confide to him his plans about his niece. The Vidame
was then in Paris, like all the rest of the court, who had come
to town to make their preparations for accompanying the
king, who was to escort the Queen of Spain. Accordingly,
Monsieur de Nemours called on the Vidame and frankly told
him everything he had kept hidden until then, except Madame
de Clèves' feelings, which he did not wish to appear to know.

The Vidame heard him with great pleasure, and answered
that, with no knowledge of his feelings, he had often, since
Madame de Clèves had become a widow, thought that she was
the only woman worthy of him. Monsieur de Nemours besought his aid in getting a chance to address her, in order to
find out her intentions.

The Vidame proposed taking him to call on her; but Monsieur de Nemours feared that she would not like this, because
she did not yet see any one. They decided that the Vidame
should invite her to come and see him on some pretext or
other, and that Monsieur de Nemours should enter by a hidden staircase, in order not to be seen. This was carried out
according to their plans. Madame de Clèves came; the Vidame
went to receive her, and led her into a small room at the end

of his apartment. Shortly after, Monsieur de Nemours came in, as if by chance. Madame de Clèves was much surprised to see him; she blushed, and tried to hide her blushes. The Vidame began to talk about unimportant subjects, and then went away, under the pretext of having some orders to give. He asked Madame de Clèves to do the honors in his place, and said he should return in a moment.

It would be impossible to express the feelings of Monsieur de Nemours and Madame de Clèves when they for the first time found themselves alone and free to talk. They remained for a long time without a word; then at last Monsieur de Nemours broke the silence. "Will you, Madame, forgive the Vidame," he said, "for having given me an opportunity to see you and to speak with you, which you have always cruelly denied me?"

"I ought not to forgive him," she replied, "for having forgotten my position and to what he exposes my reputation." As she uttered these words she started to leave; but Monsieur de Nemours delayed her, saying:

"Do not be alarmed, Madame; no one knows that I am here, and there is no danger. Listen to me, Madame,—if not through kindness, at least through love of yourself, and in order to protect yourself against the extravagances to which I shall certainly be led by an uncontrollable passion."

For the first time Madame de Clèves yielded to her tenderness for Monsieur de Nemours, and looking at him with eyes full of gentleness and charm, she said: "But what do you hope from the kindness that you ask of me? You would certainly regret obtaining it, and I should regret granting it. You deserve a happier fate than you have yet had, and can have in the future, unless you seek it elsewhere."

"I, Madame, find such happiness elsewhere! Is there any other happiness than winning your love? Although I have never spoken with you, I cannot think that you are ignorant of my affection, or that you do not know that it is truer and warmer than ever. How much it has been tried by events unknown to you, and how much by your severity!"

"Since you wish me to speak, and I decide it best," answered Madame de Clèves, sitting down, "I will do so, with a frankness that you will not always find in women. I shall not tell you that I have not noticed your attachment to me,— perhaps you could not believe me if I were to say so; I confess, then, not only that I have noticed it, but also just as you wished it to appear."

"And, Madame, if you have seen it," he interrupted, "is it possible that you have not been touched by it; and may I venture to ask if it has made no impression on your heart?"

"You should have judged of that from my conduct," she replied; "but I should be glad to know what you have thought of it."

"I should have to be in a happier condition to dare to tell you," he answered, "and my fate has too little relation with what I should say. All that I can tell you, Madame, is that you would not have confessed to Monsieur de Clèves what you concealed from me, and that you would have concealed from him what you would have let me see."

"How were you able to find out," she asked, blushing, "that I confessed anything to Monsieur de Clèves?"

"I heard it from your own lips, Madame," he replied; "but as an excuse for my boldness in listening to you, consider whether I misused what I had heard, whether my hopes were strengthened by it, whether I became bold enough to speak to you."

He began to tell her how he had heard her conversation with Monsieur de Clèves; but she interrupted him in the middle.

"Say no more," she said; "I now see how you came to know too much: that you did, was very plain to me at the dauphiness's, when she had heard the story from those to whom you had told it."

Monsieur de Nemours then explained to her how that had happened.

"Do not apologize," she resumed; "I forgave you a long time ago, before you told me how it occurred. But since you have yourself heard from me what I had meant to keep a secret from you all my life, I confess that you have inspired me with emotions unknown before I saw you, and so unfamiliar to me that they filled me with a surprise which greatly added to the agitation they produced. I confess this with the less shame because I may now do it innocently, and you have seen that my feelings did not guide my actions."

"Do you believe, Madame," exclaimed Monsieur de Nemours, falling on his knees, "that I am not ready to die at your feet with joy and rapture?"

"I only tell you," she answered, smiling, "what you already know only too well."

"Ah! Madame," he said, "what a difference between finding

something out by accident, and hearing it from you, and seeing that you wish me to know it."

"It is true," said she, "that I wish you to know it, and that I take pleasure in telling you. I am no certain that I do not tell it more from love of myself than from love of you; for certainly this avowal will have no consequences, and I shall follow the rigid rules that my condition imposes."

"You will not think of such a thing, Madame," replied Monsieur de Nemours; "you are bound by no further duty; you are free; and if I dared, I should even tell you that it depends on you so to act that your duty shall some day oblige you to preserve the feelings that you have for me."

"My duty," she replied, "forbids my ever thinking of any one, and of you last of all, for reasons unknown to you."

"Perhaps they are not, Madame," he pleaded; "but those are no true reasons. I have reason to beleve that Monsieur de Clèves thought me happier than I was, and imagined that you approved of mad freaks of mine which my passion suggested without your knowledge."

"Let us not speak of that affair," she said. "I cannot bear the thought of it; it fills me with shame, and its consequences were too painful. It is only too likely that you are the cause of Monsieur de Clèves' death; the suspicions you aroused, your inconsiderate conduct, cost him his life as truly as if you had taken it with your own hands. Think of what I should do if you had come to such extremities and the same unhappy result had followed. I know very well this is not the same thing in the eyes of the world; but in mine there is no difference, for I know it was from you he got his death, and on account of me."

"Oh! Madame," interposed Monsieur de Nemours, "what phantom of duty do you oppose to my happiness? What! Madame, a vain and baseless fancy can prevent your making happy a man you do not hate, when he has conceived the hope of passing his life with you, his fate leading him to love you as the best woman in the world, finding in you every charming trait, incurring not your hatred, and seeing in you everything that best becomes a woman,—for, Madame, there is no other woman who combines what you do. Men who marry their mistresses who love them, tremble from fear lest they should renew their misconduct with others; but nothing of the sort is to be feared in you: you are only to be admired. Can I have foreseen such felicity only to find you raising obstacles? Ah! Madame, you forget that you chose me from other men,—or rather, you did not; you made a mistake, and I have flattered myself."

"You did not flatter youself," she replied; "the reasons for my acting as I do would not, perhaps, seem to me so strong, had I not chosen you as you suspect,—and that is what makes me foresee unhappiness if I should take an interest in you."

"I have no answer," he said, "when you show me that you fear unhappiness; but I confess that, after all you have been good enough to say to me, I did not expect to be opposed by such a cruel argument."

"It is so far from uncomplimentary to you," she answered, "that I shall even find it hard to tell it to you."

"Alas! Madame, what can you fear will flatter me too much after what you have just said to me?"

"I wish still to speak to you as frankly as I began," she explained, "and I want to dispense with all the reserve and formalities that I should respect in a first conversation; but I beg of you to listen to me without interruption.

"I think it but a slight reward for your affection that I should hide from you none of my feelings, but should let you see them exactly as they are. This probably will be the only time in my life that I shall take the liberty of letting you see them; nevertheless, I cannot confess to you without deep shame that the certainty of not being loved by you as I am, seems to me a horrible misfortune; that if there were not already insurmountable claims of duty, I doubt if I could make up my mind to risk this unhappiness. I know that you are free, as I am, and that we are so situated that the world would probably blame neither of us if we should marry; but do men keep their love in these permanent unions? Ought I to expect a miracle in my case, and can I run the risk of seeing this passion, which would be my only happiness, fade away? Monsieur de Clèves was perhaps the only man in the world capable of keeping his love after marriage. My fate forbade my enjoying this blessing. Perhaps, too, his love only survived because he found none in me. But I should not have the same way of preserving yours; I believe that the obstacles you have met have made you constant; those were enough to make you yearn to conquer them, and my involuntary actions,—things you learned by chance,—gave you enough hope to keep you interested."

"Oh! Madame," replied Monsieur de Nemours, "I can no longer maintain the silence you impose on me; you do me too much injustice, and you let me see how far you are from being prejudiced in my favor."

"I confess," she said, "that I may be moved by my emotions, but they cannot blind me; nothing can prevent my seeing that you are born with every disposition for gallantry, and with all the qualities proper to secure speedy success. You have already been in love several times,—you would be again very often. I should not make you happy; I should see you interested in another as you have been in me: this would inflict on me a mortal blow, and I should never feel sure that I should not be jealous. I have said too much to try to hide from you that you have already made me feel this passion, and that I suffered cruel tortures that evening when the queen gave me that letter from Madame de Themines which was said to be directed to you, and that the impression left on me is that jealousy is the greatest unhappiness in the world.

"Vanity or taste makes all women try to secure you; there are few whom you do not please,—my own experience teaches me that there are few whom you might not please. I should always imagine that you were loved and in love, and I should not be often wrong. Yet in this condition I could only suffer,—I should not dare to complain. One may make reproaches to a lover, but can a woman reproach her husband for ceasing to love her? If I could become hardened to that misfortune, could I become hardened to imagining that I saw Monsieur de Clèves charging you with his death, reproaching me for loving you, and showing the difference between his affection and yours? It is impossible to resist such arguments; I must remain in my present position and in my immovable determination never to leave it."

"But do you think you can, Madame?" exclaimed Monsieur de Nemours. "Do you think that your resolutions can hold out against a man who worships you and is fortunate enough to please you? It is harder than you think, Madame, to resist what pleases us and one who loves us. You have done it by an austere virtue which is almost without a precedent; but this virtue no longer conflicts with your emotions, and these I hope you will follow, in spite of yourself."

"I know that there is nothing harder than what I undertake; I mistrust my own strength, supported by all my arguments. What I think due to the memory of Monsieur de Clèves would be ineffectual, if it were not reinforced by my anxiety for my own peace of mind; and these arguments need to be strengthened by those of duty. But though I mistrust myself, I think I shall never overcome my scruples, and I do not hope to overcome my interest in you. It will make me unhappy, and I shall deny myself the pleasure of seeing you, whatever pain this may cost me. I am in a position which makes that a crime which at any other time would be permissible, and mere etiquette forbids that we should meet."

Monsieur de Nemours flung himself at her feet and gave expression to all the emotion that filled him. He manifested, by his words and tears, the liveliest and tenderest passion that heart ever felt. Madame de Clèves was not unmoved; and looking at Monsieur de Nemours with eyes heavy with tears, she exclaimed,—

"Why must I charge you with the death of Monsieur de Clèves? Why did I not learn to know you when I was free; or why did I not know you before I was married? Why does fate divide us by such an insuperable obstacle?"

"There is no obstacle," pleaded Monsieur de Nemours; "you alone thwart my happiness, you alone impose a law which virtue and reason could not impose."

"It is true," she replied, "that I make a great sacrifice to a duty which exists only in my imagination. Wait to see what time will do. Monsieur de Clèves has but just died, and that fatal event is too recent for me to judge clearly. Meanwhile you have the pleasure of having won the love of a woman who would never have loved had she not seen you; be sure that my feelings for you will never change and will always survive, whatever I do.

"Good by," she said. "This conversation fills me with shame. Repeat it to the Vidame; I give my consent,—nay, I beg of you to do so."

With these words she left the room, Monsieur de Nemours being unable to prevent her. She found the Vidame in the next room. He saw her so agitated that he did not dare to speak to her, and he handed her to her carriage without a word. He went back to Monsieur de Nemours, who was in such a whirl of joy, sadness, surprise, and admiration,—in short, so possessed by all the emotions that spring from a passion full of hope and dread,—that he seemed beside himself. It was long before the Vidame got any clear notion of what they had said; finally, however, he succeeded; and Monsieur de Chartres, without being the least in love, had no less admiration for the virtue, intelligence, and worth of Madame de Clèves than had Monsieur de Nemours himself. They tried to determine the prince's probable chances; and whatever the fears that love might arouse, the prince agreed with the Vidame that it was impossible that Madame de Clèves should persist in her resolutions. Nevertheless, they agreed to follow her orders, from fear lest, if the duke's love for her should become known, she should in some way bind herself, and would not change from fear of its being thought that she had loved him while her husband was living.

Monsieur de Nemours determined to join the king, as he could no longer stay away, and he made up his mind to start without even trying to see Madame de Clèves again. He begged the Vidame to speak to her. He told him a number of things to say to her, and suggested countless arguments with which to overcome her scruples. At last a good part of the night was gone before Monsieur de Nemours thought of leaving to seek repose.

Madame de Clèves was in no condition to find rest; it was for her such a new thing to lay aside the reserve which she had imposed upon herself, to permit a man to tell her that he loved her, to confess that she too was in love, that she did not recognize herself. She was amazed at what she had done, and repented it bitterly; she was also made happy by it,—she was completely upset by love and agitation. She went over once more the arguments in defence of her duty which stood in the way of her happiness; she lamented their strength, and regretted having stated them so strongly to Monsieur de Nemours. Although the thought of marrying him had occurred to her the moment she saw him again in the garden, it had not made so deep an impression on her as had her talk with him; and at moments she could scarcely believe that she would be unhappy if she should marry him. She would have liked to be able to say that she was wrong both in her scruples about the past and in her fears for the future. At other moments reason and duty convinced her of the opposite, and decided her not to marry again or ever to see Monsieur de Nemours; but this resolution was extremely repugnant to her when her heart was so much moved and had so recently seen the joys of love. At last, in order to allay her agitation, she thought it was not necessary for her to do herself the violence of forming a decision,—etiquette left her still much time for making up her mind; but she resolved to abide by her determination to have nothing to do with Monsieur de Nemours meanwhile.

The Vidame came to see her, and pleaded his friend's cause with all possible skill and earnestness; but he could not persuade her to modify her own conduct or that which she had imposed on Monsieur de Nemours. She told him that she did not mean to change her present condition, that she knew it would be hard for her to carry out this intention, but that she hoped she should be strong enough to do so. She showed him how firmly convinced she was that Monsieur de Nemours had caused her husband's death, and that she should do wrong in marrying him; so that the Vidame feared it would not be easy to convince her of the opposite. He did not confide to this prince what he thought, and when he reported his talk with her, he let him enjoy all the hope that reason can awaken in a man who is loved. •

The next day they left to join the king. The Vidame, at the request of Monsieur de Nemours, wrote to Madame de Clèves in order to speak of him; and in a second letter, which soon followed, Monsieur de Nemours added a few lines himself. But Madame de Clèves, who did not wish to infringe her rules, and who feared the perils of correspondence, told the Vidame that she should decline to receive his letters if he continued to write about Monsieur de Nemours; and this she said so earnestly that this prince himself begged his friend never to mention his name.

The court left to escort the Queen of Spain as far as Poitou. Madame de Clèves was left to herself during their absence, and the farther she was removed from Monsieur de Nemours and from anything that could remind her of him, the more she recalled the memory of Monsieur de Clèves, which she was bent on keeping ever present before her. Her reasons for not marrying Monsieur de Nemours seemed strong so far as her duty, and irrefutable so far as her tranquillity, was concerned. The fading of his love after marriage, and all the pangs of jealousy, which she regarded as certain, showed her the misery to which she would expose herself, but she saw too that she had assumed an impossible task in undertaking to resist the most fascinating of men, whom she loved and who loved her, in a matter which offended neither virtue nor propriety. She decided that only separation could give her strength; and this she felt that she needed, not merely to maintain her determination not to marry, but also to protect herself from the sight of Monsieur de Nemours. Hence she resolved to make a long journey during the time that etiquette forced her to spend in retirement. Some large estates that she owned in the Pyrenees seemed to her the best place she could choose. She started a few days before the court returned; and just before leaving, she wrote to the Vidame to beg that no one should inquire after her or write to her.

Monsieur de Nemours was as much afflicted by her absence as another man would have been by the death of the woman he loved. The thought of this long separation from Madame de Clèves was a constant source of suffering, especially after he had tasted the pleasure of meeting her and seeing that she loved him. He could do nothing but grieve, and his grief increased daily. Madame de Clèves, as a result of all her agitation, fell seriously ill after her arrival at her country place, and news of this reached the court. Monsieur de Nemours was inconsolable, and fell into the most unabounded despair. The Vidame had great difficulty in keeping him from letting his love be seen, as well as from following after her to find out how she was. The Vidame's relationship and intimacy served as a pretext for sending constant letters. At last word came that she had passed the turning point of her dangerous illness, but was still so weak that all were very anxious.

This long and near view of death enabled Madame de Clèves to judge mundane matters in a very different spirit from that of health. Her imminent peril taught her indifference to everything, and the length of her illness enforced this upon her. Yet when she had recovered, she found that she had not wholly forgotten Monsieur de Nemours; but she summoned to her aid every argument she could devise against marrying him. The conflict was a storm one; but at last she conquered what was left of this passion, which was already diminished by her reflections during her illness. The thought of death had revived her memory of Monsieur de Clèves; and this, harmonizing with her sense of duty, made a strong impression on her heart. The affections and ties of the world appeared to her as they appear to persons of enlarged views. Her health, which was still delicate, helped her to preserve those feelings; but knowing how circumstances affect the wisest resolutions, she was unwilling to run the risk of seeing her own altered, or of returning to the place where lived the man she had loved. Under the pretext of needing change of air, she withdrew to a religious house, without making known her determination to leave the court.

When Monsieur de Nemours heard of this, he at once saw what a decisive step it was, and feared that he had no more ground for hope. Yet the destruction of his hopes did not prevent his doing his utmost to bring about her return; he made the queen write to her, and even persuaded the Vidame to visit her: but it was all to no purpose. The Vidame saw her; she did not tell him that she had resolved upon this, but he decided that she would never return. At last Monsieur de Nemours went himself, under the pretext of going to the baths. She was much moved and astonished when she heard that he had come. She sent him a message by one of her trusty companions that she begged him not to be surprised if she was unwilling to run the risk of seeing him again and of having the feelings she felt bound to maintain swept away by his presence; that she wanted him to know that having found her duty and her peace of mind unalterably opposed to her interest in him, everything else in the world seemed so indifferent that she had abandoned it entirely, had given all her thoughts to another life, and had no other feeling left but her desire to have him share the same sentiments.

Monsieur de Nemours thought he should die of grief in the presence of the woman who brought this message. He begged her twenty times to go back to Madame de Clèves, to entreat her to let him see her; but she told him that Madame de Clèves had forbidden her, not only to bring her any message from him, but even to repeat to her what he might say. At last he had to leave, as completely overwhelmed with grief as a man could be who had lost all hopes of ever seeing again a woman whom he loved with the most violent and the most natural passion possible. Yet he did not yield even then; he did everything he could to induce her to alter her decision. At last, when years had passed, time and separation allayed his grief and extinguished his passion. Madame de Clèves led such a life that it was evident she meant never to go into the world again; part of each year she spent in this religious house; and the other part at home, but in retirement, busied with severer tasks than those of the austerest convents. Her life, which was not long, furnished examples of the loftiest virtue.

THE GIRL WITH GOLDEN EYES

(*La Fille aux yeux d'or*).

by Honoré de Balzac

A giant of the 19th century novel, Honoré de Balzac at the age of 30 began a literary career which was to encompass more than 90 novels and tales. As with Flaubert, romantic and realistic strains were present in his nature and in his work, and he is justly acclaimed both for penetrating powers of observation and an unflagging imagination. Born of a bourgeois family, Balzac was a child prodigy who consumed the school library and, at the same time, betrayed no apparent brilliance as a scholar. After studies at the Sorbonne, he apprenticed himself to a law firm, but soon discovered that his interests lay elsewhere. Much to the displeasure of his family, he threw over his law studies and found himself a grubby garret in which to write. After ten years of struggling and producing innumerable pot-boilers under various pseudonyms, which won him neither fame nor wealth, Balzac, deeply in debt, produced his first successful novel, Les Chouans. *Within the next few years, he wrote several of his masterpieces, including* Colonel Chabert *and* Eugénie Grandet. *Then, in 1833, he conceived a plan to produce a huge masterwork to be titled* The Human Comedy, *which was to portray, in meticulous and all-encompassing detail, all of contemporary French society. This epic cycle of novels stands as one of the finest of literary achievements. It is informed with the basically pessimistic view that life is a constant struggle, and identifies Balzac as a precursor of realism.*

To Eugène Delacroix, Painter.

One of the most dreadful spectacles we may run across is the malignant aspect of a certain class of the Parisian populace; a class horrible to behold, pallid, yellow, tawny. Is not

Paris a vast meadow incessantly stirred by a storm of whirling diverse interests, its crop of men mowed down by death, at an earlier age than elsewhere; whose faces are distorted, twisted, rent by all the passions of the soul and its desires, the venom of which is begotten in their brain; must they not rather be called masks than faces—lying masks of courage, masks of sorrow, masks of joy, masks of hypocrisy; all emaciated, each one stamped indelibly with the mark of a gasping covetousness? What for? For gold, or for pleasure!

Whatever observations on the Paris mind may be made, it is easily explainable how the cadaverous physiognomy is come by in either of its ages—youth or decay. Its youth is a pallid youth devoid of color, a weakness painted over to appear young. Strangers who are not given to reflection may on their first impressions, most likely, give forth an opinion of dislike for this capital, this great factory of enjoyment, whence, they think to themselves, they will shortly be glad to escape; let them but remain and they will soon assume the same deformed shape as the rest. But few words are needed to depict the always infernally tinted Parisian brand; this is not all pleasantry nor raillery, for Paris in summer may justly take the name of hell. This is a fact. It is all smoke, all scorch, all sparkle, all broil, all flame; one perspires, one is dull, revives, sparkles, crackles, and dies out. Never life in any country is hotter or more afflicted. All social nature is in a state of fusion, as it were; after finishing a task, one says: "To another!" So nature says likewise to herself. Like unto nature, society, social nature, busies itself with insects, with the flowers of a day, with trifles, fancies, and, like it, also vomits fire and flame from its everlasting crater. Perhaps, before analyzing the cause of this cast of feature peculiar to each class of this intelligent, hustling people, it might be better to describe the general reason for that particular class who disclose faces with that pale, bluey-brownish appearance, not as individuals but a clan.

All take interest in courage, but the Parisian finishes by not being interested in anything. The lack of a dominant sentiment on each face is due to friction; it becomes gray, like the plaster of a house upon which is discharged all kinds of dust and smoke. In reality, like the old woman who so long as she can get drunk to-morrow does not care where, so the Parisian remains a child whatever his age may be. He grumbles at everything, he consoles everything, he mocks everything, forgets all, wishes all, tastes of all, clutches all with passion, leaves all with nonchalance: his kings, his coquettes, his glory, his idols, whether they be of bronze or glass; the same as he throws away his old stockings, his hats, and his fortune. In Paris, each feeling that is unresisted goes in the run of things, and their course can only be changed by a hard tussle, which loosens the passions: there love is a desire and hate is welcomed; he has no more a real parent than he has a thousand-franc bill; no other friend than the pawnshop. The abandoned have the door, and become the fruits of the street; these people are not absolutely useful nor altogether useless; there is always room for such, in the salon as in the street; blockheads and rogues, people of spirit or of probity.

Everything is tolerated—the government and the guillotine, religion and the cholera. You are agreeable to all the world; you are not wanted there at all. Which, then, rules in this country without morals, without belief, without sentiment, but which, on the other side, embraces all the sentiments, all the beliefs, and all the morals? Gold or pleasure! Take these two words as a light and run over this great plaster cage, this swarm of black kennels, and there see the young serpents of agitation, of insurrection, of fermentation! Look. Examine the arrival of that world which has nothing!

The worker, the proletariat, the man who stirs his feet, his hands, his tongue, his back, his one arm, his five fingers, to live; eh, well, the former must needs practice economy, it is the first principle of his life; he overdoes his strength, he harnesses his wife to some machine, he wears out his child by a too close sticking of him at the wheel. The manufacturer, by what secondary thread I know not, nor whom it is that sets him in motion to stir this people who, with their dirty hands, turn and gild porcelain, sew coats and dresses, hammer out iron, carve wood, bend steel, blend together hemp and yarn, imitate flowers, embroider woolen, do hair-dressing, stamp bronze, make crystal wreaths, plait leather and lace, cut copper, paint carriages, trim off the old-young elms, steam cotton, blow glass, cut diamonds, polish metals, transform leaves into marble, highly finish flints, design toilettes, color, whiten, and blacken everything; well, the little boss is to soon arrive in this world of sweat and will promise a study of patience, an excessive salary, be it in the name of the town's fancy or be it in the name of a monster named Speculation.

Then, these quadrumanes are ever on the alert, they pine, labor, swear, fast, march; all these weary themselves for gain which fascinates them. Afterward, careless of the future, greedy for enjoyment, relying on their strong right arm as does the painter on his palette; they sport, great lords of one day and on Monday all their money is in the taverns, which melts down the begettings in the slush of the town; girdled with the most immodest Venus, incessantly being closed and unclosed, where they are lost like the sport of fortune which this people periodically becomes, first ferocious in pleasure, then quiet at work. Therefore during five days each performs his assigned part in Paris! He books his movements to a shuffle, he swells, grows lean, pallid, spouts out a thousand schemes for his promotion. Afterward his pleasure, his repose is the weariness following a debauch; brown of skin, black with bruises, sallow with drunkenness or yellow from indigestion, who knows not from one day to another whence shall come his future bread, the week's soup, his wife's clothes, or dresses for the child who is all in rags. These men, under the force of circumstances, born, doubtless, beautiful beings (for all creation is relatively beautiful) are, in their infancy, regiments under the command of Might, under the reign of the hammer, of shears, of the cotton-mill, and become quickly vulcanized. Vulcan, with all his ugliness and his strength, is he not the emblem of this ugly yet strong race, sublime in their mechanical intelligence, patient for the most part, terrible one day in a century, as inflammable as powder and prepared for an incendiary revolution by brandy, and yet so intelligent in thought as not to kindle at a word captiously spoken which signifies naught to them: Gold or Pleasure!

In trying to understand all those who hold out their hands to charity for their legitimate wage, where five francs agree with every genus of Parisian prostitution, and all his money is well or evil-gained, these people count up to three hundred thousand individuals. Only for the taverns would not the government be overthrown every Tuesday in the year? Fortunately, on Tuesday, this people is dull, their pleasure is boxed up, they have not as much as a sou, they return to work, to dry bread, stimulated thereto by a lack of material for procreation, to which they become accustomed. Nevertheless, these people are phenomena of virtue, these real men, these unknown Napoleons, who are the type of their strength and endurance in their highest expression, and resume their social duties in an existence where thoughts and movements combine less for throwing pleasure to them than for the regulating of their acts of sorrow.

The chances are that this workman has saved, it is equally a chance that he gratifies his fancy, he has been able to cast his eyes into the future, he has met a woman, he has found that he is a father, and, after some years of hardship and privations, he ventures a little traffic in haberdashery and notions, renting a little store. If neither illness nor vice arrest him on his way, if he is prosperous, here is a rough sketch of this normal life.

But first salute this king of the moving Parisian, who holds the submission of time and space. Yes, salute this being composed of saltpetre and gas, who gives the children of France their nights of toil, increasing during the day the number in his service; the renown and pleasure of its citizens. This man solves the problem of sacrificing at the one time to an amiable wife, his household, the "Constitutionnel," his office, the National Guard, the opera, and God; but he does not object to turn into crowns the "Constitutionnel," his office, the opera, the National Guard, his wife, and God. Therefore bow before this indefatigable jack-of-all trades. Ending every day at five o'clock, he flies like a bird along the distance that separates him from his home in the Rue Montmarte. Whether it thunders or blows, rains or snows, he is off to the office of the "Constitutionnel" to attend to the sale of that journal, of which he has charge of the distribution. Indoors and out he vends this political bread with gusto. By nine o'clock he is in the bosom of his household, he retails a joke to his wife, steals a smacking kiss as payment, tastes a cup of coffee, or growls at his children. At a quarter before ten he appears at the mayor's office. There, perched on a chair like a paroquet on his pole, the stoker of the town of Paris, until four o'clock he writes down the deaths and births of the whole of the arrondissement without giving a tear or grief. The joys and the sorrows of the quarter pass under the nib of his pen, as but lately the spirit of the "Constitutionnel" journeyed on his shoulders. He gives heed to nothing. He is always right in his own eyes, he takes his patriotism as he finds it in the paper, he disputes no one, he hisses or applauds with the rest of the world; he's a bird. At some little trouble in his parish he may, in case it is an important ceremony, leave his work to a supernumerary and go to sing a Requiem in the lectern of the church, of which he is, on Sundays and saints' days, the most distinguished ornament; his voice is most imposing when he energetically twists his big mouth to thunder forth a joyous

Amen. He is the cantor. Free of his official duties at four o'clock, he proceeds to distribute pleasure and amusements in the precincts of his store, the most famous in the city.

Happy is his wife; he has no time in which to be jealous; he is more the man of action than sentiment. So, from the time he comes to allure the demoiselles of the counter, whose sparkling eyes wheedle their customers; who rejoice in the bosom of finery, fichus, lawns, all fashioned by these makers of clothing, or more especially so before their dinner hour, for he makes a practice of giving a page in the journal to be copied, or to open the door instead of the doorkeeper, to cause some delay. At six o'clock, for the whole of two days, he is faithfully at his post. Unremovable counter-tenor of the chorus, he is found at the opera quite ready to become a soldier, Arab, prisoner, savage, peasant, ghost, the foot of a camel, a lion, demon, genie, slave, a black or white eunuch, always well versed in the play presented; of its sorrows, its pities, its astonishments, to scream out its invariable shrieks, to keep silent, to hunt, to fight, to represent Rome or Egypt; but always, *in petto,* the haberdasher. At midnight he becomes again the good husband, man, and tender father; he glides into the conjugal stream, his imagination is again intent on the lissome figures of the nymphs of the opera, and makes him turn, to the benefit of conjugal love, the depravities of that world and the round, voluptuous legs of la Taglioni. In fact, if he sleeps, his sleep is lively, and he dispatches his slumber like he dispatches his life. Is it not this incessant motion that makes the man, distance incarnate, the Proteus of civilization? This man embraces everything: history, literature, politics, government, religion, militarism, art. Is he not a living ency-clopædia, a grotesque Atlas, incessantly on the march, like Paris, which knows not repose? To him everything is legs. No physiognomy can be kept pure in all this toil. Perhaps the worker, who dies an old man at thirty years of age, his stomach tanned by his successive doses of brandy, has been able to find, to speak of him as some philosophers speak of an income, no more happiness than when he was a haberdasher. But perhaps, on the other hand, he has made a successful stroke. Of his eight trades, of his shoulders, his throat, his hands, of his wife and his business, he retires from the latter. Many go on farms, with their children and some thousand francs, and there find the more laborious pleasure which always recreates the heart of man. This fortune and these children, or the children who remain to him from the prey of the superior world, he takes into his gate with his crowns and his daughter, the while his son is being educated at college, who, obtaining more education than had ever been his father's, casts ambitious looks on a higher sphere. Very frequently the youngster of a little trader will become of some object in the State.

This ambition brings us to the thoughts on the second of the Parisian spheres. Whether he has climbed up a story and gone into the entresol, or has descended from the garret and stops on the fourth floor, he at length penetrates into the world somehow; the result is the same. The wholesale merchants and their boys, their employés, the people of the young bank and of great honesty, the dishonest, the lost souls, the first and the last salesmen, clerks of the bailiff, the lawyer, the notary, in fact, all the assistant members, thinkers, speculators of the power middle-class who triturate the doings of Paris and watch over its gains, monopolize its commodities, control the products manufactured by the working-people, barrel up the fruits of the South, the fish of the sea, the wines of all bank-sides loved by the son; who spread their hands over the Orient, and scornfully take the shawls of the Turks and Russians, they reap the crops of the far-off Indies, which, as they sleep, are brought to their mart; look after their profits, count their stock, alter and increase their prices; they pack up the whole of Paris in detail, the carriage, the games of children, spy out the caprices and vices of ripe age, and wring out their maladies; well, without drinking brandy like the workman does, are they not flung to the vultures outside the barriers, all the time going beyond their strength—going further than the weight of their body permits, and their morals in addition; their desires dried up, their fast pace abated. At home, the physical tension caused by the lash of interest, under the flail of ambition which torments the world, raises in this monstrous city, the same as the workman is forced under the cruel weight of material elaborations by his incessant desires and the despotism of the "I WILL" aristocrat. There the same, obedient to the same universal master, pleasure or gold, he must devour time, is pressed for time, finding more than twenty-four hours in the day and night, he is unnerved, is killed, sells thirty years of old age for two years of sickly repose. The only difference—the workman dies in a hospital, when his last stunted term is done, while the bourgeois persists to breathe and live, but is cretinish.

You have encountered the drawn face, flat, old, without

light in the eyes, without firmness on the feet, dragging on the boulevard, with a dull, expressionless air, the ceinture of his Venus, of his cherished town. What do the bourgeois want? The steel of the National Guard, an immutable *pot-au-feu,* a decent place in Père-Lachaise cemetery, and, for their old age, a little gold legitimately earned. His Monday, to him, is Sunday; his rest is the promenade of a carriage in the coach-house; his champagne supper depends on how his wife and children joyfully swallow the coal-dust where they roast in the sun; the barrier is his restaurant in which he finds the venomous dinner of so wide renown, or some family ball in which he stifles until midnight.

Some simpletons are as much astonished as Saint-Guy when they are shown the animalculæ that a microscope makes visible in a drop of water, but yet say that the Gargantua of Rabelais, the type of an incomprehensible, sublime audacity, how this giant, fallen from a celestial sphere, amuses himself in contemplating the doings of this second Parisian life, you know the formula, eh? Have you seen their little barracks, cold even in summer, without any other fireplace than an earthen foot-warmer in winter, placed under the vast dome of copper that covers the corn-market. "Madame is there in the early morning, she is the factotum of the Market and gains by her trade twelve thousand francs per annum," says one. Monsieur, when madame has left, passes into a little, dark office ready at hand, where he loans by the *little week* to the traders of that quarter. At nine o'clock he is found at the Bureau of Passports, where he is one of the second-clerks. That evening he is in a box at the Theatre-Italiens, or some other theatre which he chooses for his pleasure. His children are put out to nurse, and afterward to college or in a boarding-school. Monsieur and madame dwell on a third-floor flat, they don't keep a cook, giving their balls in a salon twelve feet by eight, and lighted with an argand lamp; but they give one hundred and fifty thousand francs to their daughter, and rest themselves, at fifty years of age, by taking in the opera, going in a carriage to Longchamp in a faded toilette; in every sunshiny hour they promenade the boulevards or climb the steps of the fortifications. Respected in the quarter, a friend of the government, allied to the higher middle-classes, monsieur, at sixty-five, obtains the cross of the Legion of Honor, and the father of his father-in-law, the mayor of the arrondissement, is invited to his soirées.

All his work in this life is done to the profit of his children,

whom this bourgeoisie fatally endeavors to raise to a higher
social rank. Each sphere still throws its spawn into a superior
one. The son of a rich grocer is made a notary, the son of a
lumber merchant becomes a lawyer. Not one tooth of them all
but wants to bite out a new furrow, all stimulate the ascending movement by the use of money.

We have now drawn a third circle in this hell, which perhaps, some day, will have its Dante. In this third social circle,
a species of Parisian stomach in which are digested the interests of this city, and where it is there condensed under the
form called "affairs," stirred and agitated, a sharp and rancor-
ous intestinal movement of the crowd of lawyers, doctors,
notaries, barristers, agents, bankers, wholesale merchants,
speculators, judges. We meet still more of the causes of the
destruction, physical and moral, everywhere we go.

This living people, almost all, in the infected studios, in the
stiff audience halls, in the little railed-off offices, pass the day
bent under the weight of business, rising at the break of day to
be in time, not to allow any one to rob him, to gain all or not
to lose, to seize a man or his money, to make or unmake a
bargain, to take advantage of a furtive opportunity, to hang
or acquit a man. This reacts on their horses, which become
broken-down, overdriven, aged, like themselves, long before
their time. Time is their tyrant; when they need it, it is flown
away; they cannot expand it or control it. Some soul remains
great, pure, moral, generous, and, consequently, some face
dwells beautiful in the depraving exercise of a trade by which
he is compelled to support his portion of the public miseries;
does he analyze, ponder, estimate the proper rule and model?

Where does this people dispose of their heart? I don't know;
but they leave some portion, when they have one, before they
go down every morning, in the depths of the poignant pains
of their families. As for them, the point of the mystery, they
see the hell of that society of which they are the confessors,
and which they scorn. Now, what has made them besmear
themselves with that corruption at which they are horrified
and sorrowful for? whence by lassitude and some secret trans-
action they marry; indeed, it is necessary for them, they are so
vitiated in all their feelings, they are so far from men and
their institutions, from the source of which they fly like the
bloom on cadavers while they are still warm. At every hour
the man of money hangs on to life; the man of wedding-
contracts hangs on death; the man of law hangs his conscience. Compelled to speak without cessation, ever replacing

the idea by the word, the sentiment by the phrase, their soul becomes a larynx. They use it to demoralize.

Neither the great merchant; nor the judge, nor the barrister can preserve their right senses: they no longer possess them; they only apply to everything their own rules, which are essentially false. Carried away by the torrent of their life, they possess neither brides, fathers, nor lovers; they slide like a sled on the snows of existence, and, every hour they live, are jostled by the business of this great city. When they return to their homes they are under requisition to attend a ball, the opera, or some festival, or, possibly, they have an engagement with some client whom by their knowledge they can protect. To this terrible expenditure of intellectual force they oppose no genuine relaxation, save such as are insipid and afford no real contrast, such as a debauch or a frightful, secret dissipation; for they dread the scandal of the world and dare not affront society. Their immoderate eating, playing, watching, bloat their faces, which become flat and coppery in color. Their actual dullness of comprehension is hidden under a special science. They know their trade, but are ignorant of all else; then, to save appearances, they put it out of the question, criticising it as wrong and irregular; in appearance doubters, but in reality simpletons, wearing their spirits by interminable discussions. Almost every one adopts convenient social prejudices, for each is of the same opinion in dispensing with all things literary and political, the same as they place their consciences under the shelter of the Code or the Tribunal of Commerce.

Partly by the good-luck of being remarkable men, those who have deviated from the mediocrities crawl to the top of the tree. Their faces are of a pale and vinegary aspect, with an unnatural coloring; their eyes are tarnished and in deep circles; their loquacious, sensual mouths, in which the observer recognizes the debasement of their thoughts and the rotation in the circle of a specialty which kills off all the generative faculties of the brain, the boon of seeing afar, of generalizing and deducing. They are nearly all shriveled in the furnace of their business. But there is not a man lashed to or caught in the hopper or cog-wheels of these immense machines that fears he will not become great.

If he is a doctor or has a smattering of medicine, or he has made some cure, he is a Bichat who dies young. If a great merchant, he neglects some business, he is nearly a Jacques Cœur. Who but execrated Robespierre? Danton was his slothful follower. Who is there, though, but has envied the faces of Danton and Robespierre, some for their sublimity, others for their power? So, likewise, the ambition of the workman is that of the middle-classes. In Paris vanity includes every passion. The type of this class is seen in the ambitious bourgeois, who, after a life of worry and continuous scheming, passes on to the Council of State, like ants file through a fissure; some being editors of newspapers, profligate in schemes, that the King may make them peers of France, perhaps to avenge themselves on the nobility; some being notaries become mayors of their arrondissement; every one flattered by their business and who, when they arrive at their goal, arrive *killed*. In France custom enthroned the wig. Napoleon, Louis XIV., the great kings, are only the leaders of the young people to fill out their designs.

Above this sphere is the world of art. But there, again, the visages marked with the seal of originality are nobly bowed, but broken, fatigued, sinuous. Wearied by a desire to create, exceeding their expensive whims, fatigued by a devouring genius, famished for the lack of pleasure, the artists of Paris risk all to win back by excessive toil the omissions left by their slothfulness; they vainly search to conciliate the world and glory, money and art. In commencing, the artist does not pant under the creditor; but his needs bring forth debts, and his debts demand his nights. After toil, pleasure. The comedian plays up to midnight, studying all the morning, repeating his lines at noon; the sculptor lies prone under his statue: the journalist is a thought on march, like a soldier in war; the painter who is the fashion is overwhelmed with work; the painter without connection has his heart gnawed if he is a man of genius. His competitors, rivals, calumniators assassinate his talent. Some, desperate, rush into the abyss of vice; others, young and ignorant, too quickly discount their future. Few of these faces, originally sublime, retain their nobility. Some few, though, retain the radiant beauty of their head without debasement. The face of an artist is always anomalous, it is ever above or beneath conventional lines, for this is what idiots term this ideal beauty. What power of destruction. What passion. All passion in Paris blends in two terms: gold and pleasure.

Now, why don't you respire? Is it that you feel there is not space enough for the air to be purified? Here is neither labor nor pains. By whirling up the spiral stairs gold has gained the summit. Out of the depths of the sighs where their gutter begins; out of the depths of the work-shops in which stay the wretched bastards; in the heart of the counting-rooms, behind the gratings of iron-rails, gold, without figuring on marriage-portions or inheritances, is grasped by the hands of young girls or the bony hands of old men, gushing out toward the aristocratic folk, where it glitters, displays itself, and streams away.

But before quitting for the four quarters to which pertain Parisian high propriety, who desire it not, after the causes spoken of; deducing the physical reasons, and after taking an observation of the plague, leaving, so to speak, in abeyance those who constantly show by their faces the janitor, the storekeeper, or the workingman; plainly speaking of a deleterious influence whose corruption nearly equals that of the Paris administration which complacently permits it to exist.

If the atmosphere of the houses in which live the greater part of the middle-class is infected, so the atmosphere of the streets spews out cruel miasmas into the back-shops where the air is rarefied; who are these that leave this pestilence in the forty thousand houses of this great city, that bathes its feet in the filth, that can really think that it is desired seriously to inclose in walls of concrete, which are alone able to prevent the most fetid mire from filtering through the soil, of there poisoning the wells and of continuing underground to Lethe, its famous name? Half of Paris sleep in the putrid exhalations of courts, of low, close streets.

But now to the great salons, airy and light; the mansions with gardens; high society, idle, happy, rich. There the faces are emaciated and gnawed by vanity. There, nothing is genuine. They seek pleasure; do they not find weariness? People of the world founder very early in life. They have no other occupation than to manufacture enjoyment; they very speedily destroy their senses by this, the same as the workman destroys his by brandy. Pleasure is like certain medical substances; to constantly obtain the same effect it becomes necessary to double the dose, and death or stupidity is the final doom. All the lower classes sprawl before the wealthy and spy out their tastes so that they may imitate their vices and exploits. How can one resist the constant seductions that are woven in this country? So Paris has its *thériakis,** for which it plays; and gluttony or courtesans are its opium. So you see to this people happiness is a question of taste and not a passion; it is a

---

* A medicinal herb, mentioned by Bacon.

romantic fantasy of chilly love. There impotence reigns; there most of their ideas are as listless as the energies of the affectations of the boudoir are feminine make-believes.

There are beardless boys of forty, there are old doctors of sixteen. The wealthy of Paris take their intelligence ready made, their science all masticated, every opinion as formulated; they dispense with real science, spirit, and opinion. In the world their unrighteousness is equal to their feebleness and to their libertinism. They become miserly of the time as they lose their strength.

They cannot find as many affections as ideas. Their greetings are covered in a profound indifference, and their politeness is continuous scorn. They never love others. By their witless sallies, their countless indiscretions, by their gossip, by all these they consider themselves above the commonalty: for of such depth is their language. But these unfortunate "happy" ones pretend not to know that they resemble in speech and manner the truths taken from la Rochefoucauld's works; as if such a thing could not exist in their midst, in this nineteenth century, as a junction of the ever-full and an absolute void. Should some man use a pleasantry that is bright and witty, it is incomprehensible; they soon fatigue with giving without receiving, they stay at home and are content to remain in the kingdom of fools for their possession.

This hollow life, this continual waiting for pleasure that never arrives, this chronic weariness, this inanity of the spirit, the heart, and the brain, this lassitude of the great Parisian assemblies, reproducing time and again all these traits, making their cardboard faces, their premature wrinkles, this physiognomy of wealth or the grin of impotence, is the reflection of the gold, or the flown intelligence.

This view of Paris morals proves that the physical Paris cannot be other than it is. This city which wears the diadem of queen, always majestic, is envied furiously and irresistibly. Paris is the head of the whole world, a brain which craves genius and guides human civilization; a great man, an artist incessantly creating, or, on further thoughts, a politician who must necessarily have wrinkles in his brain; here are the vices of the great man, the fantasies of the artist, and the criticisms of the politician. His physiognomy undergoes a germination of good and of evil, the combat and the victory; the moral war of eighty-nine, whose trumpet sound still reëchoes in every corner of the world; and likewise the troubles of 1814. That city cannot become more moral, nor more cordial, nor more correct unless copper-bound, like those fireworks whose gushing waves you so admire. Is not Paris a noble vessel loaded with intellect? Yes, her arms sometimes are oracles that permit fatalities. THE CITY OF PARIS has a tall mast, all of bronze, sculptured with victories, and has for its lookout man Napoleon. That shipwreck sent her pitching and rolling; but she still ploughs the world, she makes fire in the hundred rings around her tribunes, she still labors in the seas of science, she bides her time, and cries aloud from the mast-head by the voice of her savants and artists: "Forward, march! follow me!"

She carries an immense array of new streamers which she has made to dress the ship. There are ship-boys and urchins laughing in the shrouds; heavy bourgeoisie form the ballast; workmen and sailors pay out the tar; in her state-rooms the happy passengers; elegant midshipmen smoke their cigars as they lean against the rail; on deck her soldiers, recruits or veterans, who vault aboard at every port, and, all willing to give their lives, asking glory what is pleasure; or of lovers, why wish for gold.

Therefore the excessive action of the proletariat, the depravity of interests which bruise the two classes of bourgeoisies, the hardships of the artists of genius, and the incessant excess of pleasure sought after by the great, explain the normal deformity of the Parisian countenance.

The Orientals only, of the whole human race, offer a magnificent portrait; but it is the effect of constant calmness caused by those profound philosophies over a long pipe, cross-legged, a twisted turban on head, which contemplates every movement with horror; while those of Paris, stunted (big and little), run, leap, and caper, scourged by an unpitying goddess, Necessity: the necessity of money, glory, and amusement. So, some fresh face, reposed, gracious, really young, is a most extraordinary exception: it is but rarely met with.

If you see one, be assured that it belongs to: a young, fervent priest or to some good, octogenarian abbé, with a triple chin; to some young person of pure nature, as is sometimes raised in certain bourgeois families; to a mother of twenty, still full of illusions, as she suckles her first-born; to a young man freshly arrived from the provinces, confided to a devoted dowager who is left without a sou; or to some shopboy, who goes to bed at midnight, thoroughly tired out with wrapping up or unwrapping calico, and who rises at seven to clean out the store; or, frequently, to a scientific man or a poetical one, who lives a sober life, quiet and chaste; or to some simpleton, satisfied with himself, nourished by his own foolishness, guzzling health, always occupied in smiling to himself; or to the happy and equable lounger species, the only really happy people in Paris, and who taste each hour the newest poesies.

However, there is in Paris one privileged class of beings who profit by this incessant motion of manufacturing interests, business, or the arts, and of gold. These beings are the women. While some even of these have a thousand secret causes, more here than elsewhere, which shall destroy their faces, still he encounters in the feminine world a little, happy tribe which lives the life of the Orientals, and these preserve their beauty; but these women are rarely seen afoot in the streets, they live concealed, like those rare plants which display their lovely petals only at certain hours, and constitute veritable exotic exceptions. Still, Paris is essentially the country of contrasts. If noble sentiments are rare there, they may yet be met with, together with boundless devotion. On this battlefield of interests and passions, in the midst of society marching along in the triumph of egoism, where each is compelled to defend himself alone, and whom we call to arms, it seems most pleasant when it is encountered and becomes sublime by its juxtaposition.

So of faces. In Paris, at times, in the higher aristocracy we find some trace of the same ravishingly clear faces, the fruits of exceptional education and environments. The youthful beauty of English blood thoroughly blended in Southern features and united to French intelligence and purity of form. The fire of their eyes, the delicious redness of their lips, the black lustre of their fine hair, a white skin, a distinguished cast to the face, render them the beautiful flowers of humanity, sublime when seen in contrast with the mass of other physiognomies—wan, drawn, weazened, crooked, grinning. So women immediately express their admiration of these young people with that greedy pleasure which makes men turn to look at a pretty person; becoming, gracious, embellished with all the virginities which our imaginations can wish to decorate the perfect girl.

If this rapid glance over the population of Paris has caused you to realize the rarity of a Raphaelistic face, and the passionate admiration that the first sight of one incites, the principal interest of our story will be fully justified. *Quod erat demonstrandum*, this is what is demonstrated, if it be allowed to apply scholastic formulæ to the science of manners.

Now, on one of those lovely mornings in spring, when the leaves are not yet green, although unfolded, when the sun begins to lighten up the roofs and when the sky is blue, when the populace of Paris come out of their shells, come buzzing on to the boulevards, gliding along like a serpent of a thousand colors, by the Rue de la Paix toward the Tuileries, saluting the splendors of wedlock which has recommenced its campaign; on one of these delightful days, then, a young man, as handsome as the day, this very day, dressed with taste, easy in manner, spoken of in secret as a love-child, the natural son of Lord Dudley and the famous Marquise de Vordac, was promenading the Broad Walk in the Tuileries.

This Adonis, named Henri de Marsay, brought to France whither Lord Dudley came to marry that young person, already the mother of Henri, to an old gentleman named M. de Marsay. This coxcomb, colorless and almost quenched, recognized the child as his own by receiving the usufruct in an interest of one hundred thousand francs; definitely describing him as his putative son; a folly which did not cost much to Lord Dudley, the French Funds being then valued at seventeen francs fifty centimes.

The old gentleman died without having known his wife. Mme. de Marsay afterward married the Marquis de Vordac; but, before she became marquise, she was rather uneasy about her and Lord Dudley's son. Just then war was declared between France and England, which separated the two lovers, and her faithfulness, "ever the same," was not nor ever will be in the style in Paris.

Then the successes of an elegant woman, pretty, universally admired, dulled in the Parisian all maternal feeling. Lord Dudley was not more careful of his offspring than was his mother. The quick infidelity of the young, ardent girl he loved had, perhaps, given a sort of aversion to everything connected with her life. It may perhaps be thought that fathers do not love their children to whom they give an ample acknowledgment; now social belief is of the utmost importance for the repose of families, that is why all bachelors hold the one opinion that the paternal is a sentiment far higher than that grown in the hot-house of woman, and is shown by both custom and law.

Poor Henri de Marsay had never met his father now in

heaven, that one of the two to whom he was not under obligations for his creation. The paternity of M. de Marsay was naturally very incomplete. These children are not, in the natural course of things, the children of a father who is concerned for only a few passing moments; and that gentleman did but imitate nature. The good man had not sold his name to be deprived of his game. He ate without compunction of the free lunches provided at the gaming-houses, and aimed at using as little as possible of what was paid him each six months by the National Treasury.

He had raised the child of an elder sister, a Demoiselle de Marsay, and gave him, from the meagre pension allowed him by his brother, a preceptor, an abbé without money or marbles, who measured out the future of the young man; and he resolved to pay him out of the hundred thousand livres of income for the care given to his pupil, to whom he had given his affection.

This preceptor he found by chance to be a true priest, one of those ecclesiastics cut out by nature for a cardinal in France, or a Borgia under the tiara. He taught the child three years and then placed him in college for ten years. Then this noble man, named the Abbé de Maronis, finished the education of his pupil by teaching him of civilization in its every phase. He nurtured him on his own experience; he drew him but little toward the church, then in a ferment; he sometimes took him through the slums, more frequently to see the courtesans; he pulled human sentiment apart piece by piece; he roasted the politics of the day in its very citadel of the salon; he sized up the government machinery, and, tempted by friendship for a noble nature which had been forsaken, endeavoured to replace him in the affections of his mother. "The church, is it not the mother of orphans?" answered the pupil of his cares.

This worthy man died a bishop in 1812; he had the profound gratification of leaving behind him under the heavens a child whose heart and spirit at sixteen could overthrow a man of forty. Who would expect to meet a heart of bronze, an alcoholic brain, under the most seducing figures of the old painters, those natural artists, who always painted a serpent in the terrestrial paradise? Still, this is nothing.

More, this good devil of a Violet had given his child a certain predilection in the knowledge of high society in Paris which can as speedily dissipate as produce, in the hands of a young man, another hundred thousand livres of income.

To conclude, this priest, wicked but politic, incredulous but wise, perfidious but amiable, feeble in appearance, but as vigorous in body as mind, was really so useful to his pupil, so complaisant to his vices, so good a calculator of all his special powers, so deep when he came to gauge humanity, so young when at table, at Frascati's, at——— you know where, that he recognized Henri de Marsay as being so little changed, in 1814, that, seeing the picture of his dear bishop, the only thing that he had been able to bequeath him, this prelate, an excellent type of man, whose genius had saved the Catholic church, Apostolic, and Roman, momentarily compromised by the weakness of its recruits and the senility of its pontiffs; but he wanted the church!

The continental war prevented young de Marsay knowing his real father, of whom it was doubtful whether he knew his name. Naturally he had little regret for his putative father. When Mademoiselle de Marsay, his only mother, had been taken to the cemetery of Père-Lachaise, where she was buried under a very pretty little tombstone, Monseigneur de Maronis had promised to this coxcomb of a widow one of the best places in heaven, insomuch that, seeing the happiness of death, Henri abandoned tears that were egotistical and did a little weeping for himself. When the abbé saw this sorrow he dried the tears of his ward, bidding him observe that the good girl took plenty of fine snuff, and had become so ugly, so deaf, so irritable, that he ought to be thankful for her death. The bishop had emancipated his pupil in 1811. Then, when the mother of M. de Marsay remarried, the priest chose, in the family council, one of those honest, headless tetrarchs, whom he constrained through the confessional, and charged him to become the administrator of the fortune and apply the revenues thereof to the needs of the youngster, but he wished him to preserve the capital intact.

Toward the close of 1814, Henri de Marsay, not having anywhere on earth a sense of obligation to any one, had the same freedom as a bird without companions. When he was twenty-two he would have passed for seventeen. Generally, his hardest rivals looked upon him as the prettiest boy in Paris.

From his father, Lord Dudley, he had taken those loving, deceitful blue eyes; from his mother, his black curly hair; from both, a pure blood, a skin like that of a young girl, a sweet and modest manner, a fine aristocratic waist, and particularly beautiful hands. For a woman to see him was to bring upon her a fit of lunacy; do you understand? Well, conceive one of those desires that gnaw the heart, but don't forget the fact of the impossibility of its being gratified, because the woman of Paris is generally without tenacity. Between themselves they say, after the manner of men, the motto of the house of Orange: JE MAIN TIEN DRAI.

Under this freshness of life, and in spite of the limpid water of his eyes, Henri had the courage of a lion, the cunning of a monkey. He could cut through a bullet on the edge of a knife at ten paces distance; he rode a horse in a manner which seemed to realize the fable of the centaur; he could drive a carriage with all the grace of a great whip; he was as lively as a cherubin and as quiet as a sheep; but he could beat any man in the faubourg by the terrible play of his feet or his cudgel; then he could finger the piano, equaling in skill the best artists when he felt in the humor; and possessed a voice of such value that Barbaja would have earned at least fifty thousand francs each season by it. Alas! all these brilliant qualities, these pretty defects, were tarnished by a dreadful vice: he believed in neither men nor women, nor in God or the devil. Capricious nature had begun this character, a priest had completed it.

So as to make this adventure understood, it is necessary to add here that Lord Dudley naturally found plenty of women anxious to have some examples and copies of this delicious portrait. His second *chef-d'œuvre* of this kind was a young girl named Euphémie, born of a Spanish lady, brought up in Havana, returning to Madrid with a young creole from the Antilles, and every taste ruined in the colonies; but happily married to an old and powerful wealthy Spanish lord, Don Hijos, Marquis of San Réal, who, since the occupation of Spain by the French troops, had been living in Paris, residing on the Rue Saint-Lazare.

More out of indifference than out of respect for the innocence of youth, Lord Dudley did not point out to his children nor advise them as to whom their creator was, or of their relationship to him, for he had children everywhere. This is a trifling inconvenience in civilization; it has its advantages, but it also has its drawbacks; it is less favorable than unfortunate for its beneficiaries. Lord Dudley, of whom we have spoken so much, came in 1816 to Paris a fugitive from English justice, after he had been to the Orient as a supercargo. This lordly traveler asked, when he saw that beautiful young man, whom he was. Then, after hearing the name:

"Ah! that is my son—what bad luck," said he.

This was the story of the young man who, toward the middle of the month of April, 1815, nonchalantly paraded the Broad Walk of the Tuileries, after the manner of all those animals who, knowing their strength, march stridently along in majesty and peace. Women of the middle-class artlessly turned around to look at him again; other women did not turn themselves but awaited his return, and engraved in their memories, for an after reminiscence, that agreeable form which made the most beautiful among them seem but ugly in comparison.

"What are you doing here on Sunday?" said the Marquis de Ronquerolles to Henri as he passed.

"I'm sizing the fish in the pond," replied the young man.

This exchange of pleasantries was accompanied by two significant looks, and only for this it might have been thought that neither de Ronquerolles nor de Marsay had the air of being known to each other. The young man examined the loungers, with a quick, eager glance and sharp hearing that is particularly Parisian, and who seem at first sight to see nothing and hear nothing, but who in reality see all and hear everything. The young man now took him by the arm.

"Well, how goes it? my dear de Marsay."

"Quite well," replied de Marsay, with a seeming affectionate manner, but which, between young Parisians, means nothing, neither for the present nor the future.

As a fact, the young people of Paris have no resemblance to the young folk of any other city. They are divided into two classes; the young man who has something and the young man who has nothing; or the young man who spends and the young man who saves.

But, and give this careful attention, the one who is drawn to Paris to go the delightful pace of high life does not act the same as he who is indigenous there. He lives there quite as well as other young men, but they are children who enter very late into Parisian existence and remain the dupes of their elders. They do not speculate, they study or they dig; say the others.

Of course there are some young men, rich or poor, who embrace careers and steadily follow them; there are a few Émile de Rousseaus, in the skins of citizens, who are never seen in society: diplomatists, as they call these particular simpletons.

Whether they are simpletons or not they augment the num-

ber of nonentities and go to make up the population of
France. They are always with us; ever ready at hand to botch
public or private business with the flat trowel of mediocrity,
boasting of their impotence, which they term morality and
honesty. This species of the "prize of excellence" of society
infest the administration, the army, the bench, the Chambers,
the Court. They thin down and flatten the country and form,
as it were, in the body politic, a lymph which overburdens it
and renders it flabby. These honest people call men of genius
flippant or immoral. So these same flippant folk pay the others for their poorly rendered services; they may be termed
humbugs, but they are respected by the multitude; happily for
France, though, these fashionable young men are unceasingly
stigmatized as dudish blockheads.

Nevertheless a mere glance suffices to assure us that there
are two species of young men found in fashionable circles—
that amiable body of which Henri de Marsay was a member.
But observers who are not satisfied with a purely superficial
view of things are soon convinced that the differences are
purely of a moral nature, and that nothing is more apt to lead
astray than a pretty exterior.

However, the whole world goes the pace just the same,
speaking at random of things, men, literature, and art;
mouthing "Pitt and Cobourg," each twelvemonth; interrupting
conversation with a pun; turning to ridicule the learning of a
scientist; scorning everything they do not understand and all
they dread; they set themselves above everybody else, insti-
tuting themselves supreme judges of all things. They are always, and for ever, mystifying their fathers and are at all
times ready to rain down their crocodile tears on the bosoms
of their mothers. As a rule, they believe in nothing; they
slander women and chaff the modest, though they are really in
subjection to dirty courtesans or some old rip of a woman. All
of these are rotten to the bone, caused by their depravity, or
have gravel, which is brought on by a brutish envy of prefer-
ment; if they are threatened with stone and are probed they
are found to have an inside of marble.

In their normal state they are outwardly very amiable, but
their friendship is only make-believe. The same slang domi-
nates the ever-changing jargon of their talk; they aim at the
fantastical in their attire; their pride is in repeating the folly
and nonsense of some popular actor or other, and they make
their entrance with some silly pun or impertinence of his to in
some sort display their knowledge of their idol; but woe to

those who cannot understand them, for they are left with the outstarting eyes of astonishment. They seem equally indifferent to the woes and scourges of their country. They resemble, in fact, the pretty white foam which tips the waves of the ocean during a tempest. On the day of the battle of Waterloo they dressed, dined, danced, and amused themselves, and they do the like during the cholera or while a revolution is on. After all, they spent as much as at other times; but here begins the comparison. Of this floating fortune and agreeable waste, one is the capital, the others the dependents thereon; they are the same journeymen, but the bills are settled by the former. Then if the one class, as it seems to those who study it, receive every kind of idea without keeping any, they are compared with those who assimilate all that is good. So those who think they know something, know nothing and understand all; they present all to those who are in need of nothing and offer nothing to those who lack anything; these secretly study the thoughts of the others and so place their money as to profit largely in their fortunes by the follies of the others. The one does not give a faithful impression of their soul on the countenance, because it is dulled as ice is by use and cannot give any reflection; but the others economize all their senses and life and show it, as one may say, through their windows.

The first, on the faith of a hope, are devoted without conviction to a system, which has the wind and sails with the current, but they skip to another political boat when the first begins to drift; the second plumb the future, they sound it and see in a faithful policy that which the English see in commercial probity—an element of success. But the young man who has something makes a pun or says something smart on the change of policy in the throne; those who have nothing make a public calculation, or meanly betray a secret, and attain all things by giving a hand to the grasp of their friends. The one never knows anything of the properties of other people, taking all their ideas for new, as if the world was on the watch for such; they have unlimited confidence in themselves, and have no enemy so cruel as themselves. But the others are armed with a continual mistrust of men whom they estimate at their real value, and are deep enough to have a thought that is deeper than that of their friends whom they exploit; then at night, when their heads are on their pillows, they weigh, like a miser, their pieces of gold.

The one is annoyed at an impertinence without brooding

over it, and afford pleasure to the diplomatists who pose before them as pulling the principal wires of these puppets—self-love—while the others respectively choose their victims and protectors. Then some day it happens that those who have nothing now have something, and those that had something then have nothing now. Those who see their parvenu comrades in a position ascribe to them cunning and bad hearts, but also as being smart men. "They are very smart" is the great eulogy decreed to those who have reached, by hook or crook, a position in the government, a wife, or a fortune. Among them are met certain young men who play this part, commencing with getting into debt, and, naturally, they are more dangerous than those who play the risky game without a sou.

The young man who was the intimate friend of Henri de Marsay was a giddy youth, just arrived from the provinces and at the time when young men were the fashion; he fully understood the art of eating up an inheritance, but he had a last cake to eat in the provinces, an inalienable estate. This was simply a small heritage, without transition, of his meagre hundred francs per month allowed him from the paternal fortune, and which, if he had not had enough intelligence to perceive that they laughed at him, he knew enough to calculate on stopping his career at two-thirds of his capital. He discovered in Paris, by means of some bills for a thousand francs, the exact value of harness, the art of not paying much respect to his gloves, which were ever extended as a token to people he met, and found that a contract was the better plan of dealing with them; he spoke powerfully and in good terms of his horses and his Pyrenean hounds; he learned to know, after the launch, to what species a woman belonged by her make-up and the appearance of her shoes; he studied *écarté,* learned some fashionable words, and conquered, by his sojourn in the Parisian world, the necessary authority to much later import into the provinces the taste for tea, plate in the English fashion, and so gave the right of those about him to scorn him for the rest of his days.

De Marsay had taken to his friendship to serve him in society, like a bold speculator employing a confidential clerk. This false or genuine friendship of de Marsay was a social position for Paul de Manerville, who, on his side, believing it was sincere and strong, exploited in his own manner his intimate friend. He lived in the reflection of his friend, he took him all the time under his umbrella, he had him in his stockings and his boots, he was gilded by his rays. When standing near Henri, the same as when walking by his side, he had the air of saying:

"Do not insult us, we are two tigers."

Very often he would allow himself to fatuously say:

"If I ask Henri such and such a thing, he is sufficiently my friend to make it known to me."

But he was very careful never to ask him anything. He was afraid, and his fear, although imperceptible, reacted on others and was of service to de Marsay.

"That de Marsay is a high-spirited man," said Paul. "Ah! you will see, he will make his mark. It will not astonish me to one day see him the minister for foreign affairs. Nothing can prevent him."

Then he would make of de Marsay, the same as Corporal Trim made of his cap, one continual play:

"Ask de Marsay, and you will learn the truth."

Or, again:

"The other day de Marsay and I were hunting together, and he did not seem to think that I could clear a bush without my horse made a running start."

Or:

"De Marsay and I were at the home of some women, and, on my word of honor, I was——," and so forth.

So Paul de Manerville cannot be classed among that clan of great, illustrious, and powerful family of ninnies who come to Paris. He would some day become a deputy. At that time he was nothing more, nothing less, than many another young man.

His friend de Marsay thus defined him: "You ask me, *whom* is this Paul? Why this is Paul de Manerville."

"I am surprised, my boy, to see you here on Sunday," said he to De Marsay.

"I might make the same rejoinder."

"Have you an intrigue?"

"An intrigue."

"Bah!"

"I can tell you without compromising my passion. A woman that comes on Sunday to the Tuileries does not value aristocratic gossip."

"Aha!"

"Stop that or I tell you nothing. You laugh too loudly, one would think we had had a too hearty breakfast. Last Thursday, here, on the Terrasse des Feuillants, I was walking along

just thinking of nothing. But when I reached the gate at the
Rue de Castiglione, by which way I was going out, I found
myself face to face with a woman, or rather with a young
person, who, even if she had not clasped me round the neck,
would, I think, have arrested me less out of humanity's sake
than for the profound astonishment with which I was struck
by her arms and legs, the latter of which ran from the back-
bone till stopped by the soles of the feet which were on the
ground. I have often experienced from different people a kind
of animal magnetism which became very strong at the moment when the affinity is respectively felt. But, my dear fellow, this was not a stupefication, nor was this a common
woman. Morally speaking, this face seemed to say: 'What!
there is my ideal, the being of my fancy, of my dreams by day
and night. How came he here? Why this morning? Why not
yesterday? Take me, I am thine,' *et cætera!*

"'Good,' I said to myself, 'I will then look into this.' Ah!
my dear fellow, talk of a figure! the unknown, this creature, is
the most adorable woman I have ever met. She belongs to that
variety of femininity that the Romans called *fulva, flava*, the
woman of flame. What most struck me at first sight, this one
with whom I am so smitten has tawny eyes like those of
tigers, yellow and luminous like living gold, of gold that
thinks, of gold which loves and which you have absolutely in
your arms."

"We know all about that, my boy!" exclaimed Paul. "She
will come here again some time, this GIRL WITH GOLDEN
EYES. She is a young woman in the neighborhood of twenty-
two, and whom I have seen here in the time of the Bourbons,
but with a woman who is a hundred thousand times better
than herself."

"Hush! you, Paul. It is impossible that any woman can
surpass that girl; she resembles a cat who wishes to come and
rub against your legs; a pale girl with charcoal tresses, slight
in appearance, who has soft threads for the third joint of her
fingers; and whose full, rounded cheeks show a white down,
whose lines, luminous as a lovely day, begin at the ears and
are lost in the throat."

"Ah! but the other, my dear de Marsay. She shows eyes of
midnight, not tearful but yet always brilliant; of black eyebrows which are joined and give her an air of giving the lie to
the inflexibility expressed in the pucker of her lips, which
seem to say that no kiss may ever settle there—such ardent,
fresh lips, too. A warm complexion by which a man is

scorched as by the sun; but, on my word of honor, she resembles you——"

"Flatterer."

"An arched waist, slender as a corvette built for the chase, and which strikes the merchantman with a French impetuosity."

"Well, my dear boy, why cannot I see it from your point of view?" said de Marsay. "Since I have studied women my unknown has the only maiden's bosom, the voluptuous and ardent form, the sole realization of the woman of my dreams, for me. She is the original of the delirious painting called 'Woman Caressing a Chimera,' the hottest, more infernal inspiration of antique genius; a saint posing as a prostitute for those who copy her for their frescoes and mosaics; for a crowd of bourgeois who cannot see in this cameo anything more than a charm to attach to their watch-chain, whereas it is all woman, an abyss of pleasure down which one may roll without ever finding the end; and yet this is that ideal woman whom one sometimes sees in reality in Spain, Italy, and even occasionally in France.

"Well, I have reviewed this girl with golden eyes, this woman caressing a chimera; I have seen her here, on Friday. I presumed that she would come again the next day at the same hour; I am not mistaken in this. I am well able to remember her without seeing her, to study that indolent walk of the unoccupied woman; but yet who reveals in her movements a sleeping voluptuousness. Well, when she returns, I shall see her again, I shall worship her anew, and start and shiver afresh. Then, I have observed the genuine Spanish duenna who guards her, a hyena who wears her jealousy as a robe, some female demon well paid to watch that suave creature. I am becoming anxious to know whether the duenna may not be tempted to desert that lovely one. Saturday I was here again. This time I am here, and as she attends this girl of whom I am the chimera, I ask myself if I am doing anything better than posing as the monster of the fresco."

"Here she is!" said Paul, "everybody is turning round to look at her——"

The unknown blushed and her eyes scintillated as she perceived Henri; she stopped a moment, then passed on.

"What do you think of that?" cried Paul, pleasantly.

The duenna looked fixedly and with attention at the two young men. When the unknown and Henri again met each other, the young girl brushed with her hand against the hand of the young man. Then she turned toward them smiling with passion; but the duenna forcibly drew her toward the gate of the Rue de Castiglione.

The two friends followed the young girl, admiring the magnificent sinuosity of that neck where it joined the head by a combination of vigorous lines, which was relieved by some stray little curls of hair. The girl with golden eyes had finely formed feet, small and rounded, which lent an added attraction to a dainty imagination. She was also elegantly attired and carried her dress like one used to the Court. As she walked she would at times turn around to look at Henri, and seemed to dislike the old woman, who at times seemed to be her mistress while she was her slave. She could beat her unmercifully without receiving a blow in return. All reached the gate together, the two friends behind the others. Two liveried valets occupied the footboard of a coupé in elegant taste and showing a coat-of-arms. The girl with golden eyes first got in, taking that side which would be nearest the two friends as the vehicle turned around; she placed her hand on the curtains and waved her handkerchief, unknown to the duenna, mocking at the curious onlookers but saying publicly, as she waved the handkerchief: "Follow me."

"Have you ever seen better play with a handkerchief than that?" said Henri to Paul de Manerville.

Then seeing a hack near by he went after the coupé, making a sign to the driver, saying:

"Follow that coupé, you shall have ten francs. Farewell, Paul."

The hack followed the coupé. That vehicle turned into the Rue Saint-Lazare and stopped at one of the handsomest mansions in the quarter.

De Marsay was not surprised. Every other young man would have obeyed a desire of at once taking some token of a girl who had realized so fully his ideas of the most luminous imprints of the women in Oriental poetry; but more adroit than to so compromise the future of his lucky fortune, he had the hack continue on down the Rue Saint-Lazare, and from there returned to his hôtel. The next day his head valet, named Laurent, a boy as wily as a Frontin of the old comedy, went around and about the house habited by the unknown, at about the time when the letters were distributed. So that he might have the chance of spying at his ease and roaming around the hôtel, he had, following the custom of police spies, disguised himself, buying the cast-off suit of an Auvergnat and trying to make his features resemble one. When the letter-carrier, who this morning did the service of the Rue Saint-Lazare, came by, Laurent pretended to be a commissioner who was looking for some person's name for whom he had a parcel, and he asked the letter-carrier. Mistaken by his appearance, this so picturesque a personage in the midst of Parisian civilization, told him that the hôtel in which lived the girl with golden eyes belonged to Don Hijos, Marquis de San-Réal, a Spanish grandee. Naturally, the Auvergnat had no business with the marquis.

"My parcel," said he, "is for the marquise."

"She is away from home," replied the letter-carrier. "Her letters are returned to London."

"The marquise has not a young girl who——?"

"Ah!" said the letter-carrier, interrupting the valet and looking attentively at him, "you are as much a commissioner as I am a ballet-girl."

Laurent slipped some pieces of gold into the letter-carrier's hand, with a pleasant jingle which made him smile.

"There, that's the name of your quarry," said he, taking out of his leather-bag a letter bearing the London postmark, and which was addressed: *A mademoiselle Paquita Valdès, Rue Saint-Lazare, hôtel San-Réal, Paris,* written in long angular characters which showed it was in a woman's hand.

"Could you punish a bottle of Chablis, with a chop and mushrooms, and preceded by about a dozen oysters?" said Laurent, who wished to secure the precious friendship of the letter-carrier.

"At half-past nine, when I have finished my round. Where?"

"At the corner of the Rue de la Chaussée-d'Antin and the Rue Neuve-des-Mathurins, at the Puits Sans Vin," said Laurent.

"Listen, my friend," said the functionary, as he joined Laurent, about an hour after their first meeting; "if your master is in love with that girl, he is undertaking a big job. I doubt that you will be able to see her. For ten years I have been a letter-carrier in Paris and have made a pretty careful study of doors, but I can safely say, without fear of being thought crazy by my comrades, that I do not know a door so mysterious as the one of Monsieur de San-Réal. No person can enter the hôtel without knowing the password; and you will further observe that it has been expressly selected for being in the centre of the garden, so as to prevent all communication with other houses.

"The janitor is an old Spaniard who cannot speak one word of French, but who has a disfigured face, which is as keen as Vidocq's in learning who is who. If the first guard could be passed by a lover by any mistake, by a robber, or by yourself, which is most unlikely, then in the first hallway, which is closed by a glass-door, you would encounter a major-domo trotting around like a footman, an old joker, who is still more savage and morose than the janitor.

"If one jumps the coach-yard gate, my major-domo sallies out and interrogates you under the gallery, and subjects you to as much questioning as a criminal. This is what happens to me, a plain letter-carrier. I should have to take a 'hemisphere' for a disguise," said he, smiling at his joke and cocking his eye. "When people call who have no legitimate reason, I can't say how they will be treated, for no one in the quarter has ever had speech with them; I don't know but what they issue tokens for those to whom they will speak; they make themselves unapproachable, whether it is that fear of being shot or that they have staked some great sum to insure their discretion. If your master loves Mademoiselle Paquita Valdès enough to surmount these obstacles, even then he is not sure of triumphing over Doña Concha Marialva, the duenna who accompanies her everywhere and who never quits her side. These two women present the appearance of being sewn together."

"That is what you tell me, my estimable letter-carrier," said Laurent, "after having swallowed your wine; you only confirm what I at first apprehended. On the faith of an honest man, I think you are making game of me. The fruit trees in front of the building—could not we get up them at night? but then I suppose dogs are kept from whom food has been withheld, so as to make them more wakeful and vicious. Those damned animals are quite capable of making a meal off one and spitting out the pieces. You speak of them being afraid of bullets, but it seems to me that they would stick at nothing."

"The porter at Monsieur le Baron de Nucingen's place, whose garden adjoins the San-Réal mansion, says that one might as well try to reach the sky as that," said the letter-carrier.

"Good! my master knows him," said Laurent. "Do you know," he went on, leering at the letter-carrier, "that I belong to a master who is a man of high spirit, and, if he took it into his head, he would plant a kiss on the feet of an empress, and that he will find some means of passing through this? If he had need of you, and I desired you, for he is very generous, could we count on you?"

"Bless my heart, Monsieur Laurent, my name is Moinot. Really my name is written the same as a *moineau**—M-o-i-n-o-t, Moinot."

"Just so," said Laurent.

"I live on the Rue des Trois-Frères, No. 11, on the fifth," continued Moinot. "I have a wife and four children. If you can show that there is nothing will hurt my conscience or interfere with my duty to the government, you understand, I am yours."

"You are a brave fellow," said Laurent, pressing his hand.

"Paquita Valdès is undoubtedly the mistress of the Marquis de San-Réal, the friend of King Ferdinand. He is an old Spanish corpse, eighty years old, and is capable of taking every conceivable precaution," said Henri, when his valet had informed him of the result of his researches.

"Monsieur," said Laurent, "unless you go there in a balloon I don't see how you are going to get into the mansion."

"You are a dummy. Is it then necessary to go into the hôtel to have Paquita, when Paquita is likely to come out at any moment?"

"But, monsieur, the duenna."

"She may keep her room for some days—your duenna."

"And then we have Paquita," said Laurent, rubbing his hands.

"Idiot!" answered Henri. "I will condemn you to the Concha if you have the impertinence to speak in that manner of a woman before I have possessed her. Look after my clothes, I am going out."

For some little time Henri sat plunged in happy thoughts. Being the darling of women, he was always able to obtain all that he pleased to desire of them; and this was when he thought of a woman without loving her: who then could resist this young man armed with beauty and strength of body and with intelligence and graciousness? But having such easy triumphs de Marsay had become weary of them; so, for the past two years, he had been sick of them. Now plunged into the depths of voluptuousness he found that he had gathered

---

* *Moineau* (sparrow) and *Moinot* are pronounced alike.

more gravel than pearls. Therefore he had come, as sovereigns do, to implore some chance obstacle to his victory; some enterprise which would demand the employment of all his moral power and active physical energies.

Although Paquita Valdès displayed to him the marvelous assemblage of perfections which he had never before seen except in detail, the attraction seemed almost null. A constant satiety had weakened the sentiment of love in his heart. Like old and worn-out men, he had no more extravagant caprices, his taste was ruined, his fancies satisfied; he no longer had any sweet memories in his heart.

Among young men love is the most beautiful of sentiments: it flourishes in the life of the soul, it arouses by a solar power the most delightful inspirations and the greatest thoughts; the first-fruits of all things have the most delicious flavor. Among men love becomes a passion: strength leads to its abuse. With the old it turns to a vice—impotence being the end. Henri was at the same time an old man and a young one.

He had failed to arouse an emotion of real love, the same as Lovelace with Clarissa Harlowe. Without the reflection of that unfindable magic pearl, he could not have those agitating passions which are the glory of the Parisian, whether it was that he himself had experienced some degree or other of corruption with a woman, or whether he was only stimulating his curiosity. Laurent's report made him willing to give an enormous price for the girl with golden eyes. He would take issue with his secret enemy, who seemed equally dangerous and subtle, and, to gain the victory, all the forces which Henri could produce would be necessary.

He was going to play that eternally old comedy, which is always new, and in which the characters were an old man, a young girl, and a lover: Don Hijos, Paquita, and de Marsay. If Laurent was as valuable as Figaro, the duenna seemed incorruptible. So this drama in real life was more strongly held by chance than had ever been the case by any dramatic author. But is there such a thing as chance to a man of genius?

"It seems necessary to play their game," said Henri.

"Well," said Paul de Manerville, who had just come in, "where are we? I came to breakfast with you."

"So," said Henri. "Why wouldn't it shock you if I were to make my toilette before you?"

"What a joke!"

"We do everything English just now, but at the same time

we won't become hypocrites and prudes like them," said Henri.

Laurent had brought out all his master's things, different suits and pretty nicknacks, which caused Paul to say:

"But you are not going out for two hours yet?"

"No," replied Henri, "not for two hours and a half."

"Well, then, between ourselves I wish you would tell me and explain to me why a superior man such as yourself, for you are a superior man, affects to overwork a foppery which is not natural to him. Why spend two hours and a half in currying yourself when a quarter of an hour is enough in which to take a bath, and in a brace of shakes you can comb your hair and dress yourself? That's my style."

"It is the fault of my great love, my precious ninny, for I confide all my best thoughts to you," said the young man, who just then was brushing his feet with a soft brush and cleansing them with English soap.

"But I have acknowledged my most sincere attachment to you," replied Paul de Manerville, "and now I find that you love another more than me."

"You must have duly observed, if you are capable of noting a moral fact, that woman likes a fop," answered de Marsay, without replying in any way to Paul's declaration.

"Do you know why it is that women love dandies? My friend, fops are the only men who properly care for themselves the same as they do. Now, by caring for one's self don't we show that we care for others? The man who does this is precisely the man whom women pet. Love is essentially an extortioner. I cannot say that this excess of propriety of theirs should make us inordinately vain. Find one who cares passionately for a 'neglected' person; don't you find a remarkable man? So this fact is the reason for it: we obey it and set it down to the account of women's envy, a most foolish idea which runs through everybody's head. On the contrary, I have seen remarkably strong men flung aside owing to the cause of their carelessness of themselves. A dude who is occupied in personal attention is taken up with a trifle, with little things. And what then is woman? a little thing, a bundle of trifles. With two words spoken in the air, can't she make you pass a few bad hours? She is sure that the fop is occupied as she is, therefore she does not think of the great things. She is not always in négligé for fame, ambition, politics, art—those great women of the public which, to her, are her rivals.

"Then the dude has the courage to cover himself with ridicule to please a woman, and her heart is full of recompenses for the man who is made ridiculous for love of her. Indeed, a fop cannot help being a fop if he has a reason for being one. These are they to whom women give a brevet rank. The dude is the colonel of love, he has good luck, he has his regiment of women, of whom he is the commander. My dear boy, in Paris all is known, and a man cannot be a fop *gratis.* You who have not got a woman, and who are perhaps the better for not having one, have you ever tried your luck as a dude? You would make yourself so ridiculous that it would be your death. You become a judge on two feet, and you are a condemned man. You might as well be executed or isolated, which is the same thing.

"To signify *silliness,* as Monsieur de la Fayette signifies *America;* Monsieur de Tallyrand, *diplomacy;* Désangiers, *singing;* Monsieur de Ségur, *romance.* If they go among those people they think more of their characteristics than themselves. Here is how we sum things up in France—every sovereignty is unjust. Monsieur de Talleyrand may be a great financier, Monsieur de la Fayette a tyrant, and Désangiers an administrator. You might have forty women next year, but not one of them would publicly acknowledge it. So therefore your simplicity, my friend Paul, is a sign of unquestioned power of conquest over the female folk.

"A man who loves a large number of women passes for possessing very superior qualities, and then this is what he will become—unfortunate. But do you think that they care nothing whether or not they have the right of coming to your salon, as they look at all the world from over their high cravats, or squinting through their eyeglasses, and can scorn the most superior man if he wears a vest which is a back number? (Laurent, you make me sick!) After breakfast, Paul, we will take in the Tuileries to see the adorable girl with golden eyes."

When, after having made an excellent repast, the two young men had surveyed the Terrasse des Feuillants and the Broad Walk of the Tuileries, they were unable to catch sight of the sublime Paquita Valdès, on account of finding themselves among fifty of the most fashionable young men in Paris —all musk, high collars, boots, spurs, whips, marching, laughing, and all given to the devil.

"By the white mass!" said Henri; "I have struck the best idea in the world. This girl receives letters from London; we might bribe or intoxicate the letter-carrier, unclose the letter, naturally to read it, then slip in a sweet little note, and reseal it. The old tyrant, *crudel tiranno,* must without a doubt know the person who writes these letters from London, and he would not have the least misgivings."

Next day de Marsay again promenaded in the sun on the Terrasse des Feuillants, and there he saw Paquita Valdès; she was more already than his passion had embellished her. He gazed with seriousness in those eyes whose flashes seemed to have the nature of the rays of the sun, and whose ardor summed up a perfect body where all was voluptuousness. De Marsay was scorched as he gazed on the dress of that seductive maiden when he met her in their promenade, but his efforts at communication were all in vain.

At the time when he again repassed Paquita and her duenna, he placed himself so that he would be on the side of the girl with golden eyes when she turned around; Paquita, no less impatient, advanced toward him with eagerness, and he felt a pressure of the hand by hers which was at the same time so quickly done and with such passionate significance that he thought he had received an electric shock. For a moment all the emotions of youth surged in his heart. When the two lovers looked at each other, Paquita seemed abashed; she lowered her eyes before Henri's gaze, but his cool survey of her feet and figure had that of those whom women, before the Revolution, called "their conqueror."

"I am resolved to have that girl for my mistress," said Henri to himself.

As he followed her to the end of the terrace, by the side of the Place Louis XV., he perceived the old Marquis de San-Réal, who was walking, supported on the arm of his valet, with all the care of a gouty and dyspeptic man. Doña Concha, who mistrusted Henri, placed Paquita between herself and the old man.

"Oh! that's it," said de Marsay, casting a look of disdain on the duenna; "if she doesn't look out she'll get a small dose of opium or some other narcotic. We know our mythology and the story of Argus."

Before getting into her carriage the girl with golden eyes exchanged a glance with her lover, a look which was anything but doubtful and which ravished Henri; but the duenna caught it and spoke sharply to Paquita, who threw herself back in the coupé with an air of desperation. For some days Paquita did not again visit the Tuileries.

Laurent, who by order of his master had been on the lookout around the San-Réal mansion, was informed by the neighbors that neither the two women nor the old marquis had gone out since the day when the duenna had surprised the glance of recognition between Henri and the young girl under her charge. The so weak tie which united the two lovers was thus already broken.

Some days after, without any person having the least idea of his doings, de Marsay had decided on his course; he had made a seal and provided some sealing-wax, an exact counterpart of the impression and wax which sealed the letters sent from London to Mlle. Valdès; also similar paper to that used by her correspondent; then he provided all the requisite articles and the stamps necessary to give the appearance of the English and French postmarks. He had written the following epistle, to which he gave every appearance of a letter sent from London:

Dearest Paquita, I cannot by words attempt to paint with what passion you have inspired me. If, to my great happiness, you partake the like sentiment, know that I have found this means of corresponding with you. My name is Adolphe de Gouges, and I reside on the Rue de l'Université, No. 54. If you are too closely watched to be able to write, or if you have neither paper nor pens, I shall know by your silence. Therefore if to-morrow, between eight o'clock in the morning and ten at night, you have not thrown a letter in reply over the wall of your garden into that of the Baron de Nucingen, where I shall remain the whole day, a man who is entirely devoted to my interests will secretly sling two phials over the wall, at the end of a cord, at ten o'clock the following morning. Manage to go out for your walk about that time. One of the phials will contain opium for sending your Argus off to sleep, six drops will be enough to give her; the other contains ink. The ink phial is of cut glass and the other is smooth. Both are thin and flat enough to be concealed in your corset. All that I have already done to enable me to correspond with you will prove to you whether I was wrong in saying that I love you. If you doubt this I vow to you that, to be given an interview of one hour with you, I would give my life for the privilege.

"They think this sort of thing is fine, these poor creatures," said de Marsay; "and they are right. What should we think of a woman who would not allow herself to be seduced by a love-letter accompanied by circumstances so convincing?"

Next day this letter was delivered by Moinot, the letter-carrier, about eight o'clock in the morning, to the janitor of the San-Réal mansion.

To be nearer the field of battle de Marsay had taken breakfast with Paul, who lived in the Rue de la Pépinière. At two o'clock, at the moment when the two friends were bursting with laughter over the discomfiture of a young man who had attempted to lead the train of fashion without having the fortune necessary to assist him, and who had just reached the end of his tether, Henri's coachman came in to seek his master at Paul's house, and to introduce to him a mysterious personage, who wished to speak to him and him alone.

This person was a mulatto, who would undoubtedly have inspired Talma for the play of Othello, if he had but met him. Never did an African show such grandeur of vengeance or such a quickness of perception, combined with an instant execution of his thoughts; he had the strength of the Moor and the indiscretion of a child. His dark eyes were fixed like those of a bird of prey and were, like those of a vulture, set in a bluish membrane devoid of eyelashes. His small, low forehead had something menacing about it. It was evident that this man was the slave of one single thought. His nervous arms seemed not to belong to him. He was accompanied by another man, one at whom all imaginations shiver and shake like Greenland, and like what is described in New England as an "unlucky man," * or something after this phrase.

This word will enable all the world to divine his appearance after the particular ideas prevailing in each country. But who can figure his pallid face, wrinkled, red at the extremities, and his long beard? Who can see his necktie like a yellow string, his greasy shirt-collar, his used-up hat, his greenish greatcoat, his piteous trousers, his vest awry, his imitation gold pin, his broken shoes, the strings of which had dabbled in the mud? Who can comprehend the immensity of his past and present poverty? Who? The Parisian alone. The man of ill-luck in Paris is the most thoroughly unlucky man in the whole world, for he still possesses the delight of knowing how unlucky he has been. The mulatto seemed to be an executioner of Louis XI., holding up a man whom he had hung.

"For which of our sins is it that we must meet these two scallawags?" said Henri.

* C'était un homme malheureux.

"By the gods! that fellow there gives me the shivers," replied Paul.

"Who are you, you that has the manner of being the better Christian of the two?" said Henri, turning to the unlucky man.

The mulatto fixed his gaze on the two young men, like a man who heard nothing, and yet who tried nevertheless to guess something of what was said by gestures and the movements of the lips.

"I am a public writer and interpreter. I live at the Palais de Justice, and my name is Poincet."

"Good. And who is that?" said Henri, pointing to the mulatto.

"I don't know; he speaks nothing but a Spanish jargon; I brought him here that he might speak to you."

The mulatto drew from his pocket the letter that Henri had written Mlle. Paquita—he, Henri!—who at once threw it on the fire.

"Well, there goes the commencement of my scheme," said he to himself. "Paul, leave us for a few moments."

"I translated that letter for him," said the interpreter, when they were alone. "When I had done this, he went, I don't know where. Then he returned and asked me to bring him here, promising me two louis if I would do so."

"What does he say to me, is it Chinese?" asked Henri.

"I could not understand him if he spoke *Chinese*," said the interpreter. "He says, monsieur," continued he after listening to the unknown, "that he would like to meet you to-morrow night at half-past ten, on the Boulevard Montmartre, near the café. You will there see a carriage into which you must get, saying to the one who opens the door the one word, *cortejo*; a Spanish word which is equivalent to saying 'lover,'" added Poincet, casting a look of congratulation on Henri.

"Well!"

The mulatto was about giving Poincet the two louis, but de Marsay would not allow him to reward the interpreter; while he himself was paying him, the mulatto spoke again.

"What does he say?"

"He cautions me," replied the unlucky man, "that if I commit the least indiscretion he will strangle me. He is a pretty gentleman, is very powerful, and has the air of being capable of doing as he says."

"I am sure of it," replied Henri, "by the way in which he spoke."

"He added," continued the interpreter, "that the person

who conducts you and yourself must exercise the greatest prudence in all your actions, both for your own and her sake; for daggers are raised above your heads which can readily be plunged into your hearts without any human power being able to prevent."

"He said that, eh? All the better; this makes it more amusing. You may come in again, Paul," he cried to his friend.

The mulatto, who had not once removed his eyes from Paquita Valdès' lover, gazed at him with a magnetic look, until he followed the interpreter from the room.

"Well, I am in for a most romantic adventure," said Henri, when Paul returned. "On the strength of having participated in a number of others, I finish by meeting in Paris with an intrigue accompanied by dangerous surroundings and perils. Ah, the deuce, how brave danger renders a woman! Restrain a woman, constrain her will, and is she not given the right and courage to in a moment leap over all barriers placed around her for years and to issue forth? Gentle creature, be it so, jump. To perish? poor girl. Of daggers? all the imagining of women. They experience all the reward which their little pleasantry is worth. Now be all my thoughts of thee, Paquita; to only think of thee, my girl! The devil take me! all I know is that she is a handsome girl; this masterpiece of nature is for me; the adventure is lost in its cream."

Notwithstanding these light words, the young man had repaired to Henri's home, who, to await the morrow without suffering, had recourse to extravagant pleasures; he played, dined, and supped with his friend; he drank like a coachman, ate like a German, and won ten or twelve thousand francs at the gaming-table. He went to the Rocher de Cancale at two o'clock in the morning, slept like a child, rising the next day as fresh as a rose, dressed himself to go to the Tuileries, and proposed a horseback ride after having seen Paquita; he gained thereby an appetite for dinner, as well as passing the time.

At the hour mentioned, Henri was on the boulevard; he saw the carriage, gave the password to a man who appeared to be the mulatto. Hearing the word, the man opened the door and quickly climbed on the box-seat. Henri was rapidly carried into Paris, but his thoughts left him but little faculty of noticing the streets through which he passed; he did not even know where he was when the carriage stopped.

The mulatto took him into a house in which the stairs were seen to be near the carriage-gate. This stairway was dark; so also was the place where Henri was obliged to wait during the time that the mulatto took in opening the door of a humid apartment, nauseous and without any light, and whose rooms were barely distinguishable by the candle which his guide found in the vestibule; it appeared empty to him, and the movables had a bad odor, like those have whose occupants are traveling. He recognized a similar sensation to the one he experienced when reading one of Anne Radcliffe's romances, where the heroes traverse the cold, dark halls of some fearful and deserted habitation.

At length the mulatto opened the door of a salon. In it there was some old furniture and older fashioned curtains, though the room was ornamented to resemble the salon of a house of ill-fame. There were the same pretensions to elegance and the same collection of things in bad taste, the same dust and dirt. On a couch, covered with red, Utrecht velvet, in the corner of the fireplace which smoked and the fire of which was buried in ashes, sat an old, badly clothed woman, her head-dress being one of those turbans which are known to have been invented by Englishwomen when they have arrived at a certain age, and who should become an infinite success in China, where the idea of beauty is a monstrosity. The salon, the old woman, the cold hearth, all these had chilled his love, if Paquita had not been here, for any cause, in a voluptuous dressing-gown, looping and throwing her glances of gold and flame, liberating and showing her rounded foot, showing freedom in her luminous movements.

This first interview was like that of all first meetings given to all passionate folk, who quickly overleap every distance to attain what they ardently desire, without the least restraint. It was impossible that he should not meet with the self-same discordant surroundings in this position, troublesome at the moment when her soul becomes the same as yours. So desire gives boldness to the man and he is disposed to care for nothing; under pain of not being a woman, his mistress will go to some extremes to see whether he really loves her; she is afraid of finding the time arrive too quickly when she will be face to face with the necessity of giving that, which for the majority of women is equivalent to a fall down a precipice, and the depths of which are to her unknown. The involuntary frigidity of that woman contrasts with her passion acknowledged and of course reacted upon by the lover with whom she is smitten. These ideas, which often float like vapors about the soul, are termed therefore naught but a passing malady.

In that sweet journey that two beings take in traveling through the beautiful land of love, that time is like a heath to cross, a heath without furze, at one time humid, at another warm, filled with ardent sands, interspersed with marshes, and which have pleasant coppices clad in roses under which love and its accompanying delights can be enjoyed on the rich carpet of fine verdure.

Very often the spiritual man finds himself saluted with a coarse jest by some brute who employs this as an answer to everything; his mind is benumbed under the glacial pressure of his desire. To him it is impossible that there can be two equally beautiful spirits—the spiritual and the animal passion; as we are now speaking of the most simple commonplace topics, such as a chance word, the thrill of a glance, the flash of a touch, a happy transition of soul which draws out the bloom of sentiment unconfined, in which they may roll without a downfall. This state of mind is always right in the violence of its feelings. Two beings who love but feebly can experience nothing like unto this. The effect of such a crisis can only be compared to that heat which is produced by a clear sky. Nature seems at first sight to be covered with a veil of gauze, the blue of the firmament appears black, an excess of light resembles shadow.

To Henri and the fair Spaniard it came with equal violence; and that static law by virtue of which two equal forces each annuls the other when they meet is precisely the same in the realm of morals. Then the embarrassment of this moment was strangely augmented by the presence of the old mummy. Everything either alarms or delights love, in everything there is a sense which presages happiness or ill-fortune. This decrepit woman was there like a poor conclusion, and figured as the horrid train of snakes by which Greek genius symbolized the followers of its chimeras and sirens; so seductive, so deceiving by their bodies, as all passions are at their inception. Although Henri was not strong-minded, a word of constant raillery, but a man of extraordinary power, a man grand beyond belief, this combination of surroundings had struck him down. The strongest men are naturally the most impressionable ones, consequently the most superstitious, so they always speak of superstition as being their judgment at first sight; whereby they do, without a doubt, perceive the result of causes hidden from other eyes, but plainly discernible to theirs.

The Spanish woman profited by this moment of stupor to fall into an infinite ecstasy of adoration which seizes the heart of a woman when she really loves and finds herself in the presence of an idol for whom she had vainly hoped. Her eyes were full of joy and happiness, which escaped in brilliant flashes. She was under the charm, fearlessly intoxicated with a felicity of which she had long dreamed. She was now able to see Henri's marvelous beauty, so that all the phantasmagoria of rags, old age, worn-out red hangings, of old green mats before the arm-chairs, the red square of carpet so badly worn, and all this infirm luxury and suffering speedily disappeared. The salon was illuminated; he no longer saw as through a floating mist that terrible harpy, fixed and mute on her red couch, whose yellow eyes betrayed the servile sentiments which had unhappily inspired him, or was she longer the cause of a vice under which he had been ensnared or she had fallen like a tyrant who has suddenly come under the flagellations of his despotism. Her eyes shone cold like those of a tiger in a cage which knows its powerlessness and finds itself compelled to swallow its envy of destruction.

"Who is that woman?" asked Henri of Paquita.

Paquita made no reply to this question. She made a sign that she did not understand French, and asked Henri if he spoke English. De Marsay then repeated the question in English.

"That is the only woman whom I dare trust, although she has already sold me," said Paquita, tranquilly. "My dear Adolphe, this is my mother, a slave who was bought in Georgia* for her rare beauty, but who now has but little to do with her owner. She speaks only her mother-tongue."

The attitude of the old woman and the envy she showed of the movements of her daughter and Henri, as she guessed what passed between them, was a sudden revelation to the young man, it made it easy of explanation.

"Paquita," said he, "are you never at liberty?"

"Never," she replied, with a wearied air. "Every day is like every other to us."

She dropped her eyes, looked at his hand, then took his right hand and placed it on the fingers of her left hand,

* Asia Minor.

pointing to her prettier ones, which were the most beautiful
that Henri had ever seen.

"One, two, three——"

She counted up to a dozen.

"Yes," said she, "we have twelve days."

"And after those?"

"After," said she, stopping, absorbed, like a feeble woman
before the executioner's axe, killed in advance by a dread
which had despoiled her of that magnificent energy with
which, as it seemed to him, nature had furnished her. But to
him it had not departed; it seemed rather to augment her
voluptuousness and transmute the grossest pleasures into endless poems.

"After!" she repeated.

Her eyes became fixed; she seemed to be contemplating
some distant, menacing object.

"I don't know," said she.

"This girl is a fool," said Henri to himself, falling into
strange reflections.

Paquita seemed to be occupied with something that had
nothing to do with him, like a fashionable woman who is
equally driven by her remorse and her passion. It might be
that she had another love in her heart which she had for the
nonce forgotten, but which had again taken its turn. In a
moment Henri was assailed by a thousand contradictory
thoughts. To him this girl had become a mystery; but as he
contemplated her with the knowing attention of an old
rounder, his passionate desires were aflame once more, like
that King of the East who demanded that a new pleasure be
invented for him, with that dreadful thirst with which all
great souls are seized.

Henri found in Paquita the richest organization that ever
Nature had delighted in making for love. The play to be
expected from that machine, the soul placed to one side, had
frightened every other man but de Marsay; but he was fasci-
nated by this rich harvest of promised delights; by that constant variety of happiness, the dream of every man, and which
every woman loves to place before her as her ambition. He
was excited by the infinite love shown so palpably, and was
transported to the most excessive of creature delights. He
most distinctly saw all this in the woman before him, more so
than when he had first seen her, for she complacently allowed
herself to be gazed at, happy in being admired. De Marsay's
admiration of her had become a secret torment, and she re-

vealed it in its entirety, throwing him a glance which was altogether Spanish, and as though she had always been used to receiving the like homage.

"If you do not become mine, and mine alone, I shall kill you," he exclaimed.

As she heard this Paquita veiled her face in her hands and naïvely cried:

"Holy Virgin! when I am thrust myself."

She arose, ran and threw herself on the red lounge, plunging her head in the rags covering her mother's bosom, and burst into tears. The old woman received her daughter without stirring out of her immobility, and not making a sign. The mother possessed to a high degree that gravity of savage folk, that impassiveness of a statue which frustrates all curiosity. Did she, or did she not, love her daughter? could not be answered. Under a mask which concealed every human feeling, good and bad alike, naught could be made of this creature. Her glance fell lightly on her daughter's beautiful hair, which was partly covered under a mantilla, and then to Henri's face, which she observed with an inexplicable curiosity. She seemed to be asking herself by what witchcraft had he come to be there; by what caprice of Nature had he been made so seductive.

"These women are mocking me!" said Henri.

At this moment Paquita raised her head, threw on him one of those glances which burn into the soul. She appeared so lovely that he swore to himself that he would possess this treasure of loveliness.

"Dear Paquita, come to me."

"Do you want to kill me?" said she, timorous, palpitating, uneasy, but drawn toward him by an inexplicable power.

"Kill you, I!" said he, smiling.

Paquita uttered a startled cry, said one word to her mother, who authoritatively took Henri's hand, then that of her daughter, looking at both of them for a long time, then tossed her head in a manner that was horribly significant.

"Come to me this evening, this moment; be mine, do not leave me; I am willing. Paquita! don't you love me? Come then!"

In a moment he said a thousand insensate words, with the rapidity of a torrent dashing down and between the rocks, repeating the same again and again in a thousand different forms.

"It is the same voice," said Paquita, with sadness; but de Marsay heard her not; "the same ardor," added she.

"Well, yes," said she, with an abandon of passion which it is impossible to express. "Yes, but not to-night. This evening, Adolphe, I gave but little opium to la Concha; should she revive before my return, I am lost. At this very moment the whole house believes that I am asleep in my own chamber. In two days go to the same place, speak the same word to the same man. That man is my foster father; Cristemio worships me and would die for me in awful torment without disclosing one word against me. Farewell!" said she, seizing Henri by the neck and entwining herself around him like a serpent.

She squeezed him from all sides at once, she placed his head on her bosom and held up her lips to his, and took a kiss that gave both of them such a dizziness that de Marsay thought that the earth had opened, and that made Paquita cry out:

"Go on!" in a voice which told plainly enough how little she was her own mistress. But still she guarded herself, although she cried out all the more: "Come on," as she led him to the stairs.

There the mulatto, whose white eyes brightened at the sight of Paquita, took the light from the hand of his idol and showed Henri to the street. He left the light under the archway of the door, opened the gate, joined Henri in the carriage, and drove him to the Boulevard des Italiens with marvelous rapidity. The horses seemed imbued with the devil.

The scene was like a dream to de Marsay, but yet one of those visions that, after vanishing away, leave in the soul a feeling of supernatural voluptuousness, after which a man runs during the rest of his life. One single kiss had sufficed. No meeting had ever been passed in a more decent manner, or more chaste or colder perhaps, in that place, horrible by what regularly took place therein, before a more hideous divinity; for that mother stayed in Henri's mind like some hellish thing, squat, cadaverous, vicious, of such savage ferocity, that all the fantasies of painters and poets have failed as yet to divine it. As a matter of fact, never had an assignation excited his senses equal to this one, neither had there ever been revealed to him an equal ardor of voluptuousness, nor had love ever gushed out from the centre of his being and diffused itself like an atmosphere around a man, like unto this. There was something sombre, mysterious, sweet, and tender; there

was something at once of constraint and expansion, a
blending of the horrible and the celestial, of paradise and hell,
which had the effect of intoxication upon de Marsay. It over-
powered him, yet he was great enough, nevertheless, to have
the power of resisting this drunkenness of delights.

For the full understanding of his conduct at the denoument
of this story, it becomes necessary to explain how his mind
was so broad at an age when young men's ordinarily shrink
up when they mix with women or are too much taken with
them. He was great by a combination of secret circumstances
which had invested him with an enormous power unknown to
others. This young man held in his hand a sceptre more puis-
sant than that wielded by any modern king, all of whom are
curbed more by the laws than their wills.

De Marsay exerted the autocratic power of an Oriental
despot.

But this power, so stupidly exercised in Asia by brutish
men, was coupled with an European intelligence, by the
French spirit, the most vital, the finest steel of all intelligent
instruments. Henri could do what he would to the advantage
of his pleasures and vanities. This invisible action on society
was the investiture of a real but secret majesty, which had no
force nor ability to turn against himself. It was his opinion
that Louis XIV. did not possess a power equal to his, but that
the most arrogant of Caliphs, of Pharaohs, of Xerxes, who
believed their line divine, was the same as his, when they
imitated God by veiling themselves before their subjects, under the pretense that their glances were death. So without
having any remorse at being at once the judge and the client,
de Marsay coolly condemned the man or woman to death
who had seriously offended him; although very often rashly
pronounced, the verdict was irrevocable.

A mistake was a misfortune, and seemed to them something like the thunderbolt which strikes some happy Parisian
in a coach, instead of crushing the old coachman who was
driving him to an assignation. So the titter and profound
pleasantry which distinguished the conversation of this young
man was generally the cause of dread to her; people did not
experience any envy when they struck against him. Women
have a prodigious liking for those men whom they call pashas
among themselves; who seem to be companions of lions and
executioners, and who walk appareled in terror. It results
among these men in a security of action, a certainty of power,

a pride of looks, a leonine spirit, which to women realizes the type of strength of which they all dream. Such was de Marsay.

Just now he was happy in the thought of his future. He became young and willowy; he had no vision of love as he went to bed. He there dreamed of the girl with golden eyes, who seemed to return to the passionate scene in which the young people had taken part. It was a dream of monstrosities, of unseizable phantasies, full of light which revealed invisible worlds, but always in an incomplete state, for a veil interposed which changed the optical conditions.

The next day, and the one following, Henri disappeared without letting any one know whither he had gone. His power did not belong to him under certain conditions, and, luckily for him, during these two days he was a simple soldier at the service of the demon whom he had taken into his talismanic existence. But, at the hour and on the evening mentioned, he awaited the carriage on the boulevard, which was not long in coming. The mulatto approached Henri to say to him, in a sentence of French he had learned by heart:

"If you would go with me, I am told by her to ask whether you will consent that I bandage your eyes?"

Cristemio held out a silk handkerchief.

"No!" said Henri, whose mind suddenly and powerfully revolted.

He made as though he would enter, but the mulatto gave a signal and the carriage started off.

"Yes!" cried de Marsay, furious at the loss of the happiness he had promised himself. Otherwise, he saw the impossibility of capitulating to a slave whose obedience was as blind as that of an executioner. Then was his anger with such an instrument becoming him?

The mulatto whistled, the carriage returned. Henri hastily sprang in. Already some curious simpletons had gathered on the boulevard. Henri was strong, he would have a game with the mulatto.

Presently the carriage started off at a round trot, then he seized him by the hands, intending by holding them to render him powerless; by thus checking his keeper, he could exercise his faculties in order to learn whither he went. Useless attempt. The eyes of the mulatto sparkled in the darkness. He repressed the cries of rage which expired in his throat, released himself by throwing off de Marsay with a hand of iron; he confined him, so to speak, at the bottom of the carriage;

then with his free hand he drew a triangular poniard, and whistled. The driver hearing the whistle at once stopped.

Henri was unarmed, he was compelled to submit; he held his head for the handkerchief. This gesture of submission appeased Cristemio, who placed the bandage over his eyes with a respect and care which bore witness to a kind of veneration for the person of the man loved by his idol. But, before taking this precaution, he had defiantly placed the poniard in the sheath at his side and buttoned himself up to the chin.

"He would have killed me, this Chinaman," said de Marsay.

The carriage again rolled rapidly along. There remained one resource to a young man who knew Paris as well as Henri did. To know whither he went it was sufficient for him to gather, by counting the number of gutters he crossed, what were passed on the boulevards and along which the carriage continued going to the right. He could thus recognize by what lateral street the carriage diverged, whether toward the Seine or toward the heights of Montmartre, and to guess the name of the street where his guide should finally stop.

But the violent emotion caused by his struggle, his rage at having his dignity compromised, his ideas of revenge to which he gave himself up, the suppositions suggested to him by the minute care taken in conducting him to this mysterious girl, all these obstacles had blunted the necessary concentration of his attention, intelligence, and the perfect perspicacity of his memory.

The journey lasted for half an hour. When the carriage stopped, it was no longer on the paved streets. The mulatto and driver took Henri by "leg and wing," lifted him, and carried him in a sort of litter fashion across a garden in which he smelt flowers and the peculiar scent of trees and grass. The silence that reigned was so profound that he was able to distinguish the noise made by some drops of water falling from the humid leaves.

The two men mounted some steps with him, here they set him down, guiding him by the hand, finally leaving him in a room the atmosphere of which was perfumed and where, under his feet, he felt a thick carpet. The hand of a woman pushed him on to a divan and removed the bandage from his eyes. Henri saw Paquita before him, but it was Paquita in her glory of female voluptuousness.

That part of the boudoir in which Henri found himself was

formed in a soft, graceful circular form, the part opposite being of a perfectly square shape, in the middle of which glittered a chimney mantel of white marble and gold. It was entered by a lateral door hidden by a curtain of rich tapestry, and was opposite a window. The veritable ornamented Turkish divan was of a horseshoe shape; that is to say, it was a low mattress, but was as large as a bed, on a divan with fifty turned feet, upholstered in white càshmere, relieved by knots of deep scarlet and black silk of lozenge shape. The back of this immense bed was elevated many inches at the upper part by the numerous cushions which enriched it, and could be arranged agreeable to the taste. This boudoir was hung with a soft red stuff, on which fluted India lawn was deftly draped into Corinthian columns, by alternate pipings of crosses and circles, being finished at top and bottom by a band of red poppy colored stuff on which a number of black arabesques were designed.

Under the lawn the scarlet became rose color, an amorous color, which matched the curtains over the window, which were of India lawn looped over rose taffeta and ornamented with scarlet and black fringes. Six silver-gilt brackets supported each two wax-candles, being attached to the tapestry at equal distances apart, for lighting the divan. The ceiling, from the centre of which hung a lustre of dull silver gilt, sparkled with whiteness, and the cornice was golden. The carpet resembled an Oriental shawl covered with designs full of the poetry of Persia, and upon which the hands of its slaves had worked.

The furniture was draped in white cashmere prettily set off with scarlet and black. The clock and candelabra were of white marble and gold. The only table there had a cashmere cover. Some elegant jardinières contained every species of roses, or red and white flowers. Indeed, the least detail seemed to have been carefully chosen with an eye to love. Never had riches coquettishly shown such a hidden elegance, expressing gracefulness and inspiring voluptuousness. Here everything would have warmed up the coldest heart. The chasteness of the ceiling, the color of which changed as the look followed it, being first all white and then all rose color, and matched with the effect of the lights which were mellowed under the diaphanous shades of lawn, producing a misty appearance in the room.

As I have never known a being who is not fond of white, so love is pleased with red, and gold flatters the passions, it has the power of realizing their fancies. So all that this man had that was vague and mysterious in himself, all his affinities that were inexplicable, he here found caressing him by their involuntary sympathies. He had here in this perfect harmony a concert of colors to which his soul responded in his voluptuous ideas, indecisive and floating.

It was in the midst of this vaporous air charged with exquisite perfumes that Paquita, dressed in a white dressing-gown, her feet bare, orange flowers in her black tresses, appeared to Henri, kneeling before him, like the worshiper when the god of the temple has deigned to visit it. Therefore de Marsay, habituated as he was to seeing Parisian luxury, was surprised at the aspect of this shell, which might have done for Venus' grotto.

Whether it was in consequence of the contrast between the darkness from which he had emerged into the light which bathed his soul, whether it was a rapid comparison made between this scene and that of his former interview, it proved one of those delicate sensations which gave birth to true poetry. Perceiving, in the centre of this little habitation, hatched by the wand of a fairy, the masterpiece of creation, this girl, whose warm-colored tint and soft skin, lightly golden by the reflection of the crimson and by the effusion of I know not what effluxion of love, which scintillated as if she reflected the rays of light and of the colors, his rage, his desire for vengeance, his wounded pride, all fell. Like an eagle which has found its prey, he pressed a live body; he seated her on his knees, and felt with an unspeakable intoxication the voluptuous pressure of this girl, whose largely developed beauties sweetly enfolded her.

"Come, Paquita!" said he, in a low voice.

"Speak up, speak without fear," said she to him. "This retreat has been built for love. No sound can escape, all has been carefully done here to prevent the loss of any accents of the best-beloved voice. Whatever outcry may be made in this citadel they can never hear it outside this *enceinte*. Here one could slay some one, their petitions and vain entreaties would be the same as if made in the middle of a desert."

"Who then has so well understood jealousy and its needs?" he asked.

"Never question me in reference to this," she replied, untying, with an unbelievably gentle touch, the cravat of the young man, that she might the better see his neck.

"Yes, there is the neck that I shall love forever," said she. "Would you do me a pleasure?"

This question, the accent of which made it almost lascivious, brought de Marsay out of a reverie into which he had been plunged, the despotic response by which Paquita had interdicted all research on the unknown person who, like a shadow, had arranged all these advantages for them.

"And if I would know who reigned here?"

Paquita looked at him and shivered.

"This has not been done for me," said he, rising and disengaging himself of the girl, whose head fell back. "Where I am concerned I would be alone."

"He will strike me, strike me!" cried the poor slave, a prey to terror.

"For what do you take me? Can you reply?"

Paquita slowly rose, with tears in her eyes, went to one or two ebony caskets, and from one took a dagger and offered it to Henri, with a gesture of submission which would have moved a tiger.

"Give me a fête such as is given by men when they love," said she, "and, then, while I sleep, kill me, for I cannot answer you. Listen! I am fastened like a poor animal to its picket; I am astonished at having been able to throw a bridge over the gulf which had separated us. Intoxicate me, then kill me.

"Ah! no, no," said she, wringing her hands, "do not kill me, I love life. Life is very beautiful to me. If I am a slave, I am also a queen. I am abashed by your words. You say that I must not love you; prove me; profit by my temporary empire to say: 'Take me as a little taste, the passing perfume of a flower in the garden of a king.' Then, after having unfolded the subtle eloquence of a woman and the wings of pleasure, after having slaked my thirst, I can then throw myself into a pit where no person can find me, and which has been dug to satisfy a vengeance without any dread of that of justice; a pit full of quicklime will consume one without leaving a trace of ever having been. You will always rest in my heart, you will always be mine."

Henri gazed at this girl without a tremor, and her look was without fear and full of joy.

"No, I am not chained. You have not fallen here into a trap, but into the heart of a woman who adores you, and it is myself who throws her into that well."

"All this seems awfully funny to me," said de Marsay,

examining himself. "But you appear to be a good girl, though of a fantastical nature; you are, on the faith of an honest man, a living charade the word of which seems particularly difficult to discover."

Paquita understood nothing of what was said by the young man; she looked at him sweetly, and with wide staring eyes not altogether unlike an animal; all she was filled with was voluptuousness.

"Now, my love," said she, returning to her first idea, "will you do me a pleasure?"

"I will do all that you wish me, and also what you may not wish me to do," replied the smiling de Marsay, who found himself at his ease, now that he had taken the resolution to leave all to the course of his good luck without looking behind him or into the future. Then, perhaps, counting on his power and on his knowledge of men and his good luck for dominating for some hours, more or less, this girl, and learning all her secrets.

"Well, then," said she to him, "leave it to me to arrange how—to my taste."

"Yes, dish yourself up to me in your own style," said Henri.

Paquita then joyously took from a cabinet a robe of scarlet velvet in which she clothed de Marsay, using for herself as head-dress a lace cap and a rich shawl *entortilla*. Giving herself up to these frivolities, done with the innocence of a child, oho burst into a convulsive laugh, which made her resemble a bird flapping its wings; but she could not see what was beyond.

It were impossible to paint the unheard-of delights which inspired these two beautiful creatures placed by heaven at that moment in a state of joyousness; it is perhaps necessary to translate metaphysically the almost fantastic and altogether extraordinary impressions of the young man.

The people who occupy the social scale in which de Marsay moved, and who live as he lived, well understand that the best thing they know is the innocence of a young girl. But, a strange thing, if the girl with the golden eyes was a virgin, she most certainly was not pure. The fantastical combination of the mysterious and real, of light and shadow, of the horrid and the beautiful, of pleasure and danger, of paradise and hell, with which he had already met in the course of this adventure, was continually shown in her play with de Marsay. All this voluptuousness, the most refined that he had ever known, showed to Henri all that poetry of the senses that is called love; but this was surpassed by the treasures unfolded by that girl, whose yellow eyes belied no promise that they had made. It was an Oriental poem, the radiant sun that shines out in the bounding strophes of Saadi and Hafiz; only that neither Saadi's rhythm nor that of Pindar could in any sense depict the ecstatic plenitude of confusion nor the stupor which had seized this *delicious* girl when he discontinued the error of using his hand of iron and allowed her to breathe.

"Death!" said she. "I am dead. Adolphe, carry me away to the end of the earth, to an island where no one can find me. Let us fly and leave no trace behind us. We shall be followed even to hell itself. My God, it is day—save yourself. I shall always revere you. Yes, to-morrow I will receive you; the cost of this so great happiness is the death of all those who look after my safety. We meet to-morrow."

She lay in his arms as in a stirrup, and he there saw all the torture of death. Then she pushed a button, which was responded to by the sound of a bell, begging de Marsay to allow her to bandage his eyes.

"And if I would rather not; if I determine to stay here?"

"You would be the cause of my speedy death," said she, "for even now I am sure of dying for you."

Henri took the chances. He recognized that the man who is gorged with pleasure is on the declivity toward oblivion; he could not be ungrateful; but a desire for liberty, a fancy to take a walk, a tinge of scorn or possibly of disgust for her idol, or, indeed, some inexplicable sentiment might have made him infamous and ignoble to her. The certainty of that confused but genuine affection among souls which are not illumined by that celestial light, nor perfumed by that holy balm which is associated with a pertinacity of sentiment, without a doubt dictated to Rousseau the adventures of Lord Edward, which conclude the letters of "la Nouvelle Héloïse." Rousseau was evidently inspired by Richardson's work; he is far from it in a thousand details which leave his monument more magnificent than the original; he is recommended to posterity by a thousand ideas which are most difficult to either explain or analyze, when, in youth, we read this work with the design of finding therein a heated description of the most physical of our feelings, while the serious and philosophical writings are not always used as the consequence or the necessity of a great thought; the adventures of Lord Edward are one of the ideas the most delicately European in that work.

Henri, a creature of the Empire, confused this sentiment, inasmuch as he had not known real love. In some way he failed in the persuasive art of comparisons, and his irresistible attractions of the memory were what brought women to his side. Above all, true love lives by the memory. The woman whose soul is not engraved upon, either by an excess of pleasure or a strength of feeling, can she ever be said to be in love? Unknown to Henri, Paquita had thus established him in two manners. But at this moment, entirely worn out with happiness, that delightful melancholy of the body, he could hardly analyze his heart as he tasted on her lips the flavor of the most delicious voluptuousness that he had ever plucked.

That morning, at a very early hour, he had found himself on the Boulevard Montmartre, looking stupidly at his runaway equipage; he drew two cigars out of his pocket and lit one at the lamp of the good woman who sold the brandy and coffee to workmen, *gamins,* hucksters, and all that Parisian population who commence life before the opening of the day; then he had gone, smoking his cigar, his hands in his trousers' pockets, with an indifference that was really disgraceful.

"What a good thing is a cigar. It is one of those things that never forsakes a man," said he.

This girl with the golden eyes, who at this time had sent crazy all the fashionable young women of Paris, he now dreamed of punishing. This idea of death was brought forth to cross his pleasure, and whose fear had again shadowed the face of this beautiful being, who took after the houris of Asia, on her mother's side, belonging to Europe by her education, to the tropics by her birth, seemed to him to be one of those seducing deceivers who do thus to make themselves more interesting.

"She is from Havana, the most Spanish of any country in the new world; she likes best of anything to play at terror, that she may throw me into much suffering, showing me the difficulty, the coquetry, or the duty, the same as Parisian women do. By her eyes of gold, I have a great desire for sleep."

He saw a hack standing at the corner of Frascati's, awaiting some gambler; he awoke the driver, telling him to drive him home; he went to bed and slept the sleep of the good-for-nothing, which, by an anachronism not a single song-writer has as yet struck, is proven to be more sound than that of innocence. Perhaps this is an effect of that proverbial axiom: "Extremes meet."

About midday de Marsay woke, stretched his arms, and felt as hungry as a famished dog, the same feeling that all old soldiers can well remember on the day following a victory. As he saw Paul de Manerville before him he was well pleased, for nothing can be more agreeable than to eat in company.

"Well," said his friend, "we can imagine all that was comprised during ten hours with the girl with golden eyes."

"The girl with golden eyes! why, I will not think of her again. By my faith, I have other fish to fry."

"Ah! you are discreet."

"Why not?" said de Marsay, smiling. "My dear fellow, discretion is easier than calculation. Listen—— but, no, I won't tell you a thing. You would not be able to understand anything; I am not disposed to cast my pearls before swine. Life is a river which facilitates commerce. For all that, my doings are the most sacred things on earth; by my cigars! I am not a professor of social economy set at the door of ninnies. Confound it. It is easier to cut an omelette than to fatigue my brain."

"Is this how you talk to your friends?"

"My dear fellow," said Henri, who rarely refused an opening for his sarcasm like that of this time, "to you above another I give the reward of discretion; that is because I like you so much. Yes, I love you. On my word of honor, you would not fail in finding me a bill for a thousand francs, by which you might hinder me heating my brains; you would find it for me, for we have nothing left to hypothecate, eh, Paul? If you should fight to-morrow, I would measure the distance and charge the pistols, in order that your arm would kill in a proper manner. Indeed, if any other person were to speak ill of you to me in your absence, he would have to take the measure of the rude gentleman whom you have found in my skin; there, that is what I call proving my friendship.

"Well, when you would have the reward of discretion, my boy, bear in mind that there are two kinds of discretion—the active and the negative. Negative discretion is that of fools and is silence—the negation, the frown, the discretion of closed doors, a true pusillanimity. Active discretion proceeds from the affirmative. If this evening, in our circle, I said: 'On the faith of an honest man, the girl with golden eyes is not worthy what she has cost me,' all of them, when I had gone out, would exclaim: 'Did you hear that dude of a de Marsay, he tried to make us believe that he was already through with the girl with the golden eyes? He wishes to be left unembarrassed with rivals; he is not very smart though.'

"Now that scheme is both vulgar and dangerous. Some would have the silliness to let this escape; it is made known to every simpleton, who all believe it. The best of all discretions is that used by clever women when they have had a change from their husbands. It consists in compromising a woman on which we have no hold, or that we do not love, or that we have not had, and thus preserving the honor of that one that we both love and respect. This is what I call the 'screen-woman.' Ah! here is Laurent. What are you bringing in?"

"Ostend oysters, Monsieur le Comte."

"Some day you will know, Paul, how amusing it is to the world to steal the secret of our affections. I find an immense satisfaction in avoiding the stupid jurisdiction of the mob, which never knows what it wants, nor what it wishes, which takes the means for the result, which by turns worships and hates, or elevates and destroys. That happiness which is aroused by the emotions they can never receive, they cannot subdue it nor make it obedient to them. If they are perhaps proud of something, is it not by what they can acquire for themselves, which we sum up as the prime cause, the effect, the principal and the result? Well, no man can tell whom I love, unless I so will it. Perhaps some time I may tell you whom I love, that will be when I want you to know, so you may learn how the drama was worked out; but allow you to see into my game?—weakness, fraud I know nothing more reprehensible than the forced play of cunning. In my smile I imitate the trade of an ambassador; is not that of the diplomatist the most difficult in life? Without a doubt. Are you ambitious? Would you become something?"

"Henri, you do but mock me; I am altogether too mediocre for that."

"Well, Paul, if you go on mocking at yourself, you will soon be mocking at all the world."

After breakfast, and as he smoked his cigar, de Marsay began to see the events of the past night in a strange light. How many great intelligences with his perspicacity and spontaneity but would try to delve to the bottom of things? Among all gentle natures there is a faculty of living beside that of the present, which expresses, as one may say, the juice which it devours; his second sight lacked one kind of slumber by which to identify causes. Cardinal de Richelieu was possessed of clairvoyance, so necessary for the conception of great undertakings. De Marsay found all the conditions, but he was unable to present arms to his profits and pleasures, and did not become one of the most profound politicians until the time arrived when he was actually saturated with pleasure, which always comes at last to all young men, and from whence, if at all, they begin to look for gold and power. This is the man of bronze: he uses woman for what woman has no power to use herself.

At this moment then de Marsay perceived that he had been played with by the girl with golden eyes, seeing in all that had happened that night whose pleasures were not of that gradually gushing-out kind, which end by pouring down in torrents. Then he could read on this page, so brilliant in effect, and guess the concealed sense. The purely physical innocence of Paquita, the astonishment of her delight, a few words, now obscure, now clear, escaped in the midst of her ravishment, all this proved to him that he was posing for some other person. How could any social corruptions be unknown to him, who professed to treat every caprice with perfect indifference, and believed himself justified by having already been given satisfaction; he was not afraid of vice, he knew how to understand a friend, but he was hurt if taken advantage of. So these presumptions were just, he had been outraged to the quick. This sole suspicion took fire; he would break the roaring tiger and scoff at the gazelle; the cry of a tiger was joined to the strength of a beast and the intelligence of a demon.

"Well, of what are you thinking?" said Paul.

"Nothing."

"I can't take that in; if I ask if you have anything against me, you answer 'Nothing;' seemingly, he is about fighting tomorrow."

"I shall not fight again," said de Marsay.

"This seems more and more tragic. Are you going to assassinate some one?"

"You mix the words. I execute."

"My dear friend," said Paul, "your jests are very well at night, but this is morning."

"What will you! voluptuousness is the same as ferocity. Why? I do not know, and I am not sufficiently inquisitive to search out the cause. These cigars are excellent. Give your friend some tea. Do you know, Paul, that I am leading the life of a brute? He would in good time choose a destiny for himself, employ his strength at something which would be full of value to his existence. Life is a strange comedy. I am afraid, I laugh at the absurdity of our social conditions. The government slices off the heads of the poor devils who kill a man, and issues diplomas to creatures who for expediency, in medical parlance, kill a dozen young men every winter. Morals are without force against a dozen vices which destroy society, and which nothing punishes.

"*Encore* the cup. On my word of honor! man is a clown who dances on the edge of a precipice. Now we speak of the immorality of 'Dangerous Liaisons,' and of I know not what other book which has the name of a chamber-maid; but there is in existence a horrible book, smutty, frightful, corrupt, always open, which one can never close; the great book of the world, without counting that other book, a thousand times more dangerous, which contains all that has been overheard, between men, or under women's fans, each evening at a ball."

"Henri, it is most certain that you have gone through some extraordinary event, and already I can see it in spite of your 'active discretion.' "

"Yes! for a fact, he was almost devoured at this time last evening. It's all in the play. Perhaps I shall have the happiness of the lost."

De Marsay rose, took a roll of bank-bills, placed them in his box of cigars, dressed, and took advantage of Paul's carriage to go to the Salon des Étrangers, where, previous to dinner, he passed the time in play and changing alternately from winner to loser, the last resort of strong organizations, when they are restrained to exercise in a void. At night he went to the rendezvous and allowed himself to be complacently bandaged about the eyes. Then with the firm will, which only really strong men have the power of concentrating, he turned his attention and applied his whole intelligence to guess by what streets he had passed in the carriage. He felt a kind of certainty of having been driven to the Rue Saint-Lazare, stopping at the wicket-gate of the garden attached to the San-Réal mansion.

When for the first time he passed this gate, and through which he had, without doubt, been carried in litter fashion by the mulatto and coachman, in the meantime he had noticed the crunching of the gravel under their feet, which showed the reason why they took such minute precautions. It could have been seen, if he had been at liberty, where he had walked by the impressions of his feet, for he pushed aside a branch of the shrubs and saw that the path was of a material which would cling to their boots; while being transported, as it were, through the air, his good fortune could only be ascribed to the raving of a dream. But, to the despair of man, he can see nothing but imperfections, whether it be good or whether it be bad. All his works, be they intellectual or physical, are signed with the sign of destruction.

A slight rain was falling, the earth was moist. During the night certain vegetable odors are much stronger than in the day; Henri had smelt the perfume of mignonette along the path by which he had been carried. This indication should render easy the researches he promised himself to make in reconnoitring the hôtel in which he believed Paquita's boudoir was to be found.

All the same he studied the route by which he had been carried to the house, and quite believed that he could afterward recall it.

He saw himself as on the previous day, when, on the ottoman before Paquita, she had unbandaged his eyes; but he saw her pale and changed. She was weeping; kneeling like an angel in prayer, but an angel that was sad and in deep melancholy, the poor girl little resembled the inquisitive, impatient, bounding creature who had taken de Marsay on her wings and transported him to the seventh heaven of love. There was something so real in the pleasure-veiled despair that the terrible de Marsay felt a further admiration for this new masterpiece of nature, and forgot for the nonce the principal concern of the assignation.

"What is the matter, my Paquita?"

"My friend," said she, "carry me off this very night. Take me to some place where no one can say on seeing me: 'There is Paquita;' where no person can reply: 'He has there a long-haired girl, with a golden glance.' There I could give you more pleasure than you can receive here from me. Then, when you did not love me any more, you could leave me, I would make no complaint, I would say nothing; and if you deserted me it would not then cause you any remorse, for one day passed near you, only one little day, will seem to me of more value than every other day of my life."

"I don't intend quitting Paris, my girl," replied Henri. "I am not going to leave it; I am bound by an oath to the fate of many people who are to me the same as I am to them. But I can make you an asylum in Paris where no human power can come near you."

"No," said she; "you forget women's power."

Never had a sentence pronounced by a human voice expressed so full a complement of terror.

"What could possibly come near you, if I stood between you and the world?"

"Poison!" said she. "Already Doña Concha is suspicious of you—— And," she continued, letting fall the tears which glistened along her cheeks, "it must be plain to be seen that I am not the same as I was. Well, if you abandon me to the fury of the monster who would devour me, if that is your saintly will —so be it. But come, let us have all the voluptuousness of life in our love; I beg, I weep, I cry; I might defend myself, I might perhaps be saved."

"Who are you imploring?" he asked.

"Silence!" said Paquita. "If I obtain my desire, this would be because of my discretion."

"Give me my scarlet robe," said Henri, insidiously.

"No, no," she quickly replied; "stay as you are, one of our angels have apprised me that I should hate you, in which I cannot see the shape of a monster, while really you are the most beautiful being under the heavens," said she, stroking Henri's hair. "You don't know how near I am to an ignoramus. I have been taught nothing. Since I was twelve years old, I have been kept closed up without having seen a soul. I do not know how to either read or write; I speak only English and Spanish."

"How comes it then that you receive letters from London?"

"Letters for me? Well, here they are," said she, taking out of a Japanese vase a quantity of papers.

She held them out to de Marsay; to the surprise of the young man these letters were covered with fantastic figures something like those seen in a rebus, traced out in blood, and which seemed to express burning sentences surcharged with passion.

"But," he exclaimed, admiring the hieroglyphics easily deciphered by jealousy, "are you under the power of an infernal genius?"

"Infernal!" she repeated.

"But how comes it, then, that you have been able to go out?"

"Ah!" said she, "they were afraid of losing me. I had Doña Concha between the fear of immediate death and a fury that would bring me to it. I have the curiosity of a demon; I wished to break the circle that had been built about me, which came between creation and myself; I made up my mind that I would see some young men, for I knew no other men than the marquis and Cristemio. Our coachman and footman who accompany us are old men——"

"But you were not always kept in seclusion? Your health would——"

"Ah!" she answered, "we took walks at times, but it was during the night and in the country, on the banks of the Seine, far from the world."

"Are you not proud of being so loved?"

"No," said she. "Although well occupied, this dark, hidden life cannot be compared to that of the light."

"What do you call the light?"

"You, my beautiful Adolphe; for I would give my life for you. All the passionate things of which I have spoken and that I inspire, I have received from you. At certain times I understand nothing of existence; but now I know how we love, and up to the present I only was loved; I love not myself. I would leave all to follow you; take me away. If you will, take me as a plaything, but leave me when you are sick of me."

"You would not regret it?"

"Not at all," said she, allowing him to read her eyes; which, tinted in gold, shone out pure and clear.

"Am I the preferred one?" said Henri to himself, who fancied she spoke truthfully, finding himself disposed to pardon the offense in favor of a love so innocent. "I really believe she is true," he thought.

If Paquita gave any thought to the past, the least memory of such in his eyes would become a crime. He had therefore the sad thought of having an idea of this, of judging his mistress, of studying her when all given up to pleasures the most entrancing that had always descended from heaven upon those who had loved him well.

Paquita seemed to have been created for love, with a special care of nature. From one night to the other her feminine genius had made the most rapid progress. Some who saw the power and insouciance of this young man taking his pleasure, in spite of the satiety of yesterday, would find in the girl with golden eyes that which we all know is created in the woman in love and to which no man is ever given up.

Paquita responded to this passion which experienced all that truly great men feel for the infinite, a mysterious passion, so dramatically expressed in "Faust," so poetically translated in "Manfred," and which enabled Don Juan to rake the hearts

of women, who expect to find ideas without setting limits to
the search or having to set up themselves that he might chase
spectres; that the learned think is found in science, and that
the mystical believe is found in God alone.

The hope of having at last the ideal being, for which he had
constantly struggled, without fatigue, quite ravished de Marsay, who, for the first time, or for a long while back, now
opened his heart. His nerves relaxed, his coolness melted in
the warm atmosphere of that brilliant soul, his sharp-edged
doctrines were annulled, and happiness colored his life, the
same as it had this boudoir with white and pink.

Feeling the sting of a superior voluptuousness, he was already constrained by the limits in which he was now inclosed
by his passion. He would not be surpassed by this woman, so
that some sort of an artificial love was formed in advance to
bring rewards to his soul, and then he found, in that vanity
which possesses man, that he would remain the conqueror by
forces unknown to this girl; but also by throwing beyond this
line, where the soul of the mistress is the same as his own, he
was lost between her delicious limbs in what the vulgar so
naïvely call the "imaginary space." It was tender, sweet, and
communicative. It made Paquita nearly crazy.

"Why should we not go to Sorrento, Nice, or Chivavari,
and there pass our lives together? Would you like this?" said
he to Paquita, in a penetrating voice.

"Why do you ask me 'will you?'" she cried. "Are you
willing? I don't care where it is, to be with you is my pleasure.
If you would choose a retreat that is worthy of us, then Asia
is the only country where love can display its wings——"

"You are right," said Henri. "We will go the Indies; there
spring is eternal, where the ground is always covered with
flowers, where man may display the clothing of sovereigns
without comment, like is done in the country of imbeciles
where they try to realize the chimera of equality. There in
that country, where we can live in the midst of a people of
slaves, where the sun for ever illuminates the white palace in
which we reside, where the scent of perfumes is ever in the
air, where the birds sing their love, and where one may die
when one loves no more."

"And where we can die together," said Paquita. "Do not
put off the going until to-morrow, let us go this instant—take
Cristemio."

"By my faith, pleasure is the most beautiful issue of life.

On to Asia; but to go there, my child, requires much gold, and to have this gold I must arrange my business."

She understood nothing of this.

"Of gold, there is enough of that here," said she, pressing his hand.

"It is not mine."

"What does that matter?" she asked. "If we need it, take it."

"It does not belong to you."

"Belong!" she repeated. "What have I that you have not? When we have taken it, it belongs to us."

He smiled.

"Poor innocent girl; you know nothing of the things of the world."

"No, but here is something that I do know," said she, drawing Henri down on herself.

At the precise moment when de Marsay had forgotten everything, and conceived the desire of appropriating this creature for ever, he received in the midst of his delight a dagger-stroke which bit by bit went to his heart, which was vexed for the first time. Paquita, who had vigorously raised herself in the air to gaze at him, now cried out:

"Oh! Margarita!"

"Margarita!" exclaimed the young man in a roar; "I now know all that I previously had doubts of."

He sprang to the cabinet in which the long dagger had been placed. Happily for Paquita and himself, the cabinet was locked. His fury was increased by this obstacle; but he recovered his tranquillity, took up his cravat, and advanced toward her with so significantly a ferocious manner, that, without knowing of what crime she was guilty, Paquita nevertheless knew that his intention was to slay her.

She made one bound and sprang to the side of the room to avoid the fatal noose which de Marsay tried to fling around her neck. There they had a contest. Each was a counterpart of the other—the suppleness, the agility, and the rage being equal. To finish the struggle Paquita threw a cushion between the legs of her lover, which flung him down, then, profiting by the respite which this advantage allowed her, she pressed the button and it was immediately responded to. The mulatto suddenly appeared. In the wink of an eye, Cristemio flung himself on de Marsay, threw him on the ground, placing his foot on his chest, with his heel turned to his throat. De Marsay at once understood that, if he struggled, he would be at that moment crushed to death on a single sign from Paquita.

"Why do you wish to kill me, my love?" she asked.

De Marsay made no reply.

"What have I done?" she went on. "Speak, explain to us."

Henri preserved the phlegmatic attitude of a strong man when he feels that he is vanquished; of cold countenance, silent, all English, which tells of the consciousness of his dignity being for that moment overthrown. Nevertheless, he was already deep in thought, in spite of the importunity of his fury, seeing how little prudence he had shown and of the injustice of killing this girl unawares without having prepared for her death in a manner proper to assure its impunity.

"My good friend," Paquita went on; "speak to me; do not leave me without a farewell of love. I will not regard the dread which you have planted in my heart. Won't you speak to me?" said she, stamping her foot with rage.

De Marsay answered by throwing her a significant look, which plainly said:

"You shall die."

Paquita threw herself on him.

"Well, do you wish to kill me? If my death will give you pleasure—kill me."

She made a sign to Cristemio, who raised his foot from the young man and allowing her to see his face, which should give a judgment of good or ill on Paquita.

"There is a man," said de Marsay, pointing to the mulatto with a sinister gesture. "He not only has devotion, but a devotedness that obeys whom it loves without question. You have a true friend in that man."

"I will give him to you, if you wish," she replied; "he would serve you with the same devotion that he has for me, if I advise him so to do."

She awaited a word in rely, then went on, in an accent full of tenderness:

"Adolphe, speak one good word to me. It will soon be day."

Henri made no reply. This young man had one sad quality, for he looked on it as being a great thing, all this concentration of strength, which is often carried by men to extravagant lengths. Henri did not know the word "Forgive." To know how to draw back, which is certainly one of the soul's graces, was in no sense his. The ferocity of men of the North, with which English blood is strongly tainted, had been transmitted to him from his sire. He was as immovable in his good as in his bad sentiments. The exclamation of Paquita was all the more horrible for him, for he had been dethroned from the sweetest triumph which had ever aggrandized the vanity of man.

The hopes, the love, and all the feelings which had exalted him, all that had flamed in his heart and mind; then these flames, lighted by the brightness of his life, had been suddenly smothered and become cold. Paquita, stupefied, had no more power in her sadness than to give the signal for him to go.

"This is useless," said she, throwing down the bandanna handkerchief. "If he loves me no more, if he hates me, all is at an end."

She waited for a look; she did not get one, and fell upon the floor half-dead. The mulatto threw a glance on Henri which was dreadfully significant, and which, for the first time in the life of this young man, caused him to tremble, for to few persons was given his rare intrepidity.

"If you have not loved her well, if you cause her the least pain, I will kill you," was in the sense of that quick glance.

De Marsay was conducted with the same servile care along a vast corridor lighted by early dawn, and out of the end of which he went by a secret door in the private stairway which ran to the garden belonging to the San-Réal hôtel. The mulatto, for precaution, walked along a tiled pathway which abutted on a wicket-gate giving on the street, which at this time was quite deserted.

De Marsay carefully noted everything; the carriage was in attendance; this time the mulatto did not accompany him; and, at the moment when Henri pushed his head through the curtains to look at the garden of the mansion, he met the white eyes of Cristemio, with whom he exchanged glances. On both sides this was a look of provocation, a defiance, an announcement of savage warfare, of a duel not guided by ordinary laws, in which treason and perfidy had at least admission.

Cristemio knew that Henri had condemned Paquita to death. Henri knew that Cristemio decreed his death before he could kill Paquita. Each considered himself the best.

"The adventure is complicated with a feature to make it more interesting," said Henri.

"To where does monsieur wish to go?" asked the coachman.

De Marsay was driven to Paul de Manerville's home.

During the greater part of this week Henri was away from home; where he was all this time no person knew, nor in what place he lived. This retreat saved him from the fury of the mulatto, and caused the ruin of the poor creature who had taken away all the hope she had of being loved, like as every other creature hopes for love on this earth.

The last day of the week, toward eleven at night, Henri went in a carriage to the wicket-gate of the garden of the mansion of San-Réal. Four men were in his company. The coachman was evidently one of his friends, for he went straight to his seat, like an attentive sentinel listening for the least noise. One of the three others rang the bell at the gate in the street; the second made into the garden, standing on the wall; the last, who held in his hand a bunch of keys, went with de Marsay.

"Henri," said his companion, "we are betrayed."

"By whom, my good Ferragus?"

"They are not asleep," said the chief of the devorants. "It shows absolutely that none in the house has drunk or eaten anything. There, see that light?"

"We have the plan of the house. Where is she?"

"I have no need of the plan to learn that," replied Ferragus; "she is in the marquise's room."

"Ah!" exclaimed de Marsay "She has, without a doubt, arrived here from London to-day. That woman has not incurred my vengeance. But, if she comes in my path, my good Gratien, we deliver her to our justice."

"S—sh, listen! the deed is done," said Ferragus to Henri.

The two friends lent their ears to the feeble cries with all the savage attention of tigers.

"Your marquise did not think that people could come to see her kill by way of the chimney," said the chief of the devorants, with the laugh of a critic, enchanted in finding a flaw in a masterpiece.

"We only, we know all things," said Henri. "Listen to me. I want to go and see how she passes up on high, in order to learn the manner of treating quarrels in their household. By the name of God, I think that she will, for a fact, be broiled on a little fire."

De Marsay lightly climbed the stairway which he knew was the way to the boudoir. When he opened the door he had that involuntary shiver which causes the most determined man to shrink from the sight of spilt blood. The spectacle offered to his gaze had, beside, for him a great meed of astonishment.

The marquise was a woman: she had calculated her vengeance with that perfection of perfidy which always distinguishes feeble animals. She had dissimulated her rage at the crime to assure its due punishment.

"Too late, my good friend," said Paquita, dying, whose pale eyes turned toward de Marsay.

The girl with golden eyes expired, weltering in her own blood. All the candles were aflame, a delicate perfume pervaded the room, a certain disorder, palpable to the eye of a clever man of the world who knows of the follies common to every passion, announced that the marquise had skillfully tortured the guilty one. This white apartment, in which the blood showed so distinctly, betrayed a long struggle. The hands of Paquita were indented in the cushions. Everywhere she had hung on for her life, everywhere she had defended herself, and everywhere she had been stricken down. Some great fragments of the fluted tapestry had been torn down by her bloody hands, which told of a terrible and long-drawn struggle.

Paquita had tried to scale the ceiling; her naked feet had marked the long back of the divan on which she had, without doubt, run. Her body, jagged with the thrusts given with the poniard by her executioner, told well with what fury she had fought for a life that Henri had made so dear to her. She lay on the floor, and had, in dying, bitten the muscles of the instep of Madame de San-Réal, who still held in her hand the poinard soaked in blood. The marquise's hair was dragged askew; she was covered with bites which bled freely; her torn dress allowed her to be seen half-naked and her bosom full of scratches.

She was in a manner sublime.

Her face, covetous and full of rage, breathed the odor of blood. Her panting mouth was partly open, and her nostrils were too small for her respirations. Certain animals, when seized with rage, spring full on their foes, seeming to have lost sight of everything else. There are others who twine about their victims, who hold them in fear so that they cannot arouse themselves, and who, like Homer's Achilles, will make nine tours around the walls of Troy and drag forth their enemies by their feet. Of such was the marquise. She did not see Henri. She was so sure of being alone that she had no fear of witnesses; then her blood was up, she was too excited by the struggle, too inflamed to see all Paris, if all the people of Paris had formed a ring around her. She would not have felt a thunderbolt. She had not even heard Paquita's last sigh, and believed that she could still be heard by the dead.

"Dead without confession," said she to her; "gone to hell, monster of ingratitude; who cares no more for a person than the devil. For the blood which you have given him, you now give all yours to me. Die, die, suffer a thousand deaths! I have been too good; I don't seem to have taken a moment in killing you; I should like to have made you experience all the sorrow you have bequeathed me. I live, I. I live unhappy; I am reduced to loving none beside God."

Awhile she stood contemplative.

"She is dead," said she, after a pause, making a violent return to herself. "Dead, ah! I shall die of grief."

The marquise would have thrown herself on the divan, overwhelmed with a despair which showed itself in her voice, but this movement was prevented by seeing Henri de Marsay.

"Who are you?" said she, rushing at him with uplifted poniard.

Henri held her arm, and they stood face to face. An awful surprise seized both of them, turning the blood in their veins to ice, and their legs shook like those of horses when they are afraid. In fact, two *Ménechmes** could not more resemble each other. They both spoke the same words together:

"Is Lord Dudley your father?"

Each nodded affirmatively.

"She was true to the blood," said Henri, pointing to Paquita.

"It is possible that for this she was the less guilty," replied Margarita-Euphémia Porrabéril, throwing herself on Paquita's body, with a cry of despair.

"Poor girl, I wish I could reanimate you. I have done wrong; forgive me, Paquita. You are dead, and I live, I. I am the more unfortunate."

At this moment appeared the horrible face of Paquita's mother.

"You came to tell me and sold her to death," cried the marquise. "I know what has brought you out of your hole. I will pay you twice over. There you are."

She took out of a drawer in an ebony cabinet a bag of gold which she flung disdainfully at the feet of the old woman. The

* Doubles, in French fiction.

sound of the gold had the power to limn an imitation of a smile on the immobile physiognomy of the Georgian slave woman.

"I came in time for you, my sister," said Henri. "The law will allow you to reclaim——"

"Nothing," replied the marquise. "Only one person could ask an account of that girl. Cristemio is dead."

"And this mother," said Henri, pointing to the old woman; "will she never tell anything?"

"She belongs to a country where women are not beings, but things which have neither goods nor will; who are bought and sold; who may be killed, who are, in fact, subject to every caprice, and whom everybody treats as so many chattels. Nevertheless, they have a passion to which every other is subordinate—even the love of maternity; so, although she loved her daughter, she had the passion——"

"Of what?" asked Henri, quickly, interrupting his sister.

"Of gambling; whom God keep," replied the marquise.

"But how comes it that you assist her," said Henri, pointing to the girl with golden eyes; "is it that she may remove the traces of this fantasy, that your law has brought about?"

"I own her mother," replied the marquise, pointing to the old Georgian, to whom she made a sign to stay.

"We shall meet again," said Henri, who began to be uneasy about his friends, and saw the necessity for going.

"No, my brother," said she; "we shall never meet again. I shall return to Spain and there enter the convent of *los Dolores.*"

"You are still young and too beautiful for that," said Henri, pressing her in his arms and kissing her.

"Farewell," said she; "nothing can ever console me for having sent a soul to be for ever lost."

Eight hours after, Paul de Manerville met de Marsay at the Tuileries, on the Terrasse des Feuillants.

"Well, what has become of our beautiful girl with the golden eyes, great rascal?"

"She is dead."

"Of what?"

"Consumption."

PARIS, *March, 1834–April, 1835.*

CARMEN
by Prosper Mérimée

Prosper Mérimée began his writing career as an enfant terrible. In 1825, at the age of 22, he published a volume of six plays entitled The Theatre of Clara Gazul, which he claimed had been written by an itinerant Spanish actress and translated by himself. In point of fact, it actually was Mérimée's own work. Two years later, he parlayed the joke with La Guzla, which purported to be a collection of Illyrian ballads. This also proved to be a literary hoax. Mérimée's readiness to poke fun at the romantic writers who were his contemporaries did not prevent him, however, from producing historical novels of his own. These were in the current fashion, full of explosive passions and set in strange romantic and exotic locales, but they are notable for brevity, objectivity and irony of tone.

An archaeologist, Mérimée, was appointed at the age of 28 to the post of Inspector General of historical monuments. As a consequence, he was able to travel widely to such colorful places as Spain, Corsica, Greece and Asia Minor. These became the background for such works as Mateo Falcone, Colomba, and Carmen, the novelette represented in this volume. Mérimée deals with primitive temperaments given to violent, romantic passions, yet the writing itself shows surprising restraint. In common with much of the best of French literature, it is precise with detail, stylistically simple, lucid and unadorned. In the hands of the composer Georges Bizet, Carmen has become one of the most beloved operas in the repertoire.

I.

I have always suspected geographers of not knowing what they were talking about when they place the battlefield of Munda in the country of the Bastuli-Pœni, near the modern Monda, some leagues to the north of Marbella. According to my own interpretation of the text of the anonymous author of "Bellum Hispaniensis," and after some information collected in the excellent library of the Duke of Osuena, I considered it necessary to seek in the environs of Montilla for the memorable spot where for the last time Cæsar played double or quits against the champions of the Republic. Finding myself in Andalusia about the beginning of the autumn of 1830, I made a rather lengthened excursion with a view to clear up the doubts which still remained in my mind on this question. A pamphlet which I shall shortly publish will, I trust, leave no uncertainty in the minds of all honest archæologists. Pending the time when my dissertation shall resolve once for all this geographical problem which keeps all scientific Europe in suspense, I wish to relate a little story, which will in no degree prejudice the interesting question of the site of Munda.

I had engaged a guide and two horses at Cordova, and set out with Cæsar's Commentaries and a few shirts as my only baggage. One day, while wandering in the elevated part of the plain of Cachena, tired out, dying of thirst, broiled by the vertical sun, I was just consigning Cæsar and the sons of Pompey to the devil, when I perceived at some distance from the path which I was following a little green space dotted with rushes and reeds. These announced the vicinity of a spring. In fact, as I approached I perceived that the seeming greensward was a marsh in which a streamlet, emerging, as it seemed, from a narrow gorge between two lofty buttresses of the Sierra di Calva, lost itself. I concluded that if I ascended a little farther I should find clearer and fresher water, and fewer leeches and frogs, with perhaps a little shade between the boulders. At the entrance of the gorge my horse neighed, and another horse, which I could not see, immediately replied.

I had scarcely advanced a hundred paces when the gorge suddenly opened out and displayed to my view a kind of natural amphitheatre, entirely shaded by the lofty cliffs which enclosed it. It was impossible to meet with any spot which promised a traveller a more agreeable resting-place. At the base of the perpendicular cliffs the stream rushed out and fell bubbling into a little basin lined with sand white as snow. Five or six beautiful and verdant oaks, always sheltered from the wind here, and watered by the stream, rose beside its source and covered it with their leafy shade; lastly, around the basin grew a rich fine grass which offered a better bed than one could find in any inn for ten leagues round.

But the honor of discovering this charming retreat did not

rest with me. A man was already reposing there, and was no doubt asleep when I penetrated thither. Awakened by the neighing of the horses, he arose and approached his steed, which had taken advantage of his master's sleeping to make a good meal of the luxuriant grass around him. His owner was a young fellow of medium height, but of robust build, and with a gloomy and proud look on his face. His complexion, which may have been good, had by exposure become even darker than his hair. In one hand he grasped the halter of his steed, in the other he held a brass blunderbuss. I must confess that at first the sight of the blunderbuss and the fierce aspect of the man surprised me; but I no longer believed in brigands, having only heard of them, but never having met any of them. Besides, I had seen so many honest farmers armed to the teeth to proceed to market that the mere sight of fire-arms was not sufficient evidence upon which to base the dishonesty of the unknown. And then I thought, what would he want with my shirts and my volume of Elzevir Commentaries?

So I saluted the man of the blunderbuss with an easy bow, and inquired with a smile whether I had disturbed him from his siesta. Without answering he measured me with his eyes from head to foot; then, as if satisfied with his scrutiny, he paid the same attention to my guide, who was approaching. I perceived the latter turn pale, and pull up with every symptom of terror. An unlucky meeting, I thought; but prudence immediately counselled me not to display any uneasiness. I dismounted, told the guide to unbridle the horses, and kneeling down beside the spring, I plunged my head and hands into it; then lying flat on the ground like the wicked soldiers of Gideon, I took a deep draught.

Nevertheless, I managed to keep an eye on the guide and the unknown. The former approached with manifest hesitation; the latter did not appear to harbor any evil intentions against us, for he had released his horse again, and his blunderbuss, which he had at first grasped horizontally and held "ready," was now held muzzle downwards.

Not thinking it worth while to be offended at the slight value put upon me, I lay down upon the grass, and in an easy manner asked the man with the blunderbuss whether he had a tinder box about him. At the same time I took out my cigar-case. The unknown, still in silence, fumbled in his pocket for the box, and taking it out, hastened to strike a light for me. He was evidently getting sociable, for he came and sat down opposite me, but without putting aside his weapon. My cigar alight, I selected the best of those remaining in my case, and inquired whether he would smoke.

"Yes, sir," he replied. These were the first words he had uttered, and I remarked that he did not pronounce the S's in the Andalusian manner*, from which circumstance I concluded that he was a traveller like myself, less the archæological inspiration.

"You will find this pretty good," I said, as I handed him a genuine regalia Habaña.

He bowed slightly, lighted his cigar from mine, thanked me with another bow, and began to smoke with every appearance of intense satisfaction.

"Ah!" he exclaimed as he permitted the smoke to escape slowly from his mouth and nostrils, "what a time it is since I have smoked!"

In Spain a cigar offered and accepted establishes friendly relations, as in the East the partaking of bread and salt ensures hospitality. My companion proved himself more communicative than I had hoped. However, although he declared himself a native of the province of Montilla, he appeared to be very slightly acquainted with the district. He did not know the name of the charming valley in which we were resting. He could not name any village in the neighborhood; and at length, in reply to my question as to whether he had not noticed in the environs some ruined walls and carved stones, he confessed that he never paid any attention to such things. On the other hand, he showed himself a connoisseur in horseflesh. He criticised my horse—which was not difficult; then he told me the pedigree of his own, which came from the famous Cordova stud: a noble animal indeed, and so insensible to fatigue that, as his master said, he had on one occasion made ninety miles in the day at speed. In the midst of this tirade the unknown suddenly checked himself, as if surprised and sorry that he had said so much.

"It was when I was in a great hurry to reach Cordova," he continued with some embarrassment, "I had to prosecute a lawsuit."

As he was speaking he looked at my guide, Antonio, who lowered his eyes.

The shade and the spring charmed me so that I recollected

* The Andalusians aspirate the *s,* and sound it as something between the *c* soft and the *z,* which the Spaniards pronounce like the English *th.* By the word Señor one can distinguish an Andalusian.

some slices of an excellent ham which my friends in Montilla had put in my guide's haversack. I made him fetch them, and invited the stranger to join me in my impromptu picnic. If he had not smoked for a long while, it seemed to me that he must have fasted for forty-eight hours, at least. He ate like a famished wolf. I thought my appearance had been quite providential for the poor devil. My guide, however, ate little, drank less, and spoke not at all, although at the beginning of our journey he had been a tremendous chatterer. The presence of our guest seemed to be a restraint upon him, and a kind of mutual distrust kept them apart; the cause of this I could not determine.

The last morsels of bread and ham had been eaten; we had each smoked a second cigar; I ordered the guide to bridle the horses, and I was about to take leave of my new acquaintance, when he asked me where I intended to pass the night.

Before I could attend to a sign from my guide, I had replied that I was making for the Venta del Cuervo.

"A bad lodging for such a person as you, sir. I am going thither, and if you will permit me to accompany you we will go together."

"Very willingly," I replied as I mounted my horse. My guide, who was holding the stirrup, made me another sign. I replied to it by shrugging my shoulders, as if to assure him that I was quite easy in my mind; and then we started.

The mysterious signs of Antonio, his uneasiness, the few words that escaped the unknown, particularly the account of the thirty-league ride, and the by no means plausible explanation which he had offered, had already formed my opinon concerning my travelling companion. I had no doubt whatever that I had to do with a *contrabandista*, perhaps with a brigand. What matter? I knew enough of the Spanish character to be certain that I had nothing to fear from a man who had eaten and smoked with me. His very presence was a protection against all untoward adventures. Moreover, I was rather glad to know what a brigand was like. One does not meet them every day, and there is a certain charm in finding oneself in company with a dangerous person, particularly when one finds him gentle and subdued.

I hoped to lead the unknown to confide in me by degrees, and notwithstanding the winks of my guide, I led the conversation to the bandits. Of course I spoke of them with all respect. There was at that time a famous bandit in Andalusia named José-Maria, whose exploits were in every one's mouth. "Suppose I am in the company of José-Maria!" I said to myself. I told all the ancedotes of this hero that I knew—all those in his praise, of course, and loudly expressed my admiration of his bravery and generosity.

"José-Maria is only a scamp," replied the stranger coldly.

"Is he doing himself justice, or is it only modesty on his part?" I asked myself; for, after considering my companion carefully, I began to apply to him the description of José-Maria which I had read posted up on the gates of many towns of Andalusia. Yes, it is he certainly. Fair hair, blue eyes, large mouth, good teeth, small hands, a fine shirt, a velvet vest with silver buttons, gaiters of white skin, a bay horse. No doubt about it. But let us respect his incognito!

We arrived at the Venta. It was just what he had described it—that is to say, one of the most miserable inns that I had ever seen. One large room served for kitchen, parlor and bedroom. A fire was burning on a flat stone in the middle of the room, and the smoke went out through a hole in the roof, or rather it stopped there, and hung in a cloud some feet above the ground. Beside the wall, on the floor, were extended five or six horsecloths, which were the beds for travellers. About twenty paces from the house—or rather from the single room which I have described—was a kind of shed, which did duty for a stable. In this delightful retreat there was for the time being no other individual besides an old woman and a little girl of ten or twelve years old, both as black as soot, and in rags.

"Here," thought I, "are all that remain of the population of the ancient Munda Bætica. O Cæsar, O Sextus Pompey, how astonished you would be if you were to return to this mundane sphere!"

When she perceived my companion the old woman uttered an exclamation of surprise.

"Ah, Señor Don José!" she cried.

Don José frowned and raised his hand with a gesture of command which made the old woman pause. I turned to my guide, and with a sign imperceptible to José made Antonio understand that I needed no information respecting the man with whom I had to pass the night. The supper was better than I had anticipated. They served up upon a small table about a foot high an old cock fricasseed with rice and pimentos, then pimentos in oil, and lastly, *gaspacho*, a kind of pimento salad. Three such highly seasoned dishes obliged us often to have recourse to the flask of Montilla, which we found delicious.

Having supped, and perceiving a mandolin hanging against the wall—there are mandolins everywhere in Spain—I asked the little girl who waited on us if she knew how to play it.

"No," she replied; "but Don José plays it very well."

"Will you be so good as to sing something?" I said to him. "I passionately love your national music."

"I can refuse nothing to so polite a gentleman, who gives me such excellent cigars," replied José good-humoredly, and being handed the mandolin he sang to his own accompaniment. His voice was harsh, but rather agreeable; the air was sad and wild; as for the words, I did not understand one of them.

"If I am not mistaken," I said, "that is not a Spanish air which you have just sung. It strikes me as resembling the *zorzicos* which I have heard in the 'Provinces,'* and the words seem to be in the Basque tongue."

"Yes," replied José with a sombre air. He placed the mandolin on the ground, and sat contemplating the dying embers with a singularly sad expression. Illumined by the lamp placed on the little table, his face, at once noble and ferocious, recalled Milton's Satan. Like him, perhaps, my companion was thinking of a heaven he had quitted—of the exile to which his sin had condemned him. I endeavored to engage him in conversation, but he did not reply, so absorbed was he in his sad reflections.

By this time the old woman had retired to rest in a corner of the room behind a primitive screen formed of a rag suspended from a cord. The little girl had followed her into this retreat reserved for the fair sex. Then my guide, rising, invited me to follow him to the stable, but at this José, as if waking up with a start, demanded in a rough tone whether he was going.

"To the stable," replied the guide.

"What for? The horses have plenty to eat. Lie down here; the gentleman will permit it."

"I am afraid the Señor's horse may be ill. I want the Señor to see it; perhaps he will know what to do."

It was evident that Antonio wished to speak to me in pri-

* The privileged provinces enjoying special *fueros*—that is to say, Alava, Biscay, Guipuzcoa, and a portion of Navarre. Basque is the language of the district.

vate, but I did not care to arouse Don José's suspicions, and under the circumstances it appeared to me that the best line to take would be to display the greatest confidence. So I informed Antonio that I knew nothing about horses, and that I was very sleepy. Don José followed the man to the stable, and soon returned alone. He told me that the horse had nothing the matter with him, but the guide valued the steed so highly that he was rubbing him with his vet to make him perspire, and intended to continue the occupation during the night. However, I was soon extended beneath the rugs, carefully wrapped in my cloak so as to avoid contact with them. After begging pardon for the liberty which he was taking in lying close to me, Don José lay down before the door, first having renewed the priming of his blunderbuss, which he took care to place beneath the haversack which served him for a pillow. Five minutes after we had wished each other good-night we were both buried in profound slumber.

I had believed that I was sufficiently tired to sleep in such a place as that, but after an hour a very disagreeable itching aroused me from my first nap. As soon as I understood the nature of the disturbing cause, I rose, firmly convinced that it would be better to pass the night in the open air than under such an inhospitable roof. I gained the door on tiptoe, and stepping over Don José, who was sleeping the sleep of the just, I managed to quit the house without arousing him. Near the door was a large wooden bench; on this I lay down and settled myself for the night as well as I could. I was about to shut my eyes for the second time, when I fancied I perceived the shadows of a man and a horse passing in front of me and not making the slightest noise. I jumped up, and thought I recognized Antonio. Surprised to see him out of the stable at such an hour I advanced to meet him. He stopped when he perceived me approaching.

"Where is he?" asked Antonio in a low voice.

"In the venta; he is asleep, he has no fear of fleas. Why have you brought the horse out?"

Then I remarked that Antonio—so as not to make any noise in quitting the shed, had carefully enveloped the horse's feet in the fragments of an old cloth.

"Speak lower, in the name of God," he said. "You do not know who that man is. He is José Navarro, the most famous bandit in Andalusia. I have been making signs to you all day which you would not understand."

"Bandit or not, what does it matter to me?" I replied. "He

has not robbed us, and I will wager that he has no intention of doing so."

"All very well, but there is a price of two hundred ducats on his head. I know where there is a detachment of lancers about a league and a half distant; and before daybreak I will bring some stout fellows here. I would have taken his horse, but he is so vicious that no one save Navarro can go near him."

"What the devil are you about?" I said. "What harm has the poor man done to you that you should betray him? Besides, are you certain that he *is* the brigand you say he is?"

"Perfectly certain. Just now he followed me into the stable and said, 'You seem to know me. If you tell this good gentleman who I am I will wring your neck!' Remain with him, sir; you have nothing to fear. So long as you are there he will have no suspicions."

While we were speaking we had got some distance from the venta, and no one in it would hear the sound of the horse's hoofs. In the twinkling of an eye Antonio took off the wrappings and prepared to mount. I endeavored to detain him by prayers, and even by threats.

"I am a poor devil, sir," he replied, "and I cannot afford to lose two hundred ducats; particularly when I can also rid the country of such vermin as is yonder. But take care! If Navarro wakes he will rush for his blunderbuss, so mind yourself. I have gone too far to retreat. You can suit yourself."

The scoundrel was already in the saddle. He spurred his horse, and was soon hidden from my view in the darkness.

I was very much annoyed with my guide, and not a little uneasy. After a moment's reflection I made up my mind what course to pursue, and reentered the venta. Don José was still asleep, repairing, no doubt, the fatigues and watches of many days preceding. I was obliged to shake him roughly before I could arouse him. Never shall I forget his fierce look and the action with which he sought to grasp his blunderbuss, which I had removed as a matter of precaution.

"Sir," said I, "I ask your pardon for disturbing you, but I have a simple question to ask. Would you be pleased to see half a dozen lancers come here?"

He leaped to his feet, and in a terrible tone said, "Who has told you that?"

"No matter whence comes the advice so that it is good."

"Your guide has betrayed me, but he shall answer for it. Where is he?"

"I do not know. In the stable, I think, but some one has told me"——

"Who told you? The old woman, perhaps?"

"Some one whom I do not know. Without more words, have you—yes or no—any reason which renders it advisable for you to avoid the soldiers? If you have, do not lose time —if not, then good-night; and I beg your pardon for awakening you."

"Ah, your guide—your guide! I suspected him at first; but his account will be settled! Adieu, sir; God reward you for the service I owe you. I am not so bad as you believe me to be; yes, there is still in me something which deserves the sympathy of a brave man. Adieu, sir, I have only one regret, and that is my inability to pay my debt to you."

"For the service which I render you, Don José, promise me to suspect no one—do not think of vengeance. Hold—here are some cigars for you. *Bon voyage!*"—and I extended my hand to him.

He shook mine without replying; seized his blunderbuss and his sack, and after saying a few words to the old woman in a slang I did not understand, he hurried to the shed. A few minutes afterwards I heard him gallop away into the open country.

As for me, I retired to my bench but I could not sleep. I interrogated myself as to whether I had any right to save a robber—perhaps a murderer—from the gallows, and that only because I had eaten with him some ham and rice. Had I not betrayed my guide, who was upholding the laws? had I not exposed myself to the revenge of a villain? But the duties of hospitality? "A prejudice of savagery," I said to myself; "I shall have to be responsible for all the crimes that the bandit hereafter may commit." However, *is* it a prejudice—this instinct of conscience which defies all reasoning? Perhaps in the delicate situation in which I was placed, I might be able to escape without remorse? I was balanced in the greatest uncertainty respecting the morality of my action when I saw half a dozen horse-soldiers returning with Antonio, who kept prudently in the rear. I met them half-way, and informed them that the bandit had escaped two hours previously. The old woman, when questioned by the corporal, replied that she knew Navarro, but that, living alone, she did not dare risk her life by denouncing him. She added that he was always in the habit of departing in the middle of the night when he came to her house. As for me, I was compelled to proceed a distance

of some leagues to show my passport, and sign a declaration
before the alcalde, after which I was permitted to resume my
archæological researches. Antonio nursed a grudge against me
—for he suspected that it was I who had prevented him from
gaining the reward of two hundred ducats. Nevertheless we
parted good friends at Cordova, where I presented him with a
gratuity as large as the condition of my finances permitted me
to give.

II.

I spent some days in Cordova. Some MS. in the Dominican library had been indicated to me, and in this I expected
to find some interesting information concerning the ancient
Munda. Being very well received by the good monks I passed
the days in their monastery; and in the evenings I walked
about the town. At Cordova at sunset there are always a
number of idlers about the quay which borders the right bank
of the Guadalquiver. There one breathes the odors of a tan-
nery which still preserves the old reputation of the country for
the preparation of leather; but on the other hand one enjoys a
sight which is well worth seeing. Some minutes before the
Angelus is rung a number of women assemble on the bank of
the river at the end of the quay, which is raised considerably.
Not a man dares to mingle with this troop. Immediately the
Angelus sounds night is supposed to have set in. At the last
stroke of the bell all the women undress and plunge into the
water. Then arise cries, laughter, and an infernal din. From the
top of the quay the men contemplate the bathers, staring at
them with open eyes, but seeing little. Nevertheless these
white and undefined forms, which are perceptible in the deep
azure waters of the river, cause poetic minds to conceive, and
with a little imagination it is not difficult to represent to oneself Diana and her nymphs in the bath, without fear of
sharing the fate of Actæon. I was informed that on one occasion some scapegraces, by bribing the bell-ringer of the ca-
thedral, induced him to ring the Angelus twenty minutes in
advance of the usual hour. Although it was broad daylight,
the nymphs of the Guadalquiver did not hesitate, and trusting
more to the Angelus than the sun, they made innocence their
bathing-dress—which is always of the simplest fashion. I was
not there. In my time the bell-ringer was incorruptible, the
twilight not very clear, and only a cat would have been able to

distinguish the oldest orange-seller from the prettiest *grisette* in Cordova.

One evening at the hour when there is nothing to be seen, I was smoking, leaning upon the parapet of the quay, when a woman ascended the steps which led down to the river, and seated herself close to me. She had in her hair a large bunch of jessamine, which emitted a strong perfume. She was simply, perhaps poorly, clad, in black, as most of the girls are in the evening. The fashionable ladies only wear black in the morning, in the evening they dress *a la Francesca*. As she approached me the bather let fall on her shoulders the mantilla with which she had covered her head, and in the starlight I could perceive that she was pretty, young, well made, and that she had very large eyes. I quickly threw away my cigar. She at once appreciated this attention—a politeness entirely French—and hastened to inform me that she liked the smell of tobacco-smoke very much, and that even she herself smoked when she could get very mild cigarettes. Fortunately I had some such in my case, and hastened to offer them to her. She condescended to take one, and lighted it at the burning end of a cork which a child brought us for a halfpenny. Smoking together we conversed so long—the pretty bather and I—that we found ourselves alone upon the quay. I did not consider that there was anything indiscreet in suggesting that we should go and have some ices at a *neveria*.* After some modest hesitation she consented, but before deciding she wished to know what time it was. I made my repeater strike the hour, and this astonished her very much. "What inventions they have in your country! What countryman are you? English, no doubt." †

"A Frenchman, and your humble servant, mademoiselle, or madame. You are probably of Cordova?"

"No."

"You are at least Andalusian? I fancy I can detect as much in your soft accent."

"If you remark people's accents so closely you ought to be able to divine who I am."

* A café furnished with an ice-house, or rather with a depot of snow. In Spain there is scarcely a village without its *neveria*.

† In Spain every traveller who does not carry samples of cottons or silks passes for an Englishman—*Inglosito*. It is the same in the East. At Chalcis I have had the honor of being announced as a Μιλόρδος Φραντξέσος.

"I believe you are of the Holy Land—a few steps from Paradise."

I had learnt this metaphor, which refers to Andalusia, from my friend Francisco Sevilla, the well-known *picador*.

"Bah!—Paradise! People here say it is not for such as we."

"Then you must be Moorish, or—" I stopped, not liking to say "a Jewess."

"Go along! go along! You see quite well that I am a gypsy. Do you wish me to tell you *la baji* (good-fortune)? Have you ever heard of La Carmencita? I am she!"

I was such an infidel at that time—it is fifteen years ago, remember—that I did not recoil with horror at finding myself in company with a sorceress. "All right," I said to myself. "Last week I supped with a bandit—a highway robber; to-day I am eating ices with a handmaiden of the devil! When travelling it is well to see everything!" I had besides another reason for cultivating her acquaintance. When I quitted the University I confess to my shame that I had lost some time in studying the occult sciences, and many times I had attempted to summon up the spirits of darkness. Although long before cured of my passion for such researches, I nevertheless still retained a certain curiosity regarding all superstitions, and it was a treat to me to ascertain to what pitch the arts of magic had attained amongst the gypsies.

As we chatted we had entered the *neveria,* and seated ourselves at a small table lighted by a wax candle placed within a glass shade. I had then plenty of opportunity to observe the *gitana,* while respectable people eating their ices were astounded to see me in such society.

I very much doubt whether Madmoiselle Carmen was of the true blood—at any rate, she was the prettiest of all the women of her race whom I ever met. To be beautiful, a woman, say the Spaniards, must unite in herself thirty points; or, if you please, you may define her by ten adjectives, each applicable to three parts of her person. For instance, she should have three black points—the eyes, the eyelids, and the eyebrows; three delicate, fine—the fingers, the lips, and the hair, &c. See Brantôme for the others. My Bohemian could not pretend to the necessary perfection. Her skin, though quite smooth, approached somewhat to the coppery tinge. Her eyes were obliquely set, but large and full; her lips rather thick, but well cut, and permitted the teeth—white as blanched almonds—to be seen. Her hair was perhaps a trifle

coarse, but had a blue sheen running through it, like that one
sees in a raven's wings, and was long and luxuriant. Not to
weary you with a detailed description, I will merely say that
with each fault she united a good point, which came out
perhaps more by virtue of the contrast. She was of a strange
and savage beauty—a face which at first surprised you, but it
was one you could never forget. Her eyes especially had an
expression at once voluptuous and fierce, which I have never
since noticed in any human eyes. "Eye of gypsy, eye of wolf"
is a Spanish saying which denotes quick observation. If you
have not time to go to the Zoological Gardens to study the
expression of the wolf's eyes, look at your cat when he is
watching a sparrow!

One felt that it would be ridiculous to have one's fortune
told in a café, so I begged the pretty sorceress to permit me to
accompany her home. She agreed without difficulty, but again
she was anxious to know how time sped, and begged me to
strike my repeater once more.

"Is it really gold?" she asked, as she gazed at the watch
attentively.

When we resumed our way it was dark night, the majority
of the shops were shut, and the streets were almost deserted.
We passed the bridge over the Guadalquiver, and at the end
of the suburb we reached a house with nothing of the palatial
about it. A child opened the door to us. The gypsy said something to her in a language unknown to me, which I have since
discovered was the Romany, or *chepe-calli,* the idiom of the
gitanos. The child immediately disappeared, leaving us in a
room of considerable dimensions, furnished with a small
table, two stools, and a chest. I must not forget a jar of water,
a pile of oranges, and a hank of onions.

As soon as we were alone the gypsy took from the chest a
pack of cards, which appeared to have seen much service, a
loadstone, a dried chameleon, and some other objects necessary
for the practice of her art. Then she bade me cross my left
hand with a piece of silver, and the magic ceremonies began.
It is useless to repeat her predictions, but by her manner of
operating it was evident that she was a practised sorceress.

Unfortunately it was not long ere we were disturbed. The
door was suddenly and violently thrown open; a man wrapped
up to the eyes in a brown cloak entered the room, and apos-
trophised the gypsy in a by no means gentle fashion. I did not
understand what he was saying, but the tone of his voice

indicated that he was in a very bad temper. The *gitana* ex-
hibited neither surprise nor anger at his appearance, but she
hastened to meet him, and with extraordinary volubility addressed some words to him in the mysterious language which
she had already made use of in my presence. The word
payllo, frequently repeated, was the only one I understood. I
was aware that by this term the gypsies designate any stranger. Supposing that it referred to me, I anticipated a rather
delicate explanation; already I had grasped one of the legs of
the stool, and was communing with myself as to the precise
moment when I should hurl it at the head of the intruder,
when the latter, pushing the girl rudely aside, advanced
towards me, and then recoiling, exclaimed—

"Ah, sir, it is *you* then!"

I looked at him in my turn, and recognized my acquaintance Don José. At that moment a feeling of regret that I had
not let him be hanged came over me.

"Ah, it is you, my brave fellow!" I exclaimed, laughing with
as little bitterness as I could manage. "You have interrupted
mademoiselle and me at the very moment when she was revealing to me some very interesting things."

"Always the same—this shall finish it!" he muttered between his teeth, and darting a furious look at her.

The gypsy nevertheless continued to address him in her
language. She got more excited by degrees. Her eyes flashed,
became suffused with blood, and terrible in their aspect; her
features contracted; she stamped her foot; it seemed to me
that she was inciting him to do something which he had some
hesitation in doing. What it was I understood only too well
when I saw her pass and repass her little hand across her
neck. I was constrained to believe that it was a question of
cutting somebody's throat, and I had some suspicion that this
throat was my own!

To all this torrent of eloquence Don José only replied
sharply in a few words. Then the gypsy darted at him a glance
of profound contempt, and seating herself *a la turque* in a
corner of the room, she selected an orange from the heap,
peeled it, and began to eat it.

Don José took me by the arm, opened the door, and led me
into the street. We proceeded about two hundred paces in
silence. Then extending his hand he said, "Keep straight on
and you will come to the bridge!"

He immediately turned his back upon me, and hurried

away. I reached my inn feeling somewhat sheepish and in bad temper. The worst of it was that when I undressed I perceived my watch was missing!

Several considerations prevented me from seeking to recover it in the morning, or to solicit the aid of the law in seeking it. I finished my work on the manuscript in the convent, and started for Seville. After several months' wandering in Andalusia I returned to Madrid and I was obliged to pass Cordova. I had no intention of making a long stay there, for I had taken a dislike to this fine city and its bathers. However, there were some friends to be visited, some commissions to be executed, which would detain me in the ancient capital of the Mussulman princes for three or four days.

As soon as I made my appearance at the convent of the Dominicans one of the fathers, who had always displayed the keenest interest in my researches concerning the site of Munda, welcomed me with open arms.

"God be praised," he said. "Welcome indeed, my dear friend. We believed you dead, and I myself have said *paters* and *aves*—which I do not regret—for the repose of your soul! So you have not been assassinated; we knew you had been robbed!"

"How so?" I inquired in surprise.

"Well, you remember you used to strike that beautiful watch of yours when we wanted to know the time in the library. It has been found, and will be returned to you"——

"That is to say," interrupted I, somewhat put out of countenance, "supposing I have lost it."

"The scoundrel is in custody," continued the friar; "and as we knew he was the kind of fellow to shoot a man in order to take a *piecette*, we were all terribly afraid he had killed you. I will go with you to the corrégidor, and we will recover your beautiful watch. And then don't say that justice is not done in Spain!"

"I confess," I replied, "that I would rather lose my watch then be instrumental in hanging a poor devil, particularly because—because"——

"Oh, do not be in the least alarmed; he is well certified to, and they cannot hang him twice. When I say hang him, I mean garotte him. This robber of yours is a *hidalgo*, and so he will be garotted the day after to-morrow without fail.*

* In 1830 the nobility still enjoyed this privilege. In the present day, under constitutional government, the common criminals have gained the right to be garotted.

You perceive that a robbery more or less can make no difference in his case. I would to Heaven it were only robbery, but he has committed many murders, each one more horrible than that which preceded it."

"What is his name?"

"He is known in this country as José Navarro, but he has another Basque name which neither you nor I shall ever succeed in pronouncing. He is a man to see, and you who love to study the curious characteristics of the country ought not to neglect the opportunity of learning how in Spain these scoundrels are sent out of the world. He is in the chapel, and Fra Martinez will conduct you thither."

My friend the Dominican insisted so strongly upon my seeing the apparatus for the *petit pendement pien choli,* that I was unable to resist him. I went to see the prisoner, furnished with a bundle of cigars, which I trusted would atone for my intrusion.

They admitted me to see Don José just as he was finishing a meal. He bowed coldly to me and thanked me politely for the cigars which I had brought him. After counting them he selected a few and returned the remainder, observing that he should not want any more than those he then had!

I inquired whether by money or some little influence I could not in some measure ameliorate his condition. At first he shrugged his shoulders, smiling sadly; but after a while changing his mind he begged that I would cause a mass to be said for his soul.

"Would you," he added, timidly, "would you have another said for a woman who injured you?"

"Assuredly," I replied, "but I do not think that any woman has injured me in this country."

He took my hand and shook it gravely. After a momentary silence, he resumed——

"Dare I venture to ask you a favor? When you return to your own land perhaps you will pass through Navarre, at least you will pass by Vittoria, which is not very far from it."

"Yes," I replied, "I shall certainly pass by Vittoria, but it is not unlikely that I shall turn aside to Pampeluna and on your account I will willingly make the *detour.*"

"Well, if you go to Pampeluna you will find more than one object of interest to detain you. It is a beautiful city. I will give you this medal (he showed me a silver medal which he wore round his neck), you will wrap it in paper"—he paused for an instant to master his emotion—"and you will send it or cause it to be sent to a good woman, whose address I will give you. You will say that I am dead, but do not tell her in what manner I died."

I promised to carry out his wishes. I saw him again on the following morning, and I passed a portion of the day with him. It was from his own lips that I learned the sad story which follows:—

III.

I was born, said he, at Elizondo, in the valley of Batzan. My name is Don José Lizarabengoa, and you know Spain well enough, sir, to understand that I am of the Basque country, and of ancient Christian lineage. If I take the title of Don it is because I have a right to it, and if I were in Elizondo I would show you my genealogy on parchment. I was destined for the Church, and compelled to study for it, but I did not profit by it. I was too fond of playing tennis and that was the ruin of me. When we Navarros play tennis we forget all else. One day when I had won a match a youth of Alava picked a quarrel with me. We fought with *maquilas*,* and still I had the advantage, but I was obliged to fly the country. I fell in with some dragoons and enlisted in the Almanza regiment of cavalry. People from our parts soon pick up the trade of a soldier. I quickly became a corporal, and was in a fair way to become quarter-master when to my misfortune I was put on guard at the tobacco manufactory of Seville. If you have ever been to Seville you have noticed that great building outside the ramparts near the Guadalquiver. It seems as if I can still see the door and the guard-house beside it. When they are off duty the Spaniards play cards or sleep, but I, a free Navarro, was always accustomed to employ myself. I made a chain of brass wire to sustain my priming-needle. One day my comrades exlaimed, "The clock is striking, the girls are going to work!" You know there are about four hundred or five hundred women employed in the cigar-making. They roll the cigars in the large room into which no man is permitted to enter without permission from the municipal magistrate, because the girls work in undress, the young ones particularly, when the weather is warm. When the young women return to work after dinner, many young fellows go to see them pass, and they are some of all sorts. There are few of these ladies

* Iron-shod sticks.

who would refuse a silk mantilla, and the inexperienced ones at this fishing have only to stoop to catch a fish. While the other men were looking on I remained on my bench near the door. I was young then and home-sick, and did not believe that there were anywhere pretty girls without the blue skirts, and the plaits of hair falling over their shoulders.* Besides, these Andalusians frightened me; I had not yet grown accustomed to their manners. They were always full of raillery, never serious or speaking a sensible word. I was working away at my chain when I heard some townspeople say, "Look at the *gitanella!*" I looked up and saw her. It was on a Friday, and I shall never forget it. I saw that Carmen, whom you know of, at whose house I found you some months ago.

She wore a red skirt, very short, which exposed to view her white silk stockings, with many a hole in them, and tiny shoes of morocco leather, tied with scarlet ribbons. She had thrown back her mantilla so as to display her shoulders, and an immense bunch of acacia blossom, which was stuck in her chemise. She also carried a flower in her mouth, and she walked with a movement of a thoroughbred filly from the Cordova stud. In my country a woman in such a costume would have made people cross themselves. At Seville every one paid some gay compliment to the girl on her appearance. She replied to them all, looking sideways as she went along, with her hand on her hip, as bold as the true gypsy she was. At first she did not take my fancy, and I continued my occupation, but she— after the nature of women and cats, which will not come when they are called and which come when they are not called—stopped in front of me and said, in the Andalusian form:—

"Gossip, will you give me your chain to hang the key of my strong box on?"

"It is to hang my priming-needle on," I replied.

"Your priming-needle! Ah, the señor makes lace, then; he requires needles."

Every one began to laugh at me. I felt myself growing red, and could make no reply.

"Well, my hearty," she continued, "make me seven ells of black lace for a mantilla, thou primer of my soul."

Then, taking the flower from between her lips, she flipped it at me with a movement of her thumb, and struck me between the eyes. Sir, I felt as if I had received a bullet in the fore-

* The ordinary costume of the peasant girls of Navarre and the Basque provinces.

head. I did not know what to do with myself; I stood as stiff as a board. When she had entered the factory I perceived the flower, which had fallen at my feet. I do not know what possessed me, but I picked it up when my comrades were not looking, and put it carefully in my vest. That was the first act of folly.

Two or three hours after, while I was still thinking of the incident, a porter arrived at the guard-house, out of breath and greatly discomposed. He told us that a woman had been assassinated in the great room of the factory, and that it was necessary to have the guard in. The sergeant ordered me to take two men and go and see what was the matter. I took the men and went up. Picture to yourself the sight that met my view when I entered—about three hundred women *en chemise,* or with as little as possible on them—screaming, crying, gesticulating, and making such a row that you couldn't have heard thunder. At one side a female was sprawling on the floor drenched in blood, with a cross—an X—cut on her face with a knife. Opposite the wounded woman, who was being tended by the best of the females, I perceived Carmen, restrained by five or six of her associates. The wounded woman kept crying out that she was dying and wanted a priest. Carmen said nothing; she clenched her teeth, and rolled her eyes like a chameleon.

"What is all this about?" I inquired. I had considerable difficulty in ascertaining what had passed, for all the women talked at once.

It would appear that the injured woman had boasted of having sufficient money in her pocket to buy a donkey at the market of Triona.

"Shut up!" exclaimed Carmen, who had a tongue of her own, "why, you haven't enough to purchase a brush."

The other, stung by the reproach, perhaps because she felt there were some suspicions concerning the article, replied that she did not know anything about brushes, not having the honor to be a gypsy or a daughter of Satan, but that Mademoiselle Carmencita would soon make the donkey's acquaintance when the corrégidor led it out for a walk with two lacqueys behind to beat the flies off.

"Well, then, for my part," replied Carmen, "I will make places for the flies to settle on your cheeks, for I will make a draught-board of them." *

* *Pinter un janeque*—to paint or chequer. The Spanish draughtboards are, for the most part, in red and white squares.

On that, criss-cross, she began, with the knife she used for cutting the cigars, to slash a St. Andrew's cross on the woman's face.

The case was perfectly clear. I seized Carmen by the arm.

"Sister," I said politely, "you must come with me."

She darted a look of recognition at me, but she said resignedly:—

"Let us go then. Where is my mantilla?"

She put it over her head in such a fashion as only to permit her fine eyes to be seen, and followed my two men as quiet as a lamb. When we reached the guard-house the quarter-master said the case was a serious one, and that he must send the culprit to prison. I was told off to conduct her. I placed her between two dragoons, and I marched behind as a corporal should do. We started for the city. At first the gypsy maintained a strict silence, but in Serpent Street—you know it, it well deserves its name with all its windings—in Serpent Street she began her manœuvres by letting her mantilla fall upon her shoulders, so as to enable me to see her winning face, and, turning towards me as far as she could, she said:—

"My officer, whither are you taking me?"

"To prison, my poor child," I replied, as gently as I could —just as a true soldier ought to talk to his prisoner, particularly when the prisoner is a woman.

"Alas! what will become of me! Señor officer, have pity on me! You are so young, so kind." Then, in a lower tone, she continued, "Let me escape. I will give you a piece of *bar lachi*, which will make you beloved by all the women."

(The *bar lachi*, sir, is a loadstone, with which the gypsies say one may work charms when one knows how to make use of it. Give a woman a pinch of it, grated, in a glass of water, and she will not be able to resist you.)

I replied, as seriously as I could—

"We are not here to talk nonsense, we must proceed to the prison; such is the order, and there is no help for it."

We Basque people have a dialect which the Spaniards can readily recognize, but there is scarcely one of them who can even say *vai jaoni* (yes, sir). Carmen, then, had no difficulty in discovering that I came from the Provinces. You know, sir, that the gypsies, having no definite country of their own, are always wandering hither and thither, speaking all languages, and the majority of them are as much at home in Portugal as in France, or in the Provinces, or Catalonia; even amongst the

Moors and the English they can make themselves understood. Carmen, then, knew the Basque dialect pretty well.

"*Laguna ene bihotsarena,* friend of my soul," she said suddenly. "Are you from the country?"

(Our language, sir, is so beautiful that when we hear it spoken in a strange place it thrills us. I wish I had a confessor from the Provinces, he muttered. Then, after a pause, he resumed:—)

"I am from Elizondo," I replied in Basque, very much moved at hearing my native tongue.

"And I am from Etchalar," she said. (That is a district some four hours' journey from us.) I was brought to Seville by the gypsies. I have been working in the factory so as to make sufficient to take me back to Navarre again to my dear mother, whose only support I am, and the little *barretcea* (garden), with its twenty cider apple-trees. Ah, if I were only there again, near the white mountains! They have insulted me because I do not belong to this country of pick-pockets, merchants of rotten oranges; and these low women are all against me because I declared that all their 'jacks' of Seville, with their knives, would not frighten one fellow from our part of the country, with only his blue *beret* and his *maquilla.*"

She was lying, sir; she has always lied. Indeed I doubt whether in all her life that girl ever spoke a word of truth. But when she spoke I believed her. She was stronger than I. She talked broken Basque, and I believed she came from Navarre. Her eyes, mouth and complexion stamped her a gypsy. I was befooled—mad—and no longer paid attention to anything. I thought that if the two Spaniards with me had said anything in disparagement of the country I would have slashed them across the face just as she had treated her comrade. In fact I was like a man intoxicated. I began to talk nonsense, and was ready to commit any folly.

"If I were to give you a push, countryman, and you were to fall down, I should have only those two Castilian conscripts to detain me," she said.

Faith, I quite forgot my orders, and I replied: "Well, my friend, my countrywoman, try it; and may Our Lady of the Mountain aid you." At that moment we were passing by one of those narrow alleys of which there are so many in Seville. Suddenly Carmen turned round and gave me a blow with her clenched hand on the chest. I fell head over heels purposely. With one bound she jumped over me and ran away, exhibiting a pair of legs such as—well: They talk of "Basque legs"—hers outshone them all. They were as quick as they were well turned! I got up immediately, but I managed to get my lance barwise across the alley, so my companions were prevented from starting in pursuit for a while. Then I set off running myself and my men after me, but there was no chance of our overtaking her, accoutred as we were with our spurs, our sabres, and lances! In less time than I take to tell you the incident, the prisoner had disappeared. Besides, all the gossips of the quarter assisted her flight and laughed at us, putting us also on the wrong scent. After much marching and counter-marching it became necessary for us to return to the guard-house without the receipt from the governor of the prison!

My men, to escape punishment, said that Carmen and I had conversed in the Basque dialect, and that it did not seem quite natural, to tell the truth, that a blow from such a little girl would knock over a man of my weight. All this looked very suspicious for me—rather too clear, in fact. When I went down stairs again I was degraded and sent to prison for a month. This was my first punishment since I had enlisted. Farewell then to the stripes of quarter master which I had already made sure of.

My first days in prison passed very sadly. When I became a soldier I had pictured to myself that I should at least reach the grade of officer. Longa, Mina, my compatriots, are even "captains-general"; Chapalangarra, who is a negro and a refu-gee like Mina in your country, Chapalangarra was a colonel, and I have played tennis twenty times with his brother, who was a poor devil, like myself. Then, I said to myself, "All that time you served without punishment is now so much time lost. You have a black mark against you; to reinstate yourself in the opinion of your superiors you will have to work ten times harder than when you were a conscript. And for what have I been punished? For a chit of a gypsy who laughs at me, and who at this moment is at large in some corner of the town." Nevertheless I could not help thinking of her. Will you believe it, sir, those stockings full of holes, which she so liberally displayed when she made her escape, were always before my eyes. I looked out between the bars of my prison window, and amongst all the women who passed in the street I did not see one who was worth that little devil. And then, in spite of myself, I would clasp the flower which she had thrown at me, and which, dried though it was, still preserved its perfume. If there are witches this girl was one of them.

One day the gaoler entered and gave me a loaf of Alcala bread.*

"Look here," he said, "see what your cousin has sent you."

I took the bread—very much surprised—for I had no cousin in Seville. It is a mistake perhaps, I thought, as I looked at the loaf, but it was so appetizing—it felt so fresh and good, that without troubling myself to find out whence it had come, or for whom it was intended, I determined to eat it. As I was cutting it my knife struck against something hard. I looked carefully and found a small English file, which had been slipped into the oven before the bread was baked. There was also in the loaf a piece of gold (two piastres.) There was no longer room for doubt. The present came from Carmen. Liberty is everything with people of her race, and they would set fire to a town to avoid a day in prison. Besides the girl was shrewd, and with that loaf had befooled the gaolers. In an hour the thickest bar could be cut with the little file, and with the assistance of the two-piastre piece I could exchange my uniform for a civilian dress at the next clothes shop. You can imagine that a man who had many times gone birds-nesting for young eaglets over our cliffs would not be much put out to descend into the street from a window less than thirty feet from the ground. But I did not want to escape. I still preserved my honor as a soldier, and desertion seemed to me a great crime. But I was touched by this token of remembrance. When one is in prison one loves to think that one has a friend outside who is interested in one. The gold piece rather offended me. I would have liked very much to have sent it back, but where could I find my creditor? That did not appear a very easy task.

After having been degraded I did not think I had anything more to suffer, but there was a humiliation in store for me. That was when, on my release from prison, I was sent to duty and put on sentry like a common soldier. You can scarcely imagine what a sensitive man feels on such an occasion as this. I believe I would rather have been shot. Then, at least, one marches along in front of the platoon; one feels of importance, every one is looking at you.

I was posted as sentry at the door of the colonel's house. He was a young man, rich, a "good fellow," who lived to

* Alcala de los Panaderos: a small town two leagues from Seville, where delicious bread is made. It is said that the water of Alcala is the cause of this excellence, and a quantity of it is carried to Seville every day.

amuse himself. All the young officers came thither and many citizens, women and actresses—so it was said. For my part, I felt as if every one in the city had agreed to meet there to stare at me. The colonel's carriage arrived, with his valet on the box. Whom did I see descend from it? *La Gitanilla!* She was decked out "as fine as fivepence," dressed up and bedizened, all gold and ribbons. A spangled dress, blue spangled shoes; flowers and trimmings all over her. She had a Basque tambourine in her hand. With her were two other gypsy women, one young and the other old. There is always an old woman to lead them. Then an old man with a guitar, also a gypsy, to play and make them dance. You know that people often amuse themselves by inviting gypsies to their parties and making them dance to the *romalis,* their characteristic dance; and often for other purposes.

Carmen recognized me, and we exchanged glances. I don't know why, but at that moment I wished myself a hundred feet underground.

"*Agur laguna* (good day, comrade). My officer, you are mounting guard like a raw recruit."

And ere I could find words to reply, she had entered the house.

All the guests were assembled in the *patio,* and, notwithstanding the crowd, I could see almost all that was passing through the railings.* I could hear the castanets, the tambourine, the laughter and applause; sometimes I could perceive *her* head when she sprang up with her tambourine. Then I heard the officers address to her remarks which made the blood mount to my face, but what she said in reply I do not know. On that day, I think, I began to love her in earnest, for three or four times came into my head the notion to rush into the *patio* and stab those coxcombs who were flirting with her. My purgatory lasted a good hour; then the gypsies came out and the carriage rolled up to fetch them. Carmen, in passing, looked at me with those eyes of hers—you know them—and said to me in a low voice—

"Countryman, when one likes good fritters one goes to Triana, to Lillas Pastia's."

* The majority of the houses in Seville have an interior court surrounded by porticoes. People live there in summer. This court is covered with an awning which is watered by day and removed at night. The street door is almost always open, and the passage leading to the court, *zaguan,* is closed by an iron grating very elegantly worked.

Lightly as a kid she sprang into the carriage, the coachman whipped his mules, and the joyous band drove off; I knew not whither.

You will guess that when I came off duty I went to Triana; but first I got shaved and brushed up, as if for a parade. She was at Lillas Pastia's. He was an old fruit-seller, a gypsy as swarthy as a Moor, at whose establishment many of the townspeople came to eat fried fish, more particularly, I believe, since Carmen had taken up her quarters there.

"Lillas," she said, when she caught sight of me, "I will do nothing more to-day. To-morrow it will be day again.* Come along, *pays;* let us have a stroll together."

She threw her mantilla over her face and we were in the street before I knew where I was going.

"Señorita," I said, "I believe I have to thank you for a present that you sent me when I was in prison. I have eaten the bread; the file served to sharpen my lance point, and I kept it in remembrance of you; but the money, here it is."

"Why, he has kept the money!" she exclaimed with a burst of laughter. "Well, so much the better, for at present I am not well in funds. But what matter? A wandering dog will not die of hunger.† Come along, let us eat it all; you shall treat me."

We had taken the road to Seville. At the entrance of Serpent Street she purchased a dozen oranges, which she made me carry in my pocket-handkerchief. A little farther on she purchased some bread, sausage, and a bottle of Manzanilla. At length she entered a confectioner's shop. There she threw upon the counter the piece of gold which I had returned to her and another which she had in her own pocket, with some silver. At last she asked me for all I had, too. I had only some small change, which I handed to her, feeling very much ashamed that I had no more. I believe she would have carried off all the stock if she could. She chose the best and the dearest articles—*yemas* (yolks of eggs, sugared), *turm* (a kind of nougat), crystallized fruits—so long as the money lasted. I had to carry all these in paper bags. Perhaps you know Candilejo Street, where is a head of Don Pedro the Justiciary.**

* *"Manana sera otro dia"*—Spanish proverb.

† *Chuquel sos pirela cocal terela*—"A wandering dog finds a bone."—Bohemian proverb.

** King Pedro, whom we call the cruel, and whom Queen Isabella the Catholic called the "Guardian of Justice," was fond of walking about the streets of Seville, seeking adventures, as the Caliph Haroun al Raschid used to do. One evening he got into a

It ought to have "given me pause." We halted before an old house in this street. She entered the walk and rapped at the ground-floor. A gypsy, a true servant of Satan, opened the door to us. Carmen said something to her in Romany. The old woman grumbled at first, but to appease her Carmen gave her two oranges and a handful of bonbons; she also permitted her to taste the wine. Then she put her cloak on her, and led her to the door, which she secured with a bar of wood. As soon as we were alone Carmen began to dance as if she were possessed, singing "You are my *rom* and I am your *romi*." *

I was standing in the middle of the room burthened with all the packages, not knowing where to put them. She threw them all upon the floor and clasping me round the neck exclaimed "I pay my debts; I pay my debts—it is the law of the Cales." †

Ah, sir—that day! that day! when I recall it I forget *to-morrow!*

dispute in a narrow street with a man who was serenading. A duel ensued, and the king killed the amorous cavalier. Hearing the clashing of the swords, an old woman looked out of a window holding a small lamp (*candilejo*) in her hand. It should be stated that the King Don Pedro, although lusty and strong, was afflicted with a curious malformation. When he walked his knee-pans "cracked" loudly. The old woman had therefore no difficulty in recognizing the King. Next day the magistrate in charge came to make his report to the sovereign. "Sire, a duel was fought last night in such a street; one of the combatants was slain." "Have you discovered the murderer?" "Yes, sire." "Why has he not been punished?" "Sire, I await your orders." "Let the law take its course!" Now the King had promulgated a decree that all duelists should be beheaded. The magistrate entered into the business like a man of spirit. He caused the head of a statue of the King to be sawn off, and exposed it in a niche in the midst of the street in which the duel had been fought. The King and all the citizens considered this a very happy thought. The street was named after the lamp held by the old woman, the sole witness of the encounter. This is the popular version. Junga relates the adventure somewhat differently (see the "Annals of Seville," vol. ii., p. 136). However this may be, Candilejo Street still exists in Seville, and in that street there is a bust in stone which they say is a likeness of Don Pedro. Unfortunately this bust is modern. The old one was very much worn away, and in the seventeenth century it was replaced by that now in existence.

* *Rom*—husband; *Romi*—wife.

† Dark people—a name the gypsies give themselves.

(The brigand was silent for a while, then after he had relighted his cigar he continued:—)

We remained together the whole of the day, eating, drinking, and—and all the rest of it. When she had devoured the sweets, like a child of six years old, she thrust her hands into the old woman's water-jar. "Now to make a *sorbet*," she said. She broke the *yemas* by dashing them against the wall—"so that the flies may leave us in peace," she remarked. There was no trick or folly that she did not perpetrate. I expressed a wish to see her dance, but where could we find castanets? She without hesitation took the old woman's only plate, smashed it in pieces, and then she danced the *romalis*, clattering the pieces of the plate as if they had been castanets of ebony or ivory. One would never feel bored with a girl like her—I can answer for that! Evening closed in, and I could hear the drums beating the "retreat."

"I must return to barracks," I said, "for roll-call."

"To barracks!" she echoed in a contemptuous tone. "So you are a negro-slave and permit yourself to be driven with the whip! You are a regular canary in appearance and disposition.* Go along with you! You have a chicken's heart!"

I stayed, resigned in advance to the police-cell. In the morning it was she who first spoke of our separation.

"Listen to me, Joseita," she said, "I have paid you, haven't I? According to our law I owed you nothing, since you are a *payllo;* but you are a good fellow, and you have pleased me. We are quits! Good-day."

I asked when I should see her again.

"When you are a little less stupid," she replied, laughing. Then in a more serious tone she continued, "Do you know, my friend, that I believe I love you a little bit? But that cannot last. Dog and wolf cannot keep house together long. Perhaps if you were to subscribe to the Egyptian law I should love to be your *romi*. But this is all nonsense—that cannot be. Bah! my lad, take my word for it, you have had the best of the bargain. You have foregathered with the devil; yes—with the devil! He is not always black, and he has not twisted your neck. I am dressed in wool, but I am not a sheep.† Go and put a taper before your *majari*.** She has well deserved it.

* The Spanish dragoons wear yellow uniforms.
† *Medicas viarda de jorpoy bus ne sino braco"*—Gypsy proverb.
** The Virgin Mary.

Come; good-bye once again. Think no more of Carmencita or she may make you marry a widow with wooden legs." *

As she ceased speaking she unfastened the bar which closed the door; and once in the street she wrapped herself in her mantilla, and showed me her heels.

She had said what was true. I would have been wise to have thought no more about her, but after that day in Candilejo Street I could not think of anything else. I walked about all day long in the hope of meeting her again. I inquired about her from the old woman and from the seller of fried fish. Both declared that she had gone to Laloro,† as they call Portugal. Probably it was in accordance with Carmen's instructions that they said so, but it was not long before I discovered that they were lying. Some weeks after my long day in Candilejo Street I was put on sentry at one of the city gates. Some little distance from this gate a breach had been made in the wall whereat people used to walk during the day, and where a sentry was posted at night to guard against smugglers. During the day I perceived Lillas Pastia lingering around the guard-house chatting with my comrades, all of whom were acquainted with him, his fish, and his fritters, which were better still. He approached me and inquired whether I had had any news of Carmen.

"No," I replied.

"Well, then, you soon will, comrade."

He was right. At night I was posted at the breach in the wall. As soon as the corporal had disappeared I perceived a woman approach my post. My heart told me it was Carmen; nevertheless I said, "Be off, you cannot pass here!"

"Come, don't be obstreperous," she replied, as she made herself known to me.

"What! are *you* there, Carmen?"

"Yes, I, countryman; let us have a little conversation together. Do you want to earn a duoro? Some people with packs are coming this way—let them pass."

"No," I replied, "I must oppose their passage. Such are my orders."

"Orders, orders! You did not think of them in Candilejo Street."

"Ah!" I replied, quite upset by the very remembrance, "that

* The gallows—widow of the last man hanged.
† The red land.

was worth the danger of forgetting my duty; but I do not want any money from smugglers."

"Let me see, then. If you do not want any money from smugglers, what do you say to going to dine at old Dorothea's house again!"

"No," I replied, half-suffocated by the effort I was making, "I cannot."

"Very well; if you are so hard to move I know to whom to apply. I will make your officer the offer to go to Dorothea's house. He seems to be a good fellow, and he will put on guard a lad who will not see more than is necessary. Good-bye, canary. I shall laugh when the order is issued for your hanging!"

I was weak enough to call her back, and I promised to permit all the gypsies to pass, if it must be so, provided I obtained the recompense I wished for. She swore to meet me on the following day, and ran off to apprise her friends, who were close by. There were five of them, one being Pastia, and all heavily laden with English goods. Carmen kept watch. She agreed to give the alarm with her castanets whenever she should perceive the rounds, but she had no need to do so. The smugglers very quickly accomplished their business.

Next day I went to Candilejo Street. Carmen was waiting for me, but in a by no means good humor.

"I do not care for people who require to be begged of," she said. "You rendered me a great service the first time without any idea that you would gain anything by it. To-day you are bartering with me. I do not know why I have come, for I don't care for you any longer. So go away; there is a duoro for your trouble!"

I was within an ace of throwing the money at her head, and was obliged to exercise a violent control over myself to avoid striking her. After we had argued for an hour I went away in a furious rage. I wandered for a long time about the city, hither and thither, like a man demented. At length I entered a church, and seating myself in the darkest corner I could find I gave way to tears. Suddenly I heard a voice say—

"A dragoon's tears! I should like to make a philtre of them!"

I looked up. There was Carmen standing before me!

"Well, countryman, are you still wishing for me? I really think I must love you still, for since you left me I have not known what to do with myself. There now, you see I am the supplicant, and want you to come to Candilejo Street."

We made it up then; but Carmen's humor was as variable as our climate. The storm is most likely to break when the sun is shining most brilliantly. She had promised to meet me once again at Dorothea's house, and she did not come, and Dorothea told me, in the calmest manner, that Carmen had gone to Laloro "on Egyptian affairs!"

Guided by experience I sought for Carmen in every place where I fancied she might be found, and I passed up and down Candilejo Street twenty times a day. One evening I was at Dorothea's house, for I had almost tamed the old woman by means of repeated glasses of anisette, when Carmen entered, followed by a young man, a lieutenant in my regiment.

"Get away at once," she said to me in the Basque tongue. I remained stupefied, rage boiling in my heart.

"What is that fellow doing here?" said the lieutenant. "Be off; get out of this!"

I could not move. I felt as if I had quite lost the use of my limbs. The officer seeing that I did not budge, and that I had not even removed my cap, took me by the collar and shook me violently. I do not know what I said. He drew his sword and I drew mine. The old woman seized my arm, and the lieutenant gave me a cut in the forehead, the scar of which remains to this day. I stepped back, and with a shove sent old Dorothea sprawling on the floor. Then, as the lieutenant followed me up, I gave him my point, and he spitted himself on my sword. Then Carmen extinguished the lamp and bade Dorothea to fly. As for myself, I rushed into the street and ran I knew not whither. It seemed to me that some one was following me. When I came to myself I found Carmen beside me. She had not left me.

"You great stupid canary," she said, "you are only good at committing follies. You see I was right when I told you I would only bring trouble upon you. Well, there is a remedy for every ill when one has a 'Fleming of Rome' * for his friend. You must begin by tying this handkerchief over your head, and giving me your sword belt. Wait for me in the alley, I will be back again in two minutes."

She disappeared and quickly returned, carrying a striped cloak for me; how she obtained it I cannot tell. She made me doff my uniform, and put the cloak on over my shirt. Thus

---

* *Flameno de Roma*—a slang term for gypsies. *Roma* in this sense does not refer to the Eternal City, but to the Romi (or married people), as the Bohemians call them. The first seen in Spain came probably from the Netherlands—hence the name Fleming.

accoutred, with the handkerchief over the cut on my head, I had something the appearance of a peasant of Valencia, of whom many come to Seville to sell their *chufas*—orangeade. Then she took me to a house, which bore a striking resemblance to Dorothea's, at the end of a narrow court. She and another gypsy woman washed me, doctored me better than the surgeon-major would have done, and gave me something —I know not what—to drink. At length they laid me on a mattress, and I fell asleep.

The women probably had put some soporific in my drink, for I did not awake until very late the next day. I had a fearful headache, and was rather feverish. It was some time before I could recall the incidents of the terrible drama in which I had taken part on the previous day.

After having dressed my wound, Carmen and her friend both crouched down beside my mattress, and exchanged a few words in *chipe calli*, which seemed to be a medical consultation. They both assured me that I would be cured before long; but, meanwhile, it was absolutely necessary to leave Seville, and as quickly as possible, for if I were arrested I would be shot, to a certainty.

"My lad," said Carmen, "you must do something; now that the king will give you neither rice nor salt cod,* you must find some means of existence. You are too stupid to rob *a pastesas,†* but you are lithe and strong. If you have courage enough go to the coast and be a contrabandist. Have I not promised to get you hanged? That is better than being shot. Besides, if you know how to look after yourself, you may live like a prince so long as the *minons‡* and the coastguard do not catch you."

It was in this pleasing way that that devil of a girl indicated to me the new career for which she destined me—and to tell the truth it was the only one which lay open to me, now that I had rendered myself liable to the punishment of death. Need I confess to you, sir, that she brought me to the decision without much trouble! It seemed to me that we should be thrown into closer contact by this existence so full of risks, and so unlawful. Thenceforth, I believed myself sure of her affection. I had often heard of the contrabandists who traversed Andalusia well-mounted, blunderbuss in hand, and with their mistresses seated behind them. I already pictured myself trot-

---

* The ordinary rations of a Spanish soldier.
† *Ustilar a pastesas,* to rob skillfully, without violence.
‡ A species of free-corps.

ting over the hills and vales with this handsome gypsy behind me. When I mentioned this to her she laughed until she was obliged to hold her sides, and told me there was nothing so pleasant as a night passed in the camp when each *rom* retired with his *romi* beneath the shelter of the little tent formed of three hoops with a blanket thrown over them.

"If I keep with you in the mountains, I shall always be sure of you," I said. "There there will be no lieutenants to share with me."

"Ah, you are jealous," she replied; "so much the worse for you. How can you be such a fool! Don't you see that I love you, since I have never asked you for any money?"

When she talked in this fashion I felt inclined to strangle her.

To cut the story short, sir, Carmen procured me a civilian dress, in which I escaped from Seville unrecognized. I proceeded to Jerez with a letter from Pastia to a seller of anisette, at whose house the smugglers used to assemble. I was presented to these gentry, whose chief, named Dancaire, received me into the company. We proceeded to Gaucin, where I again found Carmen, who had appointed to meet me there. In the expedition, she acted as a spy for us, and no one could have been a better one. She had returned from Gibraltar, and had arranged with the captain of a vessel concerning the disembarkation of the English merchandise which we expected to arrive at the coast. We went to await its arrival near Estepona; then we hid a portion of it in the mountains, and laden with the remainder proceeded to Ronda, whither Carmen had preceded us. Then she once more gave us the hint when to enter the town. This first expedition and some others were fortunate. The life of a smuggler pleased me more than that of a soldier. I made Carmen presents. I had money and a mistress. I suffered scarcely any remorse, for as the gypsies say—an itching of pleasure is no itch at all.* We were well received everywhere; my associates treated me well, and even evinced some consideration for me. This was because I had killed a man, and amongst them there was no one who had not a similar exploit to boast of. But what influenced me more than all else in my new life was the frequent presence of Carmen. She displayed more friendship for me than formerly —nevertheless, before her comrades she did not pretend that she was my mistress, and had even made me swear with all kinds of oaths not to say a word to them on the subject. I was

* *Sarapia sat pesquital ne punzaya.*

so utterly weak before this creature that I obeyed all her caprices. Besides, this was the first occasion on which she displayed any of the reserve of an "honest woman," and I was foolish enough to believe that she had abandoned all her former practices.

Our troop, which was composed of eight or ten men only, assembled together in important junctures, but were usually scattered in pairs or threes in the towns and villages. Each one of us assumed a calling or trade; one was a tinker, another a horse dealer. I was a pedlar. But I very seldom showed myself in the large towns, because of that little affair in Seville. One day, or rather one night, our rendezvous was below Vega. Dancaire and I found ourselves there before the others. He seemed in excellent spirits.

"We shall soon have another comrade," he said. "Carmen has executed one of her best moves. She has managed the escape of her *rom* from the *presidio* at Tarifa."

I was just beginning to understand the gypsy dialect, which nearly all my associates made use of, and the word *rom* gave me a chill.

"What, her husband! Is she married?" I asked.

"Yes," replied the captain, "to Garcia, the one-eyed, a gypsy as 'deep' as she is. The poor fellow was in penal servitude. Carmen got round the surgeon so cleverly that she obtained her *rom's* liberty. Ah! that girl is worth her weight in gold. It is two years since she first began to plan his escape. Nothing had succeeded until the officer was changed. With the latter it seems she quickly found the means to make herself understood."

You can imagine with what pleasure I listened to this news. I soon met Garcia the one-eyed; he was one of the most repulsive villains whom Bohemia ever reared, a dark skin and a still blacker soul. He was the most unmitigated ruffian that ever I met in my life. Carmen came with him, and when she called him her *rom* in my presence you should have seen the "eyes" she made to me, and the grimaces at him when his back was turned. I was very angry, and would not speak to her all the evening. In the morning we had made up our bales and were already on our way when we perceived that a dozen horsemen were after us. The Andalusian boasters, who always talk in the most bloodthirsty manner, showed a very firm front. There was a general stampede. Dancaire, Garcia, a fine young fellow from Edja called Remendado, and Carmen did not lose their presence of mind. The others abandoned the mules and threw themselves into the ravines, where the dragoons could not follow them. We could not save our mules, and we hastened to loose the most valuable portion of our booty and to take it on our shoulders. We then endeavored to escape over the rocks, and by the steepest and roughest slopes. We cast our bales before us, and followed them as well as we could, sliding down on our heels. All this time the enemy was firing at us. It was the first time that I had heard the whistling of bullets, and it did not make me feel quite at ease. When one has a wife in prospect there is no merit in risking death. We all escaped except poor Remendado, who got a bullet in his loins. I threw away my pack and endeavored to assist him.

"Fool!" exclaimed Garcia, "what have we to do with that carrion? Pick up your load, and don't lose the cotton stockings."

"Let him go," said Carmen to me.

Fatigue obliged me to lay the lad for a moment beneath the shelter of a rock. Garcia advanced and discharged his blunderbuss at his head.

"He will be a clever fellow who will recognize him now," he remarked, as he gazed at the features which a dozen bullets had shattered.

Such, sir, was the delightful kind of life I had embraced. In the evening we found ourselves in a thicket, and worn out with fatigue, having nothing to eat, and ruined by the loss of our mules. What did that infernal Garcia do? He took a pack of cards from his pocket and began to play with Dancaire by the light of the fire which had been kindled. Meanwhile I lay down and was watching the stars, thinking of Remendado and wishing I were in his place. Carmen was crouched near me, and from time to time she rattled her castanets, and hummed a tune. Then, approaching me, as if with the intention of whispering to me, she kissed me, almost against my will, two or three times.

"You are the devil," I said to her.

"Yes," she answered.

After some hours' rest she departed for Gaucin, and next morning a little goatherd brought us some bread. We remained all day in the same place, and at night we moved towards Gaucin. We waited for news of Carmen: none came. At daybreak we perceived a muleteer who was guiding a well-dressed woman holding a parasol, and accompanied by a little girl, who seemed to be her servant. Garcia said to us—

"There are two mules and two women which St. Nicholas has sent us. I would rather have had four mules. Never mind. This is my business."

He seized his blunderbuss and descended towards the path; hiding in the brushwood. Dancaire and I followed him a little distance. When we were within range we showed ourselves, and called to the muleteer to halt. The woman instead of being frightened—and our dress was sufficient for that—burst out laughing.

"Ah, the *lilipendi,* they take me for an *erani!*" * It was Carmen, but so well disguised that I would not have recognized her had she spoken in any other language.

She sprang from the mule and spoke for a while in a low tone with Garcia and Dancaire. Then she said to me:

"Canary, we shall meet again before you are hanged. I am going to Gibraltar on 'affairs of Egypt.' You will soon hear me talked about."

We parted after she had indicated to us a place where we could find shelter for some days. This girl was the saving of our troop. We soon received some money which she sent, and a hint, which was worth more to us, namely, that two British noblemen were about to proceed from Gibraltar to Granada by such a route. A word to the wise! They had plenty of money. Garcia wanted to kill them, but Dancaire and I were opposed to such a measure. We would relieve them of their money, their watches, and their shirts, of which last articles we had great need.

Sir, one may become a rogue without thinking about it. A pretty girl causes you to lose your head; you fight for her: a misfortune happens, it becomes necessary to dwell amid the mountains, and from a smuggler you become a robber before you are aware of the change. We concluded that it would not be well for us to remain in the environs of Gibraltar after that little business with the Englishmen, and we concealed ourselves in the Sierra de Ronda. You have mentioned José-Maria; well, it was there that I made his acquaintance. He brought his mistress with him on these expeditions. She was a pretty girl, well-behaved and modest, with good manners, never uttering an unbecoming word, and of a devotedness—! By way of compensation, he treated her very badly. He was always running after other girls, he "bullied" her, then sometimes he took it into his head to be jealous. Once he struck

* Ah, the fools! do they take me for a lady!

her with his knife. Well, she only loved him the more for that.
That is the way women, particularly Andalusians, are constituted! She was quite proud of the scar on her arm, and ex-
hibited it as one of the most beautiful things in the world.
And then José-Maria was the very worst comrade you could
possibly meet. On one expedition which we undertook he
managed so well that all the profit fell to him, and all the
blows fell on us. But I must resume my story. As we heard
nothing more of Carmen, Dancaire said:

"One of us most proceed to Gibraltar to get news of her
she ought to have prepared something. I would go willingly,
but I am too well known there."

The one-eyed fellow said:

"So am I. I have played too many tricks upon the lobsters,*
and as I have only one eye, it is not easy to escape detection."

"Then I must go," I said in my turn, delighted at the very
idea of seeing Carmen again. "Let us see; what must be
done?"

The others replied:

"You can go to St. Roque whichever way you please, and
when you have got to Gibraltar ask where a person, named
Rollona, a seller of chocolate, lives; when you have found her
out, you will find out what has happened yonder."

It was arranged that we three should start for the Sierra de
Gaucin, that I should leave my companions there and proceed
to Gibraltar as a fruit merchant. At Ronda one of our frater-
nity procured me a passport, at Gaucin I was given a donkey;
I loaded him with oranges and melons, and went on my way.
When I reached Gibraltar I found that Rollona was well
known, but that she had either died or been sent to the gal-
leys, and in my opinion her absence explained how our means
of correspondence with Carmen had failed. I put my donkey
up in a stable, and with my oranges wandered about town as
if to sell them; but, in fact, to endeavor to find some face I
knew. There are plenty of vagrants in "Gib," people from all
parts of the globe, and it is like the tower of Babel, for one
cannot go ten paces along a street without hearing as many
different languages. I met many gypsies, but I scarcely dared
to trust them. I recognized them and they recognized me. We
ascertained that we were of the same class. After two days
spent in useless search, I had learned nothing concerning ei-

* A term applied to the English, because of the color of their
uniforms.

ther Rollona or Carmen, and I was considering whether I should not return to my comrades after making some purchases, when, as I was walking down a street at sunset, I heard a woman's voice from a window say, "Here, you orange-seller!" I looked up, and on a balcony I perceived Carmen leaning over the rail beside an officer in scarlet, with gold epaulets, curled hair, and the appearance generally of a grandee. As for her, she was dressed splendidly: a shawl over her shoulders, a gold comb in her hair, attired in silk, and as cunning as ever—just the same, laughing immoderately. The Englishman, in barbarous Spanish, hailed me, and bade me come up, as madame wanted some oranges; and Carmen said to me in Basque, "Come up, and be astonished at nothing." Nothing could astonish me where she was concerned. I cannot tell whether I was the more glad or disappointed to see her again. A tall, powdered servant let me in, and ushered me into a splendid apartment. Carmen at once addressed me in Basque.

"Mind you do not understand a word of Spanish, and you do not know me."

Then, turning to the Englishman, she said, "I told you all along he was a Basque—you will hear a curious dialect. What a silly look he has, hasn't he? You would take him for a cat surprised in the larder!"

"And you," I replied in my own tongue, "have the air of a brazen-faced quean, and I am greatly disposed to gash your face before your lover."

"My lover!" she exclaimed. "So you have found out that all by yourself. And you are jealous of that fool? Why, you are a greater simpleton than you were before our evenings in Candilejo Street. Don't you see—fool that you are—that I am engaged upon affairs of Egypt, and in the most brilliant fashion? This house is mine; the lobster's guineas will be mine. I shall lead him by the nose, and bring him whence he shall never escape."

"And as for me," I replied, "if you conduct the affairs of Egypt any more in this manner I shall do something which will effectually prevent your beginning again."

"Ah, indeed! Are you my *rom* that you give me orders? The One-Eyed is satisfied. What have you seen here? Ought not you to be content to be the only one who can call himself my *minchorro?*" *

* Lover—or, rather, "fancy-man."

"What does he say?" asked the Englishman.

"He says that he is thirsty, and could manage a good drink," replied Carmen. Then she fell back upon a sofa, screaming with laughter at the translation.

Sir, when that girl laughed there was no use in trying to talk sense. Every one laughed with her. The great Englishman laughed also, like the idiot he was, and bade his people bring me something to drink.

While I was drinking, Carmen said—

"Do you see that ring on his finger? If you like, I will give it to you."

But I answered—

"I would give a finger to have my lord on the mountain, each of us with a *maquila* in our hands."

"*Maquila?* What does he mean?" asked the Englishman.

"*Maquila!*" replied Carmen, still laughing. "*Maquila* is an orange. Is it not a queer term for an orange? He says he would like to make you eat an orange."

"Yes?" replied the Englishman. "Very well, bring more *maquilas* to-morrow."

As we were conversing, the servant announced dinner. Then the Englishman offered his arm to Carmen—as if she could not go in by herself, and threw me a pistole. Carmen, laughing all the time, said to me—

"My lad, I cannot invite you to dinner; but to-morrow, as soon as you hear the drums beating for parade, come here with your oranges. You will find a room better furnished than that in Candilejo Street, and you will see that I am always your Carmencita; and then we can chat over Egyptian affairs."

I made no reply, and I was in the street when the Englishman called out, "Bring the *maquilas* to-morrow." Then I heard Carmen's laughter once more.

I went away, not knowing whither or what I was doing. I scarcely slept, and the morning found me so incensed against the traitress that I resolved to quit Gibraltar without seeing her again. But at the first roll of the drums all my fortitude deserted me. I took my straw basket of oranges and hurried to Carmen. Her jealousy was aroused, and I saw her great eyes watching me. The powdered servant let me in. Carmen sent him on an errand, and as soon as we were alone she burst into one of her peals of crocodile laughter and threw herself on my neck. I had never seen her so lovely. Dressed like a bride, perfumed, surrounded with costly furniture and silken hangings—Ah! and I like the robber that I was!

"Minchorro," said Carmen, "I have a great mind to smash everything here, to set fire to the house and be off for the Sierra!"

Then her caresses, and her laughter! She danced and tore her dress; never did ape perform more gambols, make more grimaces or play more tricks. When she had regained her composure she said—

"Listen; it is a question of Egypt. I want him to take me to Ronda, where I have a sister—a nun. (More laughter.) We will pass by a place which I will tell you of. You can fall upon him and rob him. The better way will be to murder him; but," she added with a diabolical smile which she displayed at certain times, and no one would ever be inclined to imitate it— "do you know what you must do? Let the One-Eyed appear first. Keep a little in the rear yourself. The Lobster is brave and skilful; he has good pistols. Do you understand?"

She interrupted herself with another peal of laughter which made me shiver.

"No," I replied, "I detest Garcia, but he is my comrade. One day perhaps I will relieve you of him, but we will settle our accounts after the fashion of our country. I am only an Egyptian by chance, and in certain ways I shall always remain a pure *Navarro,* as the proverb says" *Navarro fino.*

She replied, "You are a fool—an idiot—a regular *payllo.* You are like the dwarf who believed himself big because he could spit a long distance.* You do not love me—Go along with you!"

When she said "Go along!" I could not go. I promised to leave, to return with my comrades and lie in wait for the Englishman. On her side she promised to be indisposed until the time came for leaving Gibraltar for Ronda. I remained two days longer at Gibraltar. She had the audacity to come in disguise to see me at my inn. I quitted the town, for I also had my own project. I returned to our rendezvous, knowing the place and the hour at which the Englishman and Carmen would pass by. I found Dancaire and Garcia awaiting me. We passed the night in a wood by a fire of pine-cones, which burned splendidly. I proposed to Garcia to have a game of cards. He agreed. At the second game I declared he was

---

* *"Or esorjie de or narsichisle sin chismar lachinguel"*—Gypsy proverb.

cheating. He laughed. I threw the cards in his face. He went
for his blunderbuss, but I put my foot upon it and said:—

"They tell me you can brandish a knife with any Jack of
Malaga. Will you try a bout with me?"

Dancaire wanted to separate us. I had given Garcia a few
blows with my fist. Rage had made him courageous. He had
drawn his knife and I mine. We told Dancaire to stand aside
and see fair play. He saw that it was no use attempting to stop
us and he stood back. Garcia was already crouching like a cat
about to spring upon a mouse. He held his hat in his left
hand, as a guard, his knife advanced in his right. That is the
Andalusian method. I stood like the Navarros, right in front
of him, the left arm raised, the right leg advanced, the knife
held down by the right thigh. I felt stronger than a giant. He
threw himself upon me like a flash, I turned on my left foot
and he found nothing before him, but I caught him in the
throat and the knife entered so far that my hand came chock
under his chin. I drew back the blade so forcibly that it broke.
All was over! The blade was expelled from the wound in a
rush of blood as big as my arm. He fell on his face like a log.

"What have you done?" said Dancaire.

"Listen," I said. "We could not have lived together. I love
Carmen and I want to be the only one! Beside, Garcia was a
brute, and I remember how he served poor Remendado. We
are only two now, but we are good fellows. Look here; will
you have me for a comrade—for life or death?"

Dancaire held out his hand. He was a man fifty years old.

"To the devil with your love affairs," he exclaimed. "If you
had asked for Carmen he would have sold her to you for a
piastre. We are only two now—what shall we do to-morrow?"

"Let me manage it," I replied. "Now I can snap my fingers
at the whole world!"

We buried Garcia and pitched our camp two hundred paces
further on. Next day Carmen and her Englishman passed with
two muleteers and a servant. I said to Dancaire:—

"I will account for the Englishman. You can frighten the
others; they are not armed."

The Englishman was a brave fellow. If Carmen had not
jogged his arm he would have shot me. To be brief, I recon-
quered Carmen that day, and my first words were to tell
her that she was a widow. When she understood how it came
to pass, she said:—

"You will always be a *lilipendi*. Garcia ought to have killed you. Your Navarre guard is all nonsense, and he has conquered better men than you. His time had come, no doubt! Yours will come too!"

"And yours," I replied, "if you are not a true *romi* to me!"

"Well and good!" she replied. "I have seen in the coffee-grounds many a time that our destinies lie together. But he who sows reaps!" And she rattled her castanets as she was in the habit of doing when she wished to get rid of any unpleasant thoughts.

One is apt to forget others when speaking of oneself; all these details bore you no doubt, but I shall soon finish now. The life we lead will last long enough! Dancaire and I associated ourselves with some comrades more trustworthy than the former: we practised smuggling, and sometimes it must be confessed we stopped people on the highway, but only as a last resource and when we had no other means of livelihood. Besides we never ill-treated travellers and we confined ourselves strictly to taking their money.

For many months I was happy with Carmen; she continued to be useful to us in our operations and gave us notice of the good things we could "bring off." She stayed sometimes at Malaga, sometimes at Cordova, sometimes at Granada; but at a word from me she would leave any place and come to meet me in an isolated inn, or even in the camp. Once only, it was at Malaga, did she give me any uneasiness. I knew that she had thrown a glamor over a very rich merchant, with whom probably she proposed to repeat the little arrangement carried out at Gibraltar. Notwithstanding all Dancaire could say to me I went after her and got to Malaga in full daylight. I looked for Carmen, and brought her away immediately. We had some sharp words.

"Do you know," she said, "that since you have really become my *rom*, I care less for you than when you were my *fancy man*. I don't want to be worried and ordered about; what I wish is to be free and to do as I please. Take care—do not push me too far. If you trouble me too much I will find some fellow who will serve you as you served Garcia."

Dancaire reconciled us, but we said things to each other which rankled in our hearts and we were not on such good terms as formerly. A short time afterwards evil befell us. The troops surprised us. Dancaire was killed with two others of our band, two more were made prisoners. I was badly wounded, and without the aid of my trusty steed would have been left in the hands of the soldiers. Worn out by fatigue, with a bullet in my body, I hid myself with only one companion in the forest. I fainted when I dismounted, and I thought I was going to die like a wounded hare in the brushwood. My comrade carried me to a grotto which we knew and then went to seek Carmen. She was at Granada and she came back at once. For fifteen days she never quitted me for a moment. She did not close her eyes; she nursed me with a skill and attention which no woman ever before displayed for a man she loved best. As soon as I could stand up again she carried me off to Granada in secrecy. The gypsies everywhere found us safe lodging, and I passed more than six weeks in a house two doors from the official who was searching for me. More than once from behind a shutter I saw him pass by. At length my health was restored, but I had thought a great deal while on my bed of sickness and I made up my mind to amend my life. I spoke to Carmen about leaving Spain and endeavoring to live honestly in America. She laughed at me.

"We are not fitted for cabbage growing," she replied; "our destiny is to live at the expense of the *payllos*. Look here, I have just arranged a little business with Nathan-ben-Joseph, of Gibraltar. He has a cargo of cotton stuffs which only want your assistance in passing through. He knows you are alive still. He reckons upon you. What shall we say to our correspondents in Gibraltar if you break your word to them?"

I permitted myself to be persuaded and resumed my villainous career.

While I was in hiding at Granada there was a bull-fight there to which Carmen went. When she came back she spoke of a very adroit *picador* named Lucas. She knew the name of his horse and how much his embroidered vest had cost. Inanito, the comrade who had remained with me, said some days afterwards that he had seen Carmen and Lucas at the house of a tradesman of Zacatin. That alarmed me. I asked Carmen how and why she had made the acquaintance of the *picador*.

"He is a man," she said, "with whom we can do some business. The river that makes a noise has either water or pebbles.* He has won 1,200 reals at the bull-ring. One of two things must happen—we must have this money—or, as he is a good rider and a brave fellow, we must enrol him in our band. So-and-so are dead; you must replace them. Take him with you."

* *Len sos sonsi abela, Pani o rebiendani terela*—Gypsy proverb.

"I don't want either his money or himself," I replied, "and I forbid you to speak to him."

"Take care," she replied. "When people defy me to do a thing it is very soon done."

Fortunately the *picador* left for Malaga, and I set about smuggling in the Jew's cottons. I had a great deal to do in this expedition, and so had Carmen. I forgot Lucas; perhaps she also forgot him, for the time at any rate. It was about that time, sir, that I met with you first, near Montilla, then afterwards at Cordova. I will not say anything about our last interview. You perhaps know more about it than I. Carmen robbed you of your watch; she also wanted your money, and particularly the ring you wear on your finger, which she said is a magic ring, which she was very anxious to possess. We had a violent quarrel; I struck her. She turned pale and cried. This was the first time I had ever seen her weep, and her tears had a great effect upon me. I begged her pardon, but she sulked all day; and when I departed for Montilla she did not want to kiss me. I was heavy-hearted when, three days afterwards, she came to see me, as gay as a lark. All was forgotten, and we passed two days in lover-like fashion. As we were again about to part she said:—

"There is a *festa* at Cordova; I am going to see it. Then I shall find out who has money, and will tell you."

I let her go. When alone I thought of the *festa*, and this change of humor in Carmen. She must have revenged herself already, I thought, since she had yielded first. A peasant told me that there was a bull-fight in Cordova. How my blood boiled, and, like a fool, I went there. He pointed out Lucas to me, and, in a seat near the barrier, I recognized Carmen. I had only to look at her for a moment to be fully assured of the fact I had suspected. Lucas played the bull "with a light heart," as I had anticipated. He snatched the cockade from the animal and carried it to Carmen, who placed it in her hair immediately. The bull tried to avenge me! Lucas was overthrown with his horse, and the bull fell upon both of them. I looked at Carmen; she was no longer in her place. It was quite impossible for me to get out, and I was compelled to wait until the courses were run. Then I went to the house which you know of, and there I remained quite quiet all the evening and a part of the night. Towards two o'clock in the morning Carmen returned, and was somewhat astonished to see me.

"Come with me," I said.

"Very well," she replied, "let us go."

I went to fetch my horse, and I put her *en croupe*. We rode all the remainder of the night without saying a single word to each other. We halted at daybreak at a solitary inn near a small hermitage. Then I said to Carmen:—

"Listen! I forget everything; I will speak of nothing that has passed. Only swear to me that you will follow me to America, and that you will remain quietly there."

"No," she replied in a sulky tone, "I won't go to America. I like being here best."

"Because you are near Lucas," I said. "But do not imagine, even if he recover, that he will ever make old bones. Yet after all, why should I trouble about him? I am tired of killing all your lovers; it is *you* whom I shall kill."

She gazed at me steadily with her wild eyes, and said:—

"I have always imagined that you would kill me. The first time I saw you I met a priest at the door of my house, and did you see nothing to-night as we quitted Cordova? A hare crossed the road between your horse's feet. It is written!"

"Carmencita," I asked, "is it true that you no longer love me?"

She made no reply; she was seated cross-legged on a mat, tracing patterns with her finger on the floor.

"Let us change our mode of life, Carmen," I pleaded. "Let us go and live in some place where we shall never be separated. You know that we have a hundred and twenty onzas buried beneath a tree not far from here. Besides, we still have money in ben-Joseph's hands."

She smiled and replied:—

"I first, you afterwards. I knew that it would come to this."

"Reflect," I continued. "I have lost all patience with you; I am at the end of my tether! Make up your mind, and I will make up mine."

I left her and walked towards the hermitage. I found the hermit at prayer. I waited until his devotions were concluded. I wanted to pray, too, but I could not. When he rose I went up to him.

"Father," I said, "will you pray for one who is in great danger?"

"I pray for all the afflicted, my son."

"Can you pray for a soul which is about to appear before its Creator?"

"Yes," he replied, looking at me fixedly, and as there was something strange in my manner he wanted me to speak out.

"It seems to me that I have seen you before," he remarked.

I put a piastre on the bench. "When will you say mass?" I asked.

"In half an hour. The son of the inn-keeper, yonder, comes to serve it. Tell me, young man, have not you something on your conscience which is tormenting you? Will you hearken to the counsel of a Christian?"

I felt ready to cry. I said I would return, and then I got away. I lay down on the grass till I heard the bell. Then I rose and went near, but remained outside the chapel. When mass was said I returned to the inn. I almost hoped that Carmen had run away; she might have taken my horse and escaped. But I found her. She would never have it said that she was afraid of me. During my absence she had unpicked the hem of her dress, and taken out the lead. She was then sitting at the table, gazing into a bowl of water at the lead which had sunk to the bottom, and which she continued to throw in. She was so immersed in her occupation that she did not at first perceive me. Then she took a piece of the lead and turned it in all directions, with a sad expression in her face; sometimes she hummed one of the mystic songs in which gypsies invoke Marie Padilla, the mistress of Don Pedro, who was, they say, the Bari Crallisa, or great Queen of the Gypsies.*

"Carmen," I said, "will you come with me?"

She rose, threw away her bowl, and put on her mantilla as if ready to go. They brought me my horse, she mounted behind me, and we departed.

"So, my Carmen," I said, after a while, "you really wish to follow me, is it not so?"

"I will follow you to death, yes; but I will not live with you any longer!"

We were in a solitary gorge; I pulled up.

"Is it here?" she said, as she sprang to the ground. She took off her mantilla, threw it at her feet and stood motionless, her hand upon her hip, looking straight at me.

* Marie Padella is accused of bewitching Don Pedro the King. A popular tradition states that she had presented the Queen Blanche of Bourbon with a golden zone, which appeared in the King's eyes like a living serpent. That was the cause of the disgust he always evinced for the unfortunate princess.

"You are going to kill me, I see that quite well," she said. "It is fated; but you will never make me yield."

"I implore you, be reasonable," I said. "Listen to me; all the past is forgotten. Nevertheless, you know it, it is I who have lost myself; it was for your sake that I became a brigand and a murderer! Carmen, my Carmen, let me save you, and myself with you!"

"José," she replied, "you ask me to do what is impossible. I no longer love you; you love me still, and for that reason you want to kill me. I could very easily lie to you, but do not care to take the trouble. All is over between us. As my *rom* you have the right to kill your *romi*, but Carmen will always be free. Calli she was born, and Calli she will die!"

"So you love Lucas?" I said.

"Yes, I have loved him, like you, for a while; perhaps less than you. At present I love no one, and I hate myself for having loved you."

I threw myself at her feet; I took her hands in mine; bedewed them with my tears; I recalled to her mind all the happy times we had had together. I offered to remain a brigand all my life to please her. I did everything, sir, everything. I offered her all, provided that she would still love me. But she said:—

"It is impossible to love you any longer, and I do not want to live with you!"

Fury took possession of me—I drew my knife; I wished she had displayed some fear and pleaded for mercy, but the woman was a demon.

"For the last time," I exclaimed, "will you remain with me?"

"No, no, no!" she replied, stamping her foot. Then she drew from her finger a ring that I had given her, and threw it amongst the bushes.

I stabbed her twice. It was Garcia's knife, which I had appropriated after breaking my own. She fell at the second thrust without a cry. I can still fancy I see her splendid black eyes regarding me steadily; then they became troubled, and closed. I remained insensible beside the body for a good hour. Then I remembered that Carmen had often said that she would like to be buried in a wood. I excavated a grave with my knife, and placed her in it. For a long time I searched for the ring, and at length found it. I placed it in the grave with her and also a small cross. Perhaps I was wrong! Then I mounted my horse, and galloped to Cordova, and at the first guard-house I made myself known. I said I had killed Carmen, but I did not wish to divulge where I had buried her. The hermit is a holy man. He has prayed for her. He has said a mass for her soul. Poor girl! It is the Calli who are to blame for having made her what she was.

A SIMPLE HEART
by Gustave Flaubert

It was said of Gustave Flaubert that he could labor endlessly over a single page to sculpt the perfect paragraph or sentence. One of the great novelists of the 19th century, he was a prime practitioner of art for its own sake, believing as he did in the perfectibility of form and in the absolute value of the creative effort. A transitional figure, Flaubert was a romantic who nevertheless strove to portray with fine exactitude and keen observation the petty details and ordinary affairs of contemporary society. His masterpiece Madame Bovary *is considered one of the finest realistic novels ever written. It is a precise account of the bourgeois society that Flaubert knew so well and that he despised and, in the unfinished* Bouvard and Pécuchet, *satirized so effectively.*

The high standards that Flaubert set for society he also set for himself. He remained for most of his life on the family estate near Rouen, devoting himself entirely to a rigidly disciplined life of art. This hermetic existence did not prevent him, however, from cultivating many influential friends, and his letters, especially those to George Sand, are valuable exercises in literary criticism. The present work, A Simple Heart, *appeared, together with two other novelettes, in the single volume* Three Tales *in 1877. All three reveal Flaubert's exactness and precision of style and his command over this most disciplined of literary forms.*

I.

Madame Aubain's servant Félicité was coveted by the ladies of Pont-l'Évêque for half a century.

She received 100 francs a year. For that she cooked, kept the house clean, and did the sewing, washing, and ironing; she could bridle a horse, fatten poultry, and churn butter—and she remained loyal to her mistress, difficult as the latter was.

Mme. Aubain had married a handsome man without funds who died at the beginning of 1809, leaving her with two young children and a quantity of debts. She then sold all her property except the farms of Toucques and Geffosses, which earned about 5,000 francs a year at best, and left her house in Saint-Melaine for a less expensive one that had belonged to her family and was situated behind the market.

This house had a slate roof and stood between an alley and a path that went down to the river. There was a difference in the levels of the rooms that made you stumble. A narrow hall divided the kitchen from the parlor where Mme. Aubain spent the whole day, sitting in a wicker chair by the window. Against the panels, which were painted white, was a row of eight mahogany chairs. On an old piano under the barometer a pile of wooden and cardboard boxes rose like a pyramid. A stuffed armchair flanked either side of the Louis-Quinze chimney piece, which was in yellow marble with a clock in the middle of it depicting a temple of Vesta. The whole room was a little musty, as the floor was on a lower level than the garden.

The first floor housed Madame's bedroom: very large, with a pale-flowered wallpaper and a portrait of "Monsieur" as a dandy of the period. It led to a smaller room, where there were two children's cots without mattresses. Next came the drawing-room, which was always locked and full of furniture covered with sheets. Then there was a corridor leading to a study. The shelves of a large bookcase were largely filled with books and papers, and its three wings surrounded a big desk made of black wood. The two panels at the end of the room were covered with pen drawings, water-color landscapes, and engravings by Audran, all relics of better days and vanished luxury. Félicité's room on the top floor got its light from a dormer window, which looked over the meadows.

She rose at daybreak to be in time for Mass and worked till evening without stopping. Then, when dinner was over, the plates and dishes in order and the door shut fast, she thrust the log under the ashes and went to sleep in front of the hearth with her rosary in her hand. Félicité was the stubbornest of all bargainers, and as for cleanness, the polish on her saucepans was the despair of other servants. Thrifty in all things, she ate slowly, gathering off the table in her fingers the crumbs of her loaf—a 12-pound loaf especially baked for her, which lasted for 20 days.

At all seasons of the year she wore a print kerchief fastened behind with a pin, a bonnet that covered her hair, gray stockings, a red skirt, and a bibbed apron—such as hospital nurses wear—over her jacket.

Her face was thin and her voice sharp. At 25 she looked like 40. From 50 onward she seemed of indeterminate age; and with her silence, straight figure, and precise movements, she was like a woman made of wood, who functioned by clockwork.

II.

Félicité had had her love story like anyone else.

Her father, a mason, had been killed by falling off some scaffolding. Then her mother died, her sisters scattered, and a farmer took her in and employed her, while she was still quite little, to herd the cows at pasture. She shivered in rags and would lie flat on the ground to drink water from the ponds; she was beaten for nothing and finally turned out for the theft of 30 sous which she did not steal. She went to another farm, where she became dairy maid, and as she was liked by her employer, the other servants were jealous of her.

One evening in August (she was then 18) they took her to a big party at Colleville. She was dazed and stupefied immediately by the noise of the fiddlers, the lights in the trees, the gay medley of dresses, the lace, the gold crosses, and the throng of people jigging all together. While she kept shyly aside, a young man with a well-to-do air, who was leaning on the shaft of a cart and smoking his pipe, came up to ask her to dance. He treated her to cider, coffee, and cake, and bought her a silk handkerchief; and then, imagining she knew his intentions, offered to see her home. At the edge of a field of oats he pushed her down roughly. She was frightened and began to scream, and he ran off.

One evening later she was on the Beaumont road. A big hay wagon was moving along slowly. She wanted to get in front of it, and as she brushed past the wheels she recognized Théodore. He greeted her quite calmly, saying she must excuse it all because it was "the fault of the drink." She could not think of any answer and wanted to run away.

He began at once to talk about the harvest and the worthies of the commune, for his father had left Colleville for the farm at Les Écots, so that now he and she were neighbors. "Ah!" she said. He added that they thought of settling him in life.

Well, he was in no hurry; he was waiting for a wife to his fancy. She dropped her head, and then he asked her if she thought of marrying. She answered with a smile that it was mean to make fun of her.

"But I am not, I swear!"—and he put his left hand around her waist. She walked in the support of his embrace; their steps grew slower. The wind was soft, the stars glittered, the huge wagon-load of hay swayed in front of them, and dust rose from the dragging steps of the four horses. Then, without a word of command, they turned to the right. He clasped her once more in his arms, and she disappeared into the shadow.

The week after Théodore secured some assignations with her.

They met at the end of farm yards, behind a wall, or under a solitary tree. She was not innocent as young ladies are—she had learned knowledge from the animals—but her reason and the instinct of her honor would not let her fall. Her resistance exasperated Théodore's passion, so much so that to satisfy it—or perhaps quite artlessly—he made her an offer of marriage. She was in doubt whether to trust him, but he swore great oaths of fidelity.

Soon he confessed to something troublesome; the year before his parents had bought him a substitute for the army, but any day he might be taken again, and the idea of serving was a terror to him. Félicité took this cowardice of his as a sign of affection, and it redoubled hers. She stole away at night to see him, and when she reached their meeting place Théodore racked her with his anxieties and urgings.

At last he declared that he would go himself to the prefecture for information and would tell her the result on the following Sunday, between eleven and midnight.

When the moment came she sped toward her lover. Instead of him, she found one of his friends.

He told her that she would not see Théodore anymore. To ensure himself against conscription, he had married an old woman, Mme. Lehoussais of Toucques, who was very rich.

There was an uncontrollable burst of grief. She threw herself on the ground, screamed, called to the God of mercy, and moaned by herself in the fields till daylight came. Then she came back to the farm and announced that she was going to leave. And at the end of the month she received her wages, tied all her small belongings with a handkerchief, and went to Pont-l'Évêque.

In front of the inn there she made inquiries of a woman in a widow's cap, who, as it happened, was just looking for a cook. The girl did not know much, but her willingness seemed so great and her demands so small that Mme. Aubain ended by saying:

"Very well, then, I will take you."

A quarter of an hour afterward Félicité was installed in her house.

She lived there at first in a tremble, as it were, at "the style of the house" and the memory of "Monsieur" floating over it all. Paul and Virginie, the first aged seven and the other hardly four, seemed to her beings of a precious substance; she carried them on her back like a horse. It was a sorrow to her that Mme. Aubain would not let her kiss them every minute. And yet she was happy there. Her grief had melted in the pleasantness of things all round.

Every Thursday regular visitors came in for a game of "Boston," and Félicité got the cards and foot warmers ready beforehand. They arrived punctually at eight and left before the stroke of eleven.

On Monday mornings the dealer who lodged in the covered passage spread out all his old iron on the ground. Then a hum of voices began to fill the town, mingled with the neighing of horses, bleating of lambs, grunting of pigs, and the sharp rattle of carts along the street. About noon, when the market was at its height, you might see a tall, hook-nosed old countryman with his cap pushed back making his appearance at the door. It was Robelin, the farmer of Geffosses. A little later came Liébard, the farmer from Toucques—short, red, and corpulent—in a gray jacket and gaiters shod with spurs.

Both had poultry or cheese to offer their landlord. Félicité was invariably a match for their cunning, and they went away filled with respect for her.

At vague intervals Mme. Aubain had a visit from the Marquis de Gremanville, one of her uncles, who had ruined himself by debauchery and now lived at Falaise on his last remaining morsel of land. He invariably came at the luncheon hour, with a dreadful poodle whose paws left all the furniture in a mess. In spite of efforts to show his breeding, which he carried to the point of raising his hat every time he mentioned "my late father," habit was too strong for him; he poured himself out glass after glass and fired off improper remarks. Félicité edged him politely out of the house—"You have had enough, Monsieur de Gremanville! Another time!"—and she shut the door on him.

She opened it with pleasure to M. Bourais, who had been a lawyer. His baldness, his white stock, frilled shirt, and roomy brown coat, his way of rounding the arm as he took snuff— his whole person, in fact—created that disturbance of mind that overtakes us at the sight of extraordinary men.

As he looked after the property of "Madame," he remained shut up with her for hours in "Monsieur's" study, though all the time he was afraid of compromising himself. He respected the magistracy immensely and had some pretensions to Latin.

To combine instruction and amusement he gave the children a geography book made up of a series of prints. They represented scenes in different parts of the world: cannibals with feathers on their heads, a monkey carrying off a young lady, Bedouins in the desert, the harpooning of a whale, and so on. Paul explained these engravings to Félicité, and that, in fact, was the whole of her literary education. The children's education was undertaken by Guyot, a poor creature employed at the town hall, who was famous for his beautiful hand and who sharpened his penknife on his boots.

When the weather was bright, the household set off early for a day at Geffosses Farm.

Its courtyard is on a slope, with the farmhouse in the middle, and the sea looks like a gray streak in the distance.

Félicité brought slices of cold meat out of her basket, and they breakfasted in a room adjoining the dairy. It was the only surviving fragment of a country house which was now no more. The wall paper hung in tatters and quivered in the drafts. Mme. Aubain sat with bowed head, overcome by her memories; the children became afraid to speak. "Why don't you play, then?" she would say, and off they went.

Paul climbed into the barn, caught birds, played with ducks and drakes over the pond, or hammered with his stick on the big casks which boomed like drums. Virginie fed the rabbits or dashed off to pick cornflowers, her quick legs showing their embroidered little drawers.

One autumn evening they went home by the fields. The moon was in its first quarter, lighting part of the sky, and mist floated like a scarf over the windings of the Toucques. Cattle, lying out in the middle of the grass, looked quietly at the four people as they passed. In the third meadow some of them got up and made a half-circle in front of the walkers. "There's nothing to be afraid of," said Félicité, as she stroked the nearest on the back with a kind of crooning song. He wheeled around, and the others did the same. But when they crossed the next pasture, there was a formidable bellow. It was a bull, hidden by the mist. Mme. Aubain was about to run. "No, no, don't go so fast!" They mended their pace, however, and heard a loud breathing behind them which came nearer. His hoofs thudded on the meadow grass like hammers; why, he was galloping now! Félicité turned around and tore up clods of earth with both hands and threw them in his eyes. He lowered his muzzle, waved his horns, and quivered with fury, bellowing terribly. Mme. Aubain, now at the end of the pasture with the two little ones, was looking wildly for a place to get over the high bank. Félicité was retreating, still with her face to the bull, keeping up a shower of clods which blinded him and crying all the time, "Be quick! Be quick!"

Mme. Aubain went down into the ditch, pushed Virginie first and then Paul, fell several times as she tried to climb the bank, and managed it at last by dint of courage.

The bull had driven Félicité to bay against a rail fence. His slaver was streaming into her face; another second, and he would have gored her. She had just time to slip between two of the rails, and the big animal stopped short in amazement.

This adventure was talked of at Pont-l'Évêque for many a year. Félicité did not pride herself on it in the least, not having the barest suspicion that she had done anything heroic.

Virginie was the sole object of her thoughts, for the child developed a nervous complaint as a result of her fright, and M. Poupart, the doctor, advised sea-bathing at Trouville. It was not a frequented place then. Mme. Aubain collected information, consulted Bourais, and made preparations as though for a long journey.

Her luggage started a day in advance, in Liébard's cart. The next day he brought around two horses, one of which had a lady's saddle with a velvet back to it, while a cloak was rolled up to make a kind of seat on the crupper of the other. Mme. Aubain rode on that, behind the farmer. Félicité took charge of Virginie, and Paul mounted M. Lechaptois' donkey, lent on condition that great care was taken of it.

The road was so bad that its five miles took two hours. The horses sank in the mud up to their pasterns, and their haunches jerked abruptly in the effort to get out; or else they stumbled in the ruts, and at other moments had to jump. In some places Liébard's mare came suddenly to a halt. He waited patiently until she went on again, talking about the people who had properties along the road and adding moral reflections to their history. So it was that as they were in the middle of Toucques and passed under some windows bowered with nasturtiums, he shrugged his shoulders and said: "There's a Mme. Lehoussais lives there; instead of taking a young man she . . ." Félicité did not hear the rest; the horses were trotting, and the donkey galloping. They all turned down a bypath; a gate swung open, and two boys appeared. The party dismounted in front of a manure heap at the very threshold of the farmhouse door.

When Mme. Liébard saw her mistress, she gave lavish signs of joy. She served her a luncheon with a sirloin of beef, tripe, black pudding, a fricassee of chicken, sparkling cider, a fruit tart, and brandied plums, seasoning it all with compliments to Madame, who seemed in better health. Mademoiselle, who was "splendid" now, and Monsieur Paul, who had "filled out" wonderfully. Nor did she forget their deceased grandparents, whom the Liébards had known as they had been in the service of the family for several generations. The farm, like them, had the stamp of antiquity. The beams on the ceiling were worm-eaten, the walls blackened with smoke, and the window panes gray with dust. There was an oak dresser laden with every sort of useful article—jugs, plates, pewter bowls, wolf-traps, and sheep-shears, and a huge syringe made the children laugh. There was not a tree in the three court yards without mushrooms growing at the bottom of it or a tuft of mistletoe on its boughs. Several of them had been thrown down by the wind. They had taken root again at the middle, and all were bending under their wealth of apples. The thatched roofs, like brown velvet and of varying thickness, withstood the heaviest squalls. The cart shed, however, was falling into ruin. Mme. Aubain said she would see about it and ordered the animals to be saddled again.

It was another half-hour before they reached Trouville. The little caravan dismounted to pass Écores—it was an overhanging cliff with boats below it—and three minutes later they were at the end of the quay and entered the court yard of the Golden Lamb, kept by good Mme. David.

From the first days of their stay Virginie began to feel less weak, thanks to the change of air and the effect of the sea baths. These, for want of a bathing-suit, she took in her chemise, and her nurse dressed her afterward in a coast-guard's cabin which was used by the bathers.

In the afternoons they took the donkey and went off be-

yond the Black Rocks, in the direction of Hennequeville. The
path climbed at first through ground with dells in it like the
green sward of a park and then reached a plateau where
grass fields and arable fields lay side by side. Hollies rose stiffly
out of the briary tangle at the edge of the road, and here and
there a great withered tree made zigzags in the blue air with
its branches.

They nearly always rested in a meadow, with Deauville on
their left, Havre on their right, and the open sea in front. It
glittered in the sunshine, smooth as a mirror and so quiet that
its murmur was scarcely to be heard; sparrows chirped in
hiding and the immense sky arched over it all. Mme. Aubain
sat doing her needlework; Virginie plaited rushes by her side;
Félicité pulled up lavender, and Paul was bored and anxious
to start home.

Other days they crossed the Toucques in a boat and looked
for shells. When the tide went out sea-urchins, starfish, and
jellyfish were left exposed, and the children ran in pursuit of
the foam flakes which scudded in the wind. The sleepy waves
broke on the sand and unrolled all along the beach: It
stretched away out of sight, bounded on the land side by the
dunes which parted it from the Marsh, a wide meadow shaped
like an arena. As they came home that way, Trouville, on the
hillside in the background, grew bigger at every step, and its
miscellaneous throng of houses seemed to break into a gay
disorder.

On days when it was too hot they did not leave their room.
From the dazzling brilliance outside light fell in streaks between the laths of the blinds. There were no sounds in the
village, and on the pavement below not a soul. This silence
round them deepened the quietness of things. In the distance,
where men were calking, there was a tap of hammers as they
plugged the hulls, and a sluggish breeze wafted up the smell
of tar.

The chief amusement was the return of the fishing boats.
They began to tack as soon as they had passed the buoys. The
sails came down on two of the three masts, and they drew on
with the foresail swelling like a balloon, glided through the
splash of the waves, and when they had reached the middle of
the harbor they suddenly dropped anchor. Then the boats drew
up against the quay. The sailors threw quivering fish over the
side; a row of carts was waiting, and women in cotton bonnets
darted out to take the baskets and give their men a kiss.

One of them came up to Félicité one day, and she entered

the lodgings a little later in a state of delight. She had found a sister again—and then Nastasie Barette, "wife of Leroux," appeared, holding an infant at her breast and another child with her right hand, while on her left was a little cabin boy with his hands on his hips and a cap over his ear.

After a quarter of an hour Mme. Aubain sent them off; but they were always to be found hanging about the kitchen or encountered in the course of a walk. The husband never appeared.

Félicité was seized with affection for them. She bought them a blanket, some shirts, and a stove; it was clear that they were making a good thing out of her. Mme. Aubain was annoyed by this weakness of hers, and she did not like the liberties taken by the nephew, who said "thee" and "thou" to Paul. So as Virginie was coughing and the fine weather gone, she returned to Pont-l'Évêque.

There M. Bourais enlightened her on the choice of a boys' school. The one at Caen was reputed to be the best, and Paul was sent to it. He said his good-byes bravely, content enough at going to live in a house where he would have companions.

Mme. Aubain resigned herself to her son's absence as a thing that had to be. Virginie thought about it less and less. Félicité missed the noise he made. But she found an occupation to distract her; from Christmas onward she took the little girl to catechism every day.

III.

After making a genuflexion at the door, she walked up between the double row of chairs under the lofty nave, opened Mme. Aubain's pew, sat down, and began to look about her. The choir stalls were filled with the boys on the right and the girls on the left, and the curé stood by the lectern. On a painted window in the apse the Holy Ghost looked down upon the Virgin. Another window showed her on her knees before the child Jesus, and a group carved in wood behind the altar shrine represented St. Michael overthrowing the dragon.

The priest began with a sketch of sacred history. The Garden, the Flood, the Tower of Babel, cities in flames, dying nations, and overturned idols passed like a dream before her eyes, and the dizzying vision left her with reverence for the Most High and fear of his wrath. Then she wept at the story

of the Passion. Why had they crucified Him, when He loved
the children, fed the multitudes, healed the blind, and had
willed, in His meekness, to be born among the poor, on the
dunghill of a stable? The sowings, harvests, winepresses, all
the familiar things the Gospel speaks of, were a part of her
life. They had been made holy by God's passing; and she
loved the lambs more tenderly for her love of the Lamb, and
the doves because of the Holy Ghost.

She found it hard to imagine Him in person, for He was
not merely a bird but a flame as well and a breath at other
times. It may be His light, she thought, which flits at night
about the edge of the marshes, His breathing, which drives on
the clouds, His voice, which gives harmony to the bells; and
she would sit rapt in adoration, enjoying the cool walls and
the quiet of the church.

Of doctrines she understood nothing—did not even try to
understand. The curé discoursed, the children repeated their
lesson, and finally she went to sleep, waking up with a start
when their wooden shoes clattered on the flagstones as they
went away.

It was thus that Félicité, whose religious education had
been neglected in her youth, learned the catechism by dint of
hearing it; and from that time she copied all Virginie's observations, fasting as she did and confessing with her. On Corpus
Christi Day they made a festal altar together.

The first communion loomed distractingly ahead. She
fussed over the shoes, the rosary, the book and gloves; and
how she trembled as she helped Virginie's mother to dress
her!

All through the Mass she was racked with anxiety. She
could not see one side of the choir because of M. Bourais; but
straight in front of her was the flock of maidens, with white
crowns above their hanging veils, making the impression of a
field of snow; and she knew her dear child at a distance by
her dainty neck and thoughtful air. The bell tinkled. The
heads bowed, and there was silence. As the organ pealed,
singers and congregation took up the "Agnus Dei"; then the
procession of the boys began, and after them the girls rose.
Step by step, with their hands joined in prayer, they went
toward the lighted altar, knelt on the first step, received the
sacrament in turn, and came back in the same order to their
places. When Virginie's turn came Félicité leaned forward to
see her, and with the imaginativeness of deep and tender
feeling it seemed to her that she actually was the child. Virgi-

nie's face became hers, she was dressed in her clothes, it was her heart beating in her breast. As the moment came to open her mouth, she closed her eyes and nearly fainted.

She appeared early in the sacristy next morning for Monsieur the curé to give her the communion. She took it with devotion, but it did not give her the same exquisite delight.

Mme. Aubain wanted to make her daughter into an accomplished person, and as Guyot could not teach her music or English, she decided to place her in the Ursuline Convent at Honfleur as a boarder. The child made no objection. Félicité sighed and thought that Madame lacked feeling. Then she reflected that her mistress might be right; matters of this kind were beyond her.

So one day an old coach drew up at the door, and out of it stepped a nun to fetch the young lady. Félicité hoisted the luggage on to the top, admonished the driver, and put six pots of preserves, a dozen pears, and a bunch of violets under the seat.

At the last moment Virginie broke into a fit of sobbing; she threw her arms round her mother, who kissed her on the forehead, saying over and over "Come, be brave! be brave!" The step was raised, and the carriage drove off.

Then Mme. Aubain's strength gave way; and in the evening all her friends—the Lormeau family, Mme. Lechaptois, the Rochefeuille ladies, M. de Houppeville, and Bourais—came in to console her.

To be without her daughter was very painful for her at first. But she heard from Virginie three times a week, wrote to her on the other days, walked in the garden, and so filled up the empty hours.

From sheer habit Félicité went into Virginie's room in the mornings and gazed at the walls. It was boredom to her not to have to comb the child's hair now, lace up her boots, tuck her into bed—and not to see her charming face perpetually and hold her hand when they went out together. In this idle condition she tried making lace. But her fingers were too heavy and broke the threads. She could not attend to anything; she had lost her sleep and was, in her own words, "destroyed."

To "divert herself" she asked leave to have visits from her nephew Victor.

He arrived on Sundays after Mass, rosy-cheeked, bare-chested, with the scent of the country he had walked through still about him. She laid her table promptly, and they had lunch, sitting opposite each other. She ate as little as possible

herself to save expense but stuffed him with food so gener-
ously that at last he went to sleep. At the first stroke of
vespers she woke him up, brushed his trousers, fastened his
tie, and went to church, leaning on his arm with maternal
pride.

Victor was always instructed by his parents to get something out of her—a packet of moist sugar, it might be, a cake
of soap, spirits, or even money at times. He brought his things
for her to mend, and she took over the task, only too glad to
have a reason for making him come back.

In August his father took him off on a coasting voyage. It
was holiday time, and she was consoled by the arrival of the
children. Paul, however, was getting selfish, and Virginie was
too old to be called "thou" any longer; this put a constraint
and barrier between them.

Victor went to Morlaix, Dunkirk, and Brighton in succession and made Félicité a present on his return from each
voyage. It was a box made of shells the first time, a coffee cup
the next, and on the third occasion a large gingerbread man.
Victor was growing handsome. He was well made, had a hint
of a mustache, good honest eyes, and a small leather hat
pushed backward like a pilot's. He entertained her by telling
stories embroidered with nautical terms.

On a Monday, July 14, 1819 (she never forgot the date),
he told her that he had signed on for the big voyage and that
the next night he would take the Honfleur boat and join his
schooner, which was to weigh anchor from Le Havre before
long. Perhaps he would be gone two years.

The prospect of this long absence threw Félicité into deep
distress; one more good-bye she must have, and on the
Wednesday evening, when Madame's dinner was finished, she
put on her best clothes and made short work of the 12 miles
between Pont-l'Évêque and Honfleur.

When she arrived in front of the Calvary, she took the turn
to the right instead of the left, got lost in the timber yards,
and retraced her steps; some people to whom she spoke advised her to be quick. She went all round the harbor basin,
full of ships, and knocked against hawsers; then the ground
fell away, lights flashed across each other, and she thought her
wits had left her, for she saw horses up in the sky.

Others were neighing by the quay-side, frightened at the
sea. They were lifted by a tackle and deposited in a boat,
where passengers jostled each other among cider casks, cheese
baskets, and sacks of grain; fowls could be heard clucking, the

captain swore, and a cabin boy stood leaning over the bows, indifferent to it all. Félicité, who had not recognized him, called "Victor!" and he raised his head; all at once, as she was darting forward, the gangway was drawn back.

The Honfleur packet, women singing as they hauled it, passed out of harbor. Its framework creaked, and the heavy waves whipped its bows. The canvas had swung around; no one could be seen on board now, and on the moon-silvered sea the boat made a black speck which paled gradually, dipped, and vanished.

As Félicité passed by Calvary, she had a wish to commend to God what she cherished most, and she stood there praying a long time with her face bathed in tears and her eyes toward the clouds. The town was asleep, coastguards were walking to and fro, and water poured without cesation through the holes in the sluice, with the noise of a torrent. The clocks struck two.

The convent parlor would not be open before day. If Félicité were late, Madame would most certainly be annoyed; and in spite of her desire to kiss the other child she turned home. The maids at the inn were waking up as she came in to Pont-l'Évêque.

So the poor slip of a boy was going to toss for months and months at sea! She had not been frightened by his previous voyages. From England or Brittany you came back safe enough; but America, the colonies, the islands—these were lost in a dim region at the other end of the world.

Félicité's thoughts from that moment ran entirely on her nephew. On sunny days she was harassed by the idea of thirst; when there was a storm she was afraid of the lightning on his account. As she listened to the wind growling in the chimney or carrying off the slates she pictured him lashed by that same tempest, at the top of a shattered mast, with his body thrown backward under a sheet of foam; or else (with a reminiscence of the illustrated geography) he was being eaten by savages, captured in a wood by monkeys, or dying on a desert shore. And never did she mention her anxieties.

Mme. Aubain had anxieties of her own, about her daughter. The good sisters found her an affectionate but delicate child. The slightest emotion unnerved her. She had to give up the piano.

Her mother stipulated for regular letters from the convent. She lost patience one morning when the postman did not come and walked to and fro in the parlor from her armchair to the window. It was really amazing; not a word for four days!

To console Mme. Aubain by her own example Félicité remarked:

"As for me, Madame, it's six months since I heard . . ."

"From whom, pray?"

"Why . . . from my nephew," the servant answered gently.

"Oh! your nephew!" And Mme. Aubain resumed her walk with a shrug of the shoulders, as much as to say: "I was not thinking of him! And what is more, it's absurd! A scamp of a cabin boy—what does he matter? . . . whereas my daughter . . . why, just think!"

Félicité, though she had been brought up on harshness, felt indignant with Madame—and then forgot. It seemed the simplest thing in the world to her to lose one's head over the little girl. For her the two children were equally important; a bond in her heart made them one, and their destinies must be the same.

She heard from the chemist that Victor's ship had arrived at Havana. He had read this piece of news in a gazette.

Cigars—they made her imagine Havana as a place where no one does anything but smoke, and there was Victor moving among the Negroes in a cloud of tobacco. Could you, she wondered, "in case you needed," return by land? What was the distance from Pont-l'Évêque? She questioned M. Bourais to find out.

He reached for his atlas and began explaining the longitudes; Félicité's consternation provoked a fine pedantic smile. Finally he marked with his pencil a black, imperceptible point in the indentations of an oval spot and said as he did so, "Here it is." She bent over the map; the maze of colored lines wearied her eyes without conveying anything; and on an invitation from Bourais to tell him her difficulty, she begged him to show her the house where Victor was living. Bourais threw up his arms, sneezed, and laughed immensely: A simplicity like hers was a positive joy. And Félicité did not understand the reason; how could she when she expected, very likely, to see the actual image of her nephew—so stunted was her mind!

A fortnight afterward Liébard came into the kitchen at market time as usual and handed her a letter from her brother-in-law. As neither of them could read, she took it to her mistress.

Mme. Aubain, who was counting the stitches in her knitting, put the work down by her side, broke the seal of the letter, started, and said in a low voice, with a look of meaning:

"It is bad news . . . that they have to tell you. Your nephew. . . ."

He was dead. The letter said no more.

Félicité fell into a chair, leaning her head against the wainscot; and she closed her eyelids, which suddenly flushed pink. Then with bent forehead, hands hanging, and fixed eyes, she said at intervals:

"Poor little lad! poor little lad!"

Liébard watched her and heaved sighs. Mme. Aubain trembled a little.

She suggested that Félicité should go to see her sister at Trouville. Félicité answered by a gesture that she had no need.

There was a silence. The worthy Liébard thought it was time for them to withdraw.

Then Félicité said:

"They don't care, not they!"

Her head dropped again, and she took up mechanically, from time to time, the long needles on her worktable.

Women passed in the yard with a barrow of dripping linen.

As she saw them through the windowpanes, she remembered her washing; she had put it to soak the day before; today she must wring it out. And she left the room.

Her plank and tub were at the edge of the Toucques. She threw a pile of linen on the bank, rolled up her sleeves, and taking her wooden beater, dealt lusty blows whose sound carried to the neighboring gardens. The meadows were empty, the river stirred in the wind; and down below long grasses wavered, like the hair of corpses floating in the water. She kept her grief down and was very brave until the evening; but once in her room she surrendered to it utterly, lying stretched on the mattress with her face in the pillow and her hands clenched against her temples.

Much later she heard, from the captain himself, the circumstances of Victor's end. They had bled him too much at the hospital for yellow fever. Four doctors held him at once. He had died instantly, and the chief had said:

"Bah! There goes another!"

His parents had always been brutal to him. She preferred not to see them again; and they made no advances, either because they forgot her or from the callousness of the wretchedly poor.

Virginie began to grow weaker.

Tightness in her chest, coughing, continual fever, and veinings on her cheek bones betrayed some deep-seated complaint. M. Poupart had advised a stay in Provence. Mme. Aubain determined on it, and would have brought her daughter home at once but for the climate of Pont-l'Évêque.

She made an arrangement with a job-master, and he drove her to the convent every Tuesday. There is a terrace in the garden, with a view over the Seine. Virginie took walks there over the fallen vine leaves, on her mother's arm. A shaft of sunlight through the clouds made her blink sometimes, as she gazed at the sails in the distance and the whole horizon from the castle of Tancarville to the lighthouses at Le Havre. Afterward they rested in the arbor. Her mother had secured a little cask of excellent Malaga, and Virginie, laughing at the idea of getting tipsy, drank a thimblefull of it, no more.

Her strength came back visibly. The autumn glided gently away. Félicité reassured Mme. Aubain. But one evening, when she had been out on a commission in the neighborhood, she found M. Poupart's gig at the door. He was in the hall, and Mme. Aubain was tying her bonnet.

"Give me my foot warmer, purse, gloves! Quicker, come!"

Virginie had inflammation of the lungs; perhaps it was hopeless.

"Not yet!" said the doctor, and they both got into the carriage under whirling flakes of snow. Night was coming on, and it was very cold.

Félicité rushed into the church to light a taper. Then she ran after the gig, came up with it in an hour, and jumped lightly in behind. As she hung on by the fringes a thought came into her mind: "The courtyard has not been shut up; supposing burglars got in!" And she jumped down.

At dawn next day she presented herself at the doctor's. He had come in and started for the country again. Then she waited in the inn, thinking that a letter would come by some hand or other. Finally, when it was twilight, she took the Lisieux coach.

The convent was at the end of a steep lane. When she was about half-way up it, she heard strange sounds—a death-bell tolling. "It is for someone else," thought Félicité, and she pulled the knocker violently.

After some minutes there was a sound of trailing slippers, the door opened ajar, and a nun appeared.

The good sister, with an air of compunction, said that "she had just passed away." On the instant the bell of St. Leonard's tolled twice as fast.

Félicité went up to the second floor.

From the doorway she saw Virginie stretched on her back, with her hands joined, her mouth open, and head thrown back under a black crucifix that leaned toward her, between curtains that hung stiffly, less pale than was her face. Mme. Aubain, at the foot of the bed, which she clasped with her arms, was choking with sobs of agony. The mother superior stood on the right. Three candlesticks on the chest of drawers made spots of red, and the mist came whitely through the windows. Nuns came and took Mme. Aubain away.

For two nights Félicité never left the dead child. She repeated the same prayers, sprinkled holy water over the sheets, came and sat down again, and watched her. At the end of the first vigil she noticed that the face had grown yellow, the lips turned blue, the nose was sharper, and the eyes sunk in. She kissed them several times and would not have been immensely surprised if Virginie had opened them again; to minds like hers the supernatural is quite simple. She made the girl's toilette, wrapped her in her shroud, lifted her down into her bier, put a garland on her head, and spread out her hair. It was fair and extraordinarily long for her age. Félicité cut off a big lock and slipped half of it into her bosom, determined that she should never part with it.

The body was brought back to Pont-l'Évêque, as Mme. Aubain intended. She followed the hearse in a closed carriage.

It took another three-quarters of an hour after the mass to reach the cemetery. Paul walked in front, sobbing. M. Bourais was behind, and then came the chief residents, the women shrouded in black mantles, and Félicité. She thought of her nephew; and because she had not been able to pay these honors to him, her grief was doubled, as though the one were being buried with the other.

Mme. Aubain's despair was boundless. It was against God that she first rebelled, thinking it unjust of Him to have taken her daughter from her—she had never done evil, and her conscience was so clear! Ah, no!—she ought to have taken Virginie off to the south. Other doctors would have saved her. She accused herself now, wanted to join her child, and broke into cries of distress in the middle of her dreams. One dream haunted her above all. Her husband, dressed as a sailor, was returning from a long voyage, and shedding tears, he told her that he had been ordered to take Virginie away. Then they consulted how to hide her somewhere.

She came in once from the garden quite upset. A moment ago—and she pointed out the place—the father and daughter had appeared to her, standing side by side, and they did nothing, but they looked at her.

For several months after this she stayed inertly in her room. Félicité lectured her gently; she must live for her son's sake, and for the other, in remembrance of "her."

"Her?" answered Mme. Aubain, as though she were just waking up. "Ah, yes . . . yes . . . ! You do not forget her!" This was an allusion to the cemetery, where she was strictly forbidden to go.

Félicité went there every day.

Precisely at four she skirted the houses, climbed the hill, opened the gate, and came to Virginie's grave. It was a little column of pink marble with a stone underneath and a garden plot enclosed by chains. The beds were hidden under a coverlet of flowers. She watered their leaves, freshened the gravel, and knelt down to break up the earth better. When Mme. Aubain was able to come there, she felt a relief and a sort of consolation.

Then years slipped away, one like another, and their only episodes were the great festivals as they recurred—Easter, the Assumption, All Saints' Day. Household occurrences marked dates that were referred to afterward. In 1825, for instance, two glaziers whitewashed the hall; in 1827 a piece of the roof fell into the courtyard and nearly killed a man. In the summer of 1828 it was Madame's turn to offer the consecrated bread; Bourais, about this time, mysteriously absented himself; and one by one the old acquaintances passed way: Guyot, Liébard, Mme. Lechaptois, Robelin, and Uncle Gremanville, who had been paralysed for a long time.

One night the driver of the mail coach announced the Revolution of July in Pont-l'Évêque. A new subprefect was appointed a few days later—Baron de Larsonnière, who had been consul in America, and brought with him, besides his wife, a sister-in-law, and three young ladies, already growing up. They were to be seen about on their lawn, in loose blouses, and they had a Negro and a parrot. They paid a call on Mme. Aubain, which she did not fail to return. The moment they were seen in the distance Félicité ran to let her mistress know. But only one thing could really move her feelings—the letters from her son.

He was swallowed up in a tavern life and could follow no career. She paid his debts, he made new ones; and the sighs that Mme. Aubain uttered as she sat knitting by the window reached Félicité at her spinning wheel in the kitchen.

They took walks together along the espaliered wall, always talking of Virginie and wondering if such and such a thing would have pleased her and what, on some occasion, she would have been likely to say.

All her small belongings filled a cupboard in the two-bedded room. Mme. Aubain inspected them as seldom as she could. One summer day she made up her mind to it—and some moths flew out of the wardrobe.

Virginie's dresses were in a row underneath a shelf, on which there were three dolls, some hoops, a set of toy pots and pans, and the basin that she used. They took out her petticoats as well, and the stockings and handkerchiefs, and laid them out on the two beds before folding them up again. The sunshine lit up these poor things, bringing out their stains and the creases made by the body's movements. The air was warm and blue, a blackbird warbled, life seemed bathed in a deep sweetness. They found a little plush hat with thick, chestnut-colored pile; but it was eaten all over by moth. Félicité begged it for her own. Their eyes met fixedly and filled with tears; at last the mistress opened her arms, the servant threw herself into them, and they embraced each other, satisfying their grief in a kiss that made them equal.

It was the first time in their lives, Mme. Aubain's nature not being expansive. Félicité was as grateful as though she had received a favor, and cherished her mistress from that moment with the devotion of an animal and a religious worship.

The kindness of her heart enfolded.

When she heard the drums of a marching regiment in the street, she posted herself at the door with a pitcher of cider and asked the soldiers to drink. She nursed cholera patients and protected the Polish refugees; one of these even declared that he wished to marry her. They quarreled, however, for when she came back from the Angelus one morning, she found that he had got into her kitchen and made himself a vinegar salad which he was quietly eating.

After the Poles came Papa Colmiche, an old man who was supposed to have committed atrocities in '93. He lived by the side of the river in the ruins of a pigsty. The little boys watched him through the cracks in the wall, and threw pebbles at him, which fell on the pallet where he lay constantly shaken by a catarrh; his hair was very long, his eyes inflamed, and there was a tumor on his arm bigger than his head. She got him some linen and tried to clean up his miserable hole; her dream was to establish him in the bakehouse, without letting him annoy Madame. When the tumor burst, she dressed it every day; sometimes she brought him cake and would put him in the sunshine on a truss of straw. The poor old man, slobbering and trembling, thanked her in his worn-out voice, was terrified that he might lose her, and stretched out his hands when he saw her go away. He died; and she had a Mass said for the repose of his soul.

That very day a great happiness befell her; just at dinner-time appeared Mme. de Larsonnière's Negro, carrying the parrot in its cage, with perch, chain, and padlock. A note from the baroness informed Mme. Aubain that her husband had been raised to a prefecture, and they were starting that evening; she begged her to accept the bird as a memento and mark of her regard.

For a long time he had absorbed Félicité's imagination, because he came from America, and that name reminded her of Victor, so much so that she made inquiries of the Negro. She had once gone so far as to say, "How Madame would enjoy having him!"

The Negro repeated the remark to his mistress, and as she could not take the bird away with her, she chose this way of getting rid of him.

IV.

His name was Loulou. His body was green and the tips of his wings rose-pink; his forehead was blue and his throat golden.

But he had the tiresome habits of biting his perch, tearing out his feathers, sprinkling his dirt about, and spattering the water of his tub. He annoyed Mme. Aubain, and she gave him to Félicité for good.

She endeavored to train him; soon he could repeat "Nice boy! Your servant, sir! Good morning, Marie!" He was placed by the side of the door and astonished several people by not answering to the name Jacquot, for all parrots are called

Jacquot. People compared him to a turkey and a log of wood and stabbed Félicité to the heart each time. Strange obstinacy on Loulou's part!—when you looked at him he refused to speak.

Nonetheless he was eager for society; for on Sundays, while the Rochefeuille ladies, M. de Houppeville and new familiars—Onfroy the apothecary, Monsieur Varin, and Captain Mathieu—were playing their game of cards, he beat the windows with his wings and threw himself about so frantically that they could not hear each other speak.

Bourais' face undoubtedly struck him as extremely droll. When he saw it, he began to laugh—and laugh with all his might. His peals rang through the courtyard and were repeated by the echo; the neighbors came to their windows and laughed too; while M. Bourais, gliding along under the wall to escape the parrot's eye, and hiding his profile with his hat, got to the river and then entered by the garden gate. There was a lack of tenderness in the looks which he darted at the bird.

Loulou had been slapped by the bucher boy for making so free as to plunge his head into his basket; and since then he was always trying to nip him through his shirt. Fabu threatened to wring his neck, although he was not cruel, for all his tattooed arms and large whiskers. Far from it; he really rather liked the parrot, and in a jovial humour even wanted to teach him to swear. Félicité, who was alarmed by such proceedings, put the bird in the kitchen. His little chain was taken off and he roamed about the house.

His way of going downstairs was to lean on each step with the curve of his beak, raise the right foot, and then the left; and Félicité was afraid that these gymnastics brought on fits of giddiness. He fell ill and could not talk or eat any longer. There was a growth under his tongue, such as fowls have sometimes. She cured him by tearing the pellicle off with her fingernails. Mr. Paul was thoughtless enough one day to blow some cigar smoke into his nostrils, and another time when Mme. Lormeau was teasing him with the end of her umbrella, he snaped at the ferrule. Finally he got lost.

Félicité had put him on the grass to refresh him and had gone away for a minute, and when she came back—no sign of the parrot! She began by looking for him in the shrubs, by the waterside, and over the roofs, without listening to her mistress's cries of "Take care, do! You are out of your wits!" Then she investigated all the gardens in Pont-l'Évêque, and stopped the passers-by. "You don't ever happen to have seen my parrot, by any chance, do you?" And she gave a description of the parrot to those who did not know him. Suddenly, behind the mills at the foot of the hill she thought she could make out something green that fluttered. But on the top of the hill there was nothing. A hawker assured her that he had come across the parrot just before, at Saint-Melaine, in Mère Simon's shop. She rushed there; they had no idea of what she meant. At last she came home exhausted, with her slippers in shreds and despair in her soul; and as she was sitting in the middle of the garden seat at Madame's side, telling the whole story of her efforts, a lightweight dropped onto her shoulder —it was Loulou! What on earth had he been doing? Taking a walk in the neighborhood, perhaps!

She had some trouble in recovering from this, or rather never did recover. As the result of a chill, she had an attack of quinsy, and soon afterward an earache. Three years later she was deaf; and she spoke very loud, even in church. Though Félicité's sins might have been published in every corner of the diocese without dishonor to her or scandal to anybody, His Reverence the priest thought it right now to hear her confession in the sacristy only.

Imaginary noises in the head completed her upset. Her mistress often said to her, "Heavens! how stupid you are!" "Yes, Madame," she replied, and looked about for something.

Her little circle of ideas grew still narrower; the peal of church bells and the lowing of cattle ceased to exist for her. All living beings moved as silently as ghosts. One sound only reached her ears now—the parrot's voice.

Loulou, as though to amuse her, reproduced the click-clack of the turn-spit, the shrill call of a man selling fish, and the noise of the saw in the joiner's house opposite; when the bell rang he imitated Mme. Aubain's "Félicité! the door! The door!"

They carried on conversations, he endlessly reciting the three phrases in his repertory, to which she replied with words that were just as disconnected but uttered what was in her heart. Loulou was almost a son and a lover to her in her isolated state. He climbed up her fingers, nibbled at her lips, and clung to her kerchief; and when she bent her forehead and shook her head gently to and fro, as nurses do, the great wings of her bonnet and the bird's wings quivered together.

When the clouds massed and the thunder rumbled Loulou broke into cries, perhaps remembering the downpours in his native forests. The streaming rain made him absolutely mad;

he fluttered wildly about, dashed up to the ceiling, upset everything, and went out through the window to dabble in the garden; but he was back quickly to perch on one of the firedogs and hopped about to dry himself, exhibiting his tail and his beak in turn.

One morning in the terrible winter of 1837 she had put him in front of the fireplace because of the cold. She found him dead, in the middle of his cage: head downward, with his claws in the wires. He had died from congestion, no doubt. But Félicité thought he had been poisoned with parsley, and though there was no proof of any kind her suspicions inclined to Fabu.

She wept so piteously that her mistress said to her, "Well, then, have him stuffed!"

She asked advice from the chemist, who had always been kind to the parrot. He wrote to Le Havre, and a person called Fellacher undertook the business. But as parcels sometimes got lost in the coach she decided to take the parrot as far as Honfleur herself.

Along the sides of the road were leafless apple trees, one after the other. Ice covered the ditches. Dogs barked about the farms; and Félicité, with her hands under her cloak, her little black sabots and her basket, walked briskly in the middle of the road.

She crossed the forest, passed High Oak, and reached St. Gatien.

A cloud of dust rose behind her, and in it a mail coach, carried away by the steep hill, rushed down at full gallop like a hurricane. Seeing this woman who would not get out of the way, the driver stood up in front and the postilion shouted too. He could not hold in his four horses, which increased their pace, and the two leaders were grazing her when he threw them to one side with a jerk of the reins. But he was wild with rage, and lifting his arm as he passed at full speed, gave her such a lash from waist to neck with his big whip that she fell on her back.

Her first act, when she recovered consciousness, was to open her basket. Loulou was happily none the worse. She felt a burn in her right cheek, and when she put her hands against it they were red; the blood was flowing.

She sat down on a heap of stones and bound up her face with her handkerchief. Then she ate a crust of bread which she had put in the basket as a precaution, and found a consolation for her wound in gazing at the bird.

When she reached the crest of Ecquemauville, she saw the Honfleur lights sparkling in the night sky like a company of stars; beyond, the sea stretched dimly. Then a faintness overtook her, and she stopped; her wretched childhood, the disillusion of her first love, her nephew's going away, and Virginie's death all came back to her at once like the waves of an oncoming tide, rose to her throat, and choked her.

Afterward, at the boat, she made a point of speaking to the captain, begging him to take care of the parcel, though she did not tell him what was in it.

Fellacher kept the parrot a long time. He was always promising it for the following week. After six months he announced that a packing case had started, and then nothing more was heard of it. It really seemed as though Loulou was never coming back. "Ah, they have stolen him!" she thought.

He arrived at last and looked superb. There he was, erect upon a branch which screwed into a mahogany socket, with a foot in the air and his head on one side, biting a nut which the bird-stuffer—with a taste for impressiveness—had gilded.

Félicité shut him up in her room. It was a place to which few people were admitted, and held so many religious objects and miscellaneous things that it looked like a chapel and bazaar in one.

A big cupboard impeded you as you opened the door. Opposite the window commanding the garden a little round one looked into the court; there was a table by the folding bed with a water jug, two combs, and a cube of blue soap in a chipped plate. On the walls hung rosaries, medals, several benign Virgins, and a holy water vessel made out of coconut; on the chest of drawers, which was covered with a cloth like an altar, was the shell box that Victor had given her, and after that a watering can, a toy balloon, exercise books, the illustrated geography, and a pair of young lady's boots; and, fastened by its ribbons to the nail of the looking-glass, hung the little plush hat! Félicité carried observances of this kind so far as to keep one of Monsieur's frock coats. All the old rubbish which Mme. Aubain did not want any longer she laid hands on for her room. That was why there were artificial flowers along the edge of the chest of drawers and a portrait of the Comte d'Artois in the little window recess.

With the aid of a bracket Loulou was established over the chimney, which jutted into the room. Every morning when she woke up, she saw him there in the dawning light and recalled old days and the smallest details of insignificant acts in a deep quietness which knew no pain.

Holding, as she did, no communication with anyone, Félicité lived as insensibly as if she were walking in her sleep. The Corpus Christi processions roused her to life again. Then she went around begging mats and candlesticks from the neighbors to decorate the altar they put up in the street.

In church she was always gazing at the Holy Ghost in the window and observed that there was something of the parrot in him. The likeness was still clearer, she thought, on a crude color-print representing the baptism of Our Lord. With his purple wings and emerald body, he was the very image of Loulou.

She bought him and hung him up instead of the Comte d'Artois, so that she could see them both together in one glance. They were linked in her thoughts; and the parrot was consecrated by his association with the Holy Ghost, which became more vivid to her eye and more intelligible. The Father could not have chosen to express Himself through a dove, for such creatures cannot speak; it must have been one of Loulou's ancestors, surely. And though Félicité looked at the picture while she said her prayers, she swerved a little from time to time toward the parrot.

She wanted to join the Ladies of the Virgin, but Mme. Aubain dissuaded her.

And then a great event loomed up before them—Paul's marriage.

He had been a solicitor's clerk to begin with, and then tried business, the Customs, the Inland Revenue, and even made efforts to get into the Rivers and Forests. By an inspiration from heaven he had suddenly, at 36, discovered his real line—the Registrar's Office. And there he showed such marked capacity that an inspector had offered him his daughter's hand and promised him his influence.

So Paul, grown serious, brought the lady to see his mother.

She sniffed at the ways of Pont-l'Évêque, gave herself great airs, and wounded Félicité's feelings. Mme. Aubain was relieved at her departure.

The week after came news of M. Bourais' death in an inn in Lower Brittany. The rumour of suicide was confirmed and doubts arose as to his honesty. Mme. Aubain studied his accounts and soon found out the whole tale of his misdoings—embezzled arrears, secret sales of wood, forged receipts, etc.

Besides that he had an illegitimate child and "relations with a person at Dozulé."

These shameful facts distressed her greatly. In March 1853 she was seized with a pain in the chest; her tongue seemed to be covered with film, and leeches did not ease the difficult breathing. On the ninth evening of her illness she died, just at 72.

She passed as being younger, owing to the bands of brown hair which framed her pale, pock-marked face. There were few friends to regret her, for she had a stiffness of manner which kept people at a distance.

But Félicité mourned for her as one seldom mourns for a master. It upset her ideas and seemed contrary to the order of things, impossible and monstrous, that Madame should die before her.

Ten days afterward, which was the time it took to hurry there from Besançon, the heirs arrived. The daughter-in-law ransacked the drawers, chose some furniture, and sold the rest; and then they went back to their registering.

Madame's armchair, her small round table, her foot-warmer, and the eight chairs were gone! Yellow patches in the middle of the panels showed where the engravings had hung. They had carried off the two little beds and the mattresses, and all Virginie's belongings had disappeared from the cupboard. Félicité went from floor to floor dazed with sorrow.

The next day there was a notice on the door, and the apothecary shouted in her ear that the house was for sale.

She tottered, and was obliged to sit down. What distressed her most of all was to give up her room, so suitable as it was for poor Loulou. She enveloped him with a look of anguish when she was imploring the Holy Ghost, and formed the idolatrous habit of kneeling in front of the parrot to say her prayers. Sometimes the sun shone in at the attic window and caught his glass eye, and a great luminous ray shot out of it and put her in an ecstasy.

She had a pension of 15 pounds a year, which her mistress had left her. The garden gave her a supply of vegetables. As for clothes, she had enough to last her to the end of her days, and she economized in candles by going to bed at dusk.

She hardly ever went out, as she did not like passing the dealer's shop, where some of the old furniture was exposed for sale. Since her fit of giddiness she dragged one leg; and as her strength was failing, Mère Simon, whose grocery business had collapsed, came every morning to split the wood and pump water for her.

Her eyes grew feeble. The shutters ceased to be thrown open. Years and years passed, and the house was neither let nor sold.

Félicité never asked for repairs because she was afraid of being sent away. The boards on the roof rotted; her bolster was wet for a whole winter. After Easter she spat blood.

Then Mère Simon called in a doctor. Félicité wanted to know what was the matter with her. But she was too deaf to hear, and the only word which reached her was "pneumonia." It was a word she knew, and she answered softly, "Ah! Like Madame," thinking it natural that she should follow her mistress.

The time for the festal shrines was coming near. The first one was always at the bottom of the hill, the second in front of the postoffice, and the third toward the middle of the street. There was some rivalry in the matter of this one, and the women of the parish ended by choosing Mme. Aubain's courtyard.

The hard breathing and fever increased. Félicité was vexed at doing nothing for the altar. If only she could at least have put something there! Then she thought of the parrot. The neighbors objected that it would not be decent. But the priest gave her permission, which so intensely delighted her that she begged him to accept Loulou, her sole possession, when she died.

From Tuesday to Saturday, the eve of the festival, she coughed more often. By the evening her face had shriveled, her lips stuck to her gums, and she was vomiting; and at twilight next morning, feeling herself very low, she sent for a priest.

Three kindly women were around her during the Extreme Unction. Then she announced that she must speak to Fabu. He arrived in his Sunday clothes, by no means at his ease in the funereal atmosphere.

"Forgive me," she said, with an effort to stretch out her arm, "I thought it was you who had killed him."

What did she mean by such stories? She suspected him of murder—a man like him! He was indignant and was on the point of making a row.

"There," said the women, "she is no longer in her senses; you can see it well enough!"

Félicité spoke to shadows of her own from time to time. The women went away, and Mère Simon had breakfast. A little later she took Loulou and brought him close to Félicité with the words:

"Come, now, say good-bye to him!"

Loulou was not a corpse, but the worms devoured him; one of his wings was broken, and the tow was coming out of his stomach. But she was blind now; she kissed him on the forehead and kept him close against her cheek. Mère Simon took him back from her to put him on the altar.

V.

Summer scents came up from the meadows, flies buzzed, the sun made the river glitter and heated the slates. Mère Simon came back into the room and fell softly asleep.

She woke at the noise of bells; the people were coming out from vespers. Félicité's delirium subsided. She thought of the procession and saw it as if she had been there.

All the school children, the church-singers, and the firemen walked on the pavement, while in the middle of the road the verger armed with his mace and the beadle with a large cross advanced in front. Then came the schoolmaster, with an eye on the boys, and the sister, anxious about her little girls; three of the daintiest, with angelic curls, scattered rose petals in the air; the deacon controlled the band with outstretched arms; and two censer-bearers turned back at every step toward the Holy Sacrament, which was borne by Monsieur the Curé, wearing his beautiful chasuble, under a canopy of dark-red velvet held up by four churchwardens. A crowd of people pressed behind, between the white cloths covering the house walls, and they reached the bottom of the hill.

A cold sweat moistened Félicité's temples. Mère Simon sponged her with a piece of linen, saying to herself that one day she would have to go that way.

The hum of the crowd increased, was very loud for an instant, and then went farther away.

A fusillade shook the windowpanes. It was the postilions saluting the monstrance. Félicité rolled her eyes and said as audibly as she could: "Does he look well?" The parrot was weighing on her mind.

Her agony began. A death-rattle that grew more and more

convulsed made her sides heave. Bubbles of froth came at the corners of her mouth, and her whole body trembled.

Soon the booming of the ophicleides, the high voices of the children, and the deep voices of the men were distinguishable. At intervals all was silent, and the tread of feet, deadened by the flowers they walked on, sounded like a flock pattering on grass.

The clergy appeared in the courtyard. Mère Simon clambered onto a chair to reach the attic window and so looked down straight upon the shrine. Green garlands hung over the altar, which was decked with a flounce of lace. In the middle was a small frame with relics in it; there were two orange trees at the corners, and all along stood silver candlesticks and china vases, with sunflowers, lilies, peonies, foxgloves, and tufts of hortensia. This heap of blazing color slanted from the level of the altar to the carpet, which covered the pavement; and some rare objects caught the eye. There was a silver-gilt sugar basin with a crown of violets, pendants of Alençon stone glittered on the moss, and two Chinese screens displayed their landscapes. Loulou was hidden under roses and showed nothing but his blue forehead, like a plaque of lapis lazuli.

The churchwardens, singers, and children took their places around the three sides of the court. The priest went slowly up the steps and placed his great, radiant golden sun upon the lace. Everyone knelt down. There was a deep silence; and the censers glided to and fro on the full swing of their chains.

An azure vapour rose up into Félicité's room. Her nostrils met it; she inhaled it sensuously, mystically, and then closed her eyes. Her lips smiled. The beats of her heart lessened one by one, vaguer each time and softer, as a fountain sinks, an echo disappears; and when she sighed her last breath she thought she saw an opening in the heavens and a gigantic parrot hovering above her head.

YVETTE
by Guy de Maupassant

A peerless writer of short stories, Guy de Maupassant derived from the example of his master, Flaubert, the qualities of craftsmanship, precision, and dispassionate observation which distinguish his works. Like Flaubert, de Maupassant was born in Normandy, and many of his subjects are drawn from that humble peasant life. The Norman fishermen, farmers, tradesmen, and petit bourgeois provincials who people his pages are observed with almost photographic accuracy. It is this documentation and attention to detail that places de Maupassant among the French naturalists of the late 19th century, though in fact, he did not share the naturalistic concept of scientific determinism. Nor did he share the belief of this school of writing—as defined by Zola in the preface to Thérèse Raquin—*in the "scientific" novel capable of anatomizing reality as precisely as a surgical autopsy.*

Like Balzac, de Maupassant's first literary success came in his 30th year. Within the next decade, 1880 to 1890, came a prodigal output of more than 300 short stories and six novels. He wrote, in addition, some plays and travel books. All of de Maupassant's works reflect a passion for technical perfection, economy, and stylistic purity. In general, they present life pessimistically. De Maupassant himself was given to spells of morbidity and in the last years of his life suffered from a psychological deterioration that led to a total mental collapse.

CHAPTER I.
A DOVE OR A HAWK?

As they were going out of the Café Riche, Jean de Servigny said to Léon Saval:

"If you're willing, we will walk. The weather is too beautiful to take a cab."

And his friend answered:

"All right, I am willing."

Jean went on:

"It is not quite eleven; we shall arrive there long before twelve, so let us go slowly."

A lively throng was swarming on the boulevard, that summer-night crowd, full of the joy of living that moves, drinks, murmurs, and flows like a river.

Every few steps a café shed its light upon the mass of diners, whose tables, covered with bottles and glasses, were in the way of passing strollers. In the streets cabs with red, green, or blue eyes shot by in the projected light, showing, for a second, the silhouette of a trotting, lanky horse, the elevated profile of the coachman, and the somber-hued body of the carriage. Those of the Urbaine Company, with their yellow panels, were an exception to the rest when struck by this light.

The two friends walked slowly, enjoying their cigars, in full dress, their overcoats thrown on their arms, flowers in their buttonholes and hats carelessly tilted to one side, as they are often worn after a good dinner and when the breeze is slightly warm.

They were bound to one another by a strong, solid friendship that dated back to their schooldays.

Jean de Servigny, short and thin, slightly bald, somewhat frail, very elegant, with curled mustache, light eyes, delicate lips, was one of those night owls who seems to have been born and brought up on the boulevard; indefatigable and full of vigor, although he always looked exhausted. He was one of those many Parisians to whom the gymnasium, fencing, shower and vapor baths imparts a fictitious nervous energy. He was as well-known for his fast life as he was for his wit, position in society, sociability, and amiability, which seem to be peculiar to certain men.

A true Parisian, light-hearted, skeptical, changing, energetic and irresolute, capable of everything and nothing, egotistical on principle, generous by fits. He spent his income and amused himself with moderation. Indifferent yet passionate, he was always on the verge of giving into, or resisting, his whims or contrary instincts, all of which he ended by obeying; in this he followed the reasoning of the men of his type, whose windmill logic consisted of going with the wind and profiting by circumstances without giving a thought as to whence they arose.

His friend, Léon Saval, equally wealthy, was one of those superb giants who cause women to glance back despite themselves. He gave the impression of a statue come to life, a type of which models are made and sent to expositions. Too large, too handsome, too tall, too stout, his fault seemed to be that very excess of advantageous qualities. He had been the hero of many a love affair.

When they arrived in front of the Vaudeville he asked:

"Did you warn this lady you would introduce me?"

Servigny laughed.

"Warn the Marquise Obardi! Do you send word to the coachman on the corner that you are going to take his cab?"

Saval, somewhat perplexed, inquired:

"What is this person, anyway?"

"She is nothing but a common, ordinary *parvenue,* a charming thing, originating no one knows where, who appeared one day, no one knows how, in the world of adventurers, and who is equal to the most cunning of that set. But that is neither here nor there. They say that her real name, her maiden name, is Octavie Bardin, from which she derived Obardi, by preserving the first letter of her Christian name and suppressing the last of her family name.

"She is, on the whole, an amiable woman, of whom you will not fail to become the lover because of your fine physique. For when Hercules is introduced to Messalina, something is bound to happen. Though I must add that even if the admission to this house is free, one is never under obligation to buy whatever is displayed there. Love and cards are the goods handled, but you are not absolutely expected to patronize either. The exit is also free.

"She took a house in the neighborhood of the Étoile about three years ago and threw open her salon to that scum of the continents that comes to Paris to make use of various dangerous and criminal talents.

"How did I come to drop into such a set? I do not remember anymore. I went there, as we all go into such places, to gamble and to meet the women who are none too prudish and the men none too honest. I rather like that world of filibusters, with their multifarious decorations, all foreigners, all noblemen, all titled, all unknown to their embassies, except to the spies. All speak of their honor without the least instigation, brag of their ancestors, tell the story of their lives every five minutes; each and every one of them is a liar, a swindler, as dangerous as his cards, as deceiving as their names, brave by necessity, for the same reason as the assassin who cannot rob his victims without risking his own life. They are the alumni of the prisons.

"I confess to a certain sympathy and secret admiration for them. They are interesting to study, to know—above all, amusing to listen to; always witty, never insipid, like the government employee. Their wives are always pretty, with a slight smack of foreign rascality and the mystery of their past life, half of which has probably been spent in some penitentiary. As a rule, they have beautiful eyes, gorgeous hair; in fact, they seem to have been especially created for that life. They possess that seductive grace which bewilders and dazzles their victims, over whom they exercise an unwholesome, irresistible charm.

"The Marquise Obardi is a true type of these elegant sirens. Ripe, but still beautiful, bewitching and crafty, she gives the impression of being vicious to the very marrow of her bones. One certainly enjoys a fast life in that house—gambling, dancing, midnight suppers, all the usual rounds of the gay life reign supreme."

Léon Saval asked: "Have you been or are you her lover?"

Servigny answered: "I have never been and will never be her lover. I frequent this place on account of her daughter."

"She has a daughter?"

"A beauty. She is today the principal attraction of this cavern. Tall, magnificent, just right, eighteen summers, as blonde as her mother is dark, always lively, ready for fun, laughing and dancing with abandonment. Who is or who has been the lucky dog? That is still an open question. Ten are in line and await patiently the day of judgment. A girl like that in the hands of a woman like the marquise is a fortune, and she is playing a mighty good and tight game. I do not know exactly where I stand. Are they waiting for a better chance than I? Still, I am going to lie low and jump at the first opportunity.

"That girl Yvette is certainly a puzzle to me. She disconcerts me entirely. She is a mystery. If she is not a monster of perversity and keenness, she is the most marvelous phenomenon of innocence that I ever saw. She lives in such an infamous world with a quiet and tranquil ease that is either terribly criminal or frightfully naïve.

"She is the marvelous offspring of an adventuress, sprouted from the filth of that class, just like the most beautiful of roses, or else the daughter of some gentleman of high lineage, some celebrated artist, or some great nobleman, some prince, or, perhaps, some king, who was the mother's passing fancy. No one knows what she is."

Saval began to laugh.

"You are in love."

"No. I am in the ranks, and there is a world of difference. I shall introduce you to my copretenders. Though I might say here that I am in the lead. I seem to be shown special favors."

Saval repeated:

"You are really in love."

"No. She troubles, seduces, worries, attracts, and even scares me away. I am afraid of her as of a trap, and still I have the greatest longing for her, just as a thirsty man has for some beverage to quench his thrist. I am charmed by her, and still I only approach her with the apprehension that one would a man suspected of being a clever thief. When near her I experience an irresistible sympathy toward her for her possible candor and a very natural suspicion against her no less probable cunning. I feel that she is an extraordinary creature, either exquisite or detestable. I cannot say yet."

Saval insisted:

"You are in love, I say, and speak with quite a little poetic grace; really you do. Question yourself closely, and you will acknowledge it."

Servigny mused for a while.

"It may be true, after all. At all events, she is always uppermost in my mind. Yes, I do think too much about her. I see her as I doze off to sleep, and then again when I awaken. Yes, I realize that. Her image is ever with me. Is this physical obsession what they call love? Her face is so imprinted in my mind that I can at any time see it by closing my eyes, and my heart beats at such moments. But I love her in a queer manner. My strongest desire is to possess her, and yet the idea of marrying her would seem to be a folly, a stupidity, a monstrosity, even to me. I am afraid of her just as the bird is of the falcon coming down upon it. And I am jealous of her and everything that remains unknown to me in that incomprehensible heart. I am forever asking myself, 'Is she a charming child or an abominable deceiver?' She says things that would make a trooper blush, but so do parrots. She is exciting and encouraging, with the air of a true courtesan, and yet she remains as distant as the purest maiden. While seemingly in love with me, she is continually poking fun at me; to the outside world she acts as if she were my lover, and, in intimacy, she treats me worse than she would her brother or valet.

"There are times when I honestly believe she has as many

lovers as her mother. Then, again, I cannot help thinking she knows nothing of life, nothing whatever.

"She is a great reader of novels, most of which I have the honor of furnishing. She calls me her librarian, and she reads them as fast as they are printed.

"The result in the make-up of her mind must surely be a strange salad.

"That heterogeneous mixture must be one of the many causes of her strange peculiarities. When one tries to take a view of life through fifteen thousand novels, one doubtless sees it in a queer light.

"One thing remains certain; I never loved a person as I do her.

"But I will never marry her.

"If she has already had lovers, I shall merely increase the number. If not, why then I shall be number one.

"It is clear she will never marry anyone. Who would marry the daughter of the Marquise Obardi, alias Octavie Bardin? No one, and there are a thousand reasons.

"Where could she find a candidate? In society? Never. Her mother's social position is too well known, as well as the house of which the daughter is the main attraction.

"In the middle class? Still less. Besides, the marquise would not make such a poor speculation; she will never give up Yvette definitely except to a man of the higher class, whom she will never find.

"A man of the lower classes is altogether out of the question. Yvette strictly belongs to no class and can really enter through marriage none of those I named.

"She belongs by birth, education, heredity, manner of life to the gay grisettes of Paris.

"She cannot escape, unless she enters a sisterhood, which is not probable. Her profession, and her only one, then, is 'love.' She will come to it, if she has not already. That is her destiny and that is what I am waiting for.

"Many others are, too. You will see a Frenchman, Monsieur de Belvigne; a Russian, the Prince Kravalow, and an Italian, the Chevalier Valreali, all of whom are candidates; there are others, but they do not count.

"The marquise is biding her time. She knows that I have money, and that is why I think she is casting her eye on me.

"Her salon is the most striking of the kind. You will meet some men just as respectable as we are. She seems to have sorted the prettiest of the women of her class, which appar-

ently stands all by itself. Her master idea was to choose ad-
venturesses who have children, girls especially, so that any
fool or ignorant victim would surely take these persons to be
honest women."

They had reached the Avenue des Champs-Elysées by this
time. A slight breeze rocked the leaves of the trees and softly
brushed the faces of the strollers. Silent shadows moved under
the trees, while others, seated on the benches, looked like dark
spots. And these shadows spoke very low, as if confiding some
important or shameful secrets.

Servigny continued after a pause:

"You have no idea of the fantastic titles that you will hear
in this haunt.

"By the way, I must introduce you as Comte Saval. 'Saval'
all by itself would make a bad impression."

But his friend protested:

"No, sir. I shall not submit to the ridicule of borrowing a
title, not even among those people. No, sir, not for the
world."

Servigny began to laugh.

"You are stupid. They baptized me Duc de Servigny. I
cannot say how it happened, though. But the fact remains that
I am the Duc de Servigny, and I neither protest nor complain.
It makes no difference to me. While, were it not for this title,
I should be terribly despised."

Saval remained unconvinced.

"It may be all right for you, because you are a nobleman,
anyway. But with me it is totally different. I am a commoner
and must accept my lot for better or for worse. That will be
my mark of distinction and my superiority."

Servigny, nevertheless, insisted.

"But that's impossible, old man, altogether too much so. It
would appear almost monstrous. You would be made to feel
like a ragpicker in a reunion of emperors. Leave it to me, and
I shall introduce you as the Viceroy of the Upper Mississippi,
and no one will say anything."

"It is of no use. I refuse to submit to it."

"All right. And, really, I am stupid to argue with you. I
defy you to enter this house unless there is a title given to
you, just as ladies are handed bouquets in certain department
stores."

They turned to their right into the Rue de Berri, went to
the first floor of a beautiful modern house, and left their
overcoats and canes in the hands of four servants in knee-

breeches. An odor of flowers, perfumes, and women impregnated the air; one heard the confused, continuous murmur that told of crowded rooms nearby.

A sort of master of ceremonies, tall, erect, of a stately stoutness, with white burnsides, approached the newcomer and asked him, after a short, proud bow:

"Whom should I announce?"

Servigny answered:

"Monsieur Saval."

Then the man, opening the door, shouted into the crowd of guests in sonorous tones:

"The Duc de Servigny!

"The Baron Saval!"

The first parlor was filled with women. One's first gaze fell upon naked breasts set in clothes and silks of the most glaring colors.

The hostess, standing up, talking to a few friends, turned around immediately and went to greet her new guests with a certain grace in her walk and smile on her lips.

Her narrow forehead, very low, was covered with a mass of black ebony hair, tightly drawn over her head, hiding both her temples.

She was tall and inclined to be stout, a little too much so, on the other side of 30, but still maintaining the freshness of youth and possessing a warm, magnetic beauty. Two enormous black eyes shone under this helmet of hair that made one looking at her both smile and dream and wish to secure her for his very own. Her nose was rather thin and mouth a trifle large but infinitely seducing—made to command and conquer.

Her voice was her greatest personal charm. It rippled from out of her mouth, so natural, so clear, so harmonious that one experienced a physical joy to listen to it. It was a pleasure for the ear to hear the words escape. It made one think of running water in a brook, and it was a treat to the eye to see those lips, a little too red, part to let the words escape.

She held out her hand to Servigny, who kissed it, and, as she let her fan drop the full length of the golden chain to which it was tied, gave the other to Saval:

"You are welcome, as are all the friends of the duke."

Then she threw a rapid glance at the superb giant just introduced to her. She had on the upper lip a slight suspicion of a mustache that darkened as she spoke. She exhaled a delicious odor, some perfume from America or India.

Others were now arriving, all marquises, counts, or princes. Then she said to Servigny with true motherly grace:

"You will find my daughter in the other room. Enjoy yourselves, gentlemen, and be at home."

And she left them to greet other guests, not without having first thrown Saval one of those looks that women grace some fortunate ones with when the latter have had the good luck to strike their fancy. Servigny took his friend by the arm:

"I am going to pilot you. The parlor, in which you now are, is the Temple of Worldly Pleasures. Second-hand objects, as good as new, even better, rated at a high price, and obtainable by lease only. To your left, the Temple of Money. Down the other end will be found the sanctuary, the market of the young girls. There the products of the worthy friends of the marquise are displayed. In this case a legitimate union might be consented to. This is the future, the fond hope—of our nights. This department is also the most interesting in the museum of moral diseases; these youngsters, whose souls are early dislocated, as it were, just as the joints of circus children are. Come and watch them."

An orchestra was playing a waltz; they stopped at the entrance of the ballroom and surveyed the assembly. About 15 couples were turning around; the men were serious and their dancers kept a fixed smile upon their lips; like their mothers, their gowns were cut low.

Suddenly a tall young miss dashed away from the other side of the room, interrupting the couples that were in her way, and, approaching the two friends, cried:

"Ah! there is Muscade! Hello, Muscade!"

She looked supremely happy; her features seemed to be illuminated with the joy of living. Her white skin, that gilded skin of the auburn-haired girl, shone brightly. She possessed a mass of flaming red hair that she wore curled over her head, which was supported by a flexible neck that was still too thin.

She seemed to have been made to move just as her mother was to speak, so natural, noble, simple were all her gestures and motions. One could not help feeling a moral joy and physical happiness to see her walk, move, incline her head, lift her arms even.

She repeated:

"Ah, Muscade! Hello, Muscade!"

Servigny shook her hand violently, as he would have a man's, and said:

"Mam'zelle Yvette, my friend the Baron Saval."

She bowed to the stranger.

"I am very pleased to meet you, sir. Are you always as tall as that?"

Servigny answered in that sprightly, half-sarcastic tone, which he always affected with her, to hide his suspicions and doubts.

"No, indeed, mam'zelle. He put on his biggest dimensions to please your mother, who likes large masses."

The young girl then answered in a semi-comic manner:

"All right. But when you come to see me, you will please diminish a little. I do not like extremes. See, Muscade is just right!"

Turning toward Servigny, she asked:

"Do you know how to dance, Muscade? Just one dance."

Without answering, he quickly took her by the waist; they both disappeared in a furious whirl.

They danced faster than the others, turned and turned, glided over the floor, madly pivoting, seemingly one person, so closely were they bound together. To see their erect bodies, motionless and stiff limbs, one would have thought they were being operated by an invisible mechanism.

Evidently they were tireless. The other couples soon abandoned hope of keeping pace and let this mad couple have the whole floor to themselves. They were then alone but still kept on waltzing indefinitely. They seemed to have forgotten where they were, what they were doing, and to have gone away far from the ball into some ecstasy. The musicians alone followed the two madcaps and kept on playing for them. All eyes were fixed upon Servigny and Yvette, and when they stopped at last, every one applauded.

She was all flushed now, her eyes had a strange look, ardent and timid, not so bold as a little while ago, but much softer; the darkened pupils in her extremely light-blue eyes did not appear natural.

Servigny was somewhat dazed. He had to lean against a door to regain composure.

She said to him:

"Poor thing, you are dizzy. I won that time."

He laughed nervously and gave her an intimate, searching look.

She then said:

"At times you remind me of a cat when it is angry and is going to spring at you. Come, let us go find your friend."

Without answering her, he took her arm and they crossed the main parlor.

Saval was not alone. The Marquise Obardi was with him. She was carrying on a meaningless conversation in that bewitching voice which turned many a one's head. But her look, that sought to penetrate into his innermost thoughts, seemed to convey an entirely different meaning to what came from her mouth. Upon perceiving Servigny, her expression changed, and she said, smiling:

"I have just rented a cottage to spend two months at Bougival. I hope you will come to see us, with your friend. I shall be there Monday. Why don't you both come to dine Saturday and stay over Sunday?"

Servigny looked at Yvette. She smiled in her usual tranquil, serene manner and said:

"Of course, Muscade will come Saturday. That goes without saying. We shall do a lot of crazy things; we shall have a great time."

For a moment Servigny thought that she put some meaning in her last words.

The marquise then turned her large black eyes upon Saval and asked:

"You will come, too, baron?"

Her smile, at least, left no room for doubt as to what she meant. He bowed.

"I shall be only too glad to come."

Yvette murmured with a malice that was either perfidious or naïve.

"We shall shock everybody; shall we not, Muscade? And we shall tantalize my regiment."

And she designated a group of men, all of whom remained at a distance with eyes fixed upon her.

Servigny answered:

"Just as you say, mam'zelle."

When he spoke to her, he never pronounced the "mademoiselle"; that was his privilege, a sign of familiarity.

Saval inquired:

"Why do you, Mademoiselle Yvette, call Servigny 'Muscade'?"

She answered candidly:

"Because he always slips out of your hand. You always think you have a good hold on him, and yet he gets away."

The marquise spoke in an absent-minded and languorous

manner; she was evidently absorbed in some other thought, while her eyes were bent on Saval.

"These children are so funny!"

Yvette did not relish this remark.

"I am not funny; I am just frank, that is all. I like Muscade, and he always escapes me; that makes me angry."

Servigny made a deep bow:

"I am never going to leave you, neither day nor night."

She exclaimed with terror:

"No, indeed! In the daytime I do not mind, but at nighttime you would be in the way."

He asked with cold-blooded impertinence:

"Why?"

She replied with amazing and tranquil audacity:

"Because I imagine that you look at your best when dressed!"

The marquise, without a trace of emotion or surprise:

"You two surely do not pay attention to what you say. You cannot be innocent to such a degree."

Servigny added ironically:

"That is my opinion."

Yvette stared at him and, evidently hurt, said haughtily:

"You are impudently impolite, altogether too much so since a few days."

Turning around, she called:

"Chevalier, come to my rescue. I am being insulted."

A thin, dark-haired gentleman approached.

"Who is the guilty one?" said he, smiling, with a sort of constrained air.

She nodded toward Servigny.

"It is he; but I like him better than any one of you, because he's less of a bore."

The Chevalier Valreali bowed.

"We do our best. We have perhaps less advantages but surely not less devotion."

A tall, stout gentleman, with gray burnsides and stentorian voice, was coming up to them.

"Mademoiselle Yvette, your servant."

"Ah, Monsieur de Belvigne," said she.

Then, turning toward Saval, she introduced the newcomer:

"My aspirant, big, fat, rich, and stupid. That's the way I like them. A real brass-band leader. Oh, but you are taller than he. Let me see, how shall I baptize you? I shall call you

Monsieur de Rhodes Jr., because your father must have been a giant. You two must have interesting things to tell each other over everybody else's head, so good evening."

And she went toward the orchestra to tell the musicians to play a quadrille.

Mme. Obardi said distractedly, just to say something:

"You tease her all the time, and you are making her temper ugly, besides encouraging and even creating evil traits."

He replied:

"Have you not then terminated her education?"

She pretended not to understand and continued to smile serenely.

Just then, perceiving a solemn gentleman, seemingly dressed in medals, she hurried toward him.

"Ah, prince, how nice of you to come!"

While drawing Saval away, Servigny said to him:

"That is the last one of my serious rivals, the Prince Kravalow. Is she not superbly beautiful?"

"I think they are both extremely so. The mother suits me."

Servigny bowed.

"At your disposition, old man."

The quadrille was about to begin, and the two friends, being in the way, were shoved here and there by the joyous couples.

"Let us go see the Knights of the Green Cloth."

They went into the gambling parlor.

Lookers-on were gathered around the table, gazing intently at what was taking place there. Very little talking was done; the tinkle of money was the predominant sound, as if it were asserting itself above the cry of human voices.

They all wore medals, strange-colored ribbons, the same stern expression. They were especially distinguishable by their beards.

The stiff American with his horseshoe, the proud Englishman with his beard spread like a fan over his breast, the Spaniard with his jet-black hair almost hiding his eyes, the Roman with that enormous mustache which Victor Emmanuel created for Italy, the Austrian with his whiskers and shaved chin, the Russian general with bristling mustache, and Frenchmen with gallant mustaches revealed the fancy of barbers of many different parts of the world.

"Do you play?" asked Servigny.

"No. Do you?"

"Not here. Do you want to leave? We shall come back on a more quiet day. There are too many people; you cannot became acquainted properly."

As soon as they were in the street, Servigny asked:

"Well, what do you think of the place?"

"Very interesting. I prefer the ladies to all the rest."

"I should say so. Those women are the elixir of love. You feel the atmosphere at the slightest contact with them, just as you smell perfume at a perfume shop. Artistic—to their finger tips—and delicate—to a nicety. Expensive—oh, yes—but you cannot regret your money."

Saval asked:

"Who is the paymaster of these ceremonies?"

Servigny shrugged his shoulders to show his ignorance.

"I really do not know. The last one was an English peer, who disappeared three months ago. She may not derive her income from the gambling, or, possibly, from the gamblers, for she sometimes has caprices. But, tell me now, is it certain we shall go to Bougival to dine Saturday? I shall have a better opportunity in the country, where formality is comparatively absent, to study Yvette thoroughly."

Saval answered:

"I have nothing to do that day, so I am willing."

As they walked through the Champs-Elysées, Servigny kept silent, wrapt in his thoughts about Yvette. Finally he exlaimed:

"Good heavens! What I wouldn't give to be Yvette's first lover! I should give—I should give——"

Before Servigny had decided what he would give, the pair had reached the Rue Royale, where Saval bid him good night and left him to continue his way alone.

CHAPTER II.

A HOT PURSUIT

The table was set on the veranda overlooking the river. The villa, named "Spring," was midway up the hill, right at the bend of the Seine, just before arriving at Marly.

An island, Croissy by name, opposite the house, made a splendid horizon with its mass of green trees, and a considerable length of the large river could be seen as far as the floating café of the Grenouillère, which was hidden by thick foliage.

It was one of those calm evenings, vividly colored, such as

are often enjoyed on the banks of a river and that give a real sensation of happiness. Not the slightest breath of wind disturbed the branches of the trees nor the clear, mirror-like surface of the Seine. And still it was not too warm; it was just right; one felt most comfortable. A certain beneficial coolness, as it were, seemed to emanate from the banks of the river.

The sun was gradually disappearing behind the trees, bound for other countries, and one aspired, it seemed, a most delightful well-being from the earth slumbering already in the peace of this vast space.

When they left the parlor to go to dinner, they all remained in ecstasy before this grand spectacle. A sweetly softened gaiety invaded all hearts: they felt that they were going to be so happy, to dine in this landscape, with such a large river and beautiful dying day for a background, breathing in at the same time a clear and balmy air.

The marquise had taken Saval's arm, and Yvette that of Servigny.

There were just the four.

The women seemed altogether different to what they were in Paris, Yvette especially.

She hardly spoke; she appeared languorous, serious.

Saval, not recognizing her anymore, asked her:

"Is there anything the matter with you, mademoiselle? You are so changed. You have become so calm and reasonable."

She answered:

"It is the country that has produced this effect upon me. I am not the same. I feel queer. But I am never the same, not even for two consecutive days. Today I shall look like an insane person, tomorrow like an elegy. I change all the time; I do not know how. Some days I should like to kill people, not animals; I would never to kill an animal; and then other days I cry for the least little thing. A whole swarm of different ideas go through my head. It all depends upon how I rise. Every morning, when I awake, I can tell you what I am going to be like until evening. It may be our dreams that predispose us in that way. It depends also upon the book I am reading."

She was dressed in a white flannel suit, which enveloped her in the floating softness of the goods. Her loose waist, with large pleats, indicated, without showing it, and although not closely fitted, a solid and already womanly form. And her delicate neck emerged from a froth of white lace, fairer than her dress, a precious jewel of skin and flesh that bore her heavy mass of golden hair.

Servigny looked at her a long time, and finally said:

"You are adorable this evening, mam'zelle. I should like to see you always so."

She said to him, with a smack of her usual roguishness:

"Do not propose to me, Muscade. I might take it seriously, and it would be mighty costly to you."

The marquise seemed happy, very happy. All in black, nobly draped in a simple dress that enhanced her well-defined lines, a little red at her waist, a wreath of red pinks hanging from her belt, she seemed to be impregnated with an uncommon ardor, which betrayed itself in the whole of her person, in the simplicity of her dress, upon which the flowers looked as if they were bleeding; in her eyes, that fell heavily, as it were, upon the company; in her subdued voice, in her rare motions.

Saval also appeared serious, absorbed. Every now and then, taking his beard in his hand, which he stroked caressingly, he seemed lost in deep thought.

An intense silence reigned for a few minutes.

As they were passing the trout, Servigny declared:

"Silence is sometimes very agreeable. Often people are in closer contact with another when silent than when talking. Isn't that so, marquise?"

"That is true," said she, turning a little toward him. "It is delightful to think of nice things together."

And she looked at Saval; the two remained a few seconds in a staring contemplation of each other.

A slight movement, almost invisible, took place under the table.

Servigny revived the conversation.

"Mam'zelle Yvette, you will have me believe you are in love if you continue to be so serious. With whom could you be in love? Let us see, if you do not mind. I shall omit the less important of your aspirants. I shall only bother with the principal ones. With the Prince Kravalow?"

At the sound of this name Yvette was roused.

"How could you think of such a thing, Muscade? He looks like a wax figure of a Russian that has won medals in a hairdressers' and barbers' exposition."

"So much for him; but there is the Vicomte Pierre de Belvigne."

This time she broke into a peal of laughter and said:

"Do you see me clasping Raisiné around the neck"—she gave everybody nicknames—"and murmuring up his nose:

" 'My dear little Peter, my divine Pedro, my adored Pietri,

my charming Pierrot, give your big poodle head to your dearie, who wants to kiss it'?"

Servigny announced:

"Take away Number Two. Now the Chevalier Valreali, whom your mother favors."

Yvette had regained her former gaiety.

"Tearful? He is worse than the Magdalen. He is only good for funerals. Every time I see him I think I am dead."

"Is it a case of love at first sight? The Baron Saval."

"Monsieur de Rhodes? Oh, no. I should feel as if I were loving a triumphal arch."

"Then it must be with me. Modesty and prudence kept me from suggesting myself first. I have only to thank you."

She answered, gracefully joyous:

"With you, Muscade? No, indeed. I like you, but do not love you. Wait, I do not want to discourage you entirely. I do not love you—yet. You have a good chance—perhaps. Persevere, Muscade; be devoted, attentive, obedient, yielding to my strangest whims, ready to please me at all times, and—we shall see—later."

"But, mam'zelle, I should rather furnish all that after, if you do not mind."

She asked roguishly:

"After what, Muscade?"

"After you will have proved that you love me."

"Well, act as if I did love you, and believe it, if you want to."

"But——"

"Silence; that is enough about that."

He saluted military fashion.

The sun had sunk beyond the island, but the whole sky seemed still enflamed, and the calm waters of the river were apparently changed to blood. The reflected light of the horizon reddened all the houses, objects, and even the people.

As Yvette was looking away into the distance before her, the marquise put her hand, unconsciously, as it were, on that of Saval; but when the young girl moved, the marquise withdrew it and began fixing something at her waist.

Servigny, who had not lost anything of this comedy, proposed:

"If you want to, mam'zelle, we shall take a walk on the island after dinner."

"Oh, yes!" she cried joyously; "and we shall go alone, too?"

"Yes, all alone, mam'zelle."

Then silence again reigned.

The vast silence of the horizon, the sleepy restfulness of the evening benumbed all hearts, bodies, and voices. There are quiet hours, hours of meditation, when it is almost impossible to speak.

The servants served noiselessly. The fixed firmament seemed to glow less and less, and night was about to open entirely her wings over the earth. Saval asked:

"Do you expect to stay long in this country?"

The marquise emphasized each word:

"Yes. As long as I shall be happy in it."

As it became impossible to see anymore, lamps were brought out. They threw a strange, pale light on the table under the great obscurity of space; and presently a torrent of flies fell upon the tablecloth. They were small flies that went to be cremated over the lamp chimney and became a sort of light-gray dust, powdering the white linen.

One could not help drinking them in the wine, eating them in the sauces, and seeing them on the bread. They even annoyed the diners by coming in crowds and tickling their hands and faces.

The beverages had to be thrown away, the plates covered, and infinite precautions used to protect the dishes.

Yvette was much amused. Servigny did his best to protect her and her dishes from this invasion, using his napkin as a weapon. But the marquise was soon disgusted and hurried the rest of the dinner through.

Yvette, who had not forgotten Servigny's promise, said to him:

"Let us go on the island now."

Her mother recommended in languorous tones:

"Do not stay long. We shall accompany you as far as the boatman's."

And they walked in couples, the young girl and her friend being in the lead. They could hear in back of them the marquise speaking very low and fast. It was a jet-black night. But the heavens glittered with little bits of fire and apparently sowed them in the river, for the water was aglow with them.

The frogs croaked, and the robin redbreasts whistled their shrill notes in the calm air.

Yvette asked all of a sudden:

"Where are they? I do not hear them walking anymore."

And she called:

"Mother!"

No one answered.

"They cannot be far away; I heard them only a little while ago."

"They must have gone back," murmured Servigny. "Your mother may have been cold."

In front of them a light shone. It was Martinet's inn. They called for someone, and a man came out and installed them in a boat that was tied to a mass of seaweeds near the bank.

They soon reached the other side where they disappeared in the forest of trees.

A certain freshness exhaled from the wet ground and hovered above the thickly leaved branches that looked as if they carried as many birds as leaves.

Far away in the distance a piano was playing a popular waltz.

Servigny had taken Yvette's arm and little by little had wound his arm around her, softly tightening his hold.

"What are you thinking of?" said he.

"Nothing. I am so happy."

"Do you not love me?"

"Yes, yes, Muscade, I love you a great deal; only let that subject drop. This is too pleasant to stop and listen to your foolishness."

He drew her toward him, although she tried to snatch herself away, and the warmth of her body affected him. He stammered:

"Yvette."

"Well?"

"I love you."

"You are joking."

"No, I am not; I have loved you for ever so long a time."

She was continually trying to escape, attempting to withdraw her arm crushed between the two bodies. And they walked along, every which way, like two persons under the influence of liquor.

He was at a loss as to what to say to her, for he understood that she could not be dealt with as with an ordinary woman; yet he did not know whether she consented or really did not comprehend him. He racked his brain to find the right words, tender and decisive enough.

Every second he was repeating:

"Yvette, tell me, Yvette."

Then, casting away all sentiment of prudence, he kissed her upon the cheek. She stepped aside and said impatiently:

"You are simply too ridiculous. Can you not leave me alone?"

The tone of her voice was not very sharp and really did not make clear what she thought of this, nor what she wanted; perceiving she was not overirritated, he kissed her on the neck just where it started, a spot which he had long observed and worshiped. She tore away from him.

He was stupefied at her rapid escape and disappearance, and it was a few seconds before he called:

"Yvette!"

She did not answer. He searched for her, keeping an eye open for any light object which might resemble the whiteness of her garment.

"Mam'zelle Yvette!"

The robin redbreasts were no longer heard.

Vaguely annoyed, he hurried his step and strengthened his call:

"Mam'zelle Yvette! Mam'zelle Yvette!"

No sound; he stopped a moment to listen. There was not the least noise, hardly a shiver of the leaves above him. The frogs alone croaked.

He wandered from bush to bush. He even went to the bank opposite Bougival and returned to the Grenouillère, in the neighborhood of which he continued his search, repeating:

"Mam'zelle Yvette, where are you? Answer. It was only a joke. For heaven's sake, answer! Do not keep me hunting like this."

The bell of a distant clock began to ring. He counted the number of strokes—12. He had been wandering about two hours. It suddenly dawned upon him that she might have gone home alone, so he went back, too.

A servant, sleeping in the vestibule, was waiting for him.

Servigny woke him up and asked:

"When did Mademoiselle Yvette get back? I left her because I had a visit to pay."

The servant answered:

"Yes, Monsieur le Duc. Mademoiselle Yvette came back before ten o'clock."

He went to his room and then to bed.

But he remained there wide awake, unable to sleep. That stolen kiss had upset him. He mused. What did she want? What was she thinking of? How pretty, how attractive!

His desires, calmed down by the life he led, by former

conquests, by lovers of all sorts, regained their vigor before this singular child, so young, enervating, and inexplicable.

He heard the clock strike one, then two. It was useless, he could not sleep. He was uncomfortably warm and perspiring. His heart beat heavily, and so did his temples. He opened the window. A cool whiff of air came in, and he drank it in, in long draughts. It was a very dark night. But suddenly he perceived right ahead of him, in the garden, a shining speck, like a red-hot piece of coal. He thought:

"A cigar? It can only be Saval." He called:

"Léon!"

A voice answered:

"Is it you, Jean?"

"Yes. Wait a minute, and I shall come down with you."

He dressed hastily, joining his friend, who was enjoying a cigar.

"What are you doing down here at such an hour?"

Saval answered:

"Taking a rest."

He laughed. Servigny shook hands with him.

"My congratulations, old man. As for me, I am bored to death."

"That means?"

"It means that Yvette and her mother are not exactly the same."

"What happened? Tell me."

Servigny told of his unsuccessful attempt, and went on:

"That girl upsets me. Just think of it, old man, I could not go to sleep. What a queer thing a girl is! Looks simple and yet she is a puzzle. A woman of worldly experience, who has lived and loved, can be easily penetrated. But a young maiden is a riddle. I am beginning to think she is making a fool of me."

Saval was rocking his chair, but stopped to say:

"Beware! she'll bring you to wedlock. There are illustrious examples. The Comtesse de Montijo, who at least was of a good family, used similar wiles to become empress. Do not play Napoleon."

Servigny murmured:

"As far as that is concerned, I am not afraid, for I'm neither a simpleton nor an emperor. Are you sleepy?"

"No, not at all."

"Let us stroll along the river bank."

They opened the gate and went down along the river toward Marly.

It was one of those cool moments that just precede the day, the hour of deep sleep and absolute rest and calm. The light, familiar noises of the night were hushed. The robin redbreasts did not sing, and the frogs had ceased their din.

Servigny, who was at times a poet and philosopher, said all of a sudden:

"She really upsets me. In arithmetic one and one make two. In love one and one make one, and still they make two. Have you ever felt that? That need of absorbing a woman in you or disappearing in her? I do not mean the need of an embrace but that torment, both moral and mental, of becoming one with another being; of exposing before him or her your soul, your heart; and, also, of penetrating into his or her innermost thoughts. Yet you are as ignorant of that being; you never discover all the fluctuations of his or her wishes, desires, even opinions. You never really succeed in comprehending the unknown, the mystery of a soul that you feel so near you; of a soul hidden behind two eyes that look at you, limpid as the waters, transparent as if there were no secret back of them; of a soul that speaks to you through a beloved mouth; of a soul that hurls its thoughts at you, one by one, by means of words, though it still remains so far away from you as the stars from one another, even more impenetrable than they are. Curious, is it not?"

Saval answered:

"I don't go in as deeply as all that. I never try to see behind the eyes. I do not bother with what is wrapped up as much as I do with the external wrapper."

And Servigny:

"But Yvette is singular. How will she greet me this morning?"

As they reached Marly, they noticed that the sky was becoming pale.

"It is time to return," declared Saval.

They did so. When Servigny entered his room, he saw the pink horizon from his window.

He closed the shutters, pulled and carefully crossed one curtain over the other, went to bed, and finally fell asleep.

He dreamed of Yvette throughout his slumbers.

A peculiar noise woke him. He sat up, listened, but heard nothing. Then a noise like the fall of hail came to his ears.

He jumped out of bed, ran to the window, opened it, and

saw Yvette in the alley, who threw handfuls of sand in his face.

She was dressed in pink, wore a large-brimmed hat with a big feather in it, and laughed maliciously:

"Well, Muscade, are you still sleeping? What did you do last night to wake up so late? Out on an adventure, my poor Muscade?"

He was dazed by violent daylight, still tired, and, above all, surprised at the mocking composure of the young girl.

He answered:

"I shall be down presently. Just a few minutes to dress."

"Hurry up. It is ten o'clock, and I have something important to tell you about a plot we are going to form. Besides, we shall have lunch at eleven."

He found her on a bench with a book of some sort, most probably a novel. She took his arm in a frank, familiar way, as if nothing had taken place, and led him to the garden.

"Here is my proposition: We are going to disobey Mother, and you will bring me to the Grenouillère. I want to see it. Mother says that honest women should not go there. But it makes no difference to me what you should or should not do. You will bring me, will you not, Muscade? And we shall have a great time."

She exhaled a delicious odor, without his being able to determine its nature, so vague and discreet it was.

Where did it come from? Her dress, her hair, or her skin? That was what he asked himself as she was speaking to him, so near that he could smell her breath, which was equally delicious in odor. He came to the conclusion it was the perfume of her graceful and attractive youth.

She said:

"You promise, do you not, Muscade? As it's going to be very warm, Mother'll refuse to go out. We shall leave her with your friend. They shall think that we are going to the woods. Oh, how glad I shall be to see the Grenouillère!"

Just then they were at the gate in front of the Seine. The sun shone on the shining surface of the river.

Every now and then a canoe or a rowboat passed, or the shrill whistles, short or prolonged, of the trains that brought the inhabitants of Paris in the suburbs could be heard.

Lunch was announced.

No one spoke. A crushingly hot July noon oppressed everyone. The heat seemed thick, and paralyzed body and soul.

Yvette, alone, although taciturn, seemed animated, nervous, and impatient.

As soon as the dessert had been served she suggested:

"Suppose we take a walk in the woods. It would be fine under the trees."

The marquise, who looked to be very tired, murmured:

"Are you insane? How can a person go out in such weather?"

The young girl was overjoyed and said:

"Well, then, we shall let you have the baron for company. Muscade and I shall climb up the hill, and we shall lie on the grass and read."

And turning toward Servigny:

"Does that suit you?"

"At your service," answered he.

The marquise shrugged her shoulders and sighed:

"Really, she is crazy!"

Then she tendered her hand to the baron languorously, and he kissed it.

Yvette and Servigny went away. They followed the bank of the river, crossed the bridge, and sat down under the weeping willows that were on the edge of the island.

The young girl drew from her pocket a book and said:

"Muscade, you are going to read to me."

He was on the verge of running away.

"But I am unable to read aloud decently."

She replied seriously:

"No excuses, now. You are a nice aspirant. Everything for nothing! Is that your motto?"

He took the book, opened it, and was much surprised. It was the description of the ants' mode of life by an English author. And as he remained silent, thinking she was really making a fool of him, she grew impatient.

"Why don't you read?" she inquired.

"Is it a bet or a caprice?" he asked.

"I saw the book in a store. They told me it was the best on the subject, and I thought it would be interesting to learn about these small animals that run through the grass. Read!"

She lay down on the grass outstretched, resting on her elbows, her head in her hands, and eyes fixed upon the ground.

He read in monotonous tones, stopping every little while to ask:

"Is not that enough?"

She shook her little head, and, having found an ant on a piece of a torn blade of grass, she kept the insect on it to study it closely. She listened attentively to all the surprising details of information about their life and customs.

And, as if a maternal tenderness had been awakened in her, Yvette gradually became full of sympathy for this little animal, so intelligent and cunning; she even let it run along her finger and felt the desire to kiss it.

Just as Servigny was reading about the way in which they held contests of skill and strength the enthusiastic young girl tried to kiss the insect that immediately escaped and began to travel over her face. She gave a shrill cry, as if threatened with an awful danger, and tapped her face frantically. Her companion, laughing heartily, took the ant out of her hair and substituted a kiss in its place; Yvette did not turn her forehead away this time.

She rose and declared:

"That's more interesting than novels. Let's go to the Grenouillère now."

They arrived in the part of the island turned into a park full of immense trees. A few couples meandered under the high leaves, along the banks of the Seine, in which glided many rowboats. There were women with young men, working girls with their lovers in shirt-sleeves, their frock coats thrown under an arm, tilted high hats, tipsy and tired out, also *bourgeoisie* with their families.

A far-off continuous rumor of human voices, a dimly grumbling clamor, announced the favorite establishment of the boatmen.

It loomed up before them, all of a sudden. An immense boat, with a tent covering, was anchored near the shore, carrying a world of females and males, drinking or else standing up, shouting, singing, howling, dancing, cutting up capers to the noise of a screeching piano, out of tune, and vibrating like a tin can.

Tall, red-headed, licentious women, displaying themselves in their most exciting manner, meandered, staring at the men with the insistence typical of inebriate women, and coarse language upon their reddened lips.

The smell of perspiration and colognes was strongly noticeable.

The drinkers swallowed liquors of all colors and shouted, bawled, evidently yielding to the need of regular brutes, of having their ears full of these abominable noises.

Every few seconds a swimmer jumped into the water, which splashed over the nearest drinkers, who yelled savagely.

The river was full of small boats. Long, thin canoes passed swiftly by, paddled by rowers with bare arms, whose muscles twisted under their sunburnt skin.

Heavier boats also wended their way, loaded with people. A schoolboy, on a lark, trying to be smart, rowed with strokes worthy of a windmill and struck the other crafts, thus raising an outcry from their boatmen, and then he disappeared, somewhat scared, but not before he had almost drowned two bathers.

Yvette was radiant and walked arm in arm with Servigny in the midst of this noisy and mixed crowd, seemingly overjoyed at elbowing this disreputable company, especially the women, whom she observed with a calm, even sympathetic eye.

"Look at that one, Muscade; she seems to be having a great time. And what beautiful hair she has."

When a pianist, dressed in red and wearing an immense straw shade hat, started playing a waltz, Yvette suddenly grasped her companion and carried him away with the energy that characterized her dancing. They danced so long and so frantically that everybody watched them. The drinkers, standing on the tables, beat time with their feet; others used glasses; the musician seemed to have become mad; he hit the ivory keys so hard, lifted his hands so high, made all sorts of gestures, swaying his head wildly with its huge covering.

He stopped suddenly and slid to the floor, where he lay at full, hidden under his hat, as if he were thoroughly exhausted. Peals of laughter broke forth throughout the café, and all applauded.

Four friends rushed forward, as in case of accident, picked him up, each taking hold of an arm or a leg, and paraded him around the island.

A joker followed them, chanting the "De Profundis," and a procession formed, everyone following the mock corpse.

Yvette joined in, laughing heartily, talking to everybody, excited by the noise and movement. Young men stared at her, pressed against her; Servigny was growing afraid that the outing was going to end badly.

The procession kept on, gradually increasing its speed, till the four bearers began to run, with a bawling crowd at their heels. When they arrived at the banks of the river, they swung their friend in it.

A loud cry of joy came from all throats, while the dazed

pianist paddled back to shore, cursing, coughing, spitting out the water, and finally struggling desperately to emerge from the mud.

Yvette clapped her hands for joy and repeated:

"Oh, Muscade, what a grand time we're having!"

Servigny observed her seriously and was somewhat vexed, or hurt, to see her so much at home in such a crowd. His natural instinct of the born gentleman was shocked.

He said to himself in astonishment:

"You have it in the blood."

He felt like speaking familiarly to her, as one does a certain class of women at the first meeting. She was to him, then at least, of the same stock. Their obscene, filthy language did not seem to produce any effect upon Yvette.

"Muscade, I want to take a swim."

He answered curtly:

"All right, mam'zelle."

They soon had procured themselves suits. She was the first to be ready and stood on the beach, smiling, exposed to the gaze of all. Then they went together in the heated water.

She swam, wrapt in happiness, and the waters that went to and fro, softly caressing her body, gracefully rocked by the ripples of the river. Suddenly ceasing to swim, she turned over and floated. His eyes devoured her almost, as she lay on top of the water, exposing the undulating lines of her body and firm breast, enhanced by the very close-fitting bathing suit.

He was entranced by her beauty. He was again beside himself. She suddenly turned toward him and, having contemplated him awhile, began to laugh.

"You're a nice fellow," she said.

He was irritated and hurt by this mocking demeanor, and an evil spirit rose in him, a revengeful one, which made him try to be cutting, even insulting:

"Would you fancy such a life?"

"What life?"

"Come, don't try to fool me. You know what I mean."

"Upon my word, I don't."

"Stop this farce. Do you or don't you?"

"I don't understand you."

"You're not so stupid. Besides, I told you yesterday evening."

"I must have forgotten."

"That I love you."

"You?"

"I."

"What foolishness!"

"I assure you, upon my honor."

"Prove it."

"That's my greatest wish."

"Which?"

"To prove it."

"Go ahead."

"You didn't say that yesterday."

"But you didn't propose anything."

"Ridiculous."

"Besides, I am not the one to approach on that score."

"Well, that's a good one. Who is, then?"

"Mother, of course."

"Your mother? Oh, that's too comical," and he burst out laughing.

She suddenly became grave and looked straight into his eyes.

"Listen, Muscade, if you really love me enough to marry me, speak to mother first, and then I'll answer you."

Now, more than ever, he thought she was making a fool of him, and he became enraged.

"You must surely mistake me for someone else."

She again directed her clear, soft eyes upon him, and said, after some hesitation:

"I don't understand you yet."

Then he blurted out with a rough and coarse ring in his voice:

"Please put an end to this ridiculous comedy that has already lasted too long. Don't play the innocent baby; it doesn't become you. You know very well that there can be no marriage between us—only love. I told you I loved you—that's the truth—I repeat it, I love you. Now, don't pretend not to understand."

They were in the water, just keeping their heads above it, face to face. She remained motionless for a few seconds, stunned, unable to penetrate the meaning of these words; then she blushed very deeply.

The blood rushed to her head, and, without another word, she swam at top speed toward land. He was unable to catch up with her.

He saw her pick up her wrapper and rush into her cabin.

He took a long time to dress, extremely perplexed as to what to do next, whether to excuse himself or persevere.

When he was ready, she was gone. He returned home slowly, anxious, and troubled.

The marquise was strolling with the baron in the garden on the lawn.

Perceiving Servigny, she said in that languorous way which had been hers for the past two days:

"Didn't I tell you not to go out in such weather? Now Yvette is sunstruck. She's gone to bed. She's as red as a poppy and has a fearful headache. Neither of you has any sense."

The young girl did not come down to supper. When something to eat was sent to her, she answered she was not hungry and begged to be left alone. The two guests returned by the ten o'clock train, and the marquise remained silent and dreamy.

She lived for and by love, just as an enthusiastic horseman or sailor, and experienced sudden attacks of passion as one does of a disease. They enervated or left her apathetic, according to their exalted, violent, dramatic, or sentimental character.

She was born to love and be loved. Risen from a very low station in life to luxury through love, which she chose unconsciously for a profession, instinctively she accepted money as naturally as the embrace which procured it. Many men had enjoyed her caresses, without her having felt any affection, or any disgust, for them.

She tolerated their embraces indiscriminately, with tranquil indifference, as a matter of course; just as the traveler necessarily eats the differently prepared meals of many lands, for, after all is said and done, one must live. Though sometimes her heart was struck with the fire of love, and she was again and again the victim of a grand passion that lasted a few weeks or months, according to the physical or moral qualities of the man.

Those were the delightful moments of her life. She loved, body and soul, with ardor and a complete abandonment of herself. She threw herself into it as one does in a river to drown and gave up her entire self, ready to die, if need be, transported into an ecstatic happiness. The latest intrigue was, to her fervid imagination, the deepest passion of her life, and she would have been very much astonished had she been reminded of the many men who had been the object of her dreams and night watches, spent in the contemplation of the stars.

Saval had captivated her, body and soul. She thought of him, his features were photographed in her mind, and she was happy, feeling secure with a certainty of her present joy.

She heard a noise behind her. Yvette had just entered, dressed in her usual manner, but pale and with a noticeable brilliancy in the eyes, as if she had just undergone some great fatigue.

"I want to speak to you," said she.

The marquise, rather astonished, looked at her. She loved her daughter, selfishly, proud of her beauty, as of a fortune, for she was too beautiful herself to be jealous; she was too indifferent to be really guilty of the plans which were imputed to her in reference to her daughter.

"I am listening, child," said she.

Yvette looked at her piercingly, in order to catch the real effect that her words were going to produce.

"Something extraordinary took place today."

"What?"

"Monsieur de Servigny told me he loved me."

The marquise waited anxiously. As Yvette did not continue, she asked:

"How did he say it? Explain."

Then Yvette threw herself at her mother's feet in an affectionate pose that was familiar to her and, pressing her hands in her own, added:

"He asked me to marry him."

Marquise Obardi was stupefied and cried:

"Servigny? You're crazy!"

Yvette did not take her eyes off her mother, seeking to espy thoroughly her thoughts and surprise. She asked gravely:

"Why am I crazy? Why wouldn't Monsieur de Servigny marry me?"

The marquise, visibly embarrassed, stammered:

"That can't be; you are mistaken. You did not hear or understand rightly. Monsieur de Servigny is too rich for you, and too—too—Parisian to get married."

Yvette rose slowly, saying:

"But if he loves me as he says."

Her mother answered impatiently:

"I thought you were old enough, and knew enough, not to put such ideas in your head. Servigny is a man of the world and extremely selfish. He will marry a woman of his means and station. If he said he wanted to marry—he really meant to——"

The marquise was incapable of unveiling her suspicions and remained silent.

"Pshaw! Leave me alone," said she at last, "and go to bed."

"Yes, mother."

She kissed her mother on the forehead and calmly went away.

As she was about to leave the room, the marquise called her back.

"How's your sunstroke?"

"There was nothing the matter with me, except that I was troubled by Servigny's talk."

And the marquise added:

"We shall come back to that subject. Above all, henceforth, don't stay alone with him, and rest assured he will not marry you, that he merely wants to—dally with you."

That was the best way the marquise knew how to express herself. Yvette returned to her room.

Madame Obardi began to think.

For many years she had lived quietly and happily in her luxury and had cast aside all serious thoughts. She had never considered Yvette's future; that had always been a matter which she put off until the question should come up itself, imperiously demanding a solution. She well knew her daughter could never marry a rich man of good family, except by some almost impossible good fortune, which has once in a while placed an adventuress on a throne. Besides, she never hoped such a thing, and she was too busy combining plans for herself to bother about anything which did not concern her directly.

Would she follow her mother's footsteps? Why not? But the marquise had never stopped to think how that would come about.

And here came her daughter, without her expecting such a thing, with one of those questions that are practically unanswerable and which forced her to arrive at a conclusion in an affair so difficult, dangerous, delicate from all points of view, especially so perplexing to your conscience, when your own child's life is at stake, in reference to such matters.

She was too keen, though, to be mistaken as to Servigny's intentions; she knew men by experience, particularly those of his class. This knowledge, then, made her involuntarily cry:

"Servigny marry you? You're crazy!"

Why had he tried the old game, this *roué*, man of the world? What would be his next move? How could one make

Yvette understand, open her eyes? She might, perhaps, be led astray.

Who would believe that a girl of her age and education could be so innocent?

The marquise was worried, though soon tired of thinking so seriously. She sought to decide something, but in vain. The situation was far too complicated and embarrassing.

Weary of her troubles, she thought:

"Pshaw! I'll watch them more closely and await developments. If need be, I shall speak to Servigny, who will soon comprehend me."

She did not, however, ask herself what she would say, nor what he might answer, nor even what agreement might be reached; still she was happy to be thus relieved of her cares, without having had the trouble of forming a resolution, and her thoughts drifted back to Saval. She threw rapid kisses toward the direction of Paris and murmured:

"I love you! I love you!"

CHAPTER III.

A TERRIBLE REVELATION

And Yvette did not sleep. Just as her mother, she was looking out the open window, and tears, her first sad tears, filled her eyes.

Up till the present time she had lived in the reckless and serene faith of her happy childhood! Why had she thought, reflected, analyzed? Why should she not have been like all other young girls? Why did a doubt, a fear, suspicions, all painful, come to her mind?

She seemed very knowing, because, apparently, she touched upon all subjects, and had imitated the manner and tone of the people around her. But she was no wiser than a little boarding-school girl; her audacity of speech, often *risqué,* was due to her extraordinary powers of assimilation and not to any conscious science on her part.

She spoke of love as a painter's or musician's son speaks of their father's art at the age of twelve. She well knew, or rather suspected, what kind of mystery shrouded this word—too many allusions had been whispered before her to leave her entirely ignorant—but how could she know that other families were different?

People kissed her mother's hand with apparent respect. All their acquaintances bore titles, seemed rich, well connected.

Two king's sons came evenings to see her mother. How could she guess?

She was naturally naïve. She did not go to the bottom of things, nor study people, as was her mother's custom. She lived in her own happiness.

But now Servigny, by means of a few words, of which she instinctively felt the brutality, had awakened in her a sudden uneasiness, unfounded at first, but later transformed into a tantalizing apprehension.

She had shut herself up, run away like a wounded beast, hurt very deeply by those words, which she repeated ceaselessly, just to penetrate their full purport: "You well know that between us it isn't a question of marriage but of love."

What did he mean? Why this injury? Was she ignorant of some secret shame? Was she the only one who was? What was it? She was disheartened, as when one discovers a hidden infamy, the faithlessness of a beloved person, or is unhapppy in a love affair that has absorbed one's sole ambition in life.

She had cried, searched, brooded, a pitiable prey to vague fears, and doubts. Then she compared her situation to that of novels she had read, and was almost consoled by the romances which her imagination built to suit the occasion.

Was she, by chance, the natural daughter of a prince? Had her mother been seduced and abandoned by some king, the King Victor Emmanuel, perchance, and had been obliged to flee before the wrath of the royal family?

No; she was more likely a forsaken child, fruit of a guilty union, of very exalted parents, who had been entrusted to the marquise, who had adopted and brought her up.

Other conjectures also kept her mind active. She sorted them, now accepting, now rejecting their probability. She soon became, in her own eyes, a heroine of the same stamp as are found in Scribe's and George Sand's works. Her ever-changing nature was almost happy in this new situation.

She had meditated a long time, until late evening, and had eagerly worked out a scheme to worm the truth out of her mother, which succeeded in part.

She had expected a greater surprise, on her mother's part, an affecting scene, and the unveiling of a great secret.

But she was disappointed. Her mother just looked annoyed; her constrained air, her uneasy attitude that betrayed a certain degree of reticence, made the young girl understand it would be better not to insist, that the mystery was of another, baser character, which she would have to unravel herself. She went back to her room with a heavy heart, her soul and spirit really and painfully sad. She wept for a long time, with her elbows on the windowsill, her head in her hands.

The coolness of the early morning hours forced her to leave the window and go to bed.

The next and the following day saw her very reserved and melancholy. The process of reflection was becoming rapidly familiar to her; she was learning to spy, guess, and reason. She saw everything and everybody in a new light; a suspicion was rising in her mind, against all, everything she had formerly believed, even her mother. By Wednesday she had hit upon a line of conduct and action, a real system of spying. She rose Thursday morning with the intention of being as crafty as a detective and on her guard against everyone.

Saval and Servigny arrived at about ten o'clock. She greeted them with a certain reserve, without affectation, familiarly.

"How are you, Muscade?"

"Pretty well, thank you; and yourself?"

He watched her.

"What's her new game, now?" said he to himself.

The marquise took Saval's arm, and Servigny gave his to Yvette and took a walk around the lawn.

Yvette, quiet and thoughtful, looked down upon the sand in the path, apparently not listening to her companion nor answering him.

Suddenly she inquired:

"Are you a true friend, Muscade?"

"Why, surely, mam'zelle."

"But a real, faithful one?"

"Your friend, body and soul."

"True enough never to lie once to me?"

"Never."

"To the point of telling the whole, naked, bare truth?"

"Yes."

"Well, then, what do you really think, at bottom, of the Prince Kravalow?"

"Hum!"

"See, you're getting ready to lie."

"No, indeed. I am trying to find the right words. Well, he's a Russian, a real one, who speaks Russian, who may have had a passport to get into France and whose only false attributes are his name and title."

"You mean to say he is——"

He hesitated, but finally making up his mind, said:

"An adventurer, mam'zelle."

"Thanks. Chevalier Valreali is no better?"

"Just as you say."

"Monsieur de Belvigne?"

"He's of another sort. He is a gentleman—provincial, honorable—to a certain degree—slightly indebted."

"And yourself?"

He answered unhesitatingly:

"I am one of those who are vulgarly called 'rounders,' a member of a good family, having, once upon a time, possessed a certain degree of intelligence, which I wasted trying to be witty; splendid health, lost by a fast life; some intrinsic worth, which was lost through idleness. All I have left is a certain amount of money, a fair worldly knowledge, a complete absence of prejudice, a strong contempt of men, even women, a very clear realization of the usefulness of my acts, and a vast toleration for roguery. Yet I am frank at times, as you may observe, and even capable of a sincere affection, as you could ascertain if you only would. Such as I am, I gladly offer myself to you."

She was not laughing; she listened attentively to get his real meaning.

She added:

"What do you think of the Comtesse de Lammy?"

He quickly replied:

"Please excuse me from giving my opinion of the women."

"Isn't there one of them——"

"No," he interjected.

"Then you have a very poor opinion of them all. Isn't there an exception?"

He grinned insolently and with that brutal audacity he used as a weapon:

"Those who are present are always excepted."

She blushed a little but asked very composedly:

"What do you think of me?"

"I think you have much practical good sense, and that you certainly can keep your hand hidden, make fools of people, set your traps, and that you are patiently waiting to see how things are going to turn out."

"Is that all?"

"That's all."

"I'll make you change that last opinion."

She went toward her mother, who was walking with Saval, apparently holding a conversation of a very tender nature.

Idly making figures in the sand, she was speaking, without looking at him, but holding his arm and closely pressed to him. Yvette observed her mother a few seconds, and a vague doubt shot through her mind, as does the shadow of a cloud pushed along by the wind.

The bell for luncheon rang.

The meal was silent and mournful.

A storm was brewing. Big clouds seemed to be ambushed in the horizon; they were mute, but thick, and apparently full of tempest.

After the coffee had been served, the marquise asked:

"Are you going to take a walk with your friend, Servigny? Fine weather for a stroll in the woods."

After casting a rapid glance at her mother, she answered:

"I'm not going out today."

The marquise appeared annoyed and insisted:

"It would be healthful for you, child."

Then Yvette almost blurted:

"I told why I am staying home; the other night."

Madame Obardi had forgotten it in her eagerness to remain alone with Saval. She blushed, was troubled, and fearful lest she would not get a chance to be alone with her friend. She mumbled:

"That's true; I had forgotten it."

Yvette began to do some embroidery work. The men smoked. The marquise, very much irritated, eyed Saval pitifully and racked her brains to find a pretext to get her daughter out of the way. When she had to realize that she could not succeed, she said to Servigny:

"If you stay overnight, we'll all go tomorrow to Chatou and have lunch at the Fournaise."

He understood, smiled, and bowed.

"With the greatest of pleasure, marquise."

The day passed slowly and painfully, constantly threatened by the storm.

Suppertime came at last. The sky was heavy with slow and large clouds. Not a breath of air.

This meal was also silent. A certain uneasy feeling, a vague fear, seemed to render all taciturn.

They remained on the terrace after supper; the conversation was ever languishing. Night was about to fall and gave promise to continue the torture of that day's crushing and smothering heat. Suddenly the horizon was rent asunder by a fiery hook, and their faces were illuminated, for a few seconds, by a dazzling light. Then a peal of thunder broke the silence, and the heat became doubly oppressing.

Yvette rose, saying:

"I am going to retire; the storm has made me nervous."

After bidding everyone good night, she went away.

As her room was just above the terrace, its light lit up the chestnut tree in front of it, and her shadow could be seen on a green background. But soon all was dark again. Mme. Obardi heaved a sigh of relief.

"My daughter's gone to bed."

Servigny said:

"I shall do the same, with your permission, marquise."

He kissed her hand and likewise disappeared.

She remained alone with Saval, in the dead of night.

Instantly she was in his arms, pressing him to her and embracing him. In spite of his protestations, she kneeled down before him and murmured:

"I want to look at you in the flashes of lightning."

But as soon as her candle was out, Yvette, tortured by a painful and confused suspicion, went barefooted to the railing and listened.

She could see nothing, as she was above them, on the very roof of the terrace itself.

All she could hear was a confused murmur of voices; her heart beat so hard that it filled the ear with noises. A window was just being shut. Servigny must have also retired. Her mother was then alone with the other.

A second flash, dividing the sky in two for a fraction of a second, gave her a glimpse of the landscape which she knew so well; and she saw the large river, the exact color of molten lead, just as one dreams of fantastic streams. An instant later a voice under her said: "I love you."

She heard no more. A strange shiver went through her body, and her mind was all in a whirl.

A dead silence seemed to hover over the country. She could hardly breathe, oppressed as she was by something unknown and horrible. Another fiery thread enflamed the sky and lit up the horizon, immediately followed by another one, and many others still.

The voice which had been heard a few minutes before repeated in louder tones: "Oh, how I love you! How I love you!" And Yvette knew the voice well; it was her mother's.

But she had read so many novels in which women, even mothers, had erred and fallen only to rise to honor again, at the *dénouement,* that she was not astonished beyond all bounds to find herself in a situation similar to that of many novels. The violence of her first sorrow, the bewilderment of the surprise were gradually becoming attenuated in the remembrance of analogous affairs which had already been suggested to her by her readings.

She said to herself:

"I shall save my mother."

This resolution, worthy of a heroine, restored her serenity, and she felt herself strong and ready for the fray and all necessary sacrifices. Now she thought of the means she must employ. Only one expedient seemed good and in accordance with her romantic nature. And she worked herself up, as an actor does for a scene, for the conversation in which she would engage with her mother.

The sun had risen. The servants were busily active about the house. The chambermaid brought her a cup of chocolate, which Yvette had her put on the table.

"Tell my mother that I don't feel well," said she, "that I shall stay in bed until the departure of the guests, that I couldn't sleep last night, and that I'd like to be left alone, because I should like to rest, if I could."

The servant, somewhat astonished, looked at the dress, still wet, and thrown on a carpet like a castaway rag.

"Did mademoiselle go out?" said she.

"Yes; I took a walk in the rain to enjoy the coolness."

And Yvette waited, for she knew her mother would come.

The marquise jumped out of bed and went to her daughter, after hearing the servant's message, for a slight suspicion had taken hold of her, since she had heard that cry of "Mother!"

"What's the matter with you?" said she.

Yvette looked at her and stammered:

"I—I——"

Then, overcome by a sudden and terrible emotion, she began to gasp.

The marquise was astonished.

"What is the matter with you?"

The young girl forgot all her plans and carefully prepared phrases, hid her face in her hands, and stuttered:

"Oh, Mother! Oh, Mother!"

Mme. Obardi stood there before her, far too moved to understand completely, though she guessed almost everything, with that subtle instinct which constituted her greatest strength.

As Yvette could not speak, suffocated by her tears, her mother, finally irritated and feeling that the explanation which she had always avoided was no longer to be shunned, said roughly:

"Will you, or will you not, tell me what ails you?"

Yvette could hardly articulate:

"Oh, Mother! Oh, Mother!"

The marquise, whose fears and embarrassment were changing to anger, shrugged her shoulders and prepared to go away.

"I really think you're crazy. When it's all over, tell me."

But the young girl suddenly uncovered her face, moistened by her tears, and said:

"No, listen—I must speak to you. Listen. Promise—we'll go away together, very far, to some country place; we'll live like two peasants; no one will know what became of us. Do, Mother, please do; I beg you, I beseech you."

The marquise was speechless, remained dumbfounded in the middle of the room. She had common blood in her veins, easily excited. Then a sentiment of shame, of a guilty mother, mixed with a certain vague sentiment of fear and exasperation of a passionate woman whose love is threatened, made her shudder, ready to beg forgiveness or commit an act of violence.

"I don't understand you," said she.

Yvette went on:

"I saw you—Mother—last night. You mustn't anymore—if you only knew—we shall go away, together—just the both—I'll love you so much, you'll forget."

Mme. Obardi said in a trembling voice:

"Listen, girlie, there are things which you don't understand yet. Don't forget—don't forget—that I forbid you—to speak to me—of—of such things."

But the young girl, suddenly resuming her rôle of rescuer, which she had imposed upon herself, said:

"No, Mother; I am no longer a child, and I have the right to know. Now, I know that we receive people of bad reputation, adventurers, and that, for this very reason, we are not respected. I know still more. That must no longer be, do you hear? I don't want it. We are going to go away. You'll sell your jewelry; we'll work if need be, and we'll live as honest women, somewhere, far away from here. And if I am lucky enough to get married, so much the better."

Her mother looked at her with her dark eyes, evidently showing irritation. She answered:

"You are not in your senses. You will kindly do me the favor to get up and take your lunch with the rest of us."

"No, Mother. There is someone whom I will never see again. You understand me. Either he or I will leave. Choose between us."

She was sitting up on the bed, and gradually raising her voice, speaking as if on the stage, thoroughly imbued with the atmosphere of the drama which she had imagined to herself, almost forgetting her sorrow, only to better remember her mission.

The marquise, altogether stupefied, repeated again:

"But you are crazy."

That was all she could think, on the spur of the moment.

Yvette answered in her most energetic and theatrical manner:

"No, Mother; this man will leave the house, or I will, for I will not surrender."

"And where will you go—what will you do?"

"I do not know, I do not care—I want us both to be honest women."

These ever-recurring words, "honest women," angered her mother, who shouted to her:

"Keep still! I shall not allow you to speak to me like that."

Yvette, thoroughly discouraged, stammered:

"Oh, mother!"

The marquise beat her breast as a penitent in the act of confessing, and, agitated and flushed, she advanced, like a demon, toward the bed.

"When one is a beautiful girl, one must live on that beauty —or starve—there is no choice."

Then, coming back again to her original idea, she added:

"Yes, the honest women deprive themselves of us. They are the worthless creatures, because they are not driven to this life by necessity. They have all they need, and more besides; and yet they are not faithful. They are the abominable creatures."

The marquise then stopped, seeing her daughter so miserable; and she became sad, remorseful, and moved to such pity that she opened her arms, threw them around her daughter, and sobbed:

"My poor little one, if you only knew how you hurt me."

They both wept for a long time.

The marquise, who could not remain melancholy for any

length of time, rose and broke away softly from her daughter's embrace.

She spoke very low now:

"That's how it is, my dear; it can't be helped. You must take life as it comes."

Yvette kept on crying. The shock had been too sudden for her to recover her senses quickly.

The marquise continued:

"Come, dress, and come down to lunch, so that no one will notice anything."

The young girl nodded in the negative; she could not speak; finally she managed to sob out an answer:

"No, Mother, you know what I told you. I shall not change my mind. I will not go out of my room till they have gone away. I don't want to see any more of those people. If they return, you'll never see me again."

The marquise had already dried her tears and, tired from the emotions of that day, murmured faintly:

"Be good, now. Don't be unreasonable."

But, after a moment's silence, she said:

"Yes, it's better for you to rest this morning. I shall come up to see you this afternoon."

Thoroughly serene now, she kissed her daughter on the forehead and went away.

As soon as her mother had disappeared, Yvette locked her door, in order to be alone and think about what she was really to do next.

About eleven o'clock the chambermaid knocked at her door and asked:

"The marquise, your mother, would like to know if mademoiselle wishes anything, and what would she like to have for lunch?"

Yvette answered:

"I'm not hungry. All I want is to be left alone."

And she stayed in bed as if she were very sick.

At about three someone knocked again. She asked:

"Who's there?"

It was her mother's voice.

"Your mother, dearie; I came to see how you were getting along."

The marquise approached her, as one would a convalescent.

"Well, do you feel better? Would you like to eat an egg?"

"Nothing, thank you."

The marquise sat on the edge of the bed. They remained

silent for a while, but the marquise, seeing her daughter gave no sign of speaking or moving, said to her:

"Aren't you going to get up?"

Yvette answered:

"Yes, in a little while."

Then she said gravely:

"I have thought it over a great deal, Mother, and here is—here is my resolution. The past is the past, and let us forget it. But the future will be different—or else—or else I know what I should do. Now, just let this be the last of this subject."

The marquise, who thought the subject had been thrashed out before this, felt herself becoming impatient. This was really too much. This big fool of a girl ought to have understood a long time ago. But she did not answer anything and repeated:

"Are you going to dress?"

"Yes, I am ready."

Her mother took the place of her chambermaid, brought her her stockings, corset, and skirts; then she kissed her.

"Do you want to take a walk before supper?"

"Yes, Mother."

And they strolled along the bank of the river, only speaking very ordinary things.

CHAPTER IV.

THE LAST STRUGGLE

Early the next morning Yvette went to sit alone where Servigny read the story of the ants' life to her. She said to herself:

"I shall not leave this place before I've resolved to do something definite."

She soon had studied the situation in all its phases.

What would she do if her mother refused to accept her conditions and did not give up her life, acquaintances, everything, to go and hide away with her, from the world, in some far distant land?

She could leave alone—flee. But where? How? How could she live?

By working? At what? Who would give her work? But then, the humble, mournful life of the working girl seemed a little disgraceful to her. She thought of becoming a teacher in a private family, like the heroines in certain novels, and of being loved by the eldest son. But for that she ought to have been of a good family, so that she might have been able to answer the exasperated father, in a proud voice:

"I am Yvette Obardi."

That was impossible. Besides, it was too old a scheme.

The idea of entering a convent was no better. She felt no special vocation for a religious life, as her compassion was never more than fleeting and intermittent. No one could save her by marriage, being what she was. There was no possible issue, no definite resource.

Besides, she wanted to do something great, noble, really strong-minded; she thought of suicide.

She decided upon this quite calmly, as if she were going to take a trip, without reflecting, without really seeing Death, understanding that it was the end, and no chance of starting over again, the departure without a return, the eternal adieu to this earth.

She was immediately in favor of this extreme, with the light-heartedness of a young, exalted soul.

But now it was a question of choosing the method. They all seemed painful, riskful, and requiring a violent act which was most repugnant to her.

She very quickly set aside the dagger and revolver that often merely wound and disfigure and require too much familiarity with their use—the cord, as being common, a pauper's expedient, ridiculous and ugly. Poison was the next one suggested, but which? Almost all provoke suffering and have more or less of an emetic effect. Then she thought of chloroform, because she had read of how it had been used to force a girl to asphyxiate herself.

She experienced a sort of proud, intimate, and joyful sentiment at this resolution. They would all learn what she was, and what was her character.

She went to Bougival, where she stopped at the druggist's to buy some chloroform for a toothache, as she intimated. The man knew her well, so gave it to her without hesitating.

Then she went to Croissy, where she obtained another flask of the narcotic; to Chatou for a third; to Rueil for a fourth; she came home late for luncheon. Her appetite being roused by this errand, she ate heartily, like a person who had indulged in much physical exercise.

Her mother was happy to see her so hungry and was quieted. She announced at the table:

"All our friends are coming over to spend Sunday with us. I have invited the prince, the chevalier, Monsieur de Belvigne."

Yvette grew slightly pale, but answered nothing.

She went out immediately after lunch—went to the station and took a ticket for Paris.

That whole afternoon was spent in going from one pharmacy to the other to buy a few drops of chloroform.

That evening she returned home with her pockets full of these small bottles.

She did the same the next day and by some hazard was able to obtain from one apothecary a half a quart of the liquid.

Saturday she stayed home; it was a heavy, warm day; she spent the whole of it on a steamer chair on the terrace.

Being thoroughly resolved to accomplish her act, her mind was now perfectly at ease.

The next day she put on a beautiful blue gown, which became her very well, for she wanted to be pretty.

While she was contemplating herself in the mirror, she said suddenly:

"Tomorrow I'll be dead." A peculiar shudder ran through her body. "Dead! I shall speak no more, nor think, nor will anyone see me again. And I shall never see the world again, either."

She looked at herself for a long time, her face especially, as one who had never seen it before. She examined her eyes, discovered a thousand things in them which she ignored before, was astonished to find a hidden trait in her face which she was unconscious of possessing, and generally treated herself like an old friend one had not seen for some time.

She said to herself:

"Yes, it is I; my reflection in that mirror. How strange to see one's self! Without the looking-glass, we should never know ourselves. Everybody else would but ourselves."

She drew both her large tresses over her breast, following, with her eye, all her motions, poses, even gestures.

"How pretty I am!" she thought. "Tomorrow I'll be dead, over there, on my bed."

She threw a glance at her bed, imagined that she saw herself stretched on it, whiter than the sheets themselves.

"Dead! In a week this face, these eyes, these cheeks, will be but a piece of rottenness, in a box, down in the earth."

A terrible sentiment of anguish hung over her heart.

The clear sun fell in large rays over the country, and the sweet morning air came in through the window.

She sat down and repeated to herself: "Dead!" It was as if the world was going to disappear for her; but no; nothing would be changed in this world, not even in her own room. Yes, her room would remain the same, as would the bed, the chairs, the dressing-table, though she would be gone, and no one would be sad, even, except her mother perhaps.

People would say: "How pretty that little Yvette was!" and that's all. And while she looked at her hand, leaning on the arm of the armchair, she thought again of the fate of her pretty skin and flesh. This time a long shiver of horror ran through the whole of her body, and she could not bring herself to understand how she could disappear alone—without the earth doing so, too, so much did she think herself a part of it—of this country, of the air, of the sun, of life itself.

Peals of laughter, voices, calls, that noisy gaiety of week-end parties, at the outset of the reception, were heard, and she recognized the strong voice of Monsieur de Belvigne, who had just started a song.

She rose, unthinkingly, and went to see. All applauded. They were there, all five, with two other gentlemen, whom she did not know.

The bell for luncheon rang.

"I'll teach them how to die," she said.

She went down with a firm step, something of the resolution of the Christian martyrs entering the arena where the lions were awaiting them.

She shook hands with everyone affably, though haughtily. Servigny asked her:

"Are you less cranky, mam'zelle, today?"

She answered in a severe and singular manner:

"Today I am in my Paris humor. I want to do all sorts of foolish things. Look out."

Then, turning toward Belvigne:

"You'll be my victim, Malvoisie. I am going to take you all to the fair at Marly."

There was really a fair at Marly. The newcomers were introduced—the Count Tamine and Marquis de Briguetot.

Yvette was silent during the repast, saving her energy and gaiety so that no one would guess what was going to take place; everybody would be the more surprised. "Who would have thought it? She seemed so happy, so contented!"

She tried not to think of the evening, when they would all be on the terrace; this was the time she had chosen.

She drank as much wine as she could, and two glasses of fine champagne, so that she was slightly flushed, feverish, both in body and mind, and ready to do anything.

"Ready, set, march," she said.

She took De Belvigne's arm and set the pace for the others, whom she addressed:

"Come, now, you'll be my escort. Servigny, you are sergeant; you go to the right. Then you'll put in front the strangers' guard, the two exotics, the prince and chevalier, next the two recruits, who start today. March!"

They were off. Servigny began to imitate the bugle, while the newcomers imitated the drum. M. de Belvigne, slightly abashed, said:

"Ah, Mademoiselle Yvette, be reasonable; you'll compromise yourself."

She answered:

"It's you I'm compromising, Raisiné. I don't care, personally. There'll be nothing of it tomorrow. Sorry, but then you mustn't go out with such girls."

They stupefied the strollers in Bougival. Everybody turned around; the inhabitants came to the door; the passengers on the train from Rueil to Marly hissed them; the men on top of the trains shouted:

"Throw them in the water—in the water."

Yvette walked like a regular soldier, dragging Belvigne by the arm. She did not smile, but kept serious, a sort of sinister immobility in her face. Servigny interrupted his bugle to shout commands. The prince and the chevalier were much amused. The two young men played the drum uninterruptedly.

They created a sensation at the fair. Women applauded; young men mocked them; a stout gentleman, with a touch of enviousness in his voice, said:

"There are some who are certainly not bored to death."

The young girl caught a glimpse of a merry-go-round, and she forced Belvigne to mount one of the horses nearest hers, while the rest scrambled for an animal. She kept Belvigne on for five rides, much to the bystanders' amusement. He was pale and almost seasick when he got off.

Then she meandered all over. She made the men weigh themselves, among a host of spectators, and buy ridiculous toys, which they were obliged to carry in their arms wherever they went. The prince and chevalier were beginning to think that the diversion was going too far. Servigny and the two young men went on undaunted.

They arrived at the bank of the river, where Yvette had a strange fancy.

"Let him who loves me jump in," said she.

No one did. A crowd gathered. The women were stupefied, the men sarcastic.

She repeated:

"Then there isn't one of you capable of jumping in for my sake."

Servigny murmured:

"The deuce!"

And he dashed into the river.

His splash sent drops of water up on Yvette's feet. An astonished murmur of gaiety was emitted by all.

Then the young girl picked up a piece of wood, threw it in the water and cried:

"Bring it to me!"

The young man swam after it, brought it back in his mouth, and presented it to her like a dog.

"Good doggie," said she, giving him a pat on the head.

A stout lady was indignant.

"Stupid!" said she.

Another added:

"Ridiculous!"

A man rejoined:

"Watch me jump in a river for a woman."

She took Belvigne by the arm, saying:

"You missed your chance."

They came back. The gazers irritated her, and she remarked:

"How stupid all these people look!"

Staring at De Belvigne, she continued:

"You, too."

M. de Belvigne bowed. She noticed that the prince and chevalier had disappeared. Servigny, mournful and dripping wet, was taciturn, and the other two were also mute.

She laughed dryly.

"You have enough, it seems. That's what you call having great fun, isn't it? You came for that; I gave you your money's worth."

She, too, walked silently; but suddenly Belvigne noticed that she was crying. Moved himself, he inquired:

"What's the matter?"

She murmured:

"Leave me alone; it's none of your business."

But, like a fool, he insisted:

"Oh, mademoiselle, what is it? Has someone hurt you?"

She repeated impatiently:

"Keep still!"

Then, no longer able to control herself, she burst into tears.

She shook throughout her body, so violent were her sobs, seemingly choked and suffocated by them.

Belvigne was at a loss as to what to do, repeating:

"I don't know what to do."

Servigny advanced.

"Let's go back, mam'zelle. Don't let anyone see you weeping. Why do you do such foolish things, if they make you sad?"

And he dragged her home gently, where she broke away from him and locked herself in her room.

She reappeared at dinner, very pale and serious. Everyone was happy, though. Servigny was dressed as a workman and spoke just like one throughout the whole meal; his slang kept everyone hilarious.

Yvette was anxious to arrive at the end of the supper, feeling her courage wane. Immediately after the coffee had been served she retired.

She heard joyous voices under her. The chevalier was trying to amuse the company.

She listened to it all. Servigny, slightly gay himself, imitated the drunken workman; called the marquise the boss and, all of a sudden, said to Saval:

"Hey, boss!"

All joined in a fit of laughter.

Yvette was not decided. She first took out a sheet of paper and wrote:

"BOUGIVAL, Sunday, 9 P.M.

"I died so as not to become wicked."

Then, in postscript:

"Adieu, dear Mother; forgive me."

She sealed the envelope and wrote her mother's name on it.

Then she placed her long chair near the window and a table with the bottle of chloroform upon it.

Yvette was saying to herself:

"I am going to die! I'm going to die!" Her heart seemed to be about to burst, so violently did she sob, although she tried desperately not to. She felt, for a moment, the need of being saved and loved.

Servigny's voice came up to her. He was telling stories which made everyone laugh. The marquise seemed the happiest. She repeated all the time:

"Oh, how comical! How comical!"

Yvette poured some chloroform on a piece of cotton. A powerful, sweet, strange odor filled the room; she approached the wet cotton to her lips and inhaled the fumes in long draughts.

At first it seemed to her that her lungs were becoming inflated, and that her soul, heavy with grief a little while ago, was becoming light, as if the weight that had oppressed her had taken flight.

An agreeable sensation took hold of her, and she felt herself rocked by a light fever into a sea of gentle dizziness.

She noticed that the cotton was dry and was astonished not to have died yet. Her senses seemed to be more acute, subtle, alert.

Not a word that was said below escaped her ears. Prince Kravalow was telling how he killed in a duel an Austrian general.

She again moistened the cotton and inhaled more of the fumes. For a few instants she felt nothing; then the former sensation of comfort seized her again.

Twice she repeated this maneuver, for she was coming to like this physical and moral sensation of torpor in which her soul wandered happily, as it were.

It seemed to her that she had neither bones, nor flesh, nor limbs. They must have been taken away without her noticing it. The chloroform had emptied her body, leaving only her thinking powers more awake and keener than she ever had known them to be.

She remembered a thousand things, details of her childhood, little nothings that pleased her. Her mind, suddenly become most active, touched upon ideas of the most different nature; meandered through the past and lost itself in former future hopes. Her thoughts gave her a sensual pleasure. She was under the charm of a divine happiness. She was sinking and disappearing in a sort of strange fairyland.

She was on a large boat that passed by a country deluged

with flowers. She saw people on the shore, who spoke very loud, and then she was on land again, she knew not how; Servigny, as a prince, came to escort her to a bullfight.

Then everything became vague.

Finally she woke up, deliciously benumbed, and had some difficulty to remember where she was.

She was not dead yet.

She was so happy, so comfortable, she was not all in a hurry to put an end to this well-being! She would have liked to prolong the duration of the present sensation.

She breathed slowly and watched the moon in front of her, beyond the trees. Something was changed in her mind. She thought differently. The chloroform, in deadening her body and soul, had calmed her sufferings and weakened her wish to die.

Why should she not live? Why should she not be loved? Be happy? Everything was possible and easy now. Everything in life was good and charming. But, as she wanted to dream as long as possible, she used some more of the liquid, but this time with the precaution of avoiding the poisoning effect of the drug.

She gazed at the moon and saw a face in it, that of a woman. She was in the same state as if she had absorbed opium. This face was swinging to and fro in the heavens; it sang, sang with a well-known voice the *Alleluia d'Amour*.

It was the marquise, who had just gone to the piano.

Yvette had wings now. She flew, on a beautiful, clear night, above woods and rivers. She rolled herself in the air that caressed her body and went at such a speed that she saw nothing under her, and then she found herself fishing in a lake.

Something resisted, but she pulled so hard that she finally drew a beautiful pearl necklace, which she had wanted for ever so long a time. She was not astonished at this, for she saw Servigny, who was on the other bank, just drawing out of the water a wooden horse.

Then she felt herself awakening again and heard someone calling her.

Her mother was saying:

"Put out your candle."

Servigny repeated comically:

"Put out your candle, Mam'zelle Yvette."

They all repeated it in a chorus:

"Mam'zelle Yvette, put out your candle."

She again poured the liquid in the cotton and breathed the

odor, though she took care to escape the mortal properties it might contain. She then took an abandoned position, as if dead, and waited, for she knew that they were going to come up and see what was the matter.

The marquise was saying:

"I'm rather anxious. That little fool went asleep without putting out her candle. I'll send Clémence to put it out and shut the window."

Soon the chambermaid knocked at the door.

"Mademoiselle, mademoiselle!"

After a moment's silence, she said:

"Madame la marquise, your mother, wants you to put out the candle and shut the window."

Clémence waited awhile and repeated:

"Mademoiselle, mademoiselle!"

As she did not answer, the servant went to the marquise and said:

"Mademoiselle must be asleep. She has locked herself up and cannot be awakened."

Madame Obardi at once replied:

"But she shall not stay like that."

Then Servigny suggested that they all shout together: "Hip —hip—hurrah—Mam'zelle Yvette!"

As Yvette did not answer, the marquise said:

"I hope nothing has happened; I'm growing anxious."

Servigny picked a few roses and threw them into her room by the open window.

The first one almost made her jump and cry out. But the others fell upon, around her, without her moving.

The marquise shouted in a choked voice:

"Yvette, why don't you answer?"

Servigny declared:

"That's not natural. I'm going to climb up to the balcony."

The chevalier became indignant.

"Here, here, that's a favor which I wish to claim for myself; that would be too much of an advantage over us—to obtain a —rendezvous."

The others, who thought it was a prank on the young girl's part, cried:

"We protest. It's a put-up game."

But the marquise, who was anxious, repeated:

"Still, we'll have to see what's the matter."

The prince declared dramatically:

"She favors the duke; we are betrayed."

"Let's toss up," said the chevalier.

He drew a hundred-franc piece. He began with the prince.

"Tails," said he.

It was a head.

The prince threw the coin and said to Saval in turn:

"Call, sir."

Saval called heads.

It was a tail.

The prince, with the others, likewise.

Servigny declared insolently:

"Oh, he cheats!"

The Russian protested and gave the piece to Servigny, who threw it up, crying:

"Heads!"

It was the reverse.

He bowed, indicated the pillar, and said:

"Go up, prince."

But the prince looked around, apparently worried.

"What are you looking for?" said the chevalier.

"I should like—a—a ladder."

A peal of laughter broke forth. Saval advanced, saying:

"We'll help you."

He took him in his giant's arms, suggesting:

"Hang on to the balcony."

He did so and remained suspended, kicking desperately in the air.

Then Servigny pulled on his legs and dragged him down.

"Whose turn?" he asked.

"Come, Belvigne, a little courage."

"I like my bones too well."

"Chevalier, you ought to be able to climb."

"You may take my place, duke."

"Hm-m, hm-m, I don't know that I'm over eager."

At the same time Servigny was turning around the pillar.

Then with a leap he obtained a good hold on the balcony, raised himself, and jumped over the railing.

All applauded. But he reappeared instantly, crying:

"Come quickly! Yvette is unconscious!"

The daughter of the marquise was pretending to be dead. Madame Obardi, affrighted, threw her arms about her.

"What's the matter with her? What's the matter with her, say?" she stuttered.

Servigny picked the bottle of chloroform from the floor.

"She's asphyxiated."

He listened to her heart, and added:

"But she's not dead; we'll revive her. Get some ammonia."

The chambermaid, in her agitation, could not understand and repeated:

"What, sir? What, sir? What?"

"Sedative water."

"Yes, sir."

"Bring it immediately, and let some air in. Open the door!"

The marquise was on her knees, sobbing:

"Yvette, my daughter, my precious one, listen to me. Answer, Yvette, my child. Oh, what's the matter with her?"

The men, thoroughly beside themselves, moved around, doing nothing of any use, except bringing towels, water, and vinegar.

Some one said: "Undress her."

The marquise, almost unconscious of her acts, tried to do so, but she was unable to. Her hands trembled, got mixed up in the girl's garments, and she groaned:

"I cannot, I cannot!"

The servant came in the room bringing the sedative water, which Servigny poured into a handkerchief, then put it under Yvette's nose, and she almost suffocated.

"She's breathing," said he. "It will not amount to anything."

The chambermaid having undressed her, he carried her to the bed.

When she was placed in it comfortably, he rose very pale.

"She'll come to in a little while," said he. For he had heard her breathing normally. But, seeing the men eagerly staring at her, a jealous irritation prompted him to say:

"Gentlemen, there are too many of us in here; leave the marquise, Saval and I will take care of Yvette."

He spoke with a dry air of authority. The others went out immediately.

Madame Obardi threw herself into her lover's arms and said:

"Save her—save her!"

Servigny at that moment caught a glimpse of the letter, which he seized rapidly, feeling instinctively that the marquise ought not to see it.

He read its contents.

"That's curious. It needs thought."

He hid the letter in his pocket.

Then it struck him that the young woman was better, but she was ashamed to show it, fearing to be questioned.

The marquise was on her knees, near the foot of the bed, and was weeping. All of a sudden she cried: "She needs a doctor!"

But Servigny, who had just said a few words to Saval, answered: "Just leave her a minute with me, and she will kiss you when you return." The baron took her away.

Servigny sat near her and said: "Mam'zelle Yvette, listen to me."

She did not answer. She felt so comfortable in her bed that she never wished to move again. She had never been so comfortable.

The warm air came in through the window in light breezes, and whisked over her face in an imperceptible and exquisite manner. It was a caress, something like a kiss of the wind, or the breath of a fan, made up of the leaves and trees of the woods, the shadows of the night, and the vapor of the rivers, and of the flowers, too, for the roses, thrown in the room, mingled their sweet and healthful odor.

And she drank this air in, in long draughts, no longer desirous to die, but possessed of a strong will to live, be happy, above all, to be loved, yes, loved.

Servigny reiterated:

"Mam'zelle Yvette, please listen."

She finally decided to open her eyes. He continued, seeing she was revived:

"Why such foolish, rash acts?"

She murmured:

"My poor Muscade, I had so much grief."

He squeezed her hand in a paternal manner.

"That only made matters worse. Now, promise never to try it again."

She did not answer, but she made a movement to smile, which was more to be felt, by the nod of her head, than seen.

He pulled out the letter he had found on the table.

"Must your mother see this?"

She shook her head.

He did not know what else to say, for the situation seemed to be without an issue. He murmured:

"You must put up with terrible things in this world. I understand your grief, and I promise——"

"You are too good."

They were silent. He was looking at her. She seemed to be moved to tenderness; and suddenly she opened both her arms, as if to attract him toward her. He bent over her, feeling she was calling him; their lips were united.

They remained thus for a long time. But he felt he was losing control of himself, so rose for a few seconds. She smiled tenderly at him now; and with her two arms clasped on his shoulders, she brought him back.

"I'm going to call your mother," said he.

After another silence, she said, so low that he hardly heard her:

"You'll love me sincerely?"

He kneeled before the bed, and, kissing her wrist, said:

"I adore you."

But someone was near the door. He leaped up and said, in his ordinary voice, which always seemed slightly ironical:

"You can come in now. It's all over now."

The marquise opened wide her arms and frantically embraced her daughter, whose face she moistened with her tears, while the radiant Servigny went to the window to breathe some fresh air, humming to himself the famous song from *Rigoletto*, "La donna e mobile."

THE PASTORAL SYMPHONY
by André Gide

The generation that came of age in France after the First World War turned to the literature of introspection to find its own identity. Rejecting the old pieties of social, sexual, and religious morality, it found in André Gide a powerful and seminal mind seeking deliverance from the rigid orthodoxies of a puritanical Protestant upbringing. Gide, the product of a comfortable bourgeois milieu, was born in Paris in 1869. His penchant for the journal form, to which he often returned, suggests a continuing search for the truths of his own inner nature. A trip to North Africa in 1893 put him in direct contact with a culture and a morality strikingly different from his own and led him to the conviction that salvation lay in the construction of a subjective personal ethic—no matter how distasteful or immoral society might consider it. As a result, Gide turned away from the cerebral, symbolist work of his youth and, in a number of autobiographical or semibiographical works, celebrated honesty, sensual experience and the authentic inner life. Among the masterworks of this period are The Immoralist, The Counterfeiters, *and* The Pastoral Symphony.

Gide's moral and religious inquietude and his unceasing quest for personal truth often exposed him to public scandal, yet he was recognized as an influential moralist and literary philosopher, and he was awarded the Nobel Prize in 1947.

FIRST NOTEBOOK

10 February 189—

The snow has been falling continuously for the last three days and all the roads are blocked. It has been impossible for me to go to R——, where I have been in the habit of holding a service twice a month for the last fifteen years. This morning not more than thirty of my flock were gathered together in La Brévine chapel.

I will take advantage of the leisure this enforced confinement affords me to think over the past and to set down how I came to take charge of Gertrude.

I propose to write here the whole history of her formation and development, for I seem to have called up out of the night her sweet and pious soul for no other end but adoration and love. Blessed be the Lord for having entrusted me with this task!

Two years and six months ago I had just driven back one afternoon from La Chaux-de-Fonds when a little girl who was a stranger to me came up in a great hurry to take me to a place about five miles away where she said an old woman lay dying. My horse was still in the shafts, so I made the child get into the carriage and set off at once, after first providing myself with a lantern, as I thought it likely I should not be able to get back before dark.

I had supposed myself to be perfectly acquainted with the whole countryside in the neighborhood of my parish; but when we had passed La Saudraie farm, the child made me take a road that I had never ventured down before. About two miles farther on, however, I recognized on the left-hand side a mysterious little lake where I had sometimes been to skate as a young man. I had not seen it for fifteen years, for none of my pastoral duties take me that way; I could not have said where it lay and it had so entirely dropped out of my mind that when I suddenly recognized it in the golden enchantment of the rose-flecked evening sky, I felt as though I had seen it before only in a dream.

The road ran alongside the stream that falls out of the lake, cut across the extreme end of the forest, and then skirted a peat-bog. I had certainly never been there before.

The sun was setting and for a long time we had been driving in the shade when my young guide pointed out a cottage on the hillside which would have seemed uninhabited but for a tiny thread of smoke that rose from the chimney, looking blue in the shade and brightening as it reached the gold of the sky. I tied the horse up to an apple tree close by and then followed the child into the dark room where the old woman had just died.

The gravity of the landscape, the silence and solemnity of the hour had struck me to the heart. A woman still in her youth was kneeling beside the bed. The child, whom I had taken to be the deceased woman's granddaughter, but who was only her servant, lighted a smoky tallow dip and then stood motionless at the foot of the bed. During our long drive I had tried to get her to talk, but had not succeeded in extracting two words from her.

The kneeling woman rose. She was not a relation as I had first supposed, but only a neighbor, a friend, whom the servant girl had brought there when she saw her mistress's strength failing, and who now offered to watch by the dead body. The old woman, she said, had passed away painlessly. We agreed together on the arrangements for the burial and the funeral service. As often before in this out-of-the-world country, it fell to me to settle everything. I was a little uneasy, I admit, at leaving the house, in spite of the poverty of its appearance, in the sole charge of this neighbor and of the little servant girl. But it seemed very unlikely that there was any treasure hidden away in a corner of this wretched dwelling . . . and what else could I do? I inquired nevertheless whether the old woman had left any heirs.

Upon this, the woman took the candle and held it up so as to light the corner of the hearth, and I could make out crouching in the fireplace, and apparently asleep, a nondescript-looking creature, whose face was almost entirely hidden by a thick mass of hair.

"The blind girl there—she's a niece, the servant says. That's all that's left of the family, it seems. She must be sent to the poorhouse; I don't see what else can be done with her."

I was shocked to hear the poor thing's future disposed of in this way in her presence and afraid such rough words might give her pain.

"Don't wake her up," I said softly, as a hint to the woman that she should at any rate lower her voice.

"Oh, I don't think she's asleep. But she's an idiot; she can't speak or understand anything, I'm told. I have been in the room since this morning and she has hardly so much as stirred. I thought at first she was deaf; the servant thinks not, but that the old woman was deaf herself and never uttered a word to her, nor to anyone else; she hadn't opened her mouth for a long time past except to eat and drink."

"How old is she?"

"About fifteen, I suppose. But as to that, I know no more about it than you do. . . ."

It did not immediately occur to me to take charge of the poor, forlorn creature myself; but after I had prayed—or, to be more accurate, while I was still praying on my knees be-

tween the woman and the little servant girl, who were both
kneeling too—it suddenly came upon me that God had set a
kind of obligation in my path and that I could not shirk it
without cowardice. When I rose, I had decided to take the girl
away that very evening, though I had not actually asked myself what I should do with her afterward, nor into whose
charge I should put her. I stayed a few moments longer
gazing at the old woman's sleeping face, with its puckered
mouth, looking like a miser's purse with strings tightly drawn
so as to let nothing escape. Then, turning toward the blind
girl, I told the neighbor of my intention.

"Yes, it is better she should not be there tomorrow when
they come to take the body away," said she. And that was all.

Many things would be easily accomplished but for the imaginary objections men sometimes take a pleasure in invent-
ing. From our childhood upwards, how often have we been
prevented from doing one thing or another we should have
liked to do, simply by hearing people about us repeat: "He
won't be able to . . .'!

The blind girl allowed herself to be taken away like a lifeless block. The features of her face were regular, rather fine,
but utterly expressionless. I took a blanket off the mattress
where she must have usually slept, in a corner under a staircase that led from the room to the loft.

The neighbor was obliging and helped me wrap her up
carefully, for the night was very clear and chilly; after having
lighted the carriage lamp, I started home, taking the girl with
me. She sat huddled up against me—a soulless lump of flesh,
with no sign of life beyond the communication of an obscure
warmth. The whole way home I was thinking: "Is she asleep?
And what can this black sleep be like? . . . And in what way
do her waking hours differ from her sleeping? But this
darkened body is surely tenanted; an immured soul is waiting
there for a ray of Thy grace, O Lord, to touch it. Wilt Thou
perhaps allow my love to dispel this dreadful darkness? . . ."

I have too much regard for the truth to pass over in silence
the unpleasant welcome I had to encounter on my return
home. My wife is a garden of virtues; and in the times of
trouble we have sometimes gone through I have never for an
instant had cause to doubt the stuff of which her heart is
made; but it does not do to take her natural charity by surprise. She is an orderly person, careful neither to go beyond

nor to fall short of her duty. Even her charity is measured, as though love were not an inexhaustible treasure. This is the only point on which we differ. . . .

Her first thoughts when she saw me bring home the girl that evening broke from her in this exclamation:

"What kind of job have you saddled yourself with now?"

As always happens when we have to come to an understanding, I began by telling the children—who were standing round, open-mouthed and full of curiosity and surprise—to leave the room. Ah, how different this welcome was from what I could have wished! Only my dear little Charlotte began to dance and clap her hands when she understood that something new, something alive, was coming out of the carriage. But the others, who have been well trained by their mother, very soon damped the child's pleasure and made her fall into step.

There was a moment of great confusion. And as neither my wife nor the children yet knew that they had to do with a blind person, they could not understand the extreme care with which I guided her footsteps. I myself was disconcerted by the odd moans the poor afflicted creature began to utter as soon as I let go her hand, which I had held in mine during the whole drive. There was nothing human in the sounds she made; they were more like the plaintive whines of a puppy. Torn away for the first time as she had been from the narrow round of customary sensations that had formed her universe, her knees now failed her; but when I pushed forward a chair, she sank on the floor in a heap, as if she were incapable of sitting down; I then led her up to the fireplace and she regained her calm a little as soon as she was able to crouch down in the same position in which I had first seen her beside the old woman's fire, leaning against the chimney-piece. In the carriage too, she had slipped off the seat and spent the whole drive huddled up at my feet. My wife, however, whose instinctive impulses are always the best, came to my help; it is her reflection that is constantly at odds with her heart and very often gets the better of it.

"What do you mean to do with *that*?" she asked when the girl had settled down.

I shivered in my soul at this use of the word *that*, and had some difficulty in restraining a movement of indignation. As I was still under the spell of my long and peaceful meditation, however, I controlled myself. Turning toward the whole

party, who were standing round in circle again, I placed my
hand on the blind girl's head and said as solemnly as I could:

"I have brought back the lost sheep."

But Amélie will not admit that there can be anything unreasonable or superreasonable in the teaching of the Gospel. I
saw she was going to object, and it was then I made a sign to
Jacques and Sarah, who, as they are accustomed to our little
conjugal differences and have not much natural curiosity (not
enough, I often think), led the two younger children out of
the room.

Then, as my wife still remained silent and a little irritated, I
thought, by the intruder's presence: "You needn't mind
speaking before her," I said. "The poor child doesn't understand."

Upon this Amélie began to protest that she had absolutely
nothing to say—which is her usual prelude to the lengthiest
explanations—and there was nothing for her to do but to
submit, as usual, to all my most unpractical vagaries, however
contrary to custom and good sense they might be. I have
already said that I had not in the least made up my mind
what I was going to do with the child. It had not occurred to
me, or only in the vaguest way, that there was any possibility
of taking her into our house permanently, and I may almost
say it was Amélie herself who first suggested it to me by
asking whether I didn't think there were "enough of us in the
house already"? Then she declared that I always hurried on
ahead without taking any thought for those who could not
keep up with me, that for her part she considered five children quite enough, and that since the birth of Claude (who at
that very moment set up a howl from his cradle, as if he had
heard his name) she had as much as she could put up with
and that she couldn't stand any more.

At the beginning of her outburst some of Christ's words
rose from my heart to my lips; I kept them back, however,
for I never think it becoming to allege the authority of the
Holy Book as an excuse for my conduct. But when she spoke
of her fatigue, I was struck with confusion, for I must admit
it has more than once happened to me to let my wife suffer
from the consequences of my impulsive and inconsiderate
zeal. In the meantime, however, her recriminations had enlightened me as to my duty; I begged Amélie therefore, as
mildly as possible, to consider whether she would not have
done the same in my place and whether she could have possibly abandoned a creature who had been so obviously left

without anyone to help her; I added that I was under no illusion as to the extra fatigue the charge of this new inmate would add to the cares of the household, and that I regretted I was not more often able to help her with them. In this way I pacified her as best I could, begging her at the same time not to visit her anger on the innocent girl, who had done nothing to deserve it. Then I pointed out that Sarah was now old enough to be more of a help to her and that Jacques was no longer in need of her care. In short, God put into my mouth the right words to help her accept what I am sure she would have undertaken of her own accord if the circumstances had given her time to reflect and if I had not forestalled her decision without consulting her.

I thought the cause was almost gained, and my dear Amélie was already approaching Gertrude with the kindest intentions; but her irritation suddenly blazed up again higher than ever when, on taking up the lamp to look at the child more closely, she discovered her to be in a state of unspeakable dirt.

"Why, she's filthy!" she cried. "Go and brush yourself quickly. No, not here. Go and shake your clothes outside. Oh dear! Oh dear! The children will be covered with them. There's nothing in the world I hate so much as vermin."

It cannot be denied that the poor child was crawling with them; and I could not prevent a feeling of disgust as I thought how close I had kept her to me during our long drive.

When I came back a few minutes later, having cleaned myself as best I could, I found my wife had sunk into an armchair and with her head in her hands was giving way to a fit of sobbing.

"I did not mean to put your fortitude to such a test," I said tenderly. "In any case it is late to-night and too dark to do anything. I will sit up and keep the fire going and the child can sleep beside it. Tomorrow we will cut her hair and wash her properly. You need not attend to her until you have got over your repugnance." And I begged her not to say anything of that to the children.

It was supper time. My protégée, at whom our old Rosalie cast many a scowling glance as she waited on us, greedily devoured the plateful of soup I handed her. The meal was a silent one. I should have liked to relate my adventure, to talk to the children and touch their hearts by making them understand and feel the strangeness of such a condition of total deprivation. I should have liked to rouse their pity, their sympathy for the guest God had sent us; but I was afraid of reviving Amélie's irritation. It seemed as though the word had been passed to take no notice of what had happened and to forget all about it, though certainly not one of us can have been thinking of anything else.

I was extremely touched when, more than an hour after everyone had gone to bed and Amélie had left me, I saw my little Charlotte steal gently through the half-open door in her nightdress and bare feet; she flung her arms round my neck and hugged me fiercely.

"I didn't say good-night to you properly," she murmured.

Then, pointing with her little forefinger to the blind girl, who was now peacefully slumbering and whom she had been curious to see again before going to sleep:

"Why didn't I kiss her too?" she whispered.

"You shall kiss her tomorrow. We must let her be now. She is asleep," I said as I went with her to the door.

Then I sat down again and worked till morning, reading or preparing my next sermon.

"Certainly," I remember thinking, "Charlotte seems much more affectionate than the elder children, but when they were her age, I believe they all got round me too. My big boy Jacques, nowadays so distant and reserved . . . one thinks them tender-hearted, when really they are only coaxing and wheedling one."

27 February

The snow fell heavily again last night. The children are delighted because they say we shall soon be obliged to go out by the windows. It is a fact that this morning the front door is blocked and the only way out is by the washhouse. Yesterday I made sure the village was sufficiently provisioned, for we shall doubtless remain cut off from the rest of the world for some time to come. This is not the first winter we have been snowbound, but I cannot remember ever having seen so thick a fall. I take advantage of it to go on with the tale I began yesterday.

I have said that when I first brought home this afflicted child I had not clearly thought out what place she would take in our household. I knew the limits of my wife's powers of endurance; I knew the size of our house and the smallness of our income. I had acted, as usual, in the way that was natural to me, quite as much as on principle, and without for a moment calculating the expense into which my impulse might land me—a proceeding I have always thought contrary to the

Gospels' teaching. But it is one thing to trust one's cares to God and quite another to shift them onto other people. I soon saw I had laid a heavy burden on Amélie's shoulders—so heavy that at first I felt struck with shame.

I helped her as best I could to cut the little girl's hair, and I saw that she did even that with disgust. But when it came to washing and cleaning her, I was obliged to leave it to my wife; and I realized that I perforce escaped the heaviest and most disagreeable tasks.

For the rest, Amélie ceased to make the slightest objection. She seemed to have thought things over during the night and resigned herself to her new duties; she even seemed to take some pleasure in them and I saw her smile when she had finished washing and dressing Gertrude. After her head had been shaved and I had rubbed it with ointment, a white cap was put on her; some of Sarah's old clothes and some clean linen took the place of the wretched rags Amélie threw into the fire. The name of Gertrude was chose by Charlotte and immediately adopted by us all, in our ignorance of her real name, which the orphan girl herself was unaware of, and which I did not know how to find out. She must have been a little younger than Sarah, whose last year's clothes fitted her.

I must here confess the profound and overwhelming disappointment I felt during the first days. I had certainly built up a whole romance for myself on the subject of Gertrude's education, and the reality was a cruel disillusion. The indifference, the apathy of her countenance, or rather its total lack of expression froze my good intentions at their very source. She sat all day long by the fireside, seemingly on the defensive, and as soon as she heard our voices, still more when we came near her, her features appeared to harden; from being expressionless they became hostile; if anyone tried to attract her attention, she began to groan and grunt like an animal. This sulkiness only left her at meal times. I helped her myself and she flung herself on her food with a kind of bestial avidity that was most distressing to witness. And as love responds to love, so a feeling of aversion crept over me at this obstinate withholding of her soul. Yes truly, I confess that at the end of the first ten days I had begun to despair, and my interest in her was even so far diminished that I almost regretted my first impulse and wished I had never brought her home with me. And the absurd thing was that Amélie, being not unnaturally a little triumphant over feelings I was really unable to hide from her, seemed all the more lavish of care and kindness now that she saw Gertrude was becoming a burden to me, and that I felt her presence among us as a mortification.

This was how matters stood when I received a visit from my friend Dr. Martins, of Val Travers, in the course of one of his rounds. He was very much interested by what I told him of Gertrude's condition and was at first greatly astonished she should be so backward, considering her only infirmity was blindness; but I explained that in addition to this she had had to suffer from the deafness of the old woman who was her sole guardian, and who never spoke to her, so that the poor child had been utterly neglected. He persuaded me that in that case I was wrong to despair, but that I was not employing the proper method.

"You are trying to build," he said, "before making sure of your foundations. You must reflect that her whole mind is in a state of chaos and that even its first lineaments are as yet unformed. The first thing to be done is to make her connect together one or two sensations of touch and taste and attach a sound to them—a word—to serve as a kind of label. This you must repeat over and over again indefatigably and then try to get her to say it after you.

"Above all, don't go too quickly; take her at regular hours and never for very long at a time. . . .

"For the rest, this method," he added, after having described it to me minutely, "has nothing particularly magic about it. I did not invent it and other people have applied it. Don't you remember in the philosophy class at school, our professors told us of an analogous case apropos of Condillac and his animated statue—unless," he corrected himself; "I read it later in a psychological review. . . . Never mind; I was much struck by it and I even remember the name of the poor girl, who was still more afflicted than Gertrude, for she was a deaf-mute as well as blind. She was discovered somewhere in England toward the middle of the last century by a doctor who devoted himself to educating her. Her name was Laura Bridgman. The doctor kept a journal, as you ought to do, of the child's progress—or rather, in the first place, of his efforts to instruct her. For days and weeks he went on, first making her feel alternately two little objects, a pin and a pen, and then putting her fingers on the two words *pin* and *pen* printed in a Braille book for the blind. For weeks and weeks there was no result. Her body seemed quite vacant. He did not lose courage, however. 'I felt like a person,' says he, 'leaning over the edge of a deep dark well and desperately dangling a rope in the hope that a hand would catch hold of it.' For he did not for one moment doubt that someone was there at the bottom of the well and that in the end the rope would be caught hold of. And one day, at last, he saw Laura's impassive face light up with a kind of smile. I can well believe that tears of love and gratitude sprang to his eyes and that he straightway fell on his knees and gave thanks to God. Laura had understood at last what it was the doctor wanted. She was saved! From that day forward she was all attention; her progress was rapid; she was soon able to learn by herself and eventually became the head of an institution for the blind—unless that was some other person—for there have been other cases recently that the reviews and newspapers have been full of; they were all astonished—rather foolishly in my opinion—that such creatures should be happy. For it is a fact that all these walled-up prisoners were happy, and as soon as they were able to express anything, it was their *happiness* they spoke of. The journalists of course went into ecstasies and pointed the 'moral' for people who 'enjoy' all their five senses and yet have the audacity to complain. . . ."

Here an argument arose betwen Martins and me, for I objected to his pessimism and could not allow what he seemed to infer—that our senses serve in the long run only to make us miserable.

"That's not what I meant," he protested; "I merely wanted to say, first, that man's spirit imagines beauty, comfort, and harmony more eaily and gladly than it can the disorder and sin that everywhere tarnish, stain, degrade, and mar this world; and further, that this state of things is revealed to us by our five senses, which also help us to contribute to it. So that I feel inclined to put the words '*si sua mala nescient*' after Virgil's '*Fortunatos nimium,*' instead of '*si sua bona norint*' as we are taught. How happy men would be if they knew nothing of evil!"

Then he told me of one of Dickens's stories—which he thinks was directly inspired by Laura Bridgman's case; he promised to send it to me, and four days later I received *The Cricket on the Hearth,* which I read with the greatest pleasure. It is a rather lengthy but at times very touching tale of a little blind girl, maintained by her father, a poor toymaker, in an illusory world of comfort, wealth, and happiness. Dickens exerts all his art in representing this deception as an act of piety, but, thank Heaven, I shall not have to make use of any such falsehood with Gertrude.

The day after Martins's visit I began to put his method into practice with all the application I was capable of. I am sorry now I did not take notes, as he advised, of Gertrude's first steps along the twilit path where I myself at first was but a groping guide. During the first weeks more patience was needed than can well be believed, not only because of the amount of time an education of this kind requires, but also because of the reproaches it brought me. It is painful for me to have to say that these reproaches came from Amélie; but, for that matter, if I mention this here it is because it has not left in me the slightest trace of animosity or bitterness—I declare this most solemnly, in case these lines should come to her eyes later on. (Does not Christ's teaching of the forgiveness of injuries follow immediately after the parable of the lost sheep?) More than that—at the very moment when I most suffered from her reproaches, I could not feel angry with her for disapproving the length of time I devoted to Gertrude. What I chiefly deplored was that she failed to believe that my efforts would be at all successful. Yes, it was her want of faith that grieved me—without, however, discouraging me. How often I heard her repeat: "If only any good were to come of it all! . . ." And she remained stubbornly convinced that my work was labor lost; so that naturally she thought it wrong of me to devote the time to Gertrude's education which she always declared would have been better employed otherwise. And whenever I was occupied with Gertrude, she managed to make out that I was wanted at that moment for someone or something else, and that I was giving her time that ought to have been given to others. In fact, I think she felt a kind of maternal jealousy, for she more than once said to me: "You never took so much pains with any of your own children"— which was true; for though I am very fond of my children, I have never thought it my business to take much pains with them.

It has often been my experience that the parable of the lost sheep is one of the most difficult of acceptance for certain people, who yet believe themselves to be profoundly Christian at heart. That each single sheep of the flock should be in turn more precious in the eyes of the shepherd than the rest of the flock as a whole is beyond and above their power of conception. And the words: "If a man have a hundred sheep and

one of them be gone astray, doth he not leave the ninety and
nine and goeth into the mountains and seeketh that which is
gone astray?"—words all aglow with charity, such persons
would, if they dared speak frankly, declare to be abominably
unjust.

Gertrude's first smiles consoled me for everything and re-
paid me for my pains a hundredfold. For "and if so be that he
find it, verily I say unto you, he rejoiceth more of that sheep
than of the ninety and nine which went not astray." Yes,
verily, the smile that dawned for me one morning on that
marble face of hers, when she seemed suddenly touched to
understanding and interest by what I had been trying for so
many days to teach her, flooded my heart with a more sera-
phic joy than was ever given me by any child of my own.

5 March

I noted this date as if it had been a birthday. It was not so
much a smile as a transfiguration. Her features flashed into
life—a sudden illumination, like the crimson glow that pre-
cedes dawn in the high Alps, thrilling the snowy peak on
which it lights and calling it up out of darkness—such a flood
it seemed, of mystic color; and I thought too of the pool of
Bethesda at the moment the angel descends to stir the slumbering water. A kind of ecstasy rapt me at sight of the angelic
expression that came over Gertrude's face so suddenly for it
was clear to me that this heavenly visitor was not so much
intelligence as love. And in a very transport of gratitude I
kissed her forehead and felt that I was offering thanks to
God.

The progress she made after this was as rapid as the first
steps had been slow. It is only with an effort that I can now
recall our manner of proceeding; it seemed to me sometimes
that Gertrude advanced by leaps and bounds, as though in
defiance of all method. I can remember that at first I dwelt
more on the qualities of objects than on their variety—hot,
cold, sweet, bitter, rough, soft, light—and then on actions: to
pick up, to put down, to remove, to approach, to tie, to cross,
to assemble, to disperse, etc. And very soon I abandoned all
attempt at method and began to talk to her without troubling
much whether her mind was always able to follow me; but I
went slowly, inviting and provoking her questions as she
seemed inclined. Certainly her mind was at work during the
hours I left her to herself; for every time I came back to her

after an absence, it was to find with fresh surprise that the wall of darkness that separated us had grown less thick. After all, I said to myself, it is so that the warmth of the air and the insistence of spring gradually triumph over winter. How often have I wondered at the melting of the snow! Its white cloak seems to wear thin from underneath, while to all appearance it remains unchanged. Every winter Amélie falls into the trap: "The snow is as thick as ever," she declares. And indeed it still seems so, when all at once there comes a break and suddenly, in patches here and there, life once more shows through.

Fearing that Gertrude might become peaky if she continued to sit beside the fire like an old woman, I had begun to make her go out. But she refused to do this unless she held my arm. I realized from her surprise and fear when she first left the house, and before she was able to tell me so in words, that she had never as yet ventured out of doors. In the cottage where I had found her no one had cared for her further than to give her food and prevent her from dying—for I cannot say that anyone helped her to live. Her little universe of darkness was bounded by the walls of the single room she never left; she scarcely ventured on summer days as far as the threshold, when the door stood open to the great universe of light. She told me later that when she heard the birds' song she used to suppose it was simply the effect of light, like the gentle warmth which she felt on her cheeks and hands, and that, without precisely thinking about it, it seemed to her quite natural that the warm air should begin to sing, just as the water begins to boil on the fire. The truth is she did not trouble to think; she took no interest in anything and lived in a state of frozen numbness till the day I took charge of her. I remember her inexhaustible delight when I told her that the little voices came from living creatures, whose sole function apparently was to express the joy that lies broadcast throughout all nature. (It was from that day that she began to say: "I am as joyful as a bird.") And yet the idea that these songs proclaim the splendor of a spectacle she could not behold had begun by making her melancholy.

"Is the world really as beautiful as the birds say?" she would ask. "Why do people not tell us so oftener? Why do you never tell me so? Is it for fear of grieving me because I cannot see it? That would be wrong. I listen so attentively to the birds; I think I understand everything they say."

"People who can see do not hear them as well as you do, my Gertrude," I said, hoping to comfort her.

"Why don't other animals sing?" she went on. Sometimes her questions surprised me and left me perplexed for a moment, for she forced me to reflect on things I had hitherto taken for granted. It was thus it occurred to me for the first time that the closer an animal lives to the ground and the heavier its weight, the duller it is. I tried to make her understand this; and I told her of the squirrel and its gambols.

She asked me if the birds were the only animals that flew.

"There are butterflies too," I told her.

"And do they sing?"

"They have another way of telling their joy. It is painted on their wings. . . ." And I described the rainbow colors of the butterfly.

28 February

Now let me turn back a little, for yesterday I allowed myself to be carried away.

In order to teach Gertrude, I had had to learn the Braille alphabet myself; but she was soon able to read much quicker than I could; I had some difficulty in deciphering the writing, and besides found it easier to follow with my eyes than with my fingers. For that matter, I was not the only one to give her lessons. And at first I was glad to be helped in this respect, for I have a great deal to do in the parish, the houses being so widely scattered that my visits to the poor and the sick sometimes oblige me to go far afield. Jacques had managed to break his arm while skating during the Christmas holidays, which he was spending with us; for during term time he goes to Lausanne, where he received his early education, and where he is studying at the theological school. The fracture was not serious and Martins, whom I at once sent for, was easily able to set it without the help of a surgeon; but it was considered advisable for Jacques to keep indoors for some time. He now suddenly began to take an interest in Gertrude, to whom he had hitherto paid no attention, and occupied himself with helping me to teach her to read. His assistance only lasted the time of his convalescence—about three weeks —but during those weeks Gertrude's progress was very marked. She was now fired with extraordinary zeal. Her young intelligence, but yesterday so benumbed and torpid, its first steps hardly taken, and scarcely able to walk, seemed now already preparing to run. I wondered at the ease with which she succeeded in formulating her thoughts and at the rapidity with which she learned to express herself—not child-ishly, but at once correctly, conveying her ideas by the help of images, taken in the most delightful and unexpected way from the objects we had just taught her to recognize, or from others we described to her, when we could not actually put them within her grasp; for she always used things she could touch or feel in order to explain what was beyond her reach, after the method of land-surveyors measuring distances.

But I think it is unnecessary to note here all the first steps of her education, doubtless the same in the early education of all blind people. I suppose too that in each case the teacher must have been plunged into a similar perplexity by the question of colors. (And this subject led me to the reflection that there is nowhere any mention of colors in the Gospels.) I do not know how other people set about it; for my part, I began by naming the colors of the prism to her in the order in which they occur in the rainbow; but then a confusion was immediately set up in her mind between color and brightness; and I realized that her imagination was unable to draw any distinction between the *quality* of the shade and what painters, I believe, call its *"value."* She had the greatest difficulty in understanding that every color in its turn might be more or less dark and that they might be mixed one with another to an unlimited extent. It puzzled her exceedingly, and she came back to the subject again and again.

About this time the opportunity was given me of taking her to a concert at Neuchâtel. The part played by each instrument in the symphony suggested to me the idea of recurring to this question of colors. I bade Gertrude observe the different resonances of the brasses, the strings, and the wood instruments, and that each of them was able in its own way to produce the whole series of sounds, from the lowest to the highest, with varying intensity. I asked her to imagine the colors of nature in the same way—the reds and oranges analogous to the sounds of the horns and trombones; the yellows and greens like those of the violins, cellos, and double basses; the violets and blues suggested by the clarinets and oboes. A sort of inner rapture now took the place of all her doubts and uncertainties.

"How beautiful it must be!" she kept on repeating.

Then suddenly she added: "But the white? I can't understand now what the white can be like."

And I at once saw how insecure my comparison was.

"White," I tried however to explain, "is the extreme treble limit where all the tones are blended into one, just as black is the bass or dark limit."

But this did not satisfy me any more than it did her; and she pointed out at once that the wood instruments, the brasses, and the violins remain distinct in the bass as well as in the treble parts. How often I have been obliged to remain puzzled and silent, as I did then, searching about for some comparison I might appeal to.

"Well," said I at last, "imagine white as something absolutely pure, something in which color no longer exists, but only light; and black, on the contrary, something so full of color that it has become dark. . . ."

I recall this fragment of dialogue merely as an example of the difficulties I encountered only too often. Gertrude had this good point, that she never pretended to understand, as people so often do, thus filling their minds with inaccurate or false statements, which in the end vitiate all their reasoning. So long as she could not form a clear idea of any notion, it remained a cause of anxiety and discomfort to her.

As regards what I have just related, the difficulty was increased by the fact that the notion of light and that of heat began by being closely associated with each other in her mind, and I had the greatest trouble afterward in disconnecting them.

Thus, through these experiments with her, it was constantly brought home to me how greatly the visual world differs from the world of sound, and that any comparison between the two must necessarily be a lame one.

29 February

I have been so full of my comparisons that I have not yet said what immense pleasure the Neuchâtel concert gave Gertrude. It was actually the *Pastoral Symphony* that was being played. I say *actually* because, as will be easily understood, there is no work I could have more wished her to hear. For a long time after we had left the concert-room, Gertrude remained silent, as though lost in ecstasy.

"Is what you see really as beautiful as that?" she asked at last.

"As beautiful as what, dear child?"

"As that 'scene on the bank of a stream'?"

I did not answer at once, for I was reflecting that those

ineffable harmonies painted the world as it might have been, as it would be without evil and without sin, rather than the world as it really was. And I had never yet ventured to speak to Gertrude of evil and sin and death.

"Those who have eyes," I said at last, "do not know their happiness."

"But I who have not," she cried, "*I* know the happiness of hearing."

She pressed up against me as she walked and hung on to my arm in the way small children do.

"Pastor, do you feel how happy I am? No, no, I don't say so to please you. Look at me. Can't you see on people's faces whether they are speaking the truth? I always know by their voices. Do you remember the day you answered me that you weren't crying when my aunt" (that is what she called my wife) "had reproached you with being no help to her? And I cried out: 'Pastor, that's not true!' Oh, I felt at once from your voice that you weren't telling me the truth; there was no need for me to feel your cheeks to know that you had been crying." And she repeated very loud: "No, there was no need for me to feel your cheeks"—which made me turn red, for we were still in the town and the passers-by turned round to look at us. She went on, however:

"You mustn't try to deceive me, you know. First of all, because it would be very mean to try to deceive a blind person . . . and then because you wouldn't succeed," she added, laughing. "Tell me, pastor, you aren't unhappy, are you?"

I put her hand to my lips, as though to make her feel, without having to confess it, that part of my happiness came from her, and answered as I did so.

"No, Gertrude, I am not unhappy. How should I be unhappy?"

"And yet you cry sometimes?"

"I have cried sometimes."

"Not since that time?"

"No, I have not cried again since then."

"And you have not felt inclined to cry?"

"No, Gertrude."

"And tell me—have you felt inclined since then not to speak the truth to me?"

"No, dear child."

"Can you promise never to try to deceive me?"

"I promise."

"Well, tell me quickly, then—am I pretty?"

This sudden question dumbfounded me, all the more because I had studiously avoided up to then taking any notice of Gertrude's undeniable beauty; and moreover I considered it perfectly unnecessary that she should be informed of it herself.

"What can it matter to you?" I said.

"I am anxious," she went on, "I should like to know whether I do not—how shall I put it?—make too much of a discord in the symphony. Whom else should I ask, pastor?"

"It is not a pastor's business to concern himself with the beauty of people's faces," said I, defending myself as best I could.

"Why not?"

"Because the beauty of their souls suffices him."

"You had rather I thought myself ugly," was her reply with a charming pout; so that, giving up the struggle, I exclaimed:

"Gertrude, you know quite well you are pretty."

She was silent and her face took on an expression of great gravity, which did not leave her until we got home.

On our return Amélie at once managed to make me feel she disapproved of the way I had been spending my day. She might have told me so before; but she had let Gertrude and me start without a word, according to her habit of letting people do things and of reserving to herself the right to blame them afterward. For that matter, she did not actually reproach me; but her very silence was accusing; for surely it would have been natural to have inquired what we had heard, since she knew I was taking Gertrude to the concert. Would not the child's pleasure have been increased if she had felt that the smallest interest had been taken in it? But Amélie did not remain entirely silent—she merely seemed to put a sort of affectation into avoiding any but the most indifferent topics; and it was not till evening, when the little ones had gone to bed, and after I had asked her in private and with some severity if she was vexed with me for taking Gertrude to the concert, that I got the following answer:

"You do things for her you would never have done for any of your own children."

So it was always the same grievance, and the same refusal to understand that the feast is prepared for the child who returns to us, not for those who have stayed at home, as the parable shows us. It grieved me too to see that she took no account of Gertrude's infirmity—poor Gertrude, who could hope for no other kind of pleasure. And if I providentially happened to be free that afternoon—I, who am as a rule so much in request—Amélie's reproach was all the more unfair, because she knew perfectly well that the other children were busy or occupied in one way or other, and that she herself did not care for music, so that even if she had all the time in the world, it would never enter her head to go to a concert, not even if it were given at our very door.

What distressed me still more was that Amélie had actually said this in front of Gertrude; for though I had taken my wife on one side, she had raised her voice so much that Gertrude heard her. I felt not so much sad as indignant, and a few moments later, when Amélie had left us, I went up to Gertrude and, taking her frail little hand in mine, I lifted it to my face. "You see," I said, "this time I am not crying."

"No," answered she, trying to smile, "this time it is my turn." And as she looked up at me, I suddenly saw her face was flooded with tears.

8 March

The only pleasure I can give Amélie is to refrain from doing the things she dislikes. These very negative signs of love are the only ones she allows me. The degree to which she has already narrowed my life is a thing she cannot realize. Oh, would to Heaven she would demand something difficult of me! How gladly I would undertake a rash, a dangerous task for her! But she seems to have a repugnance for everything that is not usual; so that for her, progress in life consists merely in adding like days to like days. She does not desire— she will not even accept—any new virtue, nor even an increase of the old ones. When it is not with disapproval, it is with mistrust that she views every effort of the soul to find in Christianity something other than the domestication of our instincts.

I must confess that I entirely forgot, that afternoon at Neuchâtel, to go and pay our haberdasher's bill and to bring her back some spools of thread she wanted. But I was more vexed with myself for this than she could have been; especially as I had been quite determined not to forget her commissions, being very well aware that "he that is faithful in that which is least is faithful also in much," and being afraid too of the conclusions she might draw from my forgetfulness. I should even have been glad if she had reproached me with it, for I certainly deserved reproaches. But, as often happens, the imaginary grievance outweighed the definite charge. Ah, how beautiful life would be and how bearable our wretchedness if we were content with real evils without opening the doors to the phantoms and monsters of our imagination! . . . But I am straying here into observations that would do better as the subject of a sermon (Luke xii, 29: "Neither be ye of doubtful mind"). It is the history of Gertrude's intellectual and moral development that I purposed tracing here and I must now return to it.

I had hoped to follow its course step by step in this book and had begun to tell the story in detail. Not only, however, do I lack time to note all its phases with minuteness, but I find it extremely difficult at the present moment to remember their exact sequence. Carried away by my tale, I began by setting down remarks of Gertrude's and conversations with her that are far more recent; a person reading these pages would no doubt be astonished at hearing her express herself so justly and reason so judiciously in such a little while. The fact is her progress was amazingly rapid; I often wondered at the promptness with which her mind fastened on the intellectual food I offered it, and indeed on everything it could catch hold of, absorbing it all by a constant process of assimilation and maturation. The way in which she forestalled my thoughts and outstripped them was a continual surprise to me, and often from one lesson to another I ceased to recognize my pupil.

At the end of a very few months there was no appearance of her intelligence having lain dormant for so long. Even at this early stage she showed more sense and judgment than the generality of young girls, distracted as they are by the outside world and prevented from giving their best attention by a multitude of futile preoccupations. She was moreover a good deal older, I think, than we had at first supposed. Indeed, it seemed as though she were determined to profit by her blindness, so that I actually wondered whether this infirmity was not in many ways an advantage. In spite of myself I compared her with Charlotte, so easily distracted by the veriest trifles, so that many a time while hearing the child say over her lessons, as I sometimes did, I found myself thinking: "Dear me, how much better she would listen if only she could not see!"

Needless to say, Gertrude was a very eager reader, but as I

wished as far as possible to keep in touch with the development of her mind, I preferred her not to read too much—or
at any rate not much without me—and especially not the
Bible—which may seem very strange for a Protestant. I will
explain myself; but before touching on a question so important, I wish to relate a small circumstance that is connected
with music and should be placed, as far as I can remember,
shortly after the concert at Neuchâtel.

Yes, the concert, I think, took place three weeks before the
summer vacation, which brought Jacques home. In the meantime I had often sat with Gertrude at the little harmonium of
our chapel, which is usually played by Mlle de la M., with
whom Gertrude is at present staying. Louise de la M. had not
yet begun to give Gertrude music lessons. Notwithstanding
my love for music, I do not know much about it, and I felt
very little able to teach her anything when I sat beside her at
the keyboard.

"No," she had said after the first gropings, "you had better
leave me. I had rather try by myself."

And I left her all the more willingly that the chapel did not
seem to me a proper place in which to be shut up alone with
her, as much out of respect for the sanctity of the place as for
fear of gossip—though as a rule I endeavor to disregard it; in
this case, however, it is a matter that concerns not only me
but her. So when a round of visits called me in that direction,
I would take her to the church and leave her there, often for
long hours together, and then would go to fetch her on my
return. In this way she spent her time patiently hunting out
harmonies, and I would find her again toward evening pon-
dering over some concord of sounds that had plunged her into
a long ecstasy.

On one of the first days of August, barely more than six
months ago, it so happened that I had gone to visit a poor
widow in need of consolation and had not found her in. I
therefore returned at once to fetch Gertrude from the church,
where I had left her; she was not expecting me back so soon,
and I was extremely surprised to find Jacques with her.
Neither of them heard me come in, for the little noise I made
was covered by the sound of the organ. It is not in my nature
to play the spy, but everything that touches Gertrude touches
me; so stepping as softly as I could, I stole up the few steps
that lead to the gallery—an excellent post of observation. I
must say that during the whole time I was there I did not hear
a word from either of them that they might not have said

before me. But he sat very close to her, and several times I saw him take her hand in order to guide her fingers over the keys. Was it not in itself strange that she should accept instructions and guidance from him when she had previously refused them from me, preferring, she said, to practice by herself? I was more astonished, more pained, than I liked to own and was just on the point of intervening when I saw Jacques suddenly take out his watch.

"I must leave you now," he said; "my father will be coming back in a moment."

I saw him lift her unresisting hand to his lips; then he left. A few moments later I went noiselessly down the stairs and opened the church door so that she might hear me and think I had only just arrived.

"Well, Gertrude! Are you ready to go home? How is the organ getting on?"

"Very well," she answered in the most natural tone; "I have really made some progress today."

A great sadness filled my heart, but we neither of us made any allusion to the episode I have just described.

I was impatient to find myself alone with Jacques. My wife, Gertrude, and the children used as a rule to go to bed rather early after supper, while we two sat on late over our studies. I was waiting for this moment. But before speaking to him I felt my heart bursting with such a mixture of feelings that I could not—or dared not—begin on the subject that was tormenting me. And it was he who abruptly broke the silence by announcing his intention of spending the rest of the vacation with us. Now, a few days earlier he had spoken to us about a tour he wanted to make in the high Alps—a plan my wife and I heartily approved of; I knew his friend T., who was to be his traveling companion, was counting on him; it was therefore quite obvious to me that this sudden change of plan was not unconnected with the scene I had just come upon. I was at first stirred by violent indignation, but was afraid to give way to it lest it should put an end to my son's confidence altogether; I was afraid too of pronouncing words I should afterward regret; so making a great effort over myself, I said as naturally as I could:

"I thought T. was counting on you."

"Oh," he answered, "not absolutely, and besides he will have no difficulty in finding someone else to go with him. I can rest here quite as well as in the Oberland, and I really think I can spend my time better than mountaineering."

"In fact," I said, "you have found something to occupy you at home."

He noticed some irony in the tone of my voice and looked at me, but being unable as yet to guess the motive of it, went on unconcernedly:

"You know I have always liked reading better than climbing."

"Yes, my dear boy," said I, returning his glance with one as searching; "but are not lessons in harmonium-playing even more attractive than reading?"

No doubt he felt himself blush, for he put his hand to his forehead, as though to shade his eyes from the lamplight; but he recovered himself almost immediately and went on in a voice I could have wished less steady:

"Do not blame me too much, Father. I did not mean to hide anything from you and you have only forestalled by a very little the confession I was preparing to make you."

He spoke deliberately, as if he were reading the words out of a book, finishing his sentences with as much calm, it seemed, as if it were a matter in which he had no concern. The extraordinary self-possession he showed brought my exasperation to a climax. Feeling that I was about to interrupt him, he raised his hand, as much as to say: "No, you can speak afterward; let me finish first." But I seized his arm and shook it.

"Oh," I exclaimed impetuously, "I would rather never see you again than have you trouble the purity of Gertrude's soul. I don't want your confessions! To abuse infirmity, innocence, candor—what abominable cowardice! I should never have thought you capable of it. And to speak of it with such cold-blooded unconcern! . . . Understand me: it is I who have charge of Gertrude and I will not suffer you to speak to her, to touch her, to see her for one single day more."

"But, Father," he went on as calmly as ever, driving me almost beside myself, "you may be sure that I respect Gertrude as much as you can. You are making a strange mistake if you think there is anything reprehensible—I don't say in my conduct, but in my intentions and in my secret heart. I love Gertrude and respect her, I tell you, as much as I love her. The idea of troubling her, of abusing her innocence, is as abominable to me as to you."

Then he protested that what he wanted was to be her help, her friend, her husband; that he had thought he ought not to speak to me about it until he had made up his mind to marry her; that Gertrude herself did not know of his intention and that he had wanted to speak to me about it first.

"This is the confession I had to make to you," he wound up; "and I have nothing else to confess, believe me."

These words filled me with stupor. As I listened, I felt my temples throbbing. I had been prepared with nothing but reproaches, and the fewer grounds he gave me for indignation, the more at a loss I felt, so that at the end of his speech I had nothing left to say.

"Let us go to bed," I said at last, after some moments of silence. I got up and put my hand on his shoulder. "Tomorrow I will tell you what I think about it all."

"Tell me at any rate that you aren't still angry with me."

"I must have the night to think it over."

When I saw Jacques again the next morning, I seemed to be looking at him for the first time. I suddenly realized that my son was no longer a child but a young man; so long as I thought of him as a child, the love that I had accidentally discovered might appear monstrous. I had passed the whole night persuading myself that on the contrary it was perfectly natural and normal. Why was it that my dissatisfaction only became keener still? It was not till later that this became clear to me. In the meantime I had to speak to Jacques and tell him my decision. Now an instinct as sure as the voice of conscience warned me that this marriage must be prevented at all costs.

I took Jacques down to the bottom of the garden.

"Have you said anything to Gertrude?" I began by asking him.

"No," he answered; "perhaps she feels I love her, but I have not yet told her so."

"Then you must promise me not to speak of it yet awhile."

"I am determined to obey you, Father; but may I not know your reasons?"

I hesitated to give them, feeling doubtful whether those that first came into my mind were the wisest to put forward. To tell the truth, conscience rather than reason dictated my conduct.

"Gertrude is too young," I said at last. "You must reflect that she has not yet been confirmed. You know she was unhappily not like other children and did not begin to develop till very late. She is so trustful that she would no doubt be only too easily touched by the first words of love she heard;

that is why it is of importance not to say them. To take possession of what is defenseless is cowardice; I know that you are not a coward. Your feelings, you say, are in no way reprehensible; I say they are wrong because they are premature. It is our duty to be prudent for Gertrude till she is able to be prudent for herself. It is a matter of conscience."

Jacques has one excellent point—that the simple words I often used to him as a child: "I appeal to your conscience," have always been sufficient to check him. Meanwhile, as I looked at him, I thought that if Gertrude were able to see, she could not fail to admire the tall slender figure, so straight and yet so lithe, the smooth forehead, the frank look, the face, so childlike still, though now, as it were, overshadowed by a sudden gravity. He was bareheaded, and his fair hair, which was rather long at that time, curled a little at the temples and half hid his ears.

"There is another thing I want to ask you," I went on, rising from the bench where we had been sitting. "You had intended, you said, to go away the day after tomorrow; I beg you not to put off your leaving. You were to remain away a whole month at least; I beg you not to shorten your absence by a single day. Is that agreed?"

"Very well, Father, I will obey."

I thought he turned extremely pale—so pale that the color left even his lips. But I persuaded myself that such prompt submission argued no very great love, and I felt inexpressibly relieved. I was touched besides by his obedience.

"That's the child I love," I said gently. And drawing him to me, I put my lips to his forehead. There was a slight recoil on his part, but I refused to feel hurt by it.

10 March

Our house is so small that we are obliged to live more or less on top of one another, which is sometimes very inconvenient for my work, although I keep a little room for myself upstairs where I can receive my visitors in private—and especially inconvenient when I want to speak to one of the family in private, without such an air of solemnity as would be the case if the interview took place in this little parlor of mine, which the children call my "sanctum" and into which they are forbidden to enter. On that particular morning, however, Jacques had gone to Neuchâtel to buy a pair of boots for his mountaineering, and as it was very fine, the children had gone out after lunch with Gertrude, whom they take charge of, while she at the same time takes charge of them. (It is a pleasure for me to note that Charlotte is particularly attentive to her.) At tea, then, a meal we always take in the common sitting-room, I was quite naturally left alone with Amélie. This was just what I wanted, for I was longing to speak to her. It happens to me so rarely to have a tête-à-tête with her, that I felt almost shy, and the importance of what I had to say agitated me as much as if it had been a question, not of Jacques's affairs, but of my own. I felt too, before I began to speak, how two people who love each other and live practically the same life can yet remain (or become) as much of an enigma to each other as if they lived behind stone walls. Words in this case—those spoken or those heard—have the pathetic sound of vain knocking against the resistance of that dividing barrier, which, unless watch be kept, will grow more and more impenetrable. . . .

"Jacques was speaking to me last night and again this morning," I began as she poured out the tea; and my voice was as faltering as Jacques's had been steady the day before. "He told me he loved Gertrude."

"It was quite right of him to tell you," said she without looking at me and continuing her housewifely task, as if I had said the most natural thing in the world—or rather as if I had said nothing she did not already know.

"He told me he wanted to marry her; he is resolved to—"

"It was only to be expected," she murmured with a slight shrug of her shoulders.

"Then you suspected it?" I asked in some vexation.

"I've seen it coming on for a long while. But that's the kind of thing men never notice."

It would have been no use to protest, and besides there was perhaps some truth in her rejoinder, so "In that case," I simply objected, "you might have warned me."

She gave me the little crooked smile with which she sometimes accompanies and screens her reticences, and then, with a sideways nod of her head, "If I had to warn you," she said, "of everything you can't see for yourself, I should have my work cut out for me!"

What did she mean by this insinuation? I did not know or care to know, and went on, without attending to it:

"Well, but I want to hear what you think about it."

She sighed. Then: "You know, my dear, that I never approved of that child's staying with us."

I found it difficult not to be irritated by her harking back in this way to the past.

"Gertrude's staying with us is not what we are discussing," I said, but Amélie went on:

"I have always thought it would lead to no good."

With a strong desire to be conciliatory, I caught at her phrase:

"Then you think it would be no good if it led to such a marriage? That's just what I wanted to hear you say. I am glad we are of the same opinion." Then I added that Jacques had submitted quietly to the reasons I had given him, so that there was no need for her to be anxious; that it had been agreed he was to leave the next day for his trip and stay away a whole month.

"As I have no more wish than you that he should find Gertrude here when he comes back," I wound up, "I think the best thing would be to hand her over to the care of Mademoiselle de la M. and I could continue to see her there; for there's no denying that I have very serious obligations to her. I have just been to sound our friend and she is quite ready to oblige us. In this way you will be rid of a presence that is painful to you. Louise de la M. will look after Gertrude; she seemed delighted with the arrangement; she is looking forward already to giving her harmony lessons."

Amélie seemed determined to remain silent, so that I went on:

"As we shall not want Jacques to see Gertrude there, I think it would be a good thing to warn Mademoiselle de la M. of the state of affairs, don't you?"

I hoped by putting this question to get something out of her; but she kept her lips tightly shut, as if she had sworn not to speak. And I went on—not that I had anything more to add, but because I could not endure her silence:

"For that matter, perhaps Jacques will have got over his love by the time he gets back. At his age one hardly knows what one wants."

"And even later one doesn't always know," said she at last, rather oddly.

Her enigmatical and slightly oracular way of speaking irritated me, for I am too frank by nature to put up easily with mystery-making. Turning toward her, I begged her to explain what she meant to imply by that.

"Nothing, my dear," she answered sadly. "I was only

thinking that a moment ago you were wishing to be warned of the things you didn't notice yourself."

"Well?"

"Well, I was thinking that it's not always easy to warn people."

I have said that I hate mysteries and I object on principle to hints and double meanings.

"When you want me to understand you, perhaps you will explain yourself more clearly," I replied, rather brutally, perhaps, and I was sorry as soon as I had said it; for I saw her lips tremble a moment. She turned her head aside, then got up and took a few hesitating, almost tottering steps about the room.

"But, Amélie," I cried, "why do you go on being unhappy now that everything is all right again?"

I felt that my eyes embarrassed her, and it was with my back turned and my elbows on the table, resting my head in my hands, that I went on to say:

"I spoke to you unkindly just now. Forgive me."

At that I heard her come up behind me; then I felt her lay her fingers gently on my head as she said tenderly and in a voice trembling with tears:

"My poor dear!"

Then she left the room quickly.

Amélie's words, which I then thought so mysterious, became clear to me soon after this; I have written them down as they struck me at the moment; and that day I only understood that it was time Gertrude should leave.

12 March

I had imposed on myself the duty of devoting a little time daily to Gertrude—a few hours or a few minutes, according to the occupations in hand. The day after this conversation with Amélie, I had some free time, and as the weather was inviting, I took Gertrude with me through the forest to that fold in the Jura where in the clear weather one can see, through a curtain of branches and across an immense stretch of land at one's feet, the wonder of the snowy Alps emerging from a thin veil of mist. The sun was already declining on the left when we reached our customary seat. A meadow of thick, closely cropped grass sloped downwards at our feet; farther off, a few cows were grazing; each of them among these mountain herds wears a bell at its neck.

"They outline the landscape," said Gertrude as she listened to their tinkling.

She asked me, as she does every time we go for a walk, to describe the place where we had stopped.

"But you know it already," I told her; "on the fringe of the forest, where one can see the Alps."

"Can one see them clearly today?"

"Yes, in all their splendor."

"You told me they were a little different every day."

"What shall I compare them to this afternoon? To a thirsty midsummer's day. Before evening they will have melted into the air."

"I should like you to tell me if there are any lilies in the big meadows before us."

"No, Gertrude, lilies do not grow on these heights, or only a few rare species."

"Not even the lilies called the lilies of the field?"

"There are no lilies in the fields."

"Not even in the fields round Neuchâtel?"

"There are no lilies of the field."

"Then why did our Lord say: 'Consider the lilies of the field'?"

"There were some in his day, no doubt, for him to say so; but they have disappeared before men and their plows."

"I remember you have often told me that what this world most needs is confidence and love. Don't you think that with a little more confidence men would see them again? When I listen to His word, I assure you I see them. I will describe them to you, shall I? They are like bells of flame—great bells of azure, filled with the perfume of love and swinging in the evening breeze. Why do you say there are none there before use? I feel them! I see the meadow filled with them."

"They are not more beautiful than you see them, my Gertrude."

"Say they are not less beautiful."

"They are as beautiful as you see them."

" 'And yet I say unto you that even Solomon in all his glory was not arrayed like one of these,' " said she, quoting Christ's words; and when I heard her melodious voice, I felt I was listening to them for the first time. " 'In all his glory,' " she repeated thoughtfully, and was silent for a time. I went on:

"I have old you, Gertrude, that it is those who have eyes who cannot see." And a prayer rose from the bottom of my heart: "I thank Thee, O Lord, that Thou revealest to the humble what Thou hidest from the wise."

"If you knew," she exclaimed in a rapture of delight, "if you knew how easily I imagine it all! Would you like me to describe the landscape to you? . . . Behind us, above us, and around us are the great fir trees, with their scent of resin and ruddy trunks, stretching out their long dark horizontal branches and groaning as the wind tries to bend them. At our feet, like an open book on the sloping desk of the mountain, lies the broad green meadow, shot with shifting colors—blue in the shade, golden in the sun, and speaking in clear words of flowers—gentians, pulsatillas, ranunculus, and Solomon's beautiful lilies; the cows come and spell them out with their bells; and the angels come and read them—for you say that the eyes of men are closed. Below the book I see a great smoky, misty river of milk, hiding abysses of mystery—an immense river, whose only shore is the beautiful, dazzling Alps far, far away in the distance. . . . That's where Jacques is going. Tell me, is he really starting tomorrow?"

"He is to start tomorrow. Did he tell you so?"

"He didn't tell me so, but I guessed it. Will he be away long?"

"A month. . . . Gertrude, I want to ask you something. Why didn't you tell me that he used to meet you in the church?"

"He came twice. Oh, I don't want to hide anything from you; but I was afraid of making you unhappy."

"It would make me unhappy if you didn't tell me."

Her hand sought mine.

"He was sad at leaving."

"Tell me, Gertrude—did he say he loved you?"

"He didn't say so, but I can feel it without being told. He doesn't love me as much as you do."

"And you, Gertrude, does it make you unhappy that he should go away?"

"I think it is better he should go. I couldn't respond."

"But tell me, does it make you unhappy that he should go?"

"You know, pastor, that it's you I love. . . . Oh, why do you take your hand away? I shouldn't speak so if you weren't married. But no one marries a blind girl. Then why shouldn't we love each other? Tell me, pastor, do you think there's anything wrong in it?"

"It's never in love that the wrong lies."

"I feel there is nothing but good in my heart. I don't want to make Jacques suffer. I don't want to make anyone suffer. . . . I only want to give happiness."

"Jacques was thinking of asking you to marry him."

"Will you let me speak to him before he goes? I should like to make him understand that he must give up loving me. Pastor, you understand, don't you, that I can't marry anyone? You'll let me speak to him, won't you?"

"This evening."

"No, tomorrow; just before he leaves. . . ."

The sun was setting in majestic splendor. The evening air was warm. We had risen and, talking as we went, we turned back along the somber homeward path.

SECOND NOTEBOOK

25 April

I have been obliged to put this book aside for some time.

The snow melted at last and as soon as the roads were passable, there were a great many things to be done that I had been obliged to put off all the long while our village was isolated from the outer world. It was only yesterday I was able for the first time to find a few moments' leisure again.

Last night I read over everything I had written here. . . .

Now that I dare call by its name the feeling that so long lay unacknowledged in my heart, it seems almost incomprehensible that I should have mistaken it until this very day—incomprehensible that those words of Amélie's that I recorded should have appeared mysterious—that even after Gertrude's naïve declarations, I could still have doubted that I loved her. The fact is that I would not then allow that any love outside marriage could be permissible, not at the same time would I allow that there could be anything whatever forbidden in the feeling that drew me so passionately to Gertrude.

The innocence of her avowals, their very frankness, reassured me. I told myself she was only a child. Real love would not go without confusion and blushes. As far as I was concerned, I persuaded myself I loved her as one loves an afflicted child. I tended her as one tends a sick person—and so I made a moral obligation, a duty, of what was really a passionate inclination. Yes, truly, on the very evening she spoke to me in the way I have described, so happy was I, so light of heart, that I misunderstood my real feelings, and even as I transcribed our talk, I misunderstood them still. For I should have considered love reprehensible, and my conviction was that everything reprehensible must lie heavy on the soul; therefore, as I felt no weight on my soul, I had no thought of love.

These conversations not only were set down just as they occurred, but were also written while I was in the same frame of mind as when they took place; to tell the truth, it was only when I reread them last night that I understood. . . .

As soon as Jacques had gone (I had allowed Gertrude to speak to him before he left, and when he returned for the last few days of his vacation, he affected either to avoid her altogether or to speak to her only in my presence), our life slipped back into its usual peaceful course. Gertrude, as had been arranged, went to stay at Mlle Louise's, where I visited her every day. But, again in my fear of love, I made a point of not talking to her of anything likely to agitate us. I spoke to her only as a pastor and for the most part in Louise's presence, occupying myself chiefly with her religious instruction and with preparing her for Holy Communion, which she has just partaken of this Easter.

I too communicated on Easter Day.

This was a fortnight ago. To my surprise, Jacques, who was spending a week's holiday with us, did not accompany us to the Lord's Table. And I greatly regret having to say that Amélie also abstained—for the first time since our marriage. It seemed as though the two of them had come to an understanding and resolved by their abstention from this solemn celebration to throw a shadow over my joy. Here again I congratulated myself that Gertrude could not see and that I was left to bear the weight of this shadow alone. I know Amélie too well not to be aware of all the blame she wished indirectly to convey by her conduct. She never openly disapproves of me, but she makes a point of showing her displeasure by leaving me in a sort of isolation.

I was profoundly distressed that a grievance of this kind—such a one, I mean, as I shrink from contemplating—should have so affected Amélie's soul as to turn her aside from her higher interests. And when I came home I prayed for her in all sincerity of heart.

As for Jacques's abstention, it was due to quite another motive, as a conversation I had with him a little later on made clear.

3 May

Gertrude's religious instruction has led me to reread the Gospels with a fresh eye. It seems to me more and more that many of the notions that constitute our Christian faith originate not from Christ's own words but from St. Paul's commentaries.

This was, in fact, the subject of the discussion I have just had with Jacques. By disposition he is somewhat hard and rigid, and his mind is not sufficiently nourished by his heart; he is becoming traditionalist and dogmatic. He reproaches me with choosing out of the Christian doctrine "what pleases me." But I do not pick and choose among Christ's words. I simply, between Christ and St. Paul, choose Christ. He, on the contrary, for fear of finding them in opposition, refuses to dissociate them, refuses to feel any difference of inspiration between them, and makes objections when I say that in one case it is a man I hear, while in the other it is God. The more he argues, the more persuaded I am he does not feel that Christ's slightest word has a divine accent that is unique.

I search the Gospels, I search in vain for commands, threats, prohibitions. . . . All of these come from St. Paul. And it is precisely because they are not to be found in the words of Christ that Jacques is disturbed. Souls like his think themselves lost as soon as they are deprived of their props, their handrails, their fences. And besides they cannot endure others to enjoy a liberty they have resigned, and want to obtain by compulsion what would readily be granted by love.

"But, Father," he said, "I too desire the soul's happiness."

"No, my friend, you desire its submission."

"It is in submission that happiness lies."

I leave him the last word because I dislike arguing; but I know that happiness is endangered when one seeks to obtain it by what should on the contrary be the effect of happiness— and if it is true that the loving soul rejoices in a willing submission, nothing is farther from happiness than submission without love.

For the rest, Jacques reasons well, and if I were not distressed at seeing so much doctrinal harshness in so young a mind, I should no doubt admire the quality of his arguments and his unbending logic. It often seems to me that I am younger than he is—younger today than I was yesterday— and I repeat to myself the words:

"Except ye become as little children, ye shall not enter into the kingdom of heaven."

Do I betray Christ, do I slight, do I profane the Gospels when I see in them above all a *method for attaining the life of blessedness?* The state of joy, which our doubt and the hardness of our hearts prevent, is an obligation laid upon every Christian. Every living creature is more or less capable of joy. Every living creature ought to tend to joy. Gertrude's smile alone teaches me more in this respect than all my lessons teach her.

And these words of Christ's stood out before my eyes in letters of light: "If ye were blind ye should have no sin." Sin is that which darkens the soul—which prevents its joy. Gertrude's perfect happiness, which shines forth from her whole being, comes from the fact that she does not know sin. There is nothing in her but light and love.

I have put into her vigilant hands the four Gospels, the Psalms, the Apocalypse, and the three Epistles of St. John, so that she may read: "God is light, and in him is no darkness at all," as in the Gospel she has already heard the Saviour say: "I am the light of the world." I will not give her the Epistles of St. Paul, for if, being blind, she knows not sin, what is the use of troubling her by letting her read: "sin by the commandment might become exceeding sinful" (Romans vii, 13) and the whole of the dialectic that follows, admirable as it may be.

8 May

Dr. Martins came over yesterday from Chaux-de-Fonds. He examined Gertrude's eyes for a long time with the ophthalmoscope. He told me he had spoken about Gertrude to Dr. Roux, the Lausanne specialist, and is to report his observations to him. They both have an idea that Gertrude might be operated on with success. But we have agreed to say nothing about it to her as long as things are not more certain. Martins is to come and let me know what they think after they have consulted. What would be the good of raising Gertrude's hopes if there is any risk of their being immediately extinguished? And besides is she not happy as she is? . . .

10 May

At Easter Jacques and Gertrude saw each other again in my presence—at least, Jacques saw Gertrude and spoke to her, but only about trifles. He seemed less agitated than I feared; and I persuade myself afresh that if his love had really been very ardent, he would not have got over it so easily, even though Gertrude had told him last year before he went away that it was hopeless. I noticed that he no longer says "thou" to Gertrude, but calls her "you" which is certainly preferable; however, I had not asked him to do so and I am glad it was his own idea. There is undoubtedly a great deal of good in him.

I suspect, however, that this submission of Jacques's was not arrived at without a struggle. The unfortunate thing is that the constraint he has been obliged to impose on his feelings now seems to him good in itself; he would like to see it imposed on everyone; I felt this in the discussion I had with him that I have recorded farther back. Is it not La Rochefoucauld who says that the mind is often the dupe of the heart? I need not say that, knowing Jacques as I do, I did not venture to point this out to him there and then, for I take him to be one of those people who are only made more obstinate by argument; but the very same evening I found what furnished me with a reply—and from St. Paul himself (I could only beat him with his own weapons)—and left a little note in his room, in which I wrote out the text: "Let not him which eateth not judge him that eateth: for God hath received him" (Romans xiv, 3).

I might as well have copied out what follows: "I know, and am persuaded by the Lord Jesus, that there is nothing unclean of itself: but to him that esteemeth any thing to be unclean, to him it is unclean." But I did not dare to, for I was afraid that Jacques might proceed to suspect me of some wrongful interpretation with regard to Gertrude—a suspicion that must not so much as cross his imagination for a second. Evidently it is here a question of food; but in how many passages of the Scriptures are we not called on to give the words a double and triple meaning? ("If thine eye . . ." and the multiplication of the loaves, the miracle of Cana, etc.) This is not a matter of logic-chopping; the meaning of this text is wide and deep: the restriction must not be dictated by the law but by love, and St. Paul exclaims immediately afterward: "But if thy brother be grieved with thy meat, now walkest thou not charitably." It is where love fails that the chink in our armor lies. That is where the Evil One attacks us. Lord, remove from my heart all that does not belong to love. . . . For I was wrong to provoke Jacques: the next morning I found on my table the same note on which I had written out the text; Jacques had simply written on the back of it another text from the same chapter: "Destroy not him with thy meat for whom Christ died" (Romans xiv, 15).

I have reread the whole chapter. It is the starting-point for endless discussion. And is Gertude to be tormented with these perplexities? Is the brightness of her sky to be darkened with these clouds? Am I not nearer Christ, do I not keep her nearer to Him, when I teach her, when I let her believe, that the only sin is that which hurts the happiness of others or endangers our own?

Alas! There are some souls to whom happiness is uncongenial; they cannot, they do not know how to avail themselves of it. . . . I am thinking of my poor Amélie. I never cease imploring her, urging her—I wish I could force her to be happy. Yes, I wish I could lift everyone up to God. But she will none of it; she curls up like certain flowers that never open to the sun. Everything she sees causes her uneasiness and distress.

"What's the good, my dear?" she answered me the other day, "we can't all be blind."

Ah, how her irony grieves me! And what courage I need not to be disturbed by it! And yet it seems to me she ought to understand that this allusion to Gertrude's infirmity is particularly painful to me. She makes me feel, indeed, that what I admire above all in Gertrude is her infinite mildness; I have never heard her express the slightest resentment against anyone. It is true I do not allow her to hear anything that might hurt her.

And as the soul that is happy diffuses happiness around it by the radiation of love, so everything in Amélie's neighborhood becomes gloomy and morose. Amiel would say that her soul gives out black rays. When, after a harassing day of toil —visits to the sick, the poor, the afflicted—I come in at nightfall, tired out and with a heart longing for rest, affection, warmth, it is to find, more often than not, worries, recriminations and quarrels, which I dread a thousand times more than the cold, the wind, and the rain out of doors. I know well enough that our old Rosalie invariably wants her own way, but she is not always in the wrong, nor Amélie always in the right when she tries to make her give in. I know that Gaspard and Charlotte are horribly unruly; but would not Amélie get better results if she scolded them less loudly and less constantly? So much nagging, so many reprimands annd expostulations, lose their edge like pebbles on the seashore; they are far less disturbing to the children than to me. I know that Claude is teething (at least that is what his mother declares every time he sets up a howl), but does it not encourage him to howl for her or Sarah to run and pick him up and be forever petting him? I am convinced he would not howl so often if he was left to howl once or twice to his heart's content when I am not there. But I know that is the very time they spoil him most.

Sarah is like her mother, and for that reason I should have wished to send her to school. She is not, alas, what her mother was at her age, when we were first engaged, but what the material cares of life have made her—I was going to say the *cultivation* of the cares of life, for Amélie certainly does cultivate them. I find it indeed very difficult to recognize in her today the angel of those early times who smiled encouragement on every high-minded impulse of my heart, who I dreamed would be the sharer of my every hope and fear, and whom I looked on as my guide and leader along the path to heaven—or did love blind me in those days? . . . I cannot see that Sarah has any interests that are not vulgar; like her mother, she allows herself to be entirely taken up with paltry household matters; the very features of her face, unilluminated as they are by any inward flame, look dull and almost hard. She has no taste for poetry or for reading in general; I never overhear any conversation between her and her mother in which I have any inclination to take part, and I feel my isolation even more painfully when I am with them than when I retire to to my study, as it is becoming my custom to do more and more often.

And I have also fallen into the habit this autumn, encouraged by the shortness of the days, of taking tea at Mlle de la M.'s whenever my rounds permit it—that is, whenever I can get back early enough. I have not yet mentioned that since last November Louise de la M. has extended her hospitality to three little blind girls, entrusted to her care by Martins. Gertrude is teaching them to read and to work at sundry little tasks over which they have already begun to be quite clever.

How restful, how comforting I find its warm friendly atmosphere every time I re-enter the Grange, and how much I miss it if I am obliged to let two or three days pass without going there. Mlle de la M., it is hardly necessary to say, has sufficient means to take in and provide for Gertrude and the three little boarders without putting herself out in any way;

three maidservants help her with the greatest devotion and save her all fatigue. Can one imagine fortune and leisure better bestowed? Louise de la M. has always interested herself in the poor; she is a profoundly religious woman and seems hardly to belong to this earth or to live for anything but love; though her hair is already silvery under its lace cap, nothing can be more childlike than her laugh, nothing more harmonious than her movements, nothing more musical than her voice. Gertrude has caught her manners, her way of speaking, almost the intonation, not only of her voice, but of her mind, of her whole being—a likeness upon which I tease them both, but which neither of them will admit. How sweet it is, when I can find the time, to linger in their company, to see them sitting beside each other, Gertrude either leaning her head on her friend's shoulder or clasping one of her hands in hers, while I read them some lines out of Lamartine or Hugo; how sweet to behold the beauties of such poetry reflected in the mirror of their limpid souls! Even the little pupils are touched by it. These children, in this atmosphere of peace and love, develop astonishingly and make remarkable progress. I smiled at first when Mlle Louise spoke of teaching them to dance—for their health's sake as much as for their amusement —but now I admire the rhythmic grace to which they have attained, though they themselves, alas, are unable to appreciate it. And yet Louise de la M. has persuaded me that though they cannot see, they do physically perceive the harmony of their movements. Gertrude takes part in their dances with the most charming grace and sweetness, and moreover seems to take the keenest pleasure in them. Or sometimes it is Louise de la M. who directs the little girls' movements, and then Gertrude seats herself at the piano. Her progress in music has been astonishing; she plays the organ in chapel now every Sunday and preludes short improvisations to the singing of the hymns. Every Sunday she comes to lunch with us; my children are delighted to see her, notwithstanding that their tastes are growing more and more divergent. Amélie is not too irritable and we get through the meal without a hitch. After lunch the whole family goes back with Gertrude to the Grange and has tea there. It is a treat for my children, and Louise enjoys spoiling them and loading them with delicacies. Amélie, who is far from being insensible to attentions of this kind, unbends at last and looks ten years younger. I think she would find it difficult now to do without this halt in the wearisome round of her daily life.

18 May

Now that the fine weather has returned, I have been able to go out again with Gertrude—a thing I had not done for a long time (for there have been fresh falls of snow quite recently and the roads have been in a terrible state until only a few days ago), and it is a long time too since I have found myself alone with her.

We walked quickly; the sharp air colored her cheeks and kept blowing her fair hair over her face. As we passed alongside a peat-bog, I picked one or two rushes that were in flower and slipped their stalks under her béret; then I twined them into her hair so as to keep them in place.

We had scarcely spoken to each other as yet in the astonishment of finding ourselves alone together, when Gertrude turned her sightless face toward me and asked abruptly:

"Do you think Jacques still loves me?"

"He has made up his mind to give you up," I replied at once.

"But do you think he knows you love me?" she went on.

Since the conversation I have related above, more than six months had gone by without (strange to say) the slightest word of love having passed between us. We were never alone, as I have said, and it was better so. . . . Gertrude's question made my heart beat so fast that I was obliged to slacken our pace a little.

"My dear Gertrude, everyone knows I love you," I cried. But she was not to be put off.

"No, no; you have not answered my question."

And after a moment's silence she went on, with lowered head:

"Aunt Amélie knows it; and *I* know it makes her sad."

"She would be sad anyway," I protested with an unsteady voice. "It is her nature to be sad."

"Oh, you always try to reassure me," she answered with some impatience. "But I don't want to be reassured. There are a great many things, I feel sure, you don't tell me about for fear of troubling or grieving me; a great many things I don't know, so that sometimes—"

Her voice dropped lower and lower; she stopped as if for want of breath. And when, taking up her last words, I asked:

"So that sometimes—?"

"So that sometimes," she continued sadly, "I think all the happiness I owe you is founded upon ignorance."

"But, Gertrude—"

"No, let me say this: I don't want a happiness of that kind. You must understand that I don't—I don't care about being happy. I would rather know. There are a great many things—sad things assuredly—that I can't see, but you have no right to keep them from me. I have reflected a great deal during these winter months; I am afraid, you know, that the whole world is not as beautiful as you have made me believe, pastor—and, in fact, that it is very far from it."

"It is true that man has often defaced it," I argued timidly, for the rush of her thoughts frightened me and I tried to turn it aside, though without daring to hope I should succeed. She seemed to be waiting for these words, for she seized on them at once as though they were the missing link in the chain.

"Exactly!" she cried; "I want to be sure of not adding to the evil."

For a long time we walked on very quickly and in silence. Everything I might have said was checked beforehand by what I felt she was thinking; I dreaded to provoke some sentence that might set both our fates trembling in the balance. And as I thought of what Martins had said about the possibility of her regaining her sight, a dreadful anxiety gripped my heart.

"I wanted to ask you," she went on at last "—but I don't know how to say it. . . ."

Certainly she needed all her courage to speak, just as I needed all mine to listen. But how could I have foreseen the question that was tormenting her?

"Are the children of a blind woman necessarily born blind?"

I don't know which of us this conversation weighed down more, but it was necessary for us to go on.

"No, Gertrude," I said, "except in very special cases. There is in fact no reason why they should be."

She seemed extremely reassured. I should have liked in my turn to ask her why she wanted to know this; I had not the courage and went on clumsily:

"But, Gertrude, to have children, one must be married."

"Don't tell me that, pastor. I know it's not true."

"I have told you what it was proper for me to tell you," I protested. "But it is true, the laws of nature do allow what is forbidden by the laws of man and of God."

"You have often told me the laws of God were the laws of love."

"But such love as that is not the same that also goes by the name of charity."

"Is it out of charity you love me?"

"No, my Gertrude, you know it is not."

"Then you admit our love is outside the laws of God?"

"What do you mean?"

"Oh, you know well enough, and I ought not to be the one to say so."

I sought in vain for some way of evasion; the beating of my heart set all my arguments flying in confusion.

"Gertrude," I exclaimed wildly, "—you think your love wrong?"

She corrected me:

"*Our* love. . . . I say to myself I ought to think so."

"And then—?"

I heard what sounded like a note of supplication in my voice, while without waiting to take breath she went on:

"But that I cannot stop loving you."

All this happened yesterday. I hesitated at first to write it down. . . . I have no idea how our walk came to an end. We hurried along as if we were being pursued, while I held her arm tightly pressed against me. My soul was so absent from my body that I felt as if the smallest pebble in the path might send us both rolling to the ground.

19 May

Martins came back this morning. Gertrude's is a case for operation. Roux is certain of it and wishes to have her under his care for a time. I cannot refuse and yet, such is my cowardice, that I asked to be allowed to reflect. I asked to have time to prepare her gently. . . . My heart should leap for joy, but it feels inexpressibly heavy, weighed down by a sick misgiving. At the thought of having to tell Gertrude her sight may be restored to her, my heart fails me altogether.

19 May. Night

I have seen Gertrude and I have not told her. At the Grange this evening there was no one in the drawing-room; I went upstairs to her room. We were alone.

I held her long in my arms pressed to my heart. She made no attempt to resist, and as she raised her face to mine our lips met. . . .

21 May

O Lord, is it for us Thou hast clothed the night with such depth and such beauty? Is it for me? The air is warm and the moon shines in at my open window as I sit listening to the vast silence of the skies. Oh, from all creation rises a blended adoration that bears my heart along, lost in an ecstasy that knows no words. I cannot—I cannot pray with calm. If there is any limitation to love, it is set by man and not by Thee, my God. However guilty my love may appear in the eyes of men, oh, tell me that in Thine it is sacred.

I try to rise above the idea of sin; but sin seems to me intolerable, and I will not give up Christ. No, I will not admit that I sin in loving Gertrude. I could only succeed in tearing this love from my heart if I tore my heart out with it, and for what? If I did not already love her, it would be my duty to love her for pity's sake; to cease to love her would be to betray her; she needs my love. . . .

Lord, I know not. . . . I know nothing now but Thee. Be Thou my guide. Sometimes I feel that darkness is closing round me and that it is I who have been deprived of the sight that is to be restored to her.

Gertrude went into the Lausanne nursing-home yesterday and is not to come out for three weeks. I am expecting her return with extreme apprehension. Martins is to bring her back. She has made me promise not to try to see her before then.

22 May

A letter from Martins: the operation has been successful. God be thanked!

24 May

The idea that she who loved me without seeing me must now see me causes me intolerable discomfort. Will she know me? For the first time in my life I consult the mirror. If I feel her eyes are less indulgent than her heart and less loving, what will become of me? O Lord, I sometimes think I have need of her love in order to love Thee!

8 June

An unusual amount of work has enabled me to get through these last days with tolerable patience. Every occupation that takes me out of myself is a merciful one; but all day long and through all that happens her image is with me.

She is coming back tomorrow. Amélie, who during these last weeks has shown only the best side of herself and seems endeavoring to distract my thoughts, is preparing a little festivity with the children to welcome her return.

9 June

Gaspard and Charlotte have picked what flowers they could find in the woods and fields. Old Rosalie has manufactured a monumental cake, which Sarah is decorating with gilt paper ornaments. We are expecting her this morning for lunch.

I am writing to fill in the time of waiting. It is eleven o'clock. Every moment I raise my head and look out at the road along which Martins's carriage will come. I resist the temptation to go and meet them; it is better—especially for Amélie's sake—that I should not welcome her apart from the others. My heart leaps. . . . Ah, here they are!

9 June. Evening

Oh, in what abominable darkness I am plunged!

Pity, Lord, pity! I renounce loving her, but do Thou not let her die!

How right my fears were! What has she done? What did she want to do? Amélie and Sarah tell me they went with her as far as the door of the Grange, where Mlle de la M. was expecting her. So she must have gone out again. . . . What happened?

I try to put my thoughts into some sort of order. The accounts they give are incomprehensible or contradictory. My mind is utterly confused . . . Mlle de la M.'s gardener has just brought her back to the Grange unconscious; he says he saw her walking by the river, then she crossed the garden bridge, then stooped and disappeared; but as he did not at first realize that she had fallen, he did not run to her help as he should have done; he found her at the little sluice, where she had been carried by the stream. When I saw her soon afterward, she had not recovered consciousness; or at least had lost it again, for she came to for a moment, thanks to the prompt measures that were taken. Martins, who, thank Heaven, had not yet left, cannot understand the kind of stupor and lassitude in which she is now sunk. He has questioned her in vain; she seems either not to hear or else to be determined not to speak. Her breathing is very labored and Martins is afraid of pneumonia; he has ordered sinapisms and cupping and has promised to come again tomorrow. The mistake was leaving her too long in her wet clothes while they were trying to bring her round; the water of the river is icy. Mlle de la M., who is the only person who has succeeded in getting a few words from her, declares she wanted to pick some of the forget-me-nots that grow in abundance on this side of the river, and that, being still unaccustomed to measure distances, or else mistaking the floating carpet of flowers for solid ground, she suddenly lost her footing. . . . If I could only believe it! If I could only persuade myself it was nothing but an accident, what a dreadful load would be lifted from my heart! During the whole meal, though it was so gay, the strange smile that never left her face made me uneasy; a forced smile, which I had never seen her wear before, but which I tried my utmost to believe was the smile of her newly born sight; a smile that seemed to stream from her eyes onto her face like tears, and beside which the vulgar mirth of the others seemed to me offensive. She did not join in the mirth; I felt as if she had discovered a secret she would surely have confided to me if we had been alone. She hardly spoke; but no one was surprised at that, because she is often silent when she is with others, and all the more so when their merriment grows noisy.

Lord, I beseech Thee, let me speak to her. I must know or how can I continue to live? . . . And yet if she really wished to end her life, is it just because she *knew?* Knew what? Dear, what horrible thing can you have learned? What did I hide from you that was so deadly? What can you so suddenly have seen?

I have been spending two hours at her bedside, my eyes never leaving her forehead, her pale cheeks, her delicate eyelids, shut down over some unspeakable sorrow, her hair still wet and like seaweed as it lies spread round her on the pillow —listening to her difficult, irregular breathing.

10 June

Mlle Louise sent for me this morning just as I was starting to go to the Grange. After a fairly quiet night Gertrude has at last emerged from her torpor. She smiled when I went into the room and motioned to me to come and sit by her bedside. I did not dare question her, and no doubt she was dreading my questions, for she said immediately, as though to forestall anything emotional:

"What do you call those little blue flowers that I wanted to pick by the river? Flowers the color of the sky. Will you be cleverer than I and pick me a bunch of them? I should like to have them here beside my bed. . . ."

The false cheerfulness of her voice was dreadful to me; and no doubt she was aware of it, for she added more gravely:

"I can't speak to you this morning; I am too tired. Go and pick those flowers for me, will you? You can come back again later."

And when an hour later I brought her the bunch of forget-me-nots, Mlle Louise told me that Gertrude was resting and could not see me before evening.

I saw her again this evening. She was lying—almost sitting up in bed—propped against a pile of pillows. Her hair was now fastened up, with the forget-me-nots I had brought her twisted into the plaits above her forehead.

She was obviously very feverish and drew her breath with great difficulty. She kept the hand I put out to her in her burning hand; I remained standing beside her.

"I must confess something to you, pastor; because this evening I am afraid of dying," she said. "What I told you this morning was a lie. It was not to pick flowers. . . . Will you forgive me if I say I wanted to kill myself?"

I fell on my knees beside the bed, still keeping her frail hand in mine; but she disengaged it and began to stroke my forehead, while I buried my face in the sheets so as to hide my tears and stifle my sobs.

"Do you think it was very wrong?" she went on tenderly; then, as I answered nothing:

"My friend, my friend," she said, "you must see that I take up too much room in your heart and in your life. When I came back to you, that was what struck me at once—or, at any rate, that the place I took belonged to another and that it made her unhappy. My crime is that I did not feel it sooner; or rather—for indeed I knew it all along—that I allowed you to love me in spite of it. But when her face suddenly appeared to me, when I saw such unhappiness on her poor face, I could not bear the idea that that unhappiness was my work. . . . No, no, don't blame yourself for anything; but let me go, and give her back her joy."

The hand ceased stroking my forehead; I seized it and covered it with kisses and tears. But she drew it away impatiently and began to toss in the throes of some fresh emotion.

"That is not what I wanted to say to you; no, it's not that I want to say," she kept repeating, and I saw the sweat on her damp forehead. Then she closed her eyes and kept them shut for a time, as though to concentrate her thoughts or to recover her former state of blindness; and in a voice that at first was trailing and mournful, but that soon, as she reopened her eyes, grew louder, grew at last animated even to vehemence:

"When you gave me back my sight," she began, "my eyes opened on a world more beautiful than I had ever dreamed it could be; yes, truly, I had never imagined the daylight so bright, the air so brilliant, the sky so vast. But I had never imagined men's faces so full of care either; and when I went into your house, do you know what it was that struck me first? . . . Oh, it can't be helped, I must tell you: what I saw first of all was our fault, our sin. No, don't protest. You remember Christ's words: 'If ye were blind ye should have no sin.' But now I see. . . . Get up, pastor. Sit there, beside me. Listen to me without interrupting. During the time I spent in the nursing-home I read—or rather I had read to me some verses of the Bible I did not know—some you had never read me. I remember a text of St. Paul's which I repeated to myself all one day: 'For I was alive without the law once; but when the commandment came, sin revived, and I died.' "

She spoke in a state of extreme excitement and in a very loud voice, almost shouting the last words, so that I was made uncomfortable by the idea that they might be heard outside the room; then she shut her eyes and repeated in a whisper, as though for herself alone:

"Sin revived—and *I* died."

I shivered and my heart froze in a kind of terror. I tried to turn aside her thoughts.

"Who read you those texts?" I asked.

"Jacques," she said, opening her eyes and looking at me fixedly. "Did you know he was converted?"

It was more than I could bear; I was going to implore her to stop, but she had already gone on:

"My friend, I am going to grieve you very much; but there must be no falsehood between us now. When I saw Jacques, I suddenly realized it was not you I loved—but him. He had your face—I mean the face I imagined you had. . . . Ah! why did you make me refuse him? I might have married him. . . ."

"But, Gertrude, you still can," I cried with despair in my heart.

"He is entering the priesthood," she said impetuously.

Then, shaken by sobs: "Oh, I want to confess to him," she moaned in a kind of ecstasy. . . . "You see for yourself there's nothing left me but to die. I am thirsty. Please call someone. I can't breathe. Leave me. I want to be alone. Ah! I had hoped that speaking to you would have brought me more relief. You must say good-by. We must say good-by. I cannot bear to be with you any more."

I left her. I called Mlle de la M. to take my place beside her; her extreme agitation made me fear the worst, but I could not help seeing that my presence did her harm. I begged that I might be sent for if there was a change for the worse.

11 June

Alas! I was never to see her again alive. She died this morning after a night of delirium and exhaustion. Jacques, who at Gertrude's dying request was telegraphed for by Mlle de la M., arrived a few hours after the end. He reproached me cruelly for not having called in a priest while there was yet time. But how could I have done so when I was still unaware that during her stay at Lausanne, and evidently urged by him, Gertrude had abjured the Protestant faith? He told me in the same breath of his own conversion and Gertrude's. And so they both left me at the same time; it seemed as if, separated by me during their lifetime, they had planned to escape me here and be united to each other in God. But I tell myself that Jacques's conversion is more a matter of the head than the heart.

"Father," he said, "it is not fitting for me to make accusations against you; but it was the example of your error that guided me."

After Jacques had left again, I knelt down beside Amélie and asked her to pray for me, as I was in need of help. She simply repeated "Our Father . . ." but after each sentence she left long pauses, which we filled with our supplication.

I would have wept, but I felt my heart more arid than the desert.

THE GROWING STONE
by Albert Camus

Albert Camus, a winner of the Nobel Prize for Literature in 1957, was a true man of letters, distinguished as a novelist, essayist, dramatist and journalist. A classically austere and lucid stylist, his commitment to life and his self-involvement are reflected in all his works. Born in Algeria in 1913, Camus was, as a young man, a practicing journalist and a practical man of the theatre. After the German occupation of France in 1941, Camus founded and edited the Resistance newspaper Combat. *His novel,* The Plague, *is a compelling account of life in a city suffering a pestilential assault, yet on another level it can be read as a symbolic presentation of life during the German occupation. On still another level, it is an allegory of Camus' view of the human condition: that life is absurd, but that men do their best to give it meaning through individual and joint responsibility. This philosophy finds a clear expression also in the play* Caligula (1946) *and in the essay,* The Myth of Sisyphus (1942). *To Camus, the figure of hapless Sisyphus doomed eternally to roll a stone up the mountainside was a crucial metaphor for life. His philosophy in some ways bears a resemblance to the French Existentialism of Jean Paul Sartre, but Camus has himself rejected the comparison. The absurdity of Camus' own death provides a curious resonance to his lifework: he was killed in 1960 in an automobile accident.*

The automobile swung clumsily around the curve in the red sandstone trail, now a mass of mud. The headlights suddenly picked out in the night—first on one side of the road, then on the other—two wooden huts with sheet-metal roofs. On the right near the second one, a tower of coarse beams could be made out in the light fog. From the top of the tower a metal cable, invisible at its starting-point, shone as it sloped down into the light from the car before disappearing behind the embankment that blocked the road. The car slowed down and stopped a few yards from the huts.

The man who emerged from the seat to the right of the driver labored to extricate himself from the car. As he stood up, his huge, broad frame lurched a little. In the shadow beside the car, solidly planted on the ground and weighed down by fatigue, he seemed to be listening to the idling motor. Then he walked in the direction of the embankment and entered the cone of light from the headlights. He stopped at the top of the slope, his broad back outlined against the darkness. After a moment he turned around. In the light from the dashboard he could see the chauffeur's black face, smiling. The man signaled and the chauffeur turned off the motor. At once a vast cool silence fell over the trail and the forest. Then the sound of the water could be heard.

The man looked at the river below him, visible solely as a broad dark motion, flecked with occasional shimmers. A denser motionless darkness, far beyond, must be the other bank. By looking fixedly, however, one could see on that still bank a yellowish light like an oil lamp in the distance. The big man turned back toward the car and nodded. The chauffeur switched off the lights, turned them on again, then blinked them regularly. On the embankment the man appeared and disappeared, taller and more massive each time he came back to life. Suddenly, on the other bank of the river, a lantern held up by an invisible arm swung back and forth several times. At a final signal from the lookout, the chauffeur turned off his lights once and for all. The car and the man disappeared into the night. With the lights out, the river was almost visible—or at least a few of its long liquid muscles shining intermittently. On each side of the road, the dark masses of forest foliage stood out against the sky and seemed very near. The fine rain that had soaked the trail an hour earlier was still hovering in the warm air, intensifying the silence and immobility of this broad clearing in the virgin forest. In the black sky misty stars flickered.

But from the other bank rose sounds of chains and muffled plashings. Above the hut on the right of the man still waiting there, the cable stretched taut. A dull creaking began to run along it, just as there rose from the river a faint yet quite audible sound of stirred-up water. The creaking became more regular, the sound of water spread farther and then became localized, as the lantern grew larger. Now its yellowish halo could be clearly seen. The halo gradually expanded and again contracted while the lantern shone through the mist and began to light up from beneath a sort of square roof of dried palms supported by thick bamboos. This crude shelter, around which vague shadows were moving, was slowly approaching the bank. When it was about in the middle of the river, three little men, almost black, were distinctly outlined in the yellow light, naked from the waist up and wearing conical hats. They stood still with feet apart, leaning somewhat to offset the strong drift of the river pressing with all its invisible water against the side of a big crude raft that eventually emerged from the darkness. When the ferry came still closer, the man could see behind the shelter on the downstream side two tall Negroes likewise wearing nothing but broad straw hats and cotton trousers. Side by side they weighed with all their might on long poles that sank slowly into the river toward the stern while the Negroes, with the same slow motion, bent over the water as far as their balance would allow. In the bow the three mulattoes, still and silent, watched the bank approach without raising their eyes toward the man waiting for them.

The ferry suddenly bumped against something. And the lantern swaying from the shock lighted up a pier jutting into the water. The tall Negroes stood still with hands above their heads gripping the ends of the poles, which were barely stuck in the bottom, but their taut muscles rippled constantly with a motion that seemed to come from the very thrust of the water. The other ferrymen looped chains over the posts on the dock, leaped onto the boards, and lowered a sort of gangplank that covered the bow of the raft with its inclined plane.

The man returned to the car and slid in while the chauffeur stepped on the starter. The car slowly climbed the embankment, pointed its hood toward the sky, and then lowered it toward the river as it tackled the downward slope. With brakes on, it rolled forward, slipped somewhat on the mud, stopped, started up again. It rolled onto the pier with a noise of bouncing planks, reached the end, where the mulattoes, still silent, were standing on either side, and plunged slowly toward the raft. The raft ducked its nose in the water as soon as the front wheels struck it and almost immediately bobbed back to receive the car's full weight. Then the chauffeur ran the vehicle to the stern, in front of the square roof where the lantern was hanging. At once the mulattoes swung the inclined plane back onto the pier and jumped simultaneously onto the ferry, pushing it off from the muddy bank. The river strained under the raft and raised it on the surface of the water, where it drifted slowly at the end of the long drawbar running along the cable overhead. The tall Negroes relaxed their effort and drew in their poles. The man and the chauffeur got out of the car and came over to stand on the edge of the raft facing upstream. No one had spoken during the maneuver, and even now each remained in his place, motionless and quiet except for one of the tall Negroes who was rolling a cigarette in coarse paper.

The man was looking at the gap through which the river sprang from the vast Brazilian forest and swept down toward them. Several hundred yards wide at that point, the muddy, silky waters of the river pressed against the side of the ferry and then, unimpeded at the two ends of the raft, sheered off and again spread out in a single powerful flood gently flowing through the dark forest toward the sea and the night. A stale smell, come from the water or the spongy sky, hung in the air. Now the slapping of the water under the ferry could be heard, and at intervals the calls of bullfrogs from the two banks or the strange cries of birds. The big man approached the small, thin chauffeur, who was leaning against one of the bamboos with his hands in the pockets of his dungarees, once blue but now covered with the same red dust that had been blowing in their faces all day long. A smile spread over his face, all wrinkled in spite of his youth. Without really seeing them, he was staring at the faint stars still swimming in the damp sky.

But the birds' cries became sharper, unfamiliar chatterings mingled with them, and almost at once the cable began to creak. The tall Negroes plunged their poles into the water and groped blindly for the bottom. The man turned around toward the shore they had just left. Now that shore was obscured by the darkness and the water, vast and savage like the continent of trees stretching beyond it for thousands of kilometers. Between the near-by ocean and this sea of vegetation, the handful of men drifting at that moment on a wild river seemed lost. When the raft bumped the new pier it was as if, having cast off all moorings, they were landing on an island in the darkness after days of frightened sailing.

Once on land, the men's voices were at last heard. The chauffeur had just paid them and, with voices that sounded strangely gay in the heavy night, they were saying farewell in Portuguese as the car started up again.

"They said sixty, the kilometers to Iguape. Three hours more and it'll be over. Socrates is happy," the chauffeur announced.

The man laughed with a warm, hearty laugh that resembled him.

"Me too, Socrates, I'm happy too. The trail is hard."

"Too heavy, Mr. D'Arrast, you too heavy," and the chauffeur laughed too as if he would never stop.

The car had taken on a little speed. It was advancing between high walls of trees and inextricable vegetation, amidst a soft, sweetish smell. Fireflies on the wing constantly crisscrossed in the darkness of the forest, and every once in a while red-eyed birds would bump against the windshield. At times a strange, savage sound would reach them from the depths of the night and the chauffeur would roll his eyes comically as he looked at his passenger.

The road kept turning and crossed little streams on bridges of wobbly boards. After an hour the fog began to thicken. A fine drizzle began to fall, dimming the car's lights. Despite the jolts, D'Arrast was half asleep. He was no longer riding in the damp forest but on the roads of the Serra that they had taken in the morning as they left São Paulo. From those dirt trails constantly rose the red dust which they could still taste, and on both sides, as far as the eye could see, it covered the sparse vegetation of the plains. The harsh sun, the pale mountains full of ravines, the starved zebus encountered along the roads, with a tired flight of ragged urubus as their only escort, the long, endless crossing of an endless desert . . . He gave a start. The car had stopped. Now they were in Japan: fragile houses on both sides of the road and, in the houses, furtive kimonos. The chauffeur was talking to a Japanese wearing soiled dungarees and a Brazilian straw hat. Then the car started up again.

"He said only forty kilometers."

"Where were we? In Tokyo?"

"No. Registro. In Brazil all the Japanese come here."

"Why?"

"Don't know. They're yellow, you know, Mr. D'Arrast."

But the forest was gradually thinning out, and the road was becoming easier, though slippery. The car was skidding on sand. The window let in a warm, damp breeze that was rather sour.

"You smell it?" the chauffeur asked, smacking his lips. "That's the good old sea. Soon, Iguape."

"If we have enough gas," D'Arrast said. And he went back to sleep peacefully.

Sitting up in bed early in the morning, D'Arrast looked in amazement at the huge room in which he had just awakened. The lower half of the big walls was newly painted brown. Higher up, they had once been painted white, and patches of yellowish paint covered them up to the ceiling. Two rows of beds faced each other. D'Arrast saw only one bed unmade at the end of his row and that bed was empty. But he heard a noise on his left and turned toward the door, where Socrates, a bottle of mineral water in each hand, stood laughing, "Happy memory!" he said. D'Arrast shook himself. Yes, the hospital in which the Mayor had lodged them the night before was named "Happy Memory." "Sure memory," Socrates continued. "They told me first build hospital, later build water. Meanwhile, happy memory, take fizz water to wash." He disappeared, laughing and singing, not at all exhausted apparently by the cataclysmic sneezes that had shaken him all night long and kept D'Arrast from closing an eye.

Now D'Arrast was completely awake. Through the iron-latticed window he could see a little red-earth courtyard soaked by the rain that was noiselessly pouring down on a clump of tall aloes. A woman passed holding a yellow scarf over her head. D'Arrast lay back in bed, then sat up at once and got out of the bed, which creaked under his weight. Socrates came in at that moment: "For you, Mr. D'Arrast. The Mayor is waiting outside." But, seeing the look on D'Arrast's face, he added: "Don't worry; he never in a hurry."

After shaving with the mineral water, D'Arrast went out under the portico of the building. The Mayor—who had the proportions and, under his gold-rimmed glasses, the look of a nice little weasel—seemed lost in dull contemplation of the rain. But a charming smile transfigured him as soon as he saw D'Arrast. Holding his little body erect, he rushed up and tried to stretch his arms around the engineer. At that moment an automobile drove up in front of them on the other side of the low wall, skidded in the wet clay, and came to a stop on an angle. "The Judge!" said the Mayor. Like the Mayor, the Judge was dressed in navy blue. But he was much younger, or at least seemed so because of his elegant figure and his look of a startled adolescent. Now he was crossing the courtyard in their direction, gracefully avoiding the puddles. A few steps from D'Arrast, he was already holding out his arms and welcoming him. He was proud to greet the noble engineer who was honoring their poor village; he was delighted by the priceless service the noble engineer was going to do Iguape by building that little jetty to prevent the periodic flooding of the lower quarters of town. What a noble profession, to command the waters and dominate rivers! Ah, surely the poor people of Iguape would long remember the noble engineer's name and many years from now would still mention it in their prayers. D'Arrast, captivated by such charm and eloquence, thanked him and didn't dare wonder what possible connection a judge could have with a jetty. Besides, according to the Mayor, it was time to go to the club, where the leading citizens wanted to receive the noble engineer appropriately before going to inspect the poorer quarters. Who were the leading citizens?

"Well," the Mayor said, "myself as Mayor, Mr. Carvalho here, the Harbor Captain, and a few others less important. Besides, you won't have to pay much attention to them, for they don't speak French."

D'Arrast called Socrates and told him he would meet him when the morning was over.

"All right," Socrates said, "I'll go to the Garden of the Fountain."

"The Garden?"

"Yes, everybody knows. Have no fear, Mr. D'Arrast."

The hospital, D'Arrast noticed as he left it, was built on the edge of the forest, and the heavy foliage almost hung over the roofs. Over the whole surface of the trees was falling a sheet of fine rain which the dense forest was noiselessly absorbing like a huge sponge. The town, some hundred houses roofed with faded tiles, extended between the forest and the river, and the water's distant murmur reached the hospital. The car entered drenched streets and almost at once came out on a rather large rectangular square which showed, among numerous puddles in its red clay, the marks of tires, iron wheels, and horseshoes. All around brightly plastered low houses closed off the square, behind which could be seen the two round towers of a blue-and-white church of colonial style. A smell of salt water coming from the estuary dominated this bare setting. In the center of the square a few wet silhouettes were wandering. Along the houses a motley crowd of gauchos, Japanese, half-breed Indians, and elegant leading citizens, whose dark suits looked exotic here, were sauntering with slow gestures. They stepped aside with dignity to make way for the car, then stopped and watched it. When the car stopped in front of one of the houses on the square, a circle of wet gauchos silently formed around it.

At the club—a sort of small bar on the second floor furnished with a bamboo counter and iron café tables—the leading citizens were numerous. Sugar-cane alcohol was drunk in honor of D'Arrast after the Mayor, glass in hand, had wished him welcome and all the happiness in the world. But while D'Arrast was drinking near the window, a huge lout of a fellow in riding-breeches and leggings came over and, staggering somewhat, delivered himself of a rapid and obscure speech in which the engineer recognized solely the word "passport." He hesitated and then took out the document, which the fellow seized greedily. After having thumbed through the passport, he manifested obvious displeasure. He resumed his speech, shaking the document under the nose of the engineer, who, without getting excited, merely looked at the angry man. Whereupon the Judge, with a smile, came over and asked what was the matter. For a moment the drunk scrutinized the frail creature who dared to interrupt him and then, staggering even more dangerously, shook the passport in the face of his new interlocutor. D'Arrast sat peacefully beside a café table and waited. The dialogue became very lively, and suddenly the Judge broke out in a deafening voice that one would never have suspected in him. Without any forewarning, the lout suddenly backed down like a child caught in the act. At a final order from the Judge, he sidled toward the door like a punished schoolboy and disappeared.

The Judge immediately came over to explain to D'Arrast in a voice that had become harmonious again, that the uncouth individual who had just left was the Chief of Police, that he had dared to claim the passport was not in order, and that he would be punished for his outburst. Judge Carvalho then addressed himself to the leading citizens, who stood in a circle around him, and seemed to be questioning them. After a brief discussion, the Judge expressed solemn excuses to D'Arrast, asked him to agree that nothing but drunkenness could explain such forgetfulness of the sentiments of respect and gratitude that the whole town of Iguape owed him, and, finally, asked him to decide himself on the punishment to be inflicted on the wretched individual. D'Arrast said that he didn't want any punishment, that it was a trivial incident, and that he was particularly eager to go to the river. Then the Mayor spoke up to assert with much simple good-humor that a punishment was really mandatory, that the guilty man would remain incarcerated, and that they would all wait until their distinguished visitor decided on his fate. No protest could soften that smiling severity, and D'Arrast had to promise that he

would think the matter over. Then they agreed to visit the
poorer quarters of the town.

The river was already spreading its yellowish waters over
the low, slippery banks. They had left behind them the last
houses of Iguape and stood between the river and a high,
steep embankment to which clung huts made of clay and
branches. In front of them, at the end of the embankment, the
forest began again abruptly, as on the other bank. But the gap
made by the water rapidly widened between the trees until
reaching a vague grayish line that marked the beginning of
the sea. Without saying a word, D'Arrast walked toward the
slope, where the various flood levels had left marks that were
still fresh. A muddy path climbed toward the huts. In front of
them, Negroes stood silently staring at the newcomers. Several
couples were holding hands, and on the edge of the mound, in
front of the adults, a row of black children with bulging
bellies and spindly legs were gaping with round eyes.

When he arrived in front of the huts, D'Arrast beckoned to
the Harbor Captain. He was a fat, laughing Negro wearing a
white uniform. D'Arrast asked him in Spanish if it were possible to visit a hut. The Captain was sure it was, he even
thought it a good idea, and the noble engineer would see very
interesting things. He harangued the Negroes at length,
pointing to D'Arrast and to the river. They listened without
saying a word. When the Captain had finished, no one stirred.
He spoke again, in an impatient voice. Then he called upon
one of the men, who shook his head. Whereupon the Captain
said a few brief words in a tone of command. The man
stepped forth from the group, faced D'Arrast, and with a
gesture showed him the way. But his look was hostile. He was
an elderly man with short, graying hair and a thin, wizened
face; yet his body was still young, with hard wiry shoulders
and muscles visible through his cotton pants and torn shirt.
They went ahead, followed by the Captain and the crowd of
Negroes, and climbed a new, steeper embankment where the
huts made of clay, tin, and reeds clung to the ground with
such difficulty that they had to be strengthened at the base
with heavy stones. They met a woman going down the path,
sometimes slipping in her bare feet, who was carrying on her
head an iron drum full of water. Then they reached a small
irregular square bordered by three huts. The man walked
toward one of them and pushed open a bamboo door on
hinges made of tropical liana. He stood aside without saying a
word, staring at the engineer with the same impassive look. In

the hut, D'Arrast saw nothing at first but a dying fire built right on the ground in the exact center of the room. Then in a back corner he made out a brass bed with a bare, broken mattress, a table in the other corner covered with earthenware dishes, and, between the two, a sort of stand supporting a color print representing Saint George. Nothing else but a pile of rags to the right of the entrance and, hanging from the ceiling, a few loincloths of various colors drying over the fire. Standing still, D'Arrast breathed in the smell of smoke and poverty that rose from the ground and choked him. Behind him, the Captain clapped his hands. The engineer turned around and, against the light, saw the graceful silhouette of a black girl approach and hold out something to him. He took a glass and drank the thick sugar-cane alcohol. The girl held out her tray to receive the empty glass and went out with such a supple motion that D'Arrast suddenly wanted to hold her back.

But on following her out he didn't recognize her in the crowd of Negroes and leading citizens gathered around the hut. He thanked the old man, who bowed without a word. Then he left. The Captain, behind him, resumed his explanations and asked when the French company from Rio could begin work and whether or not the jetty could be built before the rainy season. D'Arrast didn't know; to tell the truth, he wasn't thinking of that. He went down toward the cool river under the fine mist. He was still listening to that great pervasive sound he had been hearing continually since his arrival, which might have been made by the rustling of either the water or the trees, he could not tell. Having reached the bank, he looked out in the distance at the vague line of the sea, the thousands of kilometers of solitary waters leading to Africa and, beyond, his native Europe.

"Captain," he asked, "what do these people we have just seen live on?"

"They work when they're needed," the Captain said. "We are poor."

"Are they the poorest?"

"They are the poorest."

The Judge, who arrived at that moment, slipping somewhat in his best shoes, said they already loved the noble engineer who was going to give them work.

"And, you know, they dance and sing every day."

Then, without transition, he asked D'Arrast if he had thought of the punishment.

"What punishment?"

"Why, our Chief of Police."

"Let him go." The Judge said that this was not possible; there had to be a punishment. D'Arrast was already walking toward Iguape.

In the little Garden of the Fountain, mysterious and pleasant under the fine rain, clusters of exotic flowers hung down along the lianas among the banana trees and pandanus. Piles of wet stones marked the intersection of paths on which a motley crowd was strolling. Half-breeds, mulattoes, a few gauchos were chatting in low voices or sauntering along the bamboo paths to the point where groves and bush became thicker and more impenetrable. There, the forest began abruptly.

D'Arrast was looking for Socrates in the crowd when Socrates suddenly bumped him from behind.

"It's holiday," he said, laughing, and clung to D'Arrast's tall shoulders to jump up and down.

"What holiday?"

"Why, you not know?" Socrates said in surprise as he faced D'Arrast. "The feast of good Jesus. Each year they all come to the grotto with a hammer."

Socrates pointed out, not a grotto, but a group that seemed to be waiting in a corner of the garden.

"You see? One day the good statue of Jesus, it came upstream from the sea. Some fishermen found it. How beautiful! How beautiful! Then they washed it here in the grotto. And now a stone grew up in the grotto. Every year it's the feast. With the hammer you break, you break off pieces for blessed happiness. And then it keeps growing and you keep breaking. It's the miracle!"

They had reached the grotto and could see its low entrance beyond the waiting men. Inside, in the darkness studded with the flickering flames of candles, a squatting figure was pounding with a hammer. The man, a thin gaucho with a long mustache, got up and came out holding in his open palm, so that all might see, a small piece of moist schist, over which he soon closed his hand carefully before going away. Another man then stooped down and entered the grotto.

D'Arrast turned around. On all sides pilgrims were waiting, without looking at him, impassive under the water dripping from the trees in thin sheets. He too was waiting in front of the grotto under the same film of water, and he didn't know for what. He had been waiting constantly, to tell the truth, for a month since he had arrived in this country. He had been waiting—in the red heat of humid days, under the little stars of night, despite the tasks to be accomplished, the jetties to be built, the roads to be cut through—as if the work he had come to do here were merely a pretext for a surprise or for an encounter he did not even imagine but which had been waiting patiently for him at the end of the world. He shook himself, walked away without anyone in the little group paying attention to him, and went toward the exit. He had to go back to the river and go to work.

But Socrates was waiting for him at the gate, lost in voluble conversation with a short, fat, strapping man whose skin was yellow rather than black. His head, completely shaved, gave even more sweep to a considerable forehead. On the other hand, his broad, smooth face was adorned with a very black beard, trimmed square.

"He's champion!" Socrates said by way of introduction. "Tomorrow he's in the procession."

The man, wearing a sailor's outfit of heavy serge, a blue-and-white jersey under the pea jacket, was examining D'Arrast attentively with his calm black eyes. At the same time he was smiling, showing all his very white teeth between his full, shiny lips.

"He speaks Spanish," Socrates said and, turning toward the stranger, added: "Tell Mr. D'Arrast." Then he danced off toward another group. The man ceased to smile and looked at D'Arrast with outright curiosity.

"You are interested, Captain?"

"I'm not a captain," D'Arrast said.

"That doesn't matter. But you're a noble. Socrates told me."

"Not I. But my grandfather was. His father too and all those before his father. Now there is no more nobility in our country."

"Ah!" the Negro said, laughing. "I understand; everybody is a noble."

"No, that's not it. There are neither noblemen nor common people."

The fellow reflected; then he made up his mind.

"No one works? No one suffers?"

"Yes, millions of men."

"Then that's the common people."

"In that way, yes, there is a common people. But the masters are policemen or merchants."

The mulatto's kindly face closed in a frown. Then he grumbled: "Humph! Buying and selling, eh! What filth! And with the police, dogs command."

Suddenly, he burst out laughing.

"You, you don't sell?"

"Hardly at all. I make bridges, roads."

"That's good. Me, I'm a ship's cook. If you wish I'll make you our dish of black beans."

"All right."

The cook came closer to D'Arrast and took his arm.

"Listen, I like what you tell. I'm going to tell you too. Maybe you will like."

He drew him over near the gate to a damp wooden bench beneath a clump of bamboos.

"I was at sea, off Iguape, on a small coastwise tanker that supplies the harbors along here. It caught fire on board. Not by my fault! I know my job! No, just bad luck. We were able to launch the lifeboats. During the night, the sea got rough; it capsized the boat and I went down. When I came up, I hit the boat with my head. I drifted. The night was dark, the waters are vast, and, besides, I don't swim well; I was afraid. Just then I saw a light in the distance and recognized the church of the good Jesus in Iguape. So I told the good Jesus that at his procession I would carry a hundred-pound stone on my head if he saved me. You don't have to believe me, but the waters became calm and my heart too. I swam slowly, I was happy, and I reached the shore. Tomorrow I'll keep my promise."

He looked at D'Arrast in a suddenly suspicious manner.

"You're not laughing?"

"No, I'm not laughing. A man has to do what he has promised."

The fellow clapped him on the back.

"Now, come to my brother's, near the river. I'll cook you some beans."

"No," D'Arrast said, "I have things to do. This evening, if you wish."

"Good. But tonight there's dancing and praying in the big hut. It's the feast for Saint George." D'Arrast asked him if he danced too. The cook's face hardened suddenly; for the first time his eyes became shifty.

"No, no, I won't dance. Tomorrow I must carry the stone.

It is heavy. I'll go this evening to celebrate the saint. And then I'll leave early."

"Does it last long?"

"All night and a little into the morning."

He looked at D'Arrast with a vaguely shameful look.

"Come to the dance. You can take me home afterward. Otherwise, I'll stay and dance. I probably won't be able to keep from it."

"You like to dance?"

"Oh, yes! I like. Besides, there are cigars, saints, women. You forget everything and you don't obey any more."

"There are women too? All the women of the town?"

"Not of the town, but of the huts."

The ship's cook resumed his smile. "Come. The Captain I'll obey. And you will help me keep my promise tomorrow."

D'Arrast felt slightly annoyed. What did that absurd promise mean to him? But he looked at the handsome frank face smiling trustingly at him, its dark skin gleaming with health and vitality.

"I'll come," he said. "Now I'll walk along with you a little."

Without knowing why, he had a vision at the same time of the black girl offering him the drink of welcome.

They went out of the garden, walked along several muddy streets, and reached the bumpy square, which looked even larger because of the low structures surrounding it. The humidity was now dripping down the plastered walls, although the rain had not increased. Through the spongy expanse of the sky, the sound of the river and of the trees reached them somewhat muted. They were walking in step, D'Arrast heavily and the cook with elastic tread. From time to time the latter would raise his head and smile at his companion. They went in the direction of the church, which could be seen above the houses, reached the end of the square, walked along other muddy streets now filled with aggressive smells of cooking. From time to time a woman, holding a plate or kitchen utensil, would peer out inquisitively from one of the doors and then disappear at once. They passed in front of the church, plunged into an old section of similar low houses, and suddenly came out on the sound of the invisible river behind the area of the huts that D'Arrast recognized.

"Good. I'll leave you. See you this evening," he said.

"Yes, in front of the church."

But the cook did not let go of D'Arrast's hand. He hesitated. Finally he made up his mind.

"And you, have you never called out, made a promise?"

"Yes, once, I believe."

"In a shipwreck?"

"If you wish." And D'Arrast pulled his hand away roughly. But as he was about to turn on his heels, he met the cook's eyes. He hesitated, and then smiled.

"I can tell you, although it was unimportant. Someone was about to die through my fault. It seems to me that I called out."

"Did you promise?"

"No. I should have liked to promise."

"Long ago?"

"Not long before coming here."

The cook seized his beard with both hands. His eyes were shining.

"You are a captain," he said. "My house is yours. Besides, you are going to help me keep my promise, and it's as if you had made it yourself. That will help you too."

D'Arrast smiled, saying: "I don't think so."

"You are proud, Captain."

"I used to be proud; now I'm alone. But just tell me: has your good Jesus always answered you?"

"Always . . . no, Captain!"

"Well, then?"

The cook burst out with a gay, childlike laugh.

"Well," he said, "he's free, isn't he?"

At the club, where D'Arrast lunched with the leading citizens, the Mayor told him he must sign the town's guest-book so that some trace would remain of the great event of his coming to Iguape. The Judge found two or three new expressions to praise, besides their guest's virtues and talents, the simplicity with which he represented among them the great country to which he had the honor to belong. D'Arrast simply said that it was indeed an honor to him and an advantage to his firm to have been awarded the allocation of this long construction job. Whereupon the Judge expressed his admiration for such humility. "By the way," he asked, "have you thought of what should be done to the Chief of Police?" D'Arrast smiled at him and said: "Yes, I have a solution." He would consider it a personal favor and an exceptional grace if the foolish man could be forgiven in his name so that his stay here in Iguape, where he so much enjoyed knowing the beautiful town and generous inhabitants, could begin in a climate of peace and friendship. The Judge, attentive and smiling, nodded his head. For a moment he meditated on the wording as an expert, then called on those present to applaud the magnanimous traditions of the great French nation and, turning again toward D'Arrast, declared himself satisfied. "Since that's the way it is," he concluded, "we shall dine this evening with the Chief." But D'Arrast said that he was invited by friends to the ceremony of the dances in the huts. "Ah, yes!" said the Judge. "I am glad you are going. You'll see, one can't resist loving our people."

That evening, D'Arrast, the ship's cook, and his brother were seated around the ashes of a fire in the center of the hut the engineer had already visited in the morning. The brother had not seemed surprised to see him return. He spoke Spanish hardly at at all and most of the time merely nodded his head. As for the cook, he had shown interest in cathedrals and then had expatiated at length on the black bean soup. Now night had almost fallen and, although D'Arrast could still see the cook and his brother, he could scarcely make out in the back of the hut the squatting figures of an old woman and of the same girl who had served him. Down below, he could hear the monotonous river.

The cook rose, saying: "It's time." They got up, but the women did not stir. The men went out alone. D'Arrast hesitated, then joined the others. Night had now fallen and the rain had stopped. The pale-black sky still seemed liquid. In its transparent dark water, stars began to light up, low on the horizon. Almost at once they flickered out, falling one by one into the river as if the last lights were trickling from the sky. The heavy air smelled of water and smoke. Near by the sound of the huge forest could be heard too, though it was motionless. Suddenly drums and singing broke out in the distance, at first muffled and then distinct, approaching closer and closer and finally stopping. Soon after, one could see a procession of black girls wearing low-waisted white dresses of coarse silk. In a tight-fitting red jacket adorned with a necklace of varicolored teeth, a tall Negro followed them and, behind him, a disorderly crowd of men in white pajamas and musicians carrying triangles and broad, short drums. The cook said they should follow the men.

The hut, which they reached by following the river a few hundred yards beyond the last huts, was large, empty, and relatively comfortable, with plastered walls. It had a dirt floor, a roof of thatch and reeds supported by a central pole, and

bare walls. On a little palm-clad altar at the end, covered with
candles that scarcely lighted half the hall, there was a
magnificent colored print in which Saint George, with alluring
grace, was getting the better of a bewhiskered dragon. Under
the altar a sort of niche decorated with rococo paper sheltered
a little statue of red-painted clay representing a horned god,
standing between a candle and a bowl of water. With a fierce
look the god was brandishing an oversized knife made of
silver paper.

The cook led D'Arrast to a corner, where they stood
against the wall near the door. "This way," he whispered, "we
can leave without disturbing." Indeed, the hut was packed
tight with men and women. Already the heat was rising. The
musicians took their places on both sides of the little altar.
The men and women dancers separated into two concentric
circles with the men inside. In the very center the black leader
in the red jacket took his stand. D'Arrast leaned against the
wall, folding his arms.

But the leader, elbowing his way through the circle of
dancers, came toward them and, in a solemn way, said a few
words to the cook. "Unfold your arms, Captain," the cook
said. "You are hugging yourself and keeping the saint's spirit
from descending." Obediently D'Arrast let his arms fall to his
sides. Still leaning against the wall, with his long, heavy limbs
and his big face already shiny with sweat, D'Arrast himself
looked like some bestial and kindly god. The tall Negro looked
at them and, satisfied, went back to his place. At once, in a
resounding voice, he intoned the opening notes of a song that
all picked up in chorus, accompanied by the drums. Then the
circles began to turn in opposite directions in a sort of heavy,
insistent dance rather like stamping, slightly emphasized by
the double line of swaying hips.

The heat had increased. Yet the pauses gradually diminished, the stops became less frequent, and the dance speeded
up. Without any slowing of the others' rhythm, without
ceasing to dance himself, the tall Negro again elbowed his
way through the circles to go toward the altar. He came back
with a glass of water and a lighted candle that he stuck in the
ground in the center of the hut. He poured the water around
the candle in two concentric circles and, again erect, turned
maddened eyes toward the roof. His whole body taut and still,
he was waiting. "Saint George is coming. Look! Look!" whispered the cook, whose eyes were popping.

Indeed, some dancers now showed signs of being in a

trance, but a rigid trance with hands on hips, step stiff, eyes staring and vacant. Others quickened their rhythm, bent convulsively backward, and began to utter inarticulate cries. The cries gradually rose higher, and when they fused in a collective shriek, the leader with eyes still raised, uttered a long, barely phrased outcry at the top of his lungs. In it the same words kept recurring. "You see," said the cook, "he says he is the god's field of battle." Struck by the change in his voice, D'Arrast looked at the cook, who, leaning forward with fists clenched and eyes staring, was mimicking the others' measured stamping without moving from his place. Then he noticed that he himself, though without moving his feet, had for some little time been dancing with his whole weight.

But all at once the drums began to beat violently and suddenly the big devil in red broke loose. His eyes flashing, his four limbs whirling around him, he hopped with bent knee on one leg after the other, speeding up his rhythm until it seemed that he must eventually fly to pieces. But abruptly he stopped on the verge of one leap to stare at those around him with a proud and terrible look while the drums thundered on. Immediately a dancer sprang from a dark corner, knelt down, and held out a short saber to the man possessed of the spirit. The tall Negro took the saber without ceasing to look around him and then whirled it above his head. At that moment D'Arrast noticed the cook dancing among the others. The engineer had not seen him leave his side.

In the reddish, uncertain light a stifling dust rose from the ground, making the air even thicker and sticking to one's skin. D'Arrast felt gradually overcome by fatigue and breathed with ever greater difficulty. He did not even see how the dancers had got hold of the huge cigars they were now smoking while still dancing; their strange smell filled the hut and rather made his head swim. He merely saw the cook passing near him, still dancing and puffing on a cigar. "Don't smoke," he said. The cook grunted without losing the beat, staring at the central pole with the expression of a boxer about to collapse, his spine constantly twitching in a long shudder. Beside him a heavy Negress, rolling her animal face from side to side, kept barking. But the young Negresses especially went into the most frightful trance, their feet glued to the floor and their bodies shaken from feet to head by convulsive motions that became more violent upon reaching the shoulders. Their heads would wag backward and forward, literally separated from a decapitated body. At the same time

all began to howl incessantly with a long collective and tone-
less howl, apparently not pausing to breathe or to introduce
modulations—as if the bodies were tightly knotted, muscles
and nerves, in a single exhausting outburst, at last giving
voice in each of them to a creature that had until then been
absolutely silent. And, still howling, the women began to fall
one by one. The black leader knelt by each one and quickly
and convulsively pressed her temples with his huge, black-
muscled hand. Then they would get up, staggering, return to
the dance, and resume their howls, at first feebly and then
louder and faster, before falling again, and getting up again,
and beginning over again, and for a long time more, until the
general howl decreased, changed, and degenerated into a sort
of coarse barking which shook them with gasps. D'Arrast,
exhausted, his muscles taut from his long dance as he stood
still, choked by his own silence, felt himself stagger. The heat,
the dust, the smoke of the cigars, the smell of bodies now
made the air almost unbreathable. He looked for the cook,
who had disappeared. D'Arrast let himself slide down along
the wall and squatted, holding back his nausea.

When he opened his eyes, the air was still as stifling but the
noise had stopped. The drums alone were beating out a
figured bass, and groups in every corner of the hut, covered
with whitish cloths, were marking time by stamping. But in
the center of the room, from which the glass and candle had
now been removed, a group of black girls in a semi-hypnotic
state were dancing slowly, always on the point of letting the
beat get ahead of them. Their eyes closed and yet standing
erect, they were swaying lightly on their toes, almost in the
same spot. Two of them, fat ones, had their faces covered
with a curtain of raffia. They surrounded another girl, tall,
thin, and wearing a fancy costume. D'Arrast suddenly recognized her as the daughter of his host. In a green dress and a
huntress's hat of blue gauze turned up in front and adorned
with plumes, she held in her hand a green-and-yellow bow
with an arrow on the tip of which was spitted a multicolored
bird. On her slim body her pretty head swayed slowly, tipped
backward a little, and her sleeping face reflected an innocent
melancholy. At the pauses in the music she staggered as if
only half awake. Yet the intensified beat of the drums provided her with a sort of invisible support around which to
entwine her languid arabesques until, stopping again together
with the music, tottering on the edge of equilibrium, she uttered a strange bird cry, shrill and yet melodious.

D'Arrast, bewitched by the slow dance, was watching the black Diana when the cook suddenly loomed up before him, his smooth face now distorted. The kindness had disappeared from his eyes, revealing nothing but a sort of unsuspected avidity. Coldly, as if speaking to a stranger, he said: "It's late, Captain. They are going to dance all night long, but they don't want you to stay now." With head heavy, D'Arrast got up and followed the cook, who went along the wall toward the door. On the threshold the cook stood side, holding the bamboo door, and D'Arrast went out. He turned back and looked at the cook, who had not moved. "Come. In a little while you'll have to carry the stone."

"I'm staying," the cook said with a set expression.

"And your promise,"

Without replying, the cook gradually pushed against the door that D'Arrast was holding open with one hand. They remained this way for a second until D'Arrast gave in, shrugging his shoulders. He went away.

The night was full of fresh aromatic scents. Above the forest the few stars in the austral sky, blurred by an invisible haze, were shining dimly. The humid air was heavy. Yet it seemed delightfully cool on coming out of the hut. D'Arrast climbed the slippery slope, staggering like a drunken man in the potholes. The forest, near by, rumbled slightly. The sound of the river increased. The whole continent was emerging from the night, and loathing overcame D'Arrast. It seemed to him that he would have liked to spew forth this whole country, the melancholy of its vast expanses, the glaucous light of its forests, and the nocturnal lapping of its big deserted rivers. This land was too vast, blood and seasons mingled here, and time liquefied. Life here was flush with the soil, and, to identify with it, one had to lie down and sleep for years on the muddy or dried-up ground itself. Yonder, in Europe, there was shame and wrath. Here, exile or solitude, among these listless and convulsive madmen who danced to die. But through the humid night, heavy with vegetable scents, the wounded bird's outlandish cry, uttered by the beautiful sleeping girl, still reached his ears.

When D'Arrast, his head in the vise of a crushing migraine, had awakened after a bad sleep, a humid heat was weighing upon the town and the still forest. He was waiting now under the hospital portico, looking at his watch, which had stopped, uncertain of the time, surprised by the broad daylight and the silence of the town. The almost clear blue sky hung low over the first dull roofs. Yellowish urubus, transfixed by the heat, were sleeping on the house across from the hospital. One of them suddenly fluttered, opened his beak, ostensibly got ready to fly away, flapped his dusty wings twice against his body, rose a few inches above the roof, fell back, and went to sleep almost at once.

The engineer went down toward the town. The main square was empty, like the streets through which he had just walked. In the distance, and on both sides of the river, a low mist hung over the forest. The heat fell vertically, and D'Arrast looked for a shady spot. At that moment, under the overhang on one of the houses, he saw a little man gesturing to him. As he came closer, he recognized Socrates.

"Well, Mr. D'Arrast, you like the ceremony?"

D'Arrast said that it was too hot in the hut and that he preferred the sky and the night air.

"Yes," Socrates said, "in your country there's only the Mass. No one dances." He rubbed his hands, jumped on one foot, whirled about, laughed uproariously. "Not possible, they're not possible." Then he looked at D'Arrast inquisitively. "And you, are you going to Mass?"

"No."

"Then, where are you going?"

"Nowhere. I don't know."

Socrates laughed again. "Not possible! A noble without a church, without anything!"

D'Arrast laughed likewise. "Yes, you see, I never found my place. So I left."

"Stay with us, Mr. D'Arrast, I love you."

"I'd like to, Socrates, but I don't know how to dance." Their laughter echoed in the silence of the empty town.

"Ah," Socrates said, "I forget. The Mayor wants to see you. He is lunching at the club." And without warning he started off in the direction of the hospital.

"Where are you going?" D'Arrast shouted.

Socrates imitated a snore. "Sleep. Soon the procession." And, half running, he resumed his snores.

The Mayor simply wanted to give D'Arrast a place of honor to see the procession. He explained it to the engineer while sharing with him a dish of meat and rice such as would miraculously cure a paralytic. First they would take their places on a balcony of the Judge's house, opposite the church, to see the procession come out. Then they would go to the

town hall in the main street leading to the church, which the
penitents would take on their way back. The Judge and the
Chief of Police would accompany D'Arrast, the Mayor being
obliged to take part in the ceremony. The Chief of Police was
in fact in the clubroom and kept paying court to D'Arrast
with an indefatigable smile, lavishing upon him incomprehensible but obviously well-meaning speeches. When D'Arrast
left, the Chief of Police hastened to make a way for him,
holding all the doors open before him.

Under the burning sun, in the still empty town, the two
men walked toward the Judge's house. Their steps were the
only sound heard in the silence. But all of a sudden a firecracker exploded in a neighboring street and flushed on every
roof the heavy, awkward flocks of bald-necked urubus. Almost at once dozens of firecrackers went off in all directions,
doors opened, and people began to emerge from the houses
and fill the narrow streets.

The Judge told D'Arrast how proud he was to receive him
in his unworthy house and led him up a handsome baroque
staircase painted chalky blue. On the landing, as D'Arrast
passed, doors opened and children's dark heads popped out
and disappeared at once with smothered laughter. The main
room, beautiful in architecture, contained nothing but rattan
furniture and large cages filled with squawking birds. The
balcony on which the Judge and D'Arrast settled overlooked
the little square in front of the church. The crowd was now
beginning to fill it, strangely silent, motionless under the heat
that came down from the sky in almost visible waves. Only
the children ran around the square, stopping abruptly to light
firecrackers, and sharp reports followed one another in rapid
succession. Seen from the balcony, the church with its plaster
walls, its dozen blue steps, its blue-and-gold towers, looked
smaller.

Suddenly the organ burst forth within the church. The
crowd, turned toward the portico, drew over to the sides of
the square. The men took off their hats and the women knelt
down. The distant organ played at length something like
marches. Then an odd sound of wings came from the forest.
A tiny airplane with transparent wings and frail fuselage, out
of place in this ageless world, came in sight over the trees,
swooped a little above the square, and, with the clacking of a
big rattle, passed over the heads raised toward it. Then the
plane turned and disappeared in the direction of the estuary.
But in the shadow of the church a vague bustle again at-

tracted attention. The organ had stopped, replaced now by brasses and drums, invisible under the portico. Black-surpliced penitents came out of the church one by one, formed groups outside the doors, and began to descend the steps. Behind them came white penitents bearing red-and-blue banners, then a little group of boys dressed up as angels, sodalities of Children of Mary with little black and serious faces. Finally, on a multicolored shrine borne by leading citizens sweating in their dark suits, came the effigy of the good Jesus himself, a reed in his hand and his head crowned with thorns, bleeding and tottering above the crowd that lined the steps.

When the shrine reached the bottom of the steps, there was a pause during which the penitents tried to line up in a semblance of order. Then it was that D'Arrast saw the ship's cook. Bare from the waist up, he had just come out under the portico carrying on his bearded head an enormous rectangular block set on a cork mat. With steady tread he came down the church steps, the stone perfectly balanced in the arch formed by his short, muscular arms. As soon as he fell in behind the shrine, the procession moved. From the portico burst the musicians, wearing bright-colored coats and blowing into beribboned brasses. To the beat of a quick march, the penitents hastened their step and reached one of the streets opening off the square. When the shrine had disappeared behind them, nothing could be seen but the cook and the last of the musicians. Behind them, the crowd got in motion amidst exploding firecrackers, while the plane, with a great rattle of its engine, flew back over the groups trailing behind. D'Arrast was looking exclusively at the cook, who was disappearing into the street now and whose shoulders he suddenly thought he saw sag. But at that distance he couldn't see well.

Through the empty streets, between closed shops and bolted doors, the Judge, the Chief of Police, and D'Arrast reached the town hall. As they got away from the band and the firecrackers, silence again enveloped the town and already a few urubus returned to the places on the roofs that they seemed to have occupied for all time. The town hall stood in a long, narrow street leading from one of the outlying sections to the church square. For the moment, the street was empty. From the balcony could be seen, as far as the eye could reach, nothing but a pavement full of potholes, in which the recent rain had left puddles. The sun, now slightly lower, was still nibbling at the windowless façades of the houses across the street.

They waited a long time, so long that D'Arrast, from staring at the reverberation of the sun on the opposite wall, felt his fatigue and dizziness returning. The empty street with its deserted houses attracted and repelled him at one and the same time. Once again he wanted to get away from this country; at the same time he thought of that huge stone; he would have liked that trial to be over. He was about to suggest going down to find out something when the church bells began to peal forth loudly. Simultaneously, from the other end of the street on their left, a clamor burst out and a seething crowd appeared. From a distance the people could be seen swarming around the shrine, pilgrims and penitents mingled, and they were advancing, amidst firecrackers and shouts of joy, along the narrow street. In a few seconds they filled it to the edges, advancing toward the town hall in an indescribable disorder—ages, races, and costumes fused in a motley mass full of gaping eyes and yelling mouths. From the crowd emerged an army of tapers like lances with flames fading into the burning sunlight. But when they were close and the crowd was so thick under the balcony that it seemed to rise up along the walls, D'Arrast saw that the ship's cook was not there.

Quick as lightning, without excusing himself, he left the balcony and the room, dashed down the staircase, and stood in the street under the deafening sound of the bells and firecrackers. There he had to struggle against the crowd of merrymakers, the taper-bearers, the shocked penitents. But, bucking the human tide with all his weight, he cut a path in such an impetuous way that he staggered and almost fell when he was eventually free, beyond the crowd, at the end of the street. Leaning against the burning-hot wall, he waited until he had caught his breath. Then he resumed his way. At that moment a group of men emerged into the street. The ones in front were walking backward, and D'Arrast saw that they surrounded the cook.

He was obviously dead tired. He would stop, then, bent under the huge stone, run a little with the hasty step of stevedores and coolies—the rapid, flat-footed trot of drudgery. Gathered about him, penitents in surplices soiled with dust and candle-drippings encouraged him when he stopped. On his left his brother was walking or running in silence. It seemed to D'Arrast that they took an interminable time to cover the space separating them from him. Having almost reached him, the cook stopped again and glanced around with dull eyes. When he saw D'Arrast—yet without appearing to recognize him—he stood still, turned toward him. An oily, dirty sweat covered his face, which had gone gray; his beard was full of threads of saliva; and a brown, dry froth glued his lips together. He tried to smile. But, motionless under his load, his whole body was trembling except for the shoulders, where the muscles were obviously caught in a sort of cramp. The brother, who had recognized D'Arrast, said to him simply: "He already fell." And Socrates, popping up from nowhere, whispered in his ear: "Dance too much, Mr. D'Arrast, all night long. He's tired."

The cook advanced again with his jerky trot, not like a man who wants to progress but as if he were fleeing the crushing load, as if he hoped to lighten it through motion. Without knowing how, D'Arrast found himself at his right. He laid his hand lightly on the cook's back and walked beside him with hasty, heavy steps. At the other end of the street the shrine had disappeared, and the crowd, which probably now filled the square, did not seem to advance any more. For several seconds, the cook, between his brother and D'Arrast, made progress. Soon a mere space of some twenty yards separated him from the group gathered in front of the town hall to see him pass. Again, however, he stopped. D'Arrast's hand became heavier. "Come on, cook, just a little more," he said. The man trembled; the saliva began to trickle from his mouth again, while the sweat literally spurted from all over his body. He tried to breathe deeply and stopped short. He started off again, took three steps, and tottered. And suddenly the stone slipped onto his shoulder, gashing it, and then forward onto the ground, while the cook, losing his balance, toppled over on his side. Those who were preceding him and urging him on jumped back with loud shouts. One of them seized the cork mat while the others took hold of the stone to load it on him again.

Leaning over him, D'Arrast with his bare hand wiped the blood and dust from his shoulder, while the little man, his face against the ground, panted. He heard nothing and did not stir. His mouth opened avidly as if each breath were his last. D'Arrast grasped him around the waist and raised him up as easily as if he had been a child. Holding him upright in a tight clasp with his full height leaning over him, D'Arrast spoke into his face as if to breathe his own strength into him. After a moment, the cook, bloody and caked with earth, detached himself with a haggard expression on his face. He staggered toward the stone, which the others were raising a little. But he stopped, looked at the stone with a vacant stare, and shook his head. Then he let his arms fall at his sides and turned toward D'Arrast. Huge tears flowed silently down his ravaged face. He wanted to speak, he was speaking, but his mouth hardly formed the syllables. "I promised," he was saying. And then: "Oh, Captain! Oh, Captain!" and the tears drowned his voice. His brother suddenly appeared behind him, threw his arms around him, and the cook, weeping, collapsed against him, defeated, with his head thrown back.

D'Arrast looked at him, not knowing what to say. He turned toward the crowd in the distance, now shouting again. Suddenly he tore the cork mat from the hands holding it and walked toward the stone. He gestured to the others to hold it up and then he loaded it almost effortlessly. His head pressed down under the weight of the stone, his shoulders hunched, and breathing rather hard, he looked down at his feet as he listened to the cook's sobs. Then with vigorous tread he started off on his own, without flagging covered the space separating him from the crowd at the end of the street, and energetically forced his way through the first rows, which stood aside as he approached. In the hubbub of bells and firecrackers he entered the square between two solid masses of onlookers, suddenly silent and gaping at him in amazement. He advanced with the same impetuous pace, and the crowd opened a path for him to the church. Despite the weight which was beginning to crush his head and neck, he saw the church and the shrine, which seemed to be waiting for him at the door. He had already gone beyond the center of the square in that direction when brutally, without knowing why, he veered off to the left and turned away from the church, forcing the pilgrims to face him. Behind him, he heard some-one running. In front of him mouths opened on all sides. He didn't understand what they were shouting, although he seemed to recognize the one Portuguese word that was being constantly hurled at him. Suddenly Socrates appeared before him, rolling startled eyes, speaking incoherently and pointing out the way to the church behind him. "To the church! To the church!" was what Socrates and the crowd were shouting at him. Yet D'Arrast continued in the direction in which he was launched. And Socrates stood aside, his arms raised in the air comically, while the crowd gradually fell silent. When D'Arrast entered the first street, which he had already taken with the cook and therefore knew it led to the river section, the square had become but a confused murmur behind him.

The stone weighed painfully on his head now and he needed all the strength of his long arms to lighten it. His shoulders were already stiffening when he reached the first streets on the slippery slope. He stopped and listened. He was alone. He settled the stone firmly on its cork base and went down with a cautious but still steady tread toward the huts. When he reached them, his breath was beginning to fail, his arms were trembling under the stone. He hastened his pace, finally reached the little square where the cook's hut stood, ran to it, kicked the door open, and brusquely hurled the stone onto the still glowing fire in the center of the room. And there, straightening up until he was suddenly enormous, drinking in with desperate gulps the familiar smell of poverty and ashes, he felt rising within him a surge of obscure and panting joy that he was powerless to name.

When the inhabitants of the hut arrived, they found D'Arrast standing with his shoulders against the back wall and eyes closed. In the center of the room, in the place of the hearth, the stone was half buried in ashes and earth. They stood in the doorway without advancing and looked at D'Arrast in silence as if questioning him. But he didn't speak. Whereupon the brother led the cook up to the stone, where he dropped on the ground. The brother sat down too, beckoning to the others. The old woman joined him, then the girl of the night before, but no one looked at D'Arrast. They were squatting in a silent circle around the stone. No sound but the murmur of the river reached them through the heavy air. Standing in the darkness, D'Arrast listened without seeing anything, and the sound of the waters filled him with a tumultuous happiness. With eyes closed, he joyfully acclaimed his own strength; he acclaimed, once again, a fresh beginning in life. At that moment, a firecracker went off that seemed very close. The brother moved a little away from the cook and, half turning toward D'Arrast but without looking at him, pointed to the empty place and said: "Sit down with us."